The Hunter's Wife

Katherine Scholes was born in Tanzania, East Africa, the daughter of a missionary doctor and an artist. She has fond memories of travelling with her parents and three siblings on long safaris to remote areas where her father operated a clinic from his Land Rover. When she was ten, the family left Tanzania, moving first to England and then settling permanently in Tasmania. As an adult, Katherine moved to Melbourne with her film-maker husband. The two worked together for many years, writing books and making films. They have now returned to Tasmania, where they live on the edge of the sea with their two sons. Katherine is the author of three international bestsellers: *The Rain Queen*, *Make Me an Idol* and *The Stone Angel*.

katherinescholes.com

Praise for Katherine Scholes:

The Stone Angel

'Scholes crafts her fiction with such care and subtlety.' *Weekend Australian*

'A truly absorbing book filled with secrets and conflicts.' *Woman's Day*

'A beautifully descriptive read and a soul-searching take on human relationships.' *New Idea*

'Scholes shows a rare ability to understand people in their specific geographical context and find within them the great surging passions of humanity.' *Sunday Tasmanian*

'Full of passion, fine writing and interesting observations about the way potent events that help shape one generation have an impact on the next. Wonderful stuff.' *Australian Women's Weekly* 'Book of the Month'

'Scholes has masterfully captured those fateful moments that can change the course of many lives. *The Stone Angel* touches the senses with its rich descriptions of coastal Tasmania and emerges as a lovingly crafted account of a home we can never run away from.' *Good Reading*

The Rain Queen

'. . . a big, sensuous, splendid novel . . .' *Overland*

'Moving and inspiring.' *Australian Good Taste*

'Utterly bewitching.' *The Independent* (France)

'A magnificent portrait of a passionate woman, a superb romantic saga. *The Rain Queen* takes us into the spectacular landscape of Africa, to discover an unknown magical world.' *Elle* (France)

'With the subtlety of Doris Lessing for the depiction of feminine nature and the vision of Karen Blixen in bringing alive a continent of dark ancestry and ancient cultures, the author of *The Rain Queen* has given us an intense vision of grief, solitude and the comfort of strangers.' *L'Express*

'Disturbing and enthralling – an authentic African voice, exotic and magical. An amazing book. Fabulous reading.'   *Madam Figaro*

'This most moving book, whose every breath is a love-song for Africa and her people, is a faultlessly woven cloth.'   *Le Monde*

'3 out of 3 stars.'   *Le Tribune*

'A superb novel . . . wonderful reading.'   *Woman* (Germany)

'Beautifully written, lively and sympathetic . . . an adventurous and highly entertaining read.'   *Bookshow* (Germany)

Make Me An Idol

'Filled with surprises . . .'   *Mach Malpause* (Germany)

Book of the Week   *Dei Zwei*

'A superb novel.'   *Cote Femme* (France)

The Hunter's Wife

KATHERINE SCHOLES

MICHAEL JOSEPH
an imprint of
PENGUIN BOOKS

MICHAEL JOSEPH

Published by the Penguin Group
Penguin Group (Australia)
250 Camberwell Road, Camberwell, Victoria 3124, Australia
(a division of Pearson Australia Group Pty Ltd)
Penguin Group (USA) Inc.
375 Hudson Street, New York, New York 10014, USA
Penguin Group (Canada)
90 Eglinton Avenue East, Suite 700, Toronto, Canada ON M4P 2Y3
(a division of Pearson Penguin Canada Inc.)
Penguin Books Ltd
80 Strand, London WC2R 0RL England
Penguin Ireland
25 St Stephen's Green, Dublin 2, Ireland
(a division of Penguin Books Ltd)
Penguin Books India Pvt Ltd
11 Community Centre, Panchsheel Park, New Delhi – 110 017, India
Penguin Group (NZ)
67 Apollo Drive, Rosedale, North Shore 0632, New Zealand
(a division of Pearson New Zealand Ltd)
Penguin Books (South Africa) (Pty) Ltd
24 Sturdee Avenue, Rosebank, Johannesburg 2196, South Africa

Penguin Books Ltd, Registered Offices: 80 Strand, London, WC2R 0RL, England

First published by Penguin Group (Australia), 2009

3 5 7 9 10 8 6 4 2

Copyright © Katherine Scholes 2009

Cover design by Debra Billson © Penguin Group (Australia)
Text design by Anne-Marie Reeves © Penguin Group (Australia)
Cover photographs by Photolibrary
Typeset in 12/18pt Fairfield LH Light by Post Pre-press Group, Brisbane, Queensland
Printed and bound in Australia by McPherson's Printing Group, Maryborough, Victoria

National Library of Australia
Cataloguing-in-Publication data:

Scholes, Katherine.
The Hunter's Wife / Katherine Scholes
ISBN 9781921518034 (pbk.)

A823.4

penguin.com.au

For my sister, Clare

ONE

1968 Central Tanzania

Mara climbed slowly up the hillside, leaning forward against the weight of a hessian bag that hung from one shoulder. She carried a rifle slung across her back, and with each step she took the hard metal of the barrel pressed against her skin. The air was still, the noonday sun burning white in a clear sky.

Passing an outcrop of boulders, Mara neared a large thorn tree. She paused, checking the branches for tawny limbs hanging down, or dark shapes crouching in the shadows. She knew well enough that wild animals prefer to leave humans alone – this had been one of the first things John had taught her about living in Africa. But still, she couldn't help thinking that the two dead guineafowl she carried in her bag marked her out as a carnivore; a predator who hunts, and who should therefore expect to be hunted in return.

Seeing no sign of danger she walked beneath the leafy canopy, taking refuge from the glare of the sun. While she caught her breath, she looked back down at the plains below her. The trees, bushes and red-earth termite mounds made a strangely neat pattern, scattered across the endless field of burnt yellow grass. She was tempted to linger for a while, enjoying the view – but she'd travelled further from home than she usually did on her own, and a glance at her watch told her if she didn't hurry back she'd end up being late for lunch. She could just imagine the scene that would unfold. Kefa, the house boy, would begin pacing the kitchen, trying to decide whether to call a tracker and send out a search party. Menelik, the cook, would not offer any opinion; he wouldn't say a word. Instead, the old man would just shake his head disapprovingly, making sure everyone understood it was no surprise to him if the Bwana's wife was causing trouble again.

The smell reached Mara first – a raw green tang that was at odds with the heat and dust. Before she had a chance to guess what it was, she reached the crest of the hill. There she stopped, mid-stride. Straight ahead of her, a fully grown tree lay on its side, roots stranded in the air. Next to it was the trunk of another tree, snapped in two. Beyond this, the damage continued, tree after tree, torn apart; debris scattered on the ground. Not far from where she stood was a dark pile of dung.

She searched quickly in all directions, straining her eyes to pick out the large grey shapes of elephants moving through the land. They were surprisingly hard to see, she knew; their muted colour blended into the haze. But eventually she was sure – they were no longer here.

Mara looked back at the ruined landscape. She told herself it was not an unusual sight: elephants often destroyed whole trees in order to take just a few mouthfuls of food; they were clumsy and wasteful. Yet she couldn't escape the thought that something more conscious and deliberate had taken place here. A flaunting of power. She could feel a potent blend of strength and anger still hanging in the air. It seemed to wrap itself around her, drawing her in.

She forced herself to move on. After a few paces she broke into a run, weaving her way between bushes and rocks. Over the next rise, she reached open savannah again. There she slowed to a walk, but kept up a brisk pace. Soon she was skirting the waterhole with its basking hippos and borders of cracked mud. Then, at last, she reached the track leading up onto the small plateau that rose beside it. Ahead, she could just see the cluster of dark-leaved mango trees gathered around the familiar red rooftops of the lodge.

Mara hurried through the parking area, where the only vehicle to be seen was an open-backed Land Rover with faded paintwork and dented panels. Vacant spaces neatly marked with white stones stretched away to each side of it. Ducking around the sign that said, *Welcome to Raynor Lodge*, Mara took a shortcut to the entrance gate. There she walked beneath a pair of weathered old elephant tusks – tall curves of ivory set into concrete pillars, their tips almost meeting above her head.

She continued up the path towards the lodge. From force of habit, she scanned the grounds and buildings, imagining she was a newly arrived guest. She checked that the diamond-shaped lead-light windows, set into the stone façade of the main house, were all sparkling clean, and the paths had been freshly raked. She glanced over at the two guest huts visible from here – traditional African rondavels with circular mudbrick walls and thatched roofs that offered an exotic contrast to the English flavour of the house. Kerosene lanterns had been hung by their doorways ready to be lit. And cane furniture was set out nearby, as if tea might be served at any moment. Everything was as it should be. Yet there was an abandoned feel to the place. The curtains were all closed, and there were no books or shoes or teacups lying about. Flowers still bloomed in the gardens, making defiant spots of colour – there were marigolds, geraniums and bougainvillea of every hue. But the parts of the lawn that usually remained green all year – fed by water that drained from the shower huts – were as dry and brown as the oat grass out on the plains.

An object near the edge of the path caught Mara's eye. She recognised the maroon leather of her husband's sunglasses case – he must have dropped it when he was preparing to leave for Dar es Salaam three days ago. She leaned to pick it up, the rifle sliding sideways onto her shoulder. As she closed her hand around the soft leather, her thoughts turned back to their parting. The way she'd held her body tense when John had leaned near to kiss her goodbye. The brief touch of his lips against her cheek. She saw, again, the look of defeat in his eyes as he'd climbed into the Land Rover – and knew it had been mirrored in her own. She'd watched in silence while the vehicle lurched away over the bumpy driveway.

The moment when John turned the corner, disappearing from view, another emotion had risen inside Mara – something more difficult to name. She prodded the memory of it, now, as if it were a wound she was testing for pain. Finally it came to her, exactly what it was that she'd felt. It was a sense of relief. Relief at the prospect of being apart from him.

She closed her eyes. Behind the chatter of birds in the mango trees, she could hear voices. She told herself she should take the guineafowl inside, let Kefa know she was back. But her body felt heavy – tired and slow.

She looked up at a sudden rustling in the trees at the edge of the garden. An African man burst onto the lawn. Mara recognised Tomba by his trademark cowboy shirt, worn over a traditional loincloth.

Tomba sprinted towards her, coming to a halt only a few steps away. In spite of his haste, he greeted Mara courteously, using an elaborate mixture of Swahili and English.

'How is your work?' he asked. 'What are you eating? How is your health?'

Mara returned the queries, trying to hide her impatience. She searched his face for signs of alarm, but saw only excitement. At last, he was finished.

'*Namna gani?* What is happening?' Mara asked. 'Is something wrong?'

'Visitors are arriving!' Tomba said. 'I have come to carry their bags!'

Mara stared at him for a second. Then she shook her head. 'You are mistaken,' she said. 'No one is coming here.'

'I am speaking the truth,' Tomba insisted. 'I have seen their Land Rover coming.' He pointed in the direction of the road to Kikuyu. 'I ran through the trees, a quick way. That is why I have arrived first. They are hunting visitors. I can tell. They are going to make a safari.' Tomba broke off, frowning. 'Why are you not pleased, Memsahib? The Bwana likes visitors. Everyone likes them.'

'We are not expecting anyone,' Mara said firmly. Tomba opened his mouth to respond, but then just looked at her in silence. Mara sensed him trying to measure out the correct degree of respect due to her. She was the Bwana's wife and a European. On the other hand, she was younger than him, and not yet a mother.

Mara studied the sunglasses case, avoiding Tomba's gaze. She felt sorry that he was going to be disappointed. It had been many weeks – perhaps months – since John's last client. Mara knew that, over the years, the people from the nearby village had come to rely on the royalties they received for big game shot in their tribal area. And some of the young people counted on the casual work they picked up at the lodge.

'They will be here, soon,' Tomba stated.

'If someone is coming for a safari,' Mara said patiently, 'they make a booking. John's agent in Dar speaks to us on the radio.'

'Ah!' Tomba eyed her knowingly. 'But your radio is not working. I have seen Bwana Stimu mending it.'

'When our radio is broken,' Mara continued, 'John's agent sends a message to the mission. And they send the message boy. If you have seen a Land Rover coming here, it is a mistake. People are lost. Or perhaps they have heard of the lodge and they think it is like a hotel.' She smiled grimly at the thought of some traveller – a geologist or government officer – calling in here to break their journey with a decent meal. Apart from the two guineafowl in her bag, and whatever was still growing in the vegetable garden, there was virtually no food in the place. Perhaps she could serve boiled wild greens – the dish the town-dwelling Africans called *sukuma wiki*, 'end of the week' or, sometimes, 'bottom of the wallet' . . .

Tomba folded his arms and stood there, undeterred. 'I am wait-ing to carry the bags.'

Mara looked over his shoulder into the distance. Uncertainty gathered inside her. What if a booking had been made – but the message had gone astray? What would she do then? She had no money to pay for fresh supplies. And John was not here.

The distant hum of an engine invaded the quiet.

A smile spread over Tomba's face. 'They are about to arrive.'

Mara spun on her heel and ran towards the compound at the rear of the lodge. Wrenching open the flywire door, she strode into the kitchen.

'Greetings of the day to you, Menelik,' she said hastily. The cook turned from his stove. He moved slowly, but not because he was nearly seventy years old. He was making a point. Ignoring Mara's obvious urgency, he made a show of looking towards the other door – the one that led into the front part of the building. The one she was meant to have used. Who did Mara think she was, entering by the back door? Some kind of kitchen hand?

'I'm looking for Kefa,' Mara continued. 'We have guests.' She dumped the hessian bag on the table, regretting there was no time to show off her guineafowl. 'I need you to find him for me. Tell him to bring the people inside and serve *chai*.'

Mara was aware of a pleading tone in her voice. She always found it difficult to issue instructions to the old man. Like many of the Amhara people of the Ethiopian highlands, he carried with him an aura of aristocracy. It was something to do with his fine cheekbones, the way he held his head. And the simple yet elegant style of his long white robes.

'We have no milk,' Menelik stated. 'It is finished completely. The Masai woman came but there was no money to pay her.'

Mara paused in the act of slipping the rifle strap over her head. 'Do we have beer?'

Menelik raised his eyebrows. 'We have two bottles only. The last ones.'

Mara shrugged helplessly. 'Let Kefa bring them out.'

In the bedroom, Mara locked away the rifle and ammunition before opening the wardrobe and grabbing her safari hostess dress from its hanger. As she struggled with the zipper, she leaned to peer through the bedroom window, watching as a new cream Land Rover drove into the car park. She relaxed a little, fairly sure, now, that the occupants were not clients of John's. The agent in Dar always used the same safari outfitter, and the vehicles he provided were invariably well-worn.

There was some writing painted on the Land Rover's side panel. *Manyala Hotel*. Mara's lips parted in surprise. Why would someone from there be coming to Raynor Lodge? She freed her long dark hair from its single plait and brushed it quickly, a surge of anger fuelling each stroke. It was because of Manyala Hotel that John was – at this moment – in Dar es Salaam, on a desperate mission to borrow money.

The big hotel had opened two and a half years ago, just as work on the new line of rondavels and huts at Raynor Lodge had been completed. Mara remembered vividly how she and John had made the journey to have a look at the place. They'd turned into a sweeping driveway that led them through a garden the size of a small park and on to a paved forecourt shaded by a blue-and-white striped awning. They'd stopped their Land Rover in front of a central lobby. Mara could still see the expression on John's face as he'd looked to the left and right, following the long sleek lines of the building's modern façade.

They'd soon learned that Manyala Hotel not only offered its guests the use of tennis courts, a swimming pool and even a game-viewing platform set above a floodlit waterhole – it also arranged tented safaris, which came complete with a team of French chefs and a choice of three professional hunters.

In the lounge bar, John and Mara had ordered a drink. As the waiter prepared it they'd stood in gloomy silence. The hotel was only a five-hour journey from the airport at Arusha, whereas their lodge was a good half-day's journey further, over some very rough roads. And although Raynor Lodge was set in beautiful country, with hidden valleys, deep gorges and a chain of lakes, there was no one special thing about the area that the agent could advertise. There was certainly nothing that could compete with the vista that would greet Manyala guests as they strolled out onto the viewing platform, for rising up beyond the near horizon was a sight unsurpassed in all of Africa – the snowy peaks of Kilimanjaro.

Mara dragged the brush through her hair one last time. She shook her head, as if to push away the pictures from the past. Then she flicked her hair back behind her shoulders and turned to the dressing-table mirror. She peered critically at her reflection. The simple dress accentuated her tall slender figure. And her dark eyes, set beneath well-defined brows, looked striking against her suntanned skin. But her face was still shiny with sweat. And there was a mark on her cheek. Licking one finger, she rubbed away a piece of grey feather-down stuck to a spot of blood. There was no time to do more.

Kefa and the visitors were not in the sitting room. Mara straightened a cushion as she crossed the room, then stepped outside onto the verandah.

She saw the house boy first, standing over near the rondavels talking to two men – an African and a European. As she moved closer, she was struck yet again by the incongruity of Kefa's title. It was true he had the lean, almost gangly appearance of a young man – but the reality was that he was middle-aged, the head of a large family. And his manner as he addressed the visitors was calm and authoritative.

Before reaching the group, Mara took a moment to assess the newcomers. The European had the prosperous, over-fed look typical of hunting clients, but in place of a safari suit he wore a loose, short-sleeved shirt printed with colourful palm trees and flowers. The African appeared small by comparison. He looked hot and over-dressed in a brown business suit.

The European seemed agitated, and did not appear to be listening to Kefa. He was running his hand through his dark hair, leaving it standing up in tufts.

'How do you do?' Mara said as she drew near to him. She heard herself emulating John's English accent. The phrase still sounded oddly formal to her – an Australian would just have said 'hello' – but she knew it was the correct greeting when you met someone for the first time.

He looked at her distractedly for a few seconds without replying. Mara wondered if perhaps he did not speak English.

The African stepped forward. 'We are very well,' he said politely. 'My name is Daudi Njoma. Let me introduce Mr Carlton Miller – from America.'

A brief smile touched the American's face. 'Hi. Pleased to meet you, ma'am.'

Mara smiled in reply. 'I'm Mrs Sutherland. The hunter's wife.'

Carlton seemed to see Mara, then, for the first time. He studied her intently for a long, silent moment.

Mara smoothed her skirt, pressing away imaginary creases.

'I'm afraid my husband is away in Dar. On business,' she said. She paused, then, but neither of the men offered any comment. 'Were you sent by the booking agent?' she asked tentatively. 'I haven't received any message, but the radio is out of order. Just temporarily. It hardly ever happens.' She smiled again, apologetically. Then she nodded in the direction of the parked Land Rover. 'I see you've come from the Manyala . . .' She let her voice rise questioningly.

'That is correct,' Daudi said. 'Everything was planned for us to stay there. But the arrangements are no longer suitable. The Head of the Game Department – Mr Kabeya – recommended that we come here.'

As she listened to his careful, correct English, Mara looked blankly at Daudi, mystified as to what could be unsuitable about Manyala Hotel. She recognised Kabeya's name, however. He was an old friend of John's. He came from the local tribe, and had spent many years of his youth serving as gunbearer to Mr

Raynor. She decided not to mention the connection, though, in case Kabeya did not like to recall that he'd once worked for a white hunter.

'You must thank him for us,' Mara said politely. 'And pass on our greetings.'

While she was speaking to Daudi, Mara was conscious of Carlton still looking at her, his eyes scanning her face and body. His gaze settled on her hands. Mara put them behind her. They were hardened from digging and watering in the vegetable garden, the nails dirty and broken.

Trying to ignore the American, she began her introduction to Raynor Lodge. She didn't bother talking about the six smaller huts – they were really just converted tin sheds John had bought from a mining company, though they had thatched roofs set above a breezeway so they were surprisingly cool inside. She focused instead on the rondavels, explaining that each had its own bathing annexe and private sundeck. Then she directed the guests' attention to the windows with their new mosquito gauze.

As she did so, she saw Daudi's eyes slide from the curtains hanging there, to the dress that she was wearing. Both were made from matching blue-patterned *kitenge* cloth. She nodded faintly, hoping to indicate that this was not a coincidence. It had been done deliberately to suggest she was wearing a kind of uniform. (For evening, she had an ankle-length version of the same dress.) The look set her apart from the wives, daughters or fiancées of the clients, who often showed off several outfits in a single day, and also from the occasional female hunter who came here. It was a reminder that Mara was the safari hostess. Other women need not fear she would compete with them in any way – including for the attention of her husband, their hunter.

'It all looks fine to me,' Carlton said. Then he turned to indicate the place where a large deep hole had been dug in the ground, raising his eyebrows questioningly.

'That's the swimming pool,' Mara explained. 'As you can see, it's still under construction.' She spoke brightly, wanting to imply that within weeks the hole would be a pool brimming with cool blue water. She hoped the visitors would not notice that plants had begun growing through cracks in the clay.

Mara moved on quickly to the subject of food – a topic that was always of interest to visitors.

'Our cook prepares meals both here at the lodge and on our tented safaris. He specialises in traditional English fare.' Mara smiled at Carlton, thinking that he looked like someone who enjoyed his food. As she glanced over his ample body, her gaze came to rest on his casual shirt: it was unironed, and the top three buttons were undone, exposing dark chest hair. She hoped Carlton would get changed before Menelik caught sight of him. The African had been schooled in correct European manners by his previous employer, an English baroness – and he would be very unimpressed.

'I shall contact my husband and make sure he returns as soon as possible. He may even be on his way already. If not, it will take two days for him to get here.'

Mara tried to sound calm and confident, but her thoughts were in turmoil. The pantry was all but empty. There was hardly any kerosene or diesel. Even candles were in short supply. And there was little point driving into Kikuyu to ask for credit at any of the shops there. John's accounts were already long overdue.

'Let's see inside the old place,' Carlton said suddenly. 'That's the important thing.'

Without waiting for Mara to lead the way, he strode off in the direction of the verandah.

Carlton stood in the middle of the main room, studying the place from all angles. Mara tried to see it through his eyes – the cushions made from locally woven cloth, furniture built from dark native timbers, the faded oriental rugs lying beside zebras and leopard skins on the floor, the picture rail draped with the vines of a climbing hoya plant. Looking down from the wall were the heads of buffalo, rhino and eland, all mounted on slabs of varnished timber. Some of them were moth-eaten and sagging. In their midst was a single elephant tusk – the last remnant of the lodge's ivory collection, and one that John could not bring himself to sell. Pinned onto the wall at eye level, so they could be examined closely, were two maps. The first was a colonial survey map of the region that included John's hunting block. The second was a map of East Africa with a large portion marked out in pink. It took in Tanganyika, Kenya and parts of some of the neighbouring countries. Written across the territory, in bold printed letters, was a single word: *SAFARILAND*.

This room was still almost exactly as it had been while its original owner, Bill Raynor, was alive. John had insisted on that – and anyway, all available energy and money had gone into completing the new guest quarters. The place had an air of simplicity and tradition that Mara found appealing, but she was acutely conscious that to the American it probably looked old-fashioned and shabby.

She tried to read Carlton's expression as he moved across to the back wall, which was covered with framed safari photographs. She followed him, ready to answer any questions. But he looked at the display in silence. Feeling awkward, hovering beside him, she pretended the pictures were of interest to her, as well. She walked along, looking, as if she were a visitor in a gallery.

The content of each photograph was roughly the same: clients posing with their weapons and the animals they had killed. Often, the professional hunter was included as well. Raynor's striking, weathered face appeared here and there. So did John's, looking as he was now, in his early thirties; and as a teenager, so young that he might still have been in school.

In pride of place was an old black and white photograph taken in 1928 during the Prince of Wales' famous safari. It showed Raynor standing beside another hunter, Denys Finch Hatton. The third person in the picture was the rotund figure of the middle-aged man the Africans referred to rather improbably as *Toto wa Kingi* – the Child of the King. Mara glanced across at Carlton to see if he wanted her to tell him about it – people usually did. But he was looking at something else.

'Who's that?' he asked, pointing to an image of a woman posing with a dead lion. She had her fingers hooked into the corners of the lion's mouth, lifting up its head for the camera. The demure expression on her face – a beautiful, delicate face – seemed at odds with the rest of the scene.

'That's Alice,' Mara said. 'She was the wife of the man who

built this lodge. Bill Raynor.' She began to tell Carlton the story of how Alice and Bill had been partners, in an era when women were virtually banned from safaris. How Alice had managed the hunting camps as effectively as any man. But how she had died, tragically young . . .

Carlton had stopped listening, though. Apparently losing interest in the photographs, he made a quick tour of the dining tables and the bar. Then he crossed to Alice's sideboard and began opening doors and drawers, looking inside. Mara fought the impulse to remind him that he did not own the place. She silently recited to herself the advice John had given her when she'd first arrived here, three years ago. *Treat them like children. Let them do whatever they want.* (He meant while they were here at the lodge, of course. Out on safari it was quite a different matter.)

There was a clink of glass meeting glass as Kefa came in, carrying a tray of drinks. Mara invited the two guests to sit down. Carlton seemed not to hear her. He abandoned his search of the cupboards and moved to stand by the door looking out onto the verandah. Mara thought perhaps he was preparing to leave.

Daudi, meanwhile, took a place on the sofa. Mara sat opposite him in a cane armchair, her legs crossed at the ankles, in the correct way, and swept just a little to one side. As Kefa handed him a tumbler of beer, Mara saw that there was no hint of condensation on the glass. She glanced towards Kefa, who was already leaving the room. Why had he not kept the beer in the fridge? It was one of the golden rules of the lodge that there must always be some cold drinks ready to serve. Then she remembered that as soon as John had left for Dar she'd ordered the fridge be turned off, to save kerosene.

Daudi seemed unconcerned. He gulped his drink appreciatively. Mara sipped her tepid water.

Still, Carlton said nothing. In the lengthening quiet, Daudi began to look uneasy. He put down his glass on a side table and cleared his throat.

Then, without warning, Carlton turned to Mara, his arms spread open in a sudden gesture of delight.

'This is perfect! The real thing . . .' He rubbed his hands together. 'We'll want the whole place to ourselves. For two weeks – maybe a bit longer. Don't worry, we'll make it worth your while if you have to cancel other bookings.'

Carlton scanned the room once more, then pointed excitedly out past the verandah. Mara looked across to where the land dropped off steeply towards the plains, only a few paces away from the edge of the deck. The waterhole could be seen down there, gleaming in the sun. A family of giraffes grazed peacefully on the far shore. Not far from them was a herd of zebras.

'The game are there,' Carlton added. He turned to Daudi, his face alight with excitement. 'We can shoot it all – right here!'

Mara jerked back her head in surprise. 'I'm sorry,' she said firmly. 'We don't allow hunting near the lodge.' She gestured towards the distant horizon where a purple escarpment rose up beyond the plains. 'The first camp is behind those hills. My husband will take you there as soon as he gets back. He can find you whatever you want. The Big Five, of course. Crocodile as well. Impala —'

'Oh, we haven't come to hunt,' said Carlton.

Mara looked at him in confusion. 'Then what . . .?'

'We're making a movie.'

Mara glanced at Daudi, seeking clues as to whether Carlton was joking, or crazy. Then she just laughed, shaking her head. John had told her stories – passed on to him by Raynor – about the way Hollywood studios made films in Africa: they mounted 300-tent safaris with convoys of lorries, mobile field hospitals and cinemas. Ten years ago, Raynor had bought a whole set of nearly new Low and Bonar tents from the outfitter who'd worked on *Mogambo*. The safari adventure film had featured not just Clark Gable but Ava Gardner and Grace Kelly as well. John never tired of telling his clients that world-famous stars had once slept in their tents.

'It's not like that,' Carlton said, as if reading her mind. 'Our main unit shoot is almost done – only two more days in Zanzibar. Then most of the company will be heading home. The second unit – coming here – is only about a dozen people. Just a basic crew and the two lead cast.' He spoke briskly, moving his hands to accentuate his words. 'We were booked into Manyala. The next location was nearby. It was a farmhouse that was going to be dressed as a hunting lodge, the kind of place Hemingway might have stayed in back in the thirties.' He looked around again, still seeming unable to believe what he was seeing. 'Somewhere exactly like this! The farmhouse looked fine in the photos they showed me. But when I came ahead to check the location – it was all wrong. There was far too much to do. And we had no time to spare. Not to mention the cost . . .' Carlton shook his head, looking anxious again. 'We've had so many problems. Just one thing after another. You can't imagine —'

'So you see,' Daudi broke in, in a calming tone. 'Now everything is okay. We have found this place.'

Carlton seemed to gather himself. 'That's right. We have. There'll be a few script changes. But basically it's a perfect set. Couldn't be better.'

Mara nodded cautiously. 'How much accommodation will you need?'

'We can make do with whatever you've got. No problem. We might have to add a few tents. When we're filming inside the lodge there'll have to be a dining tent, of course. But it can all be done.' He sighed, closing his eyes for a moment. 'Thank God. It's a life-saver! It really is.'

Mara eyed him curiously. He made it sound as if he really had been in a life-and-death predicament.

'We'll still need your husband here, of course,' Carlton contin-ued, snapping back into his business-like manner. 'We'll be doing some big landscape shots – and just because we're not hunting, doesn't mean something won't want to hunt us!'

He chuckled at his own joke. Daudi stretched his lips politely.

'But there's one key thing,' Carlton continued.

He stood a step closer to Mara. There was no hint of humour in his voice now. The look in his eye was deadly serious. 'So I must ask – can you guarantee us complete privacy while we're here?'

'I don't think that will be a problem,' she said. 'Even our radio doesn't work.'

'Great. Don't fix it. We're at the end of a long shoot. Everyone's been through a lot. The heat in Zanzibar. Crowds. Railway scenes. Lots of difficulties . . . We have some important set-ups to cover – scenes that are at the very heart of the film. One reason we chose Manyala as the base was because it's at the end of the road. No one passing through.' He broke off, looking awkward. 'Well, except for people heading out here, of course. Anyway, the point is that we just don't want to be bothered by the outside world. Our two stars are very well known. Lillian Lane and Peter Heath.'

Mara caught her breath in surprise. She'd never heard of Peter Heath – but Lillian Lane was a household name, even in Australia. People flocked to see her films, and the *Women's Weekly* often printed stories about her glamorous lifestyle.

Mara tried to picture Lillian Lane – so elegant and beauti-ful – sitting here at Raynor Lodge on one of the old cane chairs. Sipping tea from a chipped cup with *Tanganyika Railways* printed on the side. Suddenly, she saw it was a ridiculous proposal. This was no place for film stars! Ordinary Californian housewives had been known to throw tantrums here. The showers were too hot to stand under, or too cold. The water left their hair sticky. There was a stone in the rice – a tooth could have been chipped . . .

'Look, Mr . . . Carlton. I'm flattered you'd like to work here. But we're just not set up for a film company. Raynor Lodge has always offered simple accommodation. We don't try to hide the fact that we are in Africa.'

'They'll love it.' Carlton swept her concerns aside. 'And anyway, it's only for two weeks. Until now they've been staying in all the best luxury hotels. They can rough it for bit.' He grew serious. 'What you need to understand is that everyone involved in second unit is one hundred per cent committed to the project. Lillian Lane and Peter Heath have even agreed to be responsible for their own make-up and wardrobe! You see, they believe in Leonard's vision.' A hushed, almost reverent, note crept into the man's voice. 'He's the director. My brother. So you see – we're all in this together.'

Mara frowned doubtfully. 'I'm still not sure it will work . . .'

Daudi put down his glass abruptly – a movement designed to draw attention. He turned to Mara. 'Let me explain something. I am from the Ministry for Information. The minister has given his personal support to this project. Our government wants everyone to know that Tanzania is a good place for business. We do not want to hear of delays and difficulties. I know everyone will be relieved to hear our friends' problems have been solved. Even the president will be pleased when this film is successfully completed.' He leaned towards Mara, giving her a meaningful look. 'Kabeya will certainly hear of your willingness to help.'

Mara understood exactly what was being said. After Independence, President Nyerere had expressed his commitment to supporting white Tanzanians – like John – who'd stayed on. Kabeya had personally opened the way for John to take up one of the first hunting concessions under the new regime. Now it was time for John to do his duty.

Mara nodded slowly. Before she had time to speak, Carlton crossed the room and seized her hand. 'It's a deal. You won't regret it, I promise. We'll arrive in three days' time and begin filming the day after. There's no time to be lost.'

He began discussing travel arrangements with Daudi. Mara pretended to listen, but her mind was racing elsewhere. She felt a stirring of excitement as she pictured herself standing in the kitchen paying the staff the wages they were owed, and telling them they would be able to bring in their sons or daughters to take up extra work. Next, she would summon John's gunbearer, who'd been unemployed for two months. Then she'd go to Kikuyu and pay off all the overdue accounts – after that, she'd start some serious shopping. Her thoughts tumbled over one another. There were so many practical matters to be addressed – and many of them in the days before John would return.

Carlton stepped towards the doorway. The movement caught Mara's attention, and she jumped to her feet.

'Just a minute,' she said. Then she stopped, unable to frame her next words. She never discussed financial matters with clients. Neither did John. Accounts were always dealt with by the agent in Dar. There were hunter's tips, of course – dependent on the quality or quantity of the trophies – but they were offered surreptitiously, a gesture between gentlemen. Mara steeled herself. She tried pretending she was one of the wealthy clients' wives. They always seemed to know how to ask for what they wanted. She lifted her chin, as she'd seen them do, and then widened her eyes. She'd seen how effective it was – you sent two messages at once: helplessness and power.

'I shall require a cash deposit in order to hold the booking,' she heard herself say. Her tone was cool and bold. 'There will be an amount to cover food and liquor costs and also part-payment of the room fees.' She thought quickly. 'Of course, there will be other costs as well, later on.'

'Sure, sure, of course,' Carlton said. 'Location fees. Royalties to the village. All the usual stuff. We can work that out when I come back. But for now . . .' He pulled out a massive bundle of Tanzanian shillings and began peeling off notes.

Mara hid her delight at the mounting pile.

'Will that do?' Carlton asked. His hand lay over the notes. He looked up at Mara and seemed to be studying her again – her face, her hands, her body – as if she were a part of the deal.

She eyed him uneasily, her hand poised in the air.

Carlton nodded, smiling, and released the cash. 'Everything is perfect.'

Daudi led the way back out onto the verandah. As they walked to the steps, past the pots of spiky aloe vera plants, Carlton paused by a huge white skull that rose above the level of his knees. It had been neatly sawn in two.

'What's this?' he asked, crouching beside it.

'An elephant's head,' Mara said. 'You can see where the tusks fit in.' She bent to point out a gaping socket.

'So why's it in two pieces?' Carlton enquired, running his hand over the weathered bone.

'My husband uses it to show clients where the elephant's brain is,' Mara said. 'So they understand where to aim. A head shot is the best way to bring down an elephant, you see. But placement is crucial.' She leaned to point at the inner part of the skull. 'You see that sausage-shaped hole in the centre? That's where the brain is. It's about the same size as a loaf of bread.' She gave Carlton a small smile – her hostess smile. It wasn't usually her job to explain things like this. 'Now, see this honeycomb section of the skull, above the brain? That's where you aim your bullet. Right in there.' As she spoke, she saw in her mind the smashed trees out on the plain, and felt, again, the anger hanging in the air. She could hear it creeping into her voice. 'Of course, it's preferable to go for a frontal if you can. You count down the seventh wrinkle on the nose, and line up your barrel between the two tusks. When the elephant falls, there's a tradition that you should cut off the trunk first, to make sure the elephant could never survive and come back looking for you. I'm not sure if this was the Africans' idea – or one of ours . . .'

She backed away, folding her hands, the speech over. She saw Daudi and Carlton exchanging glances.

'Your husband's taught you well,' Carlton said, straightening up. He looked at Mara with new curiosity.

'John Sutherland is a very famous hunter,' Daudi commented. 'Kabeya told me he has twice won the Shaw and Hunter Trophy. He was the youngest ever to be awarded it.'

'And what's that for?' Carlton asked.

'It's given by the East African Professional Hunting Association to the hunter who has found an outstanding trophy for his client,' Daudi said. 'I believe it has only ever been awarded seventeen times. Never to an African, of course.' His eyes narrowed for a moment. Then his face became a mask again. 'I've heard other Europeans say it is the Oscar of the hunting world.'

Carlton raised his eyebrows. 'We'll be in good hands, then.'

'Yes, you will,' Mara nodded her agreement. She led the way off the verandah and along past the rondavels. A shadow of doubt crossed Carlton's face.

'It'd be good if you could make Lillian's accommodation look nice,' he said. 'Get a vase of flowers or something. No yellow flowers though. She doesn't like them. Oh – and one thing: she has to have matching towels. You know – bath and hand towels. She's very particular about that.' He pointed at the first of the rondavels. 'Give her that one and Peter Heath the other. Are they exactly the same inside?'

Mara nodded. 'Just about.'

'Good – that's good. You can put Leonard and me together in one of those other huts. We shared a room for the first ten years of our lives – it won't hurt us to do it again!'

At the Land Rover, Carlton opened the driver's door, while waving Daudi round to the passenger side. Then he paused, one foot lifted to climb in, as if something had just occurred to him.

'Oh, yes – and whereabouts is the airstrip?'

Mara looked at him in silence, then lowered her gaze, pretending to study the door-catch. The nearest airstrip was at the Mission, at least an hour away, and not an easy drive.

'Lillian and Peter will fly in, of course,' Carlton said. 'You couldn't expect them to come by road – not these roads.'

Mara chewed tensely at her bottom lip. She could see the chance of earning money disappearing as rapidly as it had arisen. Suddenly, she remembered that a particularly wealthy client had once arrived by air – he'd landed his own aircraft down on the savannah. She pointed in the direction of the plain. Through the trees the golden sweep of grassland was visible in the distance.

'Aircraft usually land over there,' she said. 'I'll get the strip checked and the windsock erected.'

She glanced across at Daudi. She was pretty sure he knew she was making it all up.

He gave her a faint nod of approval, and turned to Carlton. 'You must instruct the pilot to fly round in a circle before he lands the plane, to let people here know it is time to chase away the animals.'

'Sure, okay. Remind me when we get back,' Carlton said. He heaved himself up into the Land Rover. Moments later the engine purred smoothly into life and the vehicle pulled away, sending up a cloud of red dust.

TWO

Mara drove carefully down the main street of Kikuyu avoiding potholes and weaving between pedestrians, cyclists and battered sedans. In her rear-vision mirror she could see the bobbing heads of at least a dozen Africans who were crowded onto the open back of the vehicle. News always travelled quickly between the lodge and the village, and in the short time it had taken Mara to get ready for a trip to town, they'd all appeared in the car park, eager to make use of a lift that would turn a day's journey on foot into an hour and a half's drive.

Turning into a narrow side street, Mara passed a line of small shops, all selling *kitenge* cloths. Samples hung outside, fluttering in the breeze, the bright patterns competing for attention. Up ahead, Mara could see the jumble of tin shelters and canvas canopies that made up the market place. As she slowed to a halt, her passengers began gathering baskets and bundles, ready to disembark.

'You must stay with me,' Mara said firmly to the two boys – Kefa's nephews – who'd come along to help her with the shopping. They were sitting inside with her, both squashed into the window seat so that the middle space was empty. Mara had invited one of them to move over, but he'd just grinned in embarrassment at the thought of sitting beside her.

'Yes, Memsahib.' The two boys nodded in unison.

'We have a lot of shopping to do,' Mara added. She glanced at her watch. When they'd finished in Kikuyu, she planned to drive straight to the mission to send a radio message to John, via the agent in Dar. She'd considered going there first, but knew that the fruit and vegetable market would have closed by the time she got to town. There would not be another one until Saturday.

Mara handed empty baskets and bags to each of the boys, then led them into the market. The air was laced with the cidery smell of over-ripe fruit, backed by dust and cow dung. Soon they were surrounded on all sides by colourful displays of fruit and vegetables, piled up in little pyramids on makeshift tables or simply set out on cloths spread over the ground. Women sat beside their produce, waving away flies as they chatted and laughed with their customers.

There was no time for Mara to carry out the usual ritual of greeting each stallholder and examining all their goods before making her choices. Today, she just walked along, pointing to the things she needed. She picked out shiny purple eggplants, knobbly cassava roots and squash, and small dusty potatoes imported from the highlands. She chose whole drums full of misshapen local tomatoes and baskets of lemons and limes. She pulled leaves from pineapples to see if they were ripe, then looked at wedges cut from watermelons, and tasted slivers of guava. She accepted offers of paw paw and passionfruit, but waved away the mangoes, even though they were fresh from Kongwa – she'd grown used to eating the African variety, but knew that the stringy, strong-tasting fruit would not be acceptable to Americans.

Whenever she'd finished making her selection at a stall, she paid its owner with the smallest of the notes Carlton had given her. Even so, the African women had to scurry around swapping coins with each other to provide her with change. The boys ferried her purchases to the Land Rover, running backwards and forwards, bowed down with the weight of the loaded baskets.

'The Bwana is preparing for a very big safari!' commented one of the stallholders. She was counting out pumpkins. At the same time, she was chewing on a piece of sugar cane, stripping away stringy fibres with her teeth.

'He is,' Mara said. 'We have many guests coming.' She decided not to try and explain about the making of a film – the woman would have no idea what she was talking about. But, as she moved on, she was aware that one of Kefa's nephews was lingering at the pumpkin stall. He began talking excitedly in the local language. Mara saw him pointing in the direction of the government offices. She was puzzled for a moment, but then she remembered there was a hall there, where Indian films were sometimes shown. Mara had never been to one, but judging by the lurid posters that advertised them, they were a heady blend of romance and adventure, with plenty of dancing and singing. The pumpkin seller looked first incredulous at what the boy was telling her, then impressed. She called across to her neighbour. As Mara carried on with her shopping, she could see and hear the story travelling the length of the market. She kept picking up the Swahili word *filmi. Filmi Americani mkubwa. Very big American film.* Or was it *film of the very big American*? She wasn't sure. Either way, she understood that before long, everyone in Kikuyu would know all about the special guests that were expected at Raynor Lodge. She frowned anxiously, remembering that she'd promised Carlton privacy. But surely, she comforted herself, it could do no harm for the Africans to know about the film. It would be the presence of journalists or photographers Carlton was worried about. And there were none of them around here.

The New Tanzania Emporium stood on a corner in the middle of Kikuyu. Its narrow façade was painted in pastel icing colours, over-laid with lots of writing in Hindi script. The shop had been recently re-named and the remains of the words *Colonial Stores* were still faintly visible beneath the newer lettering. Mara could smell roasting spices and hot cooking oil wafting from the open doorway. It reminded her that she had not eaten since she'd had breakfast at dawn.

Pushing her way past a curtain of cane beads, she entered the dim interior. A dense heat closed around her as she picked her way between tin drums of cooking oil, and open sacks full of corn meal, kidney beans, lentils, peanuts, rice, flour. She passed a slow-moving electric fan mounted on the wall – it stirred the air slightly, but only seemed to make the shop feel hotter.

She had just taken out her shopping list, when a voice called from the back room behind the counter.

'Yes, yes. What do you want? Just say it. Hurry up.'

Mara recognised the lyrical Indian voice – and rudimentary Swahili – of the owner's wife.

'Bina!' she called out. 'It's me, Mara.'

A bulky figure squeezed through a doorway and stood behind the counter. She wore a hot pink sari that glowed with gold embroidery. She smiled at Mara, showing matching gold in her teeth.

'I have money,' Mara said quickly. 'I want to pay the account – and then buy some supplies.'

Bina's smile widened. 'I have heard your news, already!' She switched to English, which she spoke with much more care than she did the African language. 'I know why you are here.' She clicked her fingers, and a small, thin woman appeared at her side. Bina pointed to the paper in Mara's hand. 'You have a list.' She poked an elbow towards her assistant. 'My sister-in-law will gather your shopping. And prepare the bills. You will come and sit with me.'

Mara smiled uncertainly. She welcomed the thought of a few minutes' rest, and Bina always offered her milky *chai* flavoured with cardamom and cloves, and spicy Indian snacks. But Mara didn't want to face Menelik's disdain if she returned with the wrong provisions. She glanced over the shelves loaded with tins and bags and packets. Most items came only in brand, though – Kimbo margarine, Kilombero sugar, Brooke Bond tea – so there were only a few choices to be made.

'Okay, thank you,' Mara said finally. 'It's not a complicated list – just long.' She was about to hand over her list when she noticed bars of soap lined up on the counter. 'Except I have to decide what kind of soap to get.' She looked from the creamy bars of Palmolive, which seemed more appropriate for film stars, to the dark red slabs of Lifebuoy that Raynor Lodge had always provided for its clients – the carbolic soap didn't smell very nice, but it could be relied upon to kill germs.

'Get both of them,' Bina said. 'Offer a choice.' She waved one plump, yet delicate hand in time with her speech, as if conducting herself in song. 'That is my number-one advice, when dealing with important people. Even if two things are not good at all – if they can pick one, they are content!'

She led Mara into the sitting room, which was also her dressmaking workshop. Bolts of cloth – rainbow silks, flashing with metal thread – were stacked against the walls. Remnants of cotton and fabric and scraps of paper patterns littered the rush mats that covered the floor.

'I know all about royalty,' Bina said. She lowered herself into a broad-seated chair and waited for Mara to wash her hands in the handbasin in the corner and sit down. Bina shouted something in Hindi, in the direction of another doorway. 'My relatives in Udaipur have worked at the palace for many generations. This is my number-two advice – your staff must be well presented.' She reached towards a bowl full of buttons sewed onto cards. 'Take some of these, and instruct everyone to replace their missing buttons. They must use matching cotton, of course.'

A child appeared, carrying a tray bearing two glasses of *chai* and a plate of *samosas* garnished with slices of lime. Mara's mouth watered at the sight of the little triangles of flaky pastry, cooked to a golden brown. Inside, she knew, was a mixture of minced meat and peas, flavoured with *garam marsala*, chilli and fresh coriander.

She smiled gratefully at Bina.

'It is your favourite,' the Indian woman stated. 'You must eat many. You are too thin.'

Mara said nothing. She knew Bina was proud of the rolls of

brown flesh that bulged out between her sari skirt and her short tight bodice – she was quite certain that it was this that had attracted her husband to marry her. She and Mara would never agree on the ideal female body.

To change the subject, Mara opened her bag and took out a copy of *Woman's Day*. After Carlton had gone, she'd flicked through all the old magazines clients had left behind at the lodge until she'd finally found a photograph of Lillian Lane. It showed her standing on the deck of a luxury yacht, arm in arm with a handsome man. Though the image was small, Mara had recognised the face immediately.

Folding the magazine open at the right page, she handed it to Bina.

'That's her,' Mara said. 'She's the actress coming to Raynor Lodge.'

Bina sighed in admiration. 'She is very, very beautiful! And look at the boat. And the man.' She tilted her head, critically. 'She is too thin as well. What will you feed her? What do Americans eat?'

Mara shrugged. 'We always serve English food. Everyone seems happy with that.' Food was not something she was worried about. She had never had any complaints about Menelik's cooking. It was simple, but of a high quality. And in case the clients didn't recognise this, Mara always made a point of mentioning – before the first meal was served – the name of the baroness responsible for Menelik's training and his recipes.

Bina appeared unconvinced. 'They must have their own American dishes,' she said. 'How long are they staying?'

'Two weeks,' Mara said.

'Two weeks! That is a long time. Many meals,' said Bina.

Mara put down her *samosa*. She could feel the tension growing inside her, and she was no longer hungry.

'I know what to do.' Bina nodded wisely. 'You must have special nights. International feasts. There is an excellent Indian chef in Arusha – he comes from Gujarat, of course. I shall contact him.'

'No! That's impossible,' Mara said. 'Menelik would never agree to having another cook in his kitchen. You know what he's like.'

Bina pursed her lips. Mara was aware that the shopkeeper and the cook did not get on well together. When Menelik came here to get supplies, he refused to respond to Bina's bad Swahili, insisting on conversing in English. He treated the Indian woman with the same open disdain that she reserved for Africans.

'You could teach him a lesson,' Bina said. Then she shrugged her rounded shoulders. 'Anyway, it's not your concern.' It was one of her favourite phrases – she used it as a way of shifting the topic of conversation, even when the matter under consideration was very much the other person's concern. She settled back in her chair and cast a critical gaze over Mara's khaki work clothes. 'So,' she announced, 'you want a new dress.'

Mara looked at Bina in surprise. The thought of ordering something new to wear had not occurred to her. But now that Bina had raised it, she felt tempted by the idea. She'd not had a new dress since Bina had sewed the safari hostess outfits, two and a half years ago.

She found herself reaching for the magazine; she knew there were fashion pages at the back. She felt guilty – neither she nor John ever spent money on clothes. They didn't need to. Raynor had

34

bought a bulk supply of safari shirts, trousers and jackets when an outfitter in Arusha had closed down during World War II. For evenings at the lodge, John wore one of his two cream linen tropical suits. And Mara, of course, had her blue dresses. On the rare occasions that they went out – to a party at one of the farms, or to the church in Kikuyu at Christmas – Mara chose from the small collection of clothes she'd brought with her from Australia. They were a bit dated, perhaps, and well-worn – but perfectly fine for a hunter's wife.

She really didn't need anything new.

But with the roll of money in her pocket, and the picture of Lillian Lane in front of her, Mara felt herself being drawn along by a sense of unreality. She began flipping through the pages. Almost straightaway, an outfit caught her eye – a skirt and a matching top. She knew the style would suit her.

Bina nodded her approval. 'But please,' she said. 'No African cloth this time.'

She began pulling out patterned silks and holding them against Mara's face. Meanwhile, Mara peered past Bina as best she could, searching the shelves for something she liked. Finally she found it: a length of soft cotton, printed with a dappled pattern of greens, golds and browns. It looked like a piece of the savannah, captured on cloth.

She crossed the room and lifted the bolt from the shelf. 'This one. It's perfect. I love it . . .'

Bina frowned, but only briefly – she seemed torn between her own disappointment with the choice, and her pride in the fact that there was something in her shop Mara liked so much.

'Remove your outer garments please,' she told Mara as she reached for her measuring tape.

Mara waited for Bina to begin shaking her head as she wrote down the size of her hips. Instead, Bina commented that it was just as well Mara was thin. The pattern she'd chosen looked as if it had been designed for a boy.

Bina's arms encircled Mara's body as she passed the tape around her waist. Mara breathed in the slightly rancid smell of the woman's oiled hair, backed by the scent of sandalwood.

'And how old are you?' Bina asked suddenly. She made it sound as though the subject had already been raised.

'Twenty-seven,' Mara answered. She wondered where the question was leading. You could never guess, with Bina.

'And you've been married for three years,' Bina stated. She didn't have to ask about that – she'd been there the day Mara had arrived in Kikuyu, the new bride of John Sutherland. 'So tell me – why are there no children? Do you have medical problems?'

'No!' Mara laughed briefly. 'It's just . . . John and I don't want children yet. We've got a lot of responsibilities, with the lodge. Financial pressures.'

Bina stood back from Mara, the measuring tape dangling from her hand. 'No one puts business before children,' she said, firmly. 'I think something is wrong.' She gave Mara a searching look. 'I think your husband is not being a good husband. He is not sleeping with you.'

Mara caught her breath. A spark of outrage rose inside her, but it was dampened by the kindness she could see in Bina's face. She turned away, looking out through the window. It opened onto a private courtyard – a barren place inhabited by a single straggly palm tree. She could feel Bina's eyes, still fixed on her.

'He does. We do,' she said. Her voice sounded weak, flimsy.

She wrapped her arms over her body. She felt exposed, standing there in only her underwear, as if her skin and her bones might somehow betray the truth: that while there had been a time when she and John were careful to avoid Mara becoming pregnant – they really had wanted to get the lodge running properly before beginning a family – it was a different story now. These days, Mara deliberately went early to bed, on her own. And she lay still when her husband came in, pretending to be deeply asleep. So she would not have to endure being touched. Or feel guilty about not touching in return . . .

Bina said no more. Instead, she continued with her measurements, touching Mara gently as she ran the tape up the middle of her back and across her shoulders. Then she held up the cloth against Mara's body, smoothing it against her skin. She spoke in a low, calming voice – as though Mara herself were a child.

'You will be beautiful,' she sang softly. 'You will see.'

Mara closed her eyes tightly, pushing back tears.

Just a little way past the last proper shop in Kikuyu, where the settlement dwindled into a messy collection of rough shacks and shelters, Mara turned into a gated compound, passing beneath a large metal sign painted with the words *B.H. Wallimohammed, Supplier of Arms and Ammunition, Michelin Tyres.*

As she drew to a standstill beside a leaning stack of used car tyres, she instructed the two boys to go and sit in the back of the Land Rover, while she carried out her last errand.

'You must guard these boxes from the hotel,' she said, pointing at the crates of liquor and soft drink. 'They are very important.'

The boys scrambled to obey her. Mara knew they were responding to the brisk tone in her voice, the brittle energy in her gestures. She was being the safari hostess – the busy, efficient person who had no time to think about herself. No time to feel . . .

She headed in the direction of a long low building that overlooked the compound. It was built solidly but crudely, out of cement blocks. The windows had thick bars over them – not just running vertically, but crosswise as well. Mara made herself keep walking at a steady pace. If she faltered, she feared she might stop – and turn back.

As she reached the front step, a wiry-looking man with grey frizzy hair stepped into the doorway. He folded his arms, making his body wider – blocking her path.

'Good afternoon, Mr Wallimohammed,' Mara greeted him. She couldn't help studying his face, trying once more to guess at his nationality. He had brownish skin, which might have been the result of deep tanning, or of a mixed racial heritage – or both. He was equally fluent in English and Swahili.

He nodded at Mara, but did not reply. He rocked slightly on his feet as he watched her standing there.

'I've come to pay John's account,' she said.

The man raised his eyebrows, pushing his forehead into deep lines. 'All of it?'

Mara pulled her wad of notes from her pocket. 'How much does he owe?'

Wallimohammed whistled through gaps in his yellowed teeth. 'Come into the office.'

Mara followed him inside, trying not to breathe too deeply. Behind the smell of gun oil and diesel that hung in the air, she knew she'd be able to detect a faint strain of something else.

It came from the shed that stood behind the office building.

The first time Mara had come here – in the days when no money was owed, and John was a respected customer – Wallimohammed had invited her to have a look inside.

'This is my other business,' he'd said, leading her towards the outbuilding. 'Handbags and wastepaper baskets.'

Mara had followed him happily, not thinking fast enough to guess at what he meant. On the threshold, she'd stopped, frozen.

The floor was covered in long lines of elephant's feet. The dry, hollow shapes were like a bizarre collection of shoes, roughly cut off mid-shin. As Mara took in the scene, details fixed in her head – the lines of horny toenails, the curling edges of the hairy hide, the woodshavings stuffed inside each foot to help keep its shape.

Beyond the feet, were piles of ears. Each one was the size of a small rug, and made of rubbery-looking leather, patterned with veins. They were all the same map-of-Africa shape, but each had the distinctive tears and nicks that Mara knew marked the identity of an individual. The severed edges were dark purple, and speckled with feeding flies.

The air smelled of dried blood, and rotting flesh.

Mara had simply turned and walked away – back through the office and out into the car park, gulping fresh air. Wallimohammed had had to hurry after her, waving the boxes of ammunition John had sent her to collect.

Since that day, Mara had only visited the gun dealer when she could not avoid it. And now she intended to stay not one moment longer than necessary.

She followed Wallimohammed towards a desk pushed into a corner of the office. It was surrounded by shelves piled high with paperwork and boxes of spare car parts. As she watched the man reach for his cashbox, it suddenly occurred to her that the room appeared lighter than it usually was.

Turning to look through the window, she saw that where the roof of the shed used to rise up, obscuring the view, there was now open blue sky. Stepping closer, she discovered that where the building had stood, there was just a big heap of broken earth covered in branches and leaves. The smashed remains of the building had been stacked to one side.

Scanning the yard, she saw that the place had been virtually stripped of shrubs and trees.

'Elephants came two nights ago,' Wallimohammed said. His head was bent over a cashbook and he didn't bother looking up. 'The night watchman couldn't scare them off – or didn't try, knowing him. They broke down my shed and tore up my garden.'

There was a long moment of silence, broken only by the distant thud of maize being pounded into cornmeal. Mara stared out through the window. There was something odd, she felt, about the way the earthen floor had been dug up and built into a long mound. A knot tightened in her stomach. Something was buried there.

'What happened . . . after that?' she asked Wallimohammed.

He dug one bony finger into a page of figures, to keep his place, then looked up. 'The shed was full of wastepaper baskets and leather for handbags. Like it always is.' He broke off, frowning out through the window. 'Bloody elephants buried them – all the feet and all the ears. The whole lot. Must've used their tusks to dig up the ground. Then they brought bits of trees and branches and put them on top.

'Anyway,' he added, returning to his bookwork, 'it was an old shed. I'll make another one.' He shook his head. 'But I can tell you, it's brought out all the old elephant stories. I don't want to hear another bloody thing about bones being moved or dead babies being carried around. As far as I'm concerned they're still just animals.'

Mara stood in silence, barely hearing his words. She felt torn between horror and a deep sense of awe. She felt an impulse to go out there and touch the broken earth with her hands. To trace the shapes of footprints left behind . . .

'There'll be a job in this for John.' Wallimohammed's voice sounded loud in the stillness. 'Rogue elephants coming to town. The ranger will send him out.'

Mara turned to look at him. For a moment she couldn't make sense of his words. Then she understood.

'He's away,' she said curtly.

'Till when? They won't want to leave it too long.'

Mara shook her head. 'When he gets back, he'll be busy. We've got a booking for a dozen people, for two weeks.'

Wallimohammed looked at her sceptically but then his gaze shifted to the bundle of money in her hand: clear proof that something had changed in the fortunes of Raynor Lodge. 'Twelve clients.

He'll have to bring in some extra hunters.' He reached for the bunch of keys that hung from his belt, and opened a metal cabinet behind him. It was stacked full with boxes of cartridges and bullets. 'Do you know what he wants?'

Mara read out the order she'd written at the bottom of her list. It was mainly light-gauge ammunition for the game she and John would shoot for the kitchen, and just enough heavy gauge to load the guns that would be carried for protection.

Wallimohammed laughed. 'You'll need a bit more than that!'

'No, we won't.' Mara looked the man in the eye. 'It's not a hunting safari.'

As she said the words, she felt a sudden sense of optimism. This was what they'd planned – to turn Raynor Lodge into a place where people came to explore the land and admire the animals, not to collect trophies.

'What are they going to do, then?' Wallimohammed asked. 'Lie by the pool?'

Mara just smiled at him. She pictured herself standing beside John in the weeks that lay ahead. Together they would tackle the many problems, big and small, that she knew would arise once Carlton and the other Americans arrived. In the midst of chaos or mishaps, they would throw encouraging glances at one another. People would see how they loved and respected one another – how, as husband and wife, they were a perfect team. Like Raynor and Alice had been.

It would be just the way Mara had dreamed, when she'd first come out here to Africa – before everything went wrong . . .

The fig tree spread its broad limbs over the mission quadrangle, shading the crowds of outpatients waiting for the clinic to open. Two children chased one another around the base of the tree trunk, jumping over the exposed roots; but most of the others just sat listlessly on the ground, ignoring the flies that crawled over their eyes and noses. Their mothers watched with tired resignation. Mara guessed many of them had walked long hours in the heat to get here, with barely any food to sustain them. She hoped they could not see her Land Rover, loaded up with more food than most families would eat in years, and an unimaginable supply of luxury goods as well.

As she followed the path that led to the main building, Mara saw the doctor's wife, Helen, and her three little daughters, all of whom were wearing matching dresses made of red and white checked cotton. These were their school uniforms, Mara knew – they'd explained to her, one day, how they always wore them on weekdays, even though they did their lessons at home in the mission bungalow.

Mara lifted a hand in greeting and Helen waved back, smiling. Mara felt – as always – the slight distance that lay between them. Helen had a busy, useful life, supporting her husband in his medical work and raising three children. In her spare hours, she taught African girls to sew. Mara, by contrast, spent her time providing for the comfort of wealthy foreigners. She knew it was the missionaries' view that the clients of Raynor Lodge set a bad example to the Africans by drinking alcohol. And that they corrupted the local people by handing out extravagant tips. It was hardly surprising that John and Mara didn't pay social visits to the mission, or that Helen and her husband had never been to the lodge.

But there was still an unspoken connection between the two white women. Mara sensed that Helen was intrigued by Mara's life. She sometimes asked about the things that clients did, the sort of clothes they wore, the kinds of people they were. She seemed drawn by some vision of glamour. For Mara's part, she envied Helen her life of certainty and simplicity. At the mission, it seemed, every-thing was clear. There was sickness and healing; life and death. Right was right and wrong was wrong, and there was a clear line in between.

When the children reached Mara, they took turns to say hello, beginning with the youngest. Helen observed them fondly, letting them tell Mara all about their new pet tortoise before suggesting they return to their lessons.

'They must be so excited about the trip,' Mara said, as the girls ran off towards the bungalow. The last time she'd called in at the mission, Helen was planning to take them home to England for a holiday. They were going to meet their grandparents for the first time.

A shadow crossed Helen's face. 'We're not going, now. It's just too expensive. We're all very disappointed.' There was a catch in her voice, suggesting she might be close to tears.

'I'm really sorry,' Mara said.

Helen sighed, then turned away to look out over the crowd of outpatients. After a moment she shook her head slightly, as if to remind herself that her own problems were insignificant compared with those displayed before her.

'I'm just on my way to the radio room,' Mara said.

Helen nodded slowly, still preoccupied. 'Actually, a message came for you this morning. Joseph was going to send it out with the runner.'

'I've been in Kikuyu,' Mara said. She felt a spike of tension. It would almost certainly be from John. But did it mean he had good news from the bank – or bad?

'Here's Joseph now,' said Helen. 'Ask him. He was on duty this morning.'

A short, dark-skinned African hurried up to them. After exchanging brief European greetings, he held out a piece of folded paper and, bowing slightly from the hips, handed it over.

Mara frowned nervously. She spread the paper open, running her gaze quickly over the words handwritten there in large capital letters.

NO SUCCESS WITH SLOAN OR RANJIT. HAVE
TAKEN JOB FOR FIVE WEEKS. FOOT SAFARI
IN THE SELOUS. LEAVING IMMEDIATELY.
NO RADIO CONTACT. JOHN

Mara re-read the blunt message, her lips moving helplessly as its meaning became clear. Sloan was the representative at the Lloyd's of London bank. Ranjit was an Indian trader who dabbled in money-lending – he was to have been John's last resort if the bank refused his application.

No success . . . So that was that – there would be no loan.

Mara moved on to process the second part of the message.

Five weeks in the Selous! The Selous Reserve was a vast tract of uninhabited land, in one of the most remote parts of Tanzania – of Africa, in fact. No contact would mean just that.

'Is everything all right?' Helen asked.

Mara could hear curiosity in her voice, but it was blended with concern. For a moment, Mara was tempted to share her worries with Helen. But she knew John would be outraged at the breach of privacy.

'Yes, fine, thanks,' she said. 'Just a message from John. Nothing important.'

She forced a farewell smile, and walked back towards the Land Rover. She shook her head slowly. It seemed a bitter irony. At last the lodge would be full of guests – and John would not be there. He'd be at the other end of the country, at the head of a long line of porters, leading some eccentric hunting party on a back-to-the-good-old-days foot safari.

Mara stopped. A shiver ran through her as the full meaning of the news sank in. John could not be brought back. The film company was going to arrive. And she would have to deal with all that was about to happen, on her own.

Back at the lodge, Mara entered by the front door. Instead of throwing her sun hat quickly into her bedroom, she placed it on the hall table where John usually put his.

She walked down the hallway towards the kitchen. The solid timber door was always kept closed, but a hum of conversation filtered through the crack beneath it. She recognised the voices of Kefa and Menelik, but there were at least two others as well.

By the eager tone of their chatter, she guessed they were talking about the American film company that was soon to arrive. She suspected that amongst the villagers, excitement and expectation were escalating out of all proportion.

Outside the door, Mara paused for a moment, then opened it wide and strode in. Four faces spun towards her. She waited for Menelik to glance at the back door – proving that nothing she did would ever be right. But he just looked at her in surprise, one eyebrow faintly raised.

'I have news,' she told them bluntly. 'It is not possible to contact the Bwana. He has gone on a long safari. He is not coming back for five weeks.'

Kefa opened his mouth, but seemed unable to speak for a moment. His eyes widened in alarm. 'But guests are coming! We need him.'

'We will have to manage without him,' Mara said. She tried to keep her voice steady, her gaze firm.

'That is not possible,' stated Kefa. 'There is always a bwana. Every place must have one. We need him to tell us all what to do. We need him to shoot the guns.'

'I will arrange for the Game Department to send a ranger,' Mara said. 'And we can call in John's gunbearer from the village. He can be second gun.'

Kefa shook his head. 'That is not allowed.'

'I know. But we will not be hunting. It is only for protection. You saw the man from the government. The president himself is supporting us. If something happens, we will contact Kabeya straightaway.'

Kefa was unmoved. 'It is not correct. The Bwana would not like it. He would not agree to having a ranger sent here – someone he himself has not chosen.'

Mara took a deep breath. 'The Bwana is not here,' she said. She spoke quietly, like John did out on the trail. All four men leaned towards her, just a fraction. She thrust her hand into the pocket of her trousers and pulled out the roll of money. It was a lot thinner than it had been a few hours ago – but it still looked impressive. She saw the men exchanging glances.

She looked at Kefa and Menelik in turn. 'This money was given to me. It is mine. I am going to pay you what you are owed already. Then, I am going to pay you a double wage, for the hard work that is coming. But you must do whatever I ask. *Sasa hivi*. Straightaway. I am the Bwana now.'

The men looked from Mara to the money, and back. In the tense quiet, a fly buzzed against the window. Menelik shrugged faintly – a gesture that said it was up to Kefa to respond. After all, the old man was the cook. He had always been in charge of his kitchen – here in the lodge, or out on safari – whether the Bwana was here, or not. But he was watching closely, Mara knew – waiting to see how Kefa would react to the challenge.

Finally Kefa seemed to reach a decision. He pulled himself up to his full height, holding his arms stiffly at his side.

'Yes, Memsahib,' he said. 'Bwana Memsahib.'

'Thank you,' Mara said. 'Thank you very much.'

THREE

The mattresses lay out in the sun, side by side on the lawn. Kefa's nephews crouched beside them examining each one in turn, looking for signs of bedbugs, and pinching out any seeds from the kapok stuffing that might be poking through the ticking covers.

Mara dropped a pile of freshly washed mosquito nets beside them. She picked out two nylon ones.

'These are for Hut One and Hut Two,' she said. She pointed at the rest of the nets – old-fashioned cottons ones, which shed bits of fluff into the air and were spotted here and there with brown stains where people had squashed blood-filled mosquitoes against them. 'Everyone else can have these.'

'Yes, Bwana Memsahib,' they said. For a moment, she thought they were going to jump to their feet before replying. Since they'd been officially employed as hut boys, Kefa had given each of them a bush shirt and a pair of khaki shorts out of Raynor's store. The garments were too big – the wide sleeves made the boys' arms look thin, their elbows bony. But they obviously felt important dressed in their uniforms. Bina would approve, Mara thought – there were certainly no buttons missing; though nearly twenty years old, the clothes were brand new.

Mara watched the two work for a while, to see if they were being thorough. Beds were important, she knew – guests tended to be preoccupied during the day, but found any night-time discomfort intolerable. Instead of lying awake, enjoying the sound of the bush coming alive – the velvet-pad of stealthy footsteps, the secret rustlings, the eerily beautiful whooping of hyenas – they focused on any small annoyance. Mara could always tell by the expressions on their faces in the morning, if they'd been bitten, or frightened, or kept awake by insects.

'Did you check the flywire?' she asked. She spoke in English, testing their command of the language – hut boys had to be able to communicate with the guests at least at a basic level. 'Not just on the windows, but up at the top?' She pointed to the closest rondavel and the screened breezeway between the roof and the walls. 'It would be very bad if a bat came inside.' Once, a client's wife had disturbed a bat in her room. As the creature flew around in panic it had become entangled in her long teased hair. By the time it had beaten itself free she'd been hysterical. At first light, she and her husband had left for the Manyala Hotel.

Mara crossed the lawn, the brown *kikuyu* grass crunching beneath her feet. She paused for a moment beneath the drooping branches of a peppercorn tree, savouring its shade. A frond of feathery leaves brushed her cheek as she breathed in the spicy fragrance of the seeds.

She thought back over all the tasks that had been carried out in the two days since Carlton's visit. This outburst of activity at the lodge contrasted almost bizarrely with the quietness of the preceding months. As she'd moved about, giving instructions, Mara often felt as though she had dreamt this whole venture. But the money was real enough, she reminded herself. The smiles on the faces of the staff were proof of that. And when they'd returned from the trip to Kikuyu, it had taken the boys over an hour to unload all the supplies from the Land Rover.

Walking back out into the heat and glare, Mara headed for the compound behind the lodge. She could see Menelik, with his greying hair and slightly stooped shoulders, standing in his herb garden, watching over the kitchen boy who was carefully watering each plant in turn. She almost stepped on a rooster as it strolled in the direction of the new hencoop that had been built to house the collection of chickens soon to arrive from the village.

Mara pulled open the door to the corrugated-iron shed that housed the generator. The air inside was several degrees hotter than it was in the yard, and smelled strongly of diesel. The engine was a dark shape in the middle of the gloomy space. It stood quiet and still. Even when guests were in residence the generator only ran from dusk until everyone had gone to bed.

'Are you there, Bwana Stimu?' Mara called, peering around. She still found the man's name slightly amusing. She remembered when John had first introduced her to him.

'This is Bwana Stimu, the electricity expert. Our *fundi wa umeme*,' he'd said.

Mara had thought Stimu was a family name. But the African had proudly explained to her that he had inherited the title from his father. He'd operated the generator at Raynor Lodge back in the days when the engines ran on steam. His son, he'd told Mara, would one day be called Mr Steam as well.

Bwana Stimu emerged from behind a forty-four gallon drum, rubbing his hands on a rag. He smiled broadly. Mara knew how pleased he was to have plenty of fuel again.

They exchanged greetings. When she had enquired after the wellbeing of Bwana Stimu's family, Mara came to the reason for her visit. 'How is the health of the Lister engine?' she asked.

Bwana Stimu looked fondly at the generator. 'He is very strong, very clean inside and outside. Very happy.'

'That's good,' Mara said. 'I think you will be very busy when the American guests arrive.'

Bwana Stimu nodded eagerly.

'They might bring their own generator with them,' Mara said. She had vague memories of having seen photographs of films being made – they always seemed to have big lights beaming onto the actors. 'Perhaps they will need some help from you.'

Bwana Stimu frowned, puzzled, as he processed her words. 'How can they bring a generator with them?'

Mara shrugged. 'Maybe in a special truck. I don't know.'

Bwana Stimu whistled through his teeth and shook his head wonderingly.

Mara smiled. She understood that he saw the idea of a mobile generator as being the ultimate example of European indulgence – having whole suitcases full of shirts and shoes and jackets paled by comparison.

'Of course,' Mara added, 'they might have their own electricity expert. It's hard to know.' For the twentieth time that day she thought how hard it was to plan for an event she knew so little about. She stared blankly at the generator, mind racing, until suddenly she became aware of tension in the air. When she turned to Bwana Stimu his eyes were wide with outrage. He drew himself up to his full height.

'I am the electricity expert at Raynor Lodge.'

'Yes, yes, indeed you are,' Mara said quickly, regretting her thoughtless words. 'They are the ones who must help you.'

Bwana Stimu seemed comforted by that. But Mara sensed that he was still trying to decide how he felt about the possibility of having another electrician – and even another generator – in his territory. He rested his hands on the rounded surface of the old Lister, stroking it gently.

Mara peeled a hardboiled egg as she walked towards the last hut in the line. There had been no time for proper meals today, but Menelik had prepared a bowl of snacks that she could eat when she had time. The gesture had surprised her. Usually, he seemed to care only whether the Bwana had eaten. She'd rewarded him by making sure she'd entered his domain by the correct door, all day.

Mara lifted the latch and stepped inside. The air smelled musty and stale. This end hut had originally been furnished as a bedroom, but since there had never been anything approaching a full booking at the lodge, it had gradually turned into a storeroom. Mara began pulling out boxes and pieces of timber and piles of old newspapers. She threw them all outside the door, so the hut boys could carry them away.

She dragged out several sacks of the rough salt they used to preserve the animal hides in preparation for their journey to the taxidermist in Dar. She tried not to think about how the fresh skins looked – all folded up like clothes, with salt between the layers. Or how the grey-white crystals turned pink over time, as they absorbed the fluid that wept from the hides.

Behind the final sack, she saw a cardboard box. Not recognising it, she lifted the flaps and looked inside, peering cautiously, in case a snake was coiled there. A pearly glow met her gaze.

Her wedding dress.

She stood still, looking down at it lying there, shimmering gently. With sudden clarity, she recalled the touch of the silk skirt caressing her legs, the hushing sigh the dress made as she let it fall over her shoulders, settling over the curves of her body.

On the day of her wedding she'd put on the gown in a room at the Kikuyu Hotel. The fragrance of lavender, wafting from the folds of silk, had reminded her of her mother, so far away in Tasmania. With tears in her eyes, she'd thought of how carefully Lorna had cut out and sewn this dress, staying up late at night and rising early in the morning to get it finished during her daughter's brief trip home from Melbourne to say goodbye. There had been a fierceness to Lorna's movements as she worked; she'd wielded her needle like a weapon, ignoring the cold looks Mara's father kept sending her way.

Ted had made no secret of the fact that he disapproved of the marriage. It was bad enough – in his view – that his daughter had moved away to work on the mainland. He'd always believed she would soon discover her mistake and come home. Now, instead,

Mara was going off to Africa to marry someone no one knew. It simply made no sense to him, he kept saying. After all, there were plenty of farmer's sons with solid prospects who lived much closer to home.

Mara's mother did not argue with him. She just sewed and sewed. In the Hamilton family, only the head of the household was free to speak his mind. Lorna communicated through gestures: a cup of hot chocolate for a child who had been punished; a new pair of socks tucked under the pillow of a girl who had brought home a disappointing school report. Then there were the regular retreats to her bedroom, a glass of water and an aspirin in hand.

When the last stitch in the hem was finished, Mara tried on the gown in the kitchen. Only then did she see how much the wide sleeves resembled the wings of an angel – as if their creator wanted to make sure Mara would have all the help she needed to make good her final escape.

'Thank you,' Mara whispered. 'It's beautiful.'

Lorna took one long look at the girl dressed up as a bride – then she helped remove the gown, before packaging it in layers of tissue paper sprinkled with dried lavender from the garden. She watched in silence as Mara added it to her loaded suitcase. She didn't say, 'I wish I could be there,' because the notion of taking a trip abroad was so absurd – even leaving aside her husband's attitude to the marriage. No one in the Hamilton family had ever travelled outside Australia; most of them had not even made the journey from their island state across to the mainland.

'I'll write,' Mara promised Lorna. 'I'll tell you all about everything.'

When the time came for Mara to leave, the whole family gathered outside the front door to the farmhouse. Mara's brothers were quiet and subdued; her father stood with hunched shoulders, looking confused, as though he'd never really thought his daughter would depart. Mara kissed them goodbye, one by one, reaching her mother last.

'I hope you will have a happy life,' Lorna said. There was a note of longing in her voice. Mara knew exactly what her words meant.

Be happier than I am. Seize this chance. Go after your dreams – before they are turned to dust . . .

'And I was happy.' Mara spoke aloud in the stillness of the hut, the walls creaking as they expanded in the heat. *I was happy.*

The words circled through her head as she thought back to her first meeting with the man who was now her husband, remembering the excitement and sense of romance that had burst into her life that day.

She was working in Melbourne at the Museum. Her job was described as curator's assistant, but it seemed mainly to involve typing letters or taking minutes at endless meetings. Only occasionally did Mara get the chance to go into the archives. She used to walk along the dusty shelves, looking at specimens – bones, insects, carvings, rocks, stuffed animals – collected from all the corners of the globe. She liked to read the labels on the bags and boxes – the exotic, magical words. *Olduvai Gorge. Amazon Basin. Upper Volta. Outer Mongolia.* She would linger down there, breathing air tainted with formaldehyde and naphthalene. Beyond the overlay of chemicals, she imagined she could pick up a vestige of something wild and unknown and far away . . .

One ordinary winter's morning she'd been heading back to her desk in the main office with a box of rock samples under her arm. To prolong her escape from the typewriter, she took a detour through the Great Hall. She expected the room to be deserted at this hour, but there was a man in there – a tall figure, dressed in a light suit. He was examining the mounted elephant that was the centrepiece of the room. Just as Mara approached him from behind, ready to offer friendly information about the Natural History collection, he stepped over the velvet rope that cordoned off the exhibit, and squatted down by the elephant's front foot.

'Excuse me, sir!' Mara called out. 'You aren't allowed to do that.'

The man straightened up, and turned to look at her. His blue eyes stood out against a tanned face and sun-bleached hair.

'I was just taking a closer look,' he said. She noticed his English accent immediately. It seemed to match the slightly old-fashioned linen suit he wore. He pointed to a pale jagged line that circled the huge grey foot. 'That scar was made by a poacher's snare.'

'Poor thing,' Mara said.

'It was early in his life. He nearly starved while he was recovering. You can see it in the ivory. But it was a bullet that killed him.' The man moved his hand up, reaching towards the elephant's side. 'You can see where it entered. Right there. He was quite old by then – past mating.'

'I see,' Mara said. 'Elephants are your speciality.'

The man nodded slowly. His gaze travelled the length of the long curving tusks. 'You could say that.'

Mara tried to remember if she'd heard any mention of a visiting zoologist – academics came here all the time, to examine the collection and give lectures. But she didn't think she'd heard of an expert on elephants.

'Which university do you come from?' she asked.

He looked puzzled for a moment – then guarded. When he spoke next, his tone was muted. 'I don't,' he said. 'I'm a hunter.'

Mara stared at him in surprise. She knew big-game hunters worked for museums, filling orders for various specimens that were wanted for the collections. But they didn't hand-deliver their animals. Mara had never met one before.

As the man climbed over the velvet rope, then walked round to the hind legs of the elephant, she found herself following him. She was struck by the fluid, careful way he moved. She could imagine him stalking through a jungle, his gun held ready in his hand . . .

As if he could feel her gaze, he looked back towards her. Mara smiled, embarrassed by being caught staring at him. He smiled in reply.

For a long moment, they just looked at one another. The Great Hall was a silent, lofty presence around them. The glass eyes of a hundred dead animals seemed to be watching them, waiting for something to happen . . .

Then a door banged in the foyer outside. There was the sound of school children's voices. The spell was broken.

Mara gave the man a small wave and hurried away. Her shoes made a loud tapping sound on the parquet floor. She felt sure he was watching her. She fought an impulse to smooth down her skirt or tidy her hair.

At lunchtime, she'd seen the hunter again. He was standing near the entrance to the Museum when she stepped out into the sunshine, her novel and an apple in her hand. In the bustle of the city street, he looked less at ease. He kept glancing around him, seeming unsure what to do next. He reminded Mara of a boy at a new school – there was an air of vulnerability about him that was at odds with his powerful stature. He appeared to be waiting for someone to rescue him.

She felt, suddenly, as though he were her responsibility. She walked up to him, offering a friendly smile. 'Are you lost? Or waiting for someone?' As the words left her lips, she blushed, afraid he would think she was suggesting he might have been waiting for her. But he just smiled back at her.

'I was going to have lunch,' he said. 'Somewhere . . .'

'There's quite a good café just down the street,' Mara said, pointing in its direction.

The man nodded, but made no move. There was a brief, dense quiet – then he drew a breath. 'Perhaps you'd like to — Would you consider joining me?' He looked immediately embarrassed by his suggestion, and waved a hand as if to wipe out his words. 'Of course, you're probably busy.'

Mara smiled at him again. 'Not at all. I'd love to join you.'

Over sandwiches and coffee, they had swapped names.

'John Sutherland,' the hunter said.

'My name's Mara. Mara Hamilton.'

'Mara . . .' he repeated, a lilt of surprise in his voice. 'That's an unusual name.'

'My mother chose it from a baby book,' Mara explained. She laughed. 'It hasn't got a very nice meaning, though. I looked it up, once. It's Hebrew for "bitter".'

'That's not what it means to me,' John said. 'The Masai Mara is one of the most beautiful places in the world. You share the same name. One day you must go there.'

Mara stared at him, then. The way he spoke made it sound like a prophecy – a foretelling of a future that was already mapped out.

The certainty of it lingered in the air, long after they began to talk of other things. John explained that he'd travelled all the way here from East Africa to deliver a collection of Stone Age African artefacts, bequeathed to the Museum by an old friend who had recently died.

'Couldn't they have been sent by mail?' Mara asked. 'It seems a very long way to come.'

'It is,' John agreed. 'But my friend asked me to bring them in person. It was all written down in his will. He thought it would be a good idea for me to get out of Africa for a while – take a holiday – before I decided what I wanted to do next. He left me a property, you see, in Tanzania. A hunting lodge.'

'And what did you decide?' Mara asked. It did not seem odd to be talking so easily, when they'd just met. It just felt right and good.

In reply, John took a photograph from his pocket: a small black and white picture with a deckled border. He held it out towards Mara.

'That's the lodge,' he said. 'There's nothing in the world that would tempt me to live anywhere else.'

Mara looked down at the image of a stone house, set amongst large trees. It looked imposing, yet comfortable – exotic, but friendly. An African man was standing by the front door. He was holding a large shotgun. Near him, on the ground, lay a collection of leopard skins. Mara frowned, struggling to bring together in her mind the attractiveness of the lodge and the reality of hunting big game.

'It's not going to be a hunting lodge any more,' John said, as if he could read her mind. 'I've given up that kind of shooting.'

He went on to explain his new vision for Raynor Lodge. How he was going to lead safaris on foot, so that people would really experience the African bush. They would stalk the big game with all the skill and rigour of the hunter, but they would only look at the animals. Cameras would be discouraged. Photographs were trophies, too, he told Mara; people who were thinking about what they could take home with them were not fully engaged in the present. His eyes shone with conviction as he laid out his plan. It sounded so simple – and so good.

They kept on talking long after their coffee cups were empty, and the lunch crowds had thinned away. Mara told John about her childhood spent in Tasmania; about her noisy crowd of brothers; about the farm that she loved and yet had always known she had to escape from.

Finally they stood up to leave.

'If you ever make it to East Africa,' John said. 'Come and stay at Raynor Lodge.'

He wrote down his postal address. As their eyes met over the scrap of paper that passed between them, Mara felt sure he knew – just as she did – that although they were about to say goodbye, their story was not over. It had only just begun.

The next day, in fact, John was waiting for Mara outside the Museum at noon. Over a second long lunch, she asked more about his life. When he described going out on tented safaris, she told him how she'd gone camping every summer for years, with the Girl Guides. She spoke of how free she always felt away from the routines of home, with nothing but a canvas between her and the outside world.

'If I had my way,' Mara said, 'I'd live in a tent.'

She was joking, but when John nodded, it was with a serious sense of recognition. The moment seemed to bring them suddenly close, the lure of shared dreams winding around them, like silken threads, soft but strong.

Ten months later, Mara was sitting in a plane for the first time in her life, on a BOAC flight to Nairobi. In her hand luggage was a bundle of letters. The papers were soft and ragged from being read so many times – especially the one in which John Sutherland had asked her to come to Tanzania, and marry him.

She'd written back the day she'd received John's proposal – saying yes. She'd never doubted she was making the right decision. And neither, she believed, had John.

He loved her. She loved him. It had been as clear and certain and bright as the sun climbing towards noon. Mara closed her eyes. The memory of joy gave way to a dull wave of pain.

She reached down into the box, burying her hands in the mound of white cloth, as if by touching the dress she might magically be able to go back to her wedding day – and begin the journey again.

Lifting it up by the lace-trimmed bodice, she shook out the skirt and held it up to the light. A jolt of shock ran through her body.

The silk was dotted with hundreds of small ragged holes. As she watched, chewed fragments fell into the air, drifting to the ground. It was only the work of white ants, she told herself. The dress should never have been left in a box on the floor.

Anyway, it was only a dress – and not one she ever needed to wear again.

It didn't matter.

She forced her mind back to the bright picture she had conjured – the joy of the wedding ceremony. The vivid pink of the flowers she'd held in her hand. The gentle, singsong voice of the African official as he read from his prayer book, addressing John: 'Do you promise to love, honour, cherish and protect her, forsaking all others and holding only unto her?'

Mara had looked up into John's eyes as he'd replied, his voice ringing out in the small room, 'I do.'

Forsaking all others.

The words were still strong and clear in Mara's mind, echoing in her head, as she tossed the ruined dress back into the box – then walked out into the sunshine.

The hut boys stood on the front bumper of the Land Rover as Mara drove at a slow walking pace. The red oat grass was sparse at this time of the year – hungry zebra and giraffe and buffalo herds had grazed it almost to the ground. Stones, roots, anthills and piles of dung were all easy to see. When the boys spotted a potential obstacle they banged on the bonnet, and Mara stopped while they jumped off. Whatever they could not chop into small pieces with their *pangas* they tossed into the back of the vehicle. Looking in the rear-vision mirror, Mara could see that most of the area they'd marked out for the runway was now smooth and flat. Over to one side, Kefa was raising a long pole for the windsock.

Soon, she reached the last stretch. While the boys hacked down a thorn bush, she looked across to the waterhole. On the far side she could see the black mound of a hippo's back, with a family of white birds perched there. Not far away, a small herd of gazelles picked their way delicately through the mud to reach the water, the black silt staining the creamy skin of their legs. It was a typically peaceful scene. Mara was struck again by how in the life of animals everything seemed always to be drawn towards a place of calm. Terror and flight erupted when a predator attacked, but as soon as the danger had passed, the prey settled quickly back into their wandering and grazing. The world of humans, by contrast, seemed a place of constant turbulence. Mara watched a flock of white waterbirds fly down and settle on the shore. She imagined herself joining them – walking into the water and resting in its buoyant coolness – all her troubles forgotten . . .

When the boys were finished, Mara sent them to join Kefa.

'Help your uncle, now,' she said. 'You have done a good job.'

They raced off, arms outspread, along the runway, making the buzzing sound of a distant aircraft. The gazelles lifted their heads from the water to watch.

Mara drove back towards the place where the track opened onto the plain. She passed the remains of old cattle *bomas* – thickets of thorn bush piled into fences, reinforced with barbed wire. They were left over from the days when Raynor had tried to farm cattle on the grasslands, before he'd discovered he could make a better living as a hunter.

Not far from the last of the *bomas*, Mara stopped the Land Rover and climbed out. She walked towards two piles of stones, set side by side on a small rise overlooking the plains and the waterhole. Even at a distance she could see that weeds had grown up around them: tough, bitter-leaved plants that none of the animals would eat. She was surprised John had not removed them – the stone cairns were sacred sites to him. The older one, built decades ago, marked the grave of Alice Raynor; the more recently constructed one, which had been concreted together, stood over the burial place of the old hunter himself.

John had never met Alice – she had died from complications following a miscarriage long before he'd come to live at Raynor Lodge. But he still had a deep and fond respect for her, adopted from Bill. And as for the old hunter himself – John had loved him like a father.

Mara knelt by Alice's grave and began pulling out weeds and replacing stones that had been dislodged by animals. She used her sleeve to wipe the dust from the wooden plaque near the base of the cairn. It had been carved from ebony, probably by the father of today's village woodworker. The epitaph was brief:

Alice Raynor
Love is forever

Mara looked at the words Bill Raynor had chosen. Their meaning was so clear and bold. He had loved only Alice. And the man had meant what he'd written. After her death, he'd remained single for all the long years that had made up the remainder of his life.

Mara dragged a tough thornbush plant from the dry ground. When it came free, its roots were still clutching a hard ball of earth. She tore out another. When all the weeds were gone, she moved to the newer grave. It was marked with a plaque made of brass. The surface gleamed in the sun and Mara had to squint to read the words engraved there.

In memory of Bill Raynor
Erected by the East African Professional Hunters Association
Nec timor nec temeritas

The last line was the association's motto: Without fear or rashness. John had explained its meaning to Mara, the first time he'd brought her to the graves. Every hunter begins by being afraid, he'd said. Then they become cocky, and make rash decisions. Then they find the middle ground, where only acceptable risks are taken. That's when they are fit to be a professional.

Mara bent to wipe a white splash of bird droppings from the brass. It was not much wonder John had been unable to face coming here in recent months, she thought, with the future of the lodge in such serious doubt. It was not his fault that his plans for the place had failed – he had not been rash; he had taken an acceptable risk. But Mara knew that this would be of no comfort to him. He had let the Raynors down.

Mara turned her head to listen into the distance. A faint rhythmic thud was coming from the village – the talking drums at work. Mara guessed they were passing on to distant neighbours the good news of the day. She sighed, feeling suddenly weary. It was easy to be swept up in the excitement of the preparations, to imagine that the arrival of Carlton and his colleagues was going to change the fortunes of Raynor Lodge. In reality it would bring only a temporary reprieve. Together with whatever John got paid for the Selous safari, he and Mara would now be able to pay off their debt to the local moneylender and hopefully have a little cash left over. But it would not solve their ongoing problems.

The lodge would still have to close.

Mara shivered in spite of the warmth of late afternoon. No one would buy the place. The lease would revert to the government and the villagers would take over the lodge. She pictured the old stone house and the line of neat guest huts inhabited by the local families. Chickens would roost on Raynor's teak windowsills. Smoke from cooking fires would be seen billowing from the breezeways of the rondavels. Whitewashed walls would turn grey. Trees would be cut down for fuel. The bush would invade the garden, erasing the flowerbeds.

Mara looked away towards the horizon. Where would they go, she and John? What would they do? She tried to picture herself standing beside her husband in another place. Somewhere else in Tanzania, perhaps? Or Australia, or England . . .

But she could not even begin to form an image in her mind. There was just a frightening blankness. It came to her, then – as she stared into the distance – that the future for her marriage looked no brighter than the grim prospect faced by the lodge. Something that had once been solid and precious was now so damaged, it was hard to imagine in what form it could survive.

FOUR

Mara stood in the space that was normally occupied by her dressing table. Balls of dust lay on the floor around her, and the chair – standing on the small threadbare rug nearby – looked stranded with nothing beside it. She used a hand-mirror to check her appearance, moving it around so that she could see different sections of her body. The blue dress was clean and freshly ironed. Her hair was pulled back from her face in a tidy ponytail. Her face had just been washed. She knew this could well be the last time she welcomed a new party of guests to the lodge, and she was determined to do the job of safari hostess as well as she were able.

She reached down to pick up a lipstick and powder compact from a basket on the floor. Then she perched the mirror on the window ledge and bent over until she could see her face. She dabbed powder onto her nose and forehead, and ran the lipstick over her lips. All the while, she was listening out for Tomba's call – he'd promised to wait in his lookout position, then warn the lodge when the visitors were about to arrive.

Mara rubbed her lips together to even out the colour. The

lipstick had been left behind at the lodge by the fiancée of one of John's clients. Mara looked at the tone critically. It was too bright, she decided – and anyway, wearing lipstick was probably a bad idea. It might look as though she were trying to attract attention to herself.

She was just beginning to rub it off when she heard a distant shout.

Within a few minutes, every member of the staff was waiting near the entrance to the lodge. Kefa had them all lined up, ranged to each side of the archway formed by the tusks – even the night watchman was there, looking barely awake. The staff consisted only of men or boys – the women of the village spent their time working hard in the family *shambas* and only came to the lodge to sell spare eggs, milk or vegetables. Kefa must have held a clothing inspection. Everyone was wearing some form of safari dress. The garments were of different styles and different ages, but all were in shades of khaki, and all had been washed and ironed.

Mara walked along the lines, smiling nervously as she checked her workers one by one. She felt touched by the efforts they'd made, the new haircuts, the polished belts. Several people had also sewn on Bina's new buttons, though some had carried out the task rather roughly.

When Mara reached Menelik, she lowered her gaze. She didn't want to appear to be inspecting him – even if she was standing in for the Bwana. It was not just the old man's appearance that intimidated Mara, or his age, or even the judgemental manner that he adopted towards her. It was more the fact that she was always aware that he remembered Alice. When he'd come to work at Raynor

Lodge – after the baroness had returned to England – Alice had been here. The man couldn't help but compare the two memsahibs. And Mara knew she must seem inferior.

Mara went to stand near Kefa. A tense quiet settled over the waiting group. The usual daytime sounds of hens clucking and birds rustling in the trees sounded over-loud. Then Tomba appeared, his cowboy shirt a flash of red and blue as he sprinted across the lawn.

When he reached Mara he bent over at the waist, breathing heavily, to indicate how hard and fast he'd run to bring his message.

'They are about to arrive,' he announced.

Everyone turned to gaze expectantly along the driveway. From the corner of her eye, Mara saw Kefa waving Tomba away from the staff line-up and directing him towards the shadows of the peppercorn tree.

A Land Rover came into view, jolting along the track. The black and white paintwork, designed to mimic the stripes on a zebra's hide, was coated with red dust.

As it drew to a halt, a second vehicle appeared – a large truck with a covered back. Mara glanced at Bwana Stimu, guessing there might be a generator inside.

The passenger-side door of the Land Rover opened first. A man climbed down and walked straight towards Mara.

'Hi, I'm Leonard,' he announced. 'The director.'

Mara looked at him in surprise. He was nothing like his brother. Where Carlton was on the short side, and overweight, Leonard had long, lean limbs and a bony face. The two men both had dark hair, but Leonard's was a mop of tight curls, and Carlton's was straight. Mara noticed that as Leonard moved, he shot glances all around him, as if he were trying to gain the maximum information about his surroundings in the shortest possible time.

'How do you do?' she said.

Leonard flung out one arm, ready to shake her hand. 'Great, just great. How're you going?'

'Fine thanks.' Mara smiled warmly. She liked the casual manners Americans displayed. John could never really get used to them, but they felt quite familiar to her – Australian ways were not all that different.

Kefa stepped forward. 'Welcome to Raynor Lodge.'

Leonard grinned. 'Thanks. It looks great here!'

'This is our house boy, Kefa,' Mara said.

Leonard reached to shake his hand as well. The gesture took Kefa by surprise. Mara noticed him automatically placing his left hand in the elbow of his right arm as he held it out – the traditional way of showing one was not carrying any kind of weapon.

'Pleased to meet you,' Leonard said, but his attention had already shifted back to his surroundings. 'The other vehicle is a couple of hours behind us,' he said, as he looked past Mara's shoulder towards the lodge buildings. 'They had a flat tyre, and then engine trouble as well. It's being fixed by some kind of village mechanic – at least I hope it is . . .'

Closer up, Mara could see grey shadows beneath the man's eyes, but these hints of exhaustion were denied by the way he moved around constantly, apparently brimming with energy.

He strode across to the elephant tusks and ran his fingers up and down the ivory. Then he tipped back his head to look up at the long curves rising above him.

As she watched him, Mara heard vehicle doors opening and closing, and the sounds of people emerging. Then she became aware of Daudi standing near her. He was still dressed in the brown suit he'd worn when he'd come here with Carlton. He greeted her politely, but briefly, in the European way. He motioned towards a group of people that was gathering behind him.

'Let me introduce everybody,' he said. He turned first to a man with blonde hair that hung in curls around his ears.

'This is Mr Rudi.'

'Just call me Rudi,' the man responded. 'I'm standby props. Except on this unit I'm about five people – dresser, props master, set decorator, art director. I'm the whole department!'

Daudi gestured towards Mara. 'This is Mrs Sutherland.'

Mara took a breath, ready to speak. She wanted to suggest that everyone should call her by her first name – just as Rudi had done – but she wasn't certain what was appropriate.

The introductions continued. There was a dour-looking man described as the gaffer. It took Mara some time to establish that he was actually the person in charge of lighting – and the generator. She decided to let Kefa bring him and Bwana Stimu together, in due course. There were a couple of Africans, described as construction workers. They had the impressive height and ink-dark skin typical of Somalis and were dressed in casual European clothes that looked fashionable and new. They greeted Mara courteously, but cast dismissive eyes over the lodge staff. Mara saw Menelik and Kefa exchanging looks of veiled outrage. Glancing at Daudi, she sensed that he was picking up every nuance of this interaction and was ready to assert his authority if any conflict arose. He would make a very useful ally, Mara noted. She hoped John's friendship with Kabeya would count in her favour and bring Daudi onto her side if it ever became necessary.

The last of the Americans appeared from behind the truck. He had sandy red hair and freckles, and his nose had the raw pink look of skin that had been burned too many times. He glanced suspiciously at the sun as he walked across to where everyone was standing. His green eyes fixed on Leonard.

'What's going to happen about my problem?' he demanded.

Leonard looked at him blankly.

The red-haired man sighed with exasperation. 'I – have – no – boom – operator. Remember?'

Daudi leaned towards Mara and spoke in an undertone. 'He's the sound recordist. Mr Jamie. Bwana *Matata*,' he added. Mister Trouble.

'He didn't show up,' Jamie continued. He looked around him, as if unsure whom he was addressing. 'He's gone back home. Lucky him.'

Leonard nodded thoughtfully. 'I think I heard Carlton say something about training up a local. I'm sure you can manage. Half of the shots are going to be shot mute anyway.'

'Don't remind me,' Jamie said in a gloomy voice.

Leonard turned to Mara. 'Perhaps you can help. We need someone to work with Jamie – someone to hold the boom. They need to be able to speak a bit of English. Apart from that we just need someone smart, strong, on the ball.'

Before Mara had a chance to respond, Tomba was standing at her side. He stepped forward. Very deliberately, he turned his gaze from Leonard to Jamie and back.

'I will be this person,' he announced in a confident voice. 'I will be someone to hold the boom.'

Mara pressed her lips together to hide a smile. She knew Tomba had no idea what a boom even was. She had only a vague idea herself.

Leonard strode up and patted Tomba on the shoulder. 'Done. You're on!'

Jamie cast a doubtful eye over Tomba's sleeveless shirt, his loincloth and the pair of ancient tennis shoes on his feet. But then he appeared to focus on the well-defined muscles of Tomba's arms. He shrugged. 'I guess you'll do. What's your name?'

Tomba grinned widely, showing two rows of white teeth. 'Bwana Boom.'

Leonard led the way along the path towards the front door. Mara hastened her step to walk alongside him, and Kefa cut across the lawn so he could be standing by the entrance to welcome the guests.

Leonard glanced sideways at Mara. 'I can see what Carlton means,' he said. 'With darkened hair, you could look just like her.'

Mara nodded politely while she tried to guess at his meaning. Then she gave up. 'Like who?' she asked.

'Lillian Lane,' Leonard said.

Mara looked at him in confusion. 'What do you mean?'

Leonard stopped walking and turned to face Mara. A look of irritation passed briefly across his face. 'I guess I assumed it had all been discussed with you. I thought Carlton had worked it all out.'

'Worked what out?' Mara asked warily. She felt a thread of anxiety stirring inside her.

'It's no big deal,' Leonard said. He began moving on along the path. 'We just need you to act as a double, now and then. You're tall, like Lillian, and your hair is long. You've got the same build, too. We can get you to climb up over some rocks, say, or walk through the bush. We film you from behind, or in wide shot, so you're just a small figure in the distance. No one can see that it's not her.'

'Why would you want to do that?' Mara asked.

'Lillian's tired, that's all,' Leonard said in a matter-of-fact tone. 'We're near the end of a long shoot. We need her to save her energy for the important scenes.' He glanced sideways at Mara again. 'Also, you'll look more comfortable in the landscape. This is your home. You can always tell, you know, when something's authentic. Actors can imitate – that's their craft. But you are the real thing.' He smiled admiringly. 'You'll be paid a fee, of course. Carlton will make a deal with you.' He lowered his gaze. 'Show me your hands – he said you've got great hands.'

Mara held them out in front of her. She felt like a little girl showing her mother her clean hands before sitting at the table. Except now, her hands had rough skin and ragged broken fingernails, from working in the vegetable garden.

As Leonard nodded his approval, Mara snatched her hands back, out of sight. She was not a little girl, after all. She didn't just have to do as she was told. She turned away from Leonard, cutting herself off from his stream of energy.

She found herself facing Daudi. His eyes met hers. He didn't need to speak, in order to remind her of what he'd said the last time he was here.

Even the president will be pleased when this film is successfully completed.

She didn't want to jeopardise John's future in this country – whatever it might hold. Nor could she afford to turn down the chance to earn an extra fee. She turned back to Leonard as she drew a slow breath. 'I'm happy to help in any way that I can.'

'Do you know how to handle a gun?'

'Of course,' Mara said. 'A twenty-two. And a shotgun.'

'Good. Good. We need to get some big landscape shots – you know, the "we're really here, in Africa" shots.'

They'd reached the lodge, now, but Leonard didn't seem to notice Kefa standing ready to usher him through the open door.

'Have you seen David Lean's movie, *Lawrence of Arabia?*' he asked Mara.

'Yes,' she said. 'I saw it just before I left Australia. It was wonderful.'

After the film, she'd walked out into the cold drizzle of a Melbourne winter's day and looked in surprise at the grey buildings that surrounded the cinema. The heat and dust of the desert, the mystique of the Arab horsemen, the fear and chaos of war – and Lawrence himself – had become so real to her that she didn't feel she belonged in her own world any more.

'Well, you must remember how he treated the desert,' Leonard said. 'It was a character in the movie – as much as Lawrence was. That's what I'm after. I want the savannah to be a real presence in the scenes we shoot here. And not just because we're in the wilds of Africa – it's much more than that.' Leonard gestured with his hands to emphasise his words. 'The openness of the plains mirrors the moral landscape of the story. It's the setting that demands honesty between the characters – in contrast to the closed-in secrecy of Zanzibar, with all those narrow lanes and shuttered windows. Do you follow me?'

Leonard spoke urgently, as though it were a matter of great importance that Mara understand him. Mara found it flattering. She was not surprised that the actors and crew – and Carlton – wanted to help this man bring his vision into reality.

She remembered, then, his query about a gun. 'You won't need me to provide protection,' she said. 'The Game Department promised to send a ranger from Arusha.'

'Yes, but we're gonna have animals in shot with you, when you're standing in for Lillian.' He laughed. 'We certainly wouldn't be risking her out there with lions and elephants! But if it's you, there's no problem. Maggie – that's the name of the character – would be carrying a gun anyway.' He smiled to himself, clearly pleased with his plan. 'Of course,' he added after a moment, 'it's only an extra precaution. Your husband will be there as well – standing out of frame, but close enough to step in if necessary.'

Mara frowned. 'I'm afraid he won't be here,' she said. 'I can't contact him. But as I said, the Game Department is sending a ranger.' She could hear herself talking too fast, wanting to make sure there would be no room for Leonard to express his dismay. 'They've chosen someone who came from this region – he'll know the country well enough. So it's not a problem,' she finished. Then a thought came to her. 'Unless . . . Unless you wanted John to be a double as well?'

'That's not necessary,' Leonard said. 'Peter Heath likes to do everything himself, even stunts, sometimes. He loves being out-doors. I think it reminds him of his childhood. You'd never know it, listening to him, but he's Australian.' He threw Mara a quick smile. 'Like you.'

Menelik stood by the big table in the kitchen, his legs planted wide, hands poised for action. He had his treasured knife laid out in front of him – the one with the Damascus blade. Mara had heard him telling the kitchen boy that during the forging the metal had been folded over a thousand times. This had the almost magical effect of creating a blade that sharpened itself – as though it were alive. The cook had bought it as a young man from an Arab trader. Lying there on the scrubbed timber, it looked sharp and dangerous.

'I will prepare Avocado Soup for the first course,' Menelik said. 'It is the Baroness's own recipe. It must be served cold. After that, I shall present Jugged Venison.'

Mara nodded distractedly. She hadn't come to discuss the menu – she trusted Menelik completely to make the best choices. She was more concerned with the question of how they could make sure that no one ended up drinking unboiled water and getting ill. In spite of the staff being lectured on how delicate Europeans were, there was room for mistakes. And Carlton had made it clear the film company was working on a tight schedule. She was also worried about what Leonard might be doing – she'd made him promise not to leave the grounds of the lodge until the ranger arrived to go with him, but she wasn't sure she could trust him to keep his word.

'I know what you are thinking,' Menelik said. 'You wish to know what kind of animal is this venison made from?' He was speaking in Swahili, today, with the slightly awkward phrasing of someone conversing in a foreign tongue. Mara could never anticipate which language he was going to use – English or Swahili or a mixture of both. She suspected it was a ploy to keep her on her toes.

'It is impala,' Menelik continued. 'It came from the village. The animal was only a little damaged by the arrow. Truly, the meat is good. I have butchered it. But now you must unlock the wine safe and give me some red wine. Burgundy would be the correct one to choose.'

'Yes, of course,' Mara agreed. She looked up, suddenly, at the sound of an engine. Could it be Leonard, driving off to explore?

Just then, the kitchen boy ran in. 'More Americans are coming!' He sang out his words, giving emphasis to each one. He'd never been to school as far as Mara knew, but he sounded oddly like a student chanting lessons. She often found herself trying not to smile when he spoke. It didn't help that his name was Dudu – the Swahili word for 'insect' – and that, with his stick-thin arms and rounded belly, he looked just like one.

'Does Kefa know?' Mara asked.

'Yes, Bwana Memsahib. Kefa is talking to them.'

'Good.' Mara decided not to go out and greet the new arrivals. She still had a lot to do to ensure that everything was in order by the time Carlton arrived with the actress and actor. The plane was due in just a few hours' time.

She saw that Dudu was about to run off, so she put her hand on his shoulder. 'You must stay here,' she said. 'Open your ears and listen. Menelik is very busy. You must behave like an adult and carry out your duties very carefully.'

Dudu stared solemnly at her as she went on. She reminded him that the grease trap would have to be cleaned out each day, when there were so many people staying at the lodge. That it was important always to test eggs for freshness by making sure they sank to the bottom of a bowl of water and did not float. That milk must be sieved to remove hairs and pieces of grass – and then boiled, of course. And that rice must be washed before cooking and searched very carefully for stones. The same went for lentils and dried beans.

Menelik pretended to ignore her as she ran through her list of concerns, but Mara knew he was listening to see if she missed anything. When she was finished, she was pleased to see him give a brief nod of approval. As she left the room, she heard him speak to Dudu.

'Did you hear everything the Bwana Memsahib has said to you? Then be careful. If you make a mistake she will beat you very badly!'

Mara walked along the line of tin huts, beginning at the far end where Daudi had already settled in. Through the open doorway she could see his brown suit jacket draped over one of the single bunks. He was going to share his room with the ranger, when he arrived. Mara wondered uneasily what John would think about having Africans staying in the guest quarters. It had never happened before. Out on safari, a camaraderie bordering on real intimacy often arose between the white hunter and his clients and the native gunbearers and trackers. It was born of the shared danger and excitement of the hunt, and the Africans' evident superiority in their knowledge of the land and its animals. But back at the lodge there had always been a different protocol. Mara had been unsure about how to accommodate the Africans who had arrived with the film company – she'd been glad to let Kefa take charge. He'd decided that Daudi and the ranger would stay in one of these huts and share meals with the Europeans in the dining room. He'd given the construction workers rooms in the old farm-labourers' cottage at the back of the lodge, where they would sleep as well as eat. Mara hoped the right choices had been made. This was no longer Tanganyika – it was independent Tanzania. New rules were needed about many things, but no one seemed quite sure what they should be.

She reached the second of the mudbrick rondavels, the one where Peter Heath would stay. She could see the hut boys inside hanging up a stained old mosquito net.

'*Namna gani?*' she demanded in a burst of annoyance. Then she remembered she should be encouraging them to use English. 'What do you think you are doing?' she asked. 'This is an old net. It is dirty! It has holes in it as well.' She felt herself being influenced by Menelik's approach to the kitchen boy. 'This room is for the big boss actor. If he is not happy, he is going to cause very bad trouble!'

Moving further into the room she stopped abruptly, noticing that a European man was standing near the bed. He had his back to her and was holding up the frame for the net. Mara noted his dusty shoes and the streaks of dirt on his blue linen shirt. Near his feet some well-worn duffel bags had been dumped on the floor.

'I'm sorry,' she said. 'This room is reserved for Peter Heath.' She forced an impatient smile as she waved an arm in the direction of the tin huts. 'You may choose any of the others down that way.'

Passing the net frame to one of the hut boys, the man stepped towards her. As he moved into a shaft of sunlight, Mara froze. The face suddenly looked familiar. It took her a second to realise that it wasn't that she'd seen this actual face before; it was more that – lit from the side – it matched some image of perfection that she instinctively recognised. His features were so finely moulded; his eyes a striking blue-green, set against sun-streaked brown hair and olive skin.

She let her arm fall to her side. Without having to ask, she knew. It had to be him. The actor.

'Hi,' he said. 'I'm Peter Heath.'

'I'm so sorry.' Mara could feel a blush rising up her body and flaming in her cheeks. 'I thought . . . I was told you'd be coming by plane, some time after lunch.' She gathered herself. 'I'm Mara Sutherland. How do you do?'

'I'm fine, thanks,' Peter said, giving her a friendly smile.

'Your room's not quite ready, I'm afraid. But we can have it fixed in a few minutes.'

'Don't worry about it,' Peter said. 'I'm in no hurry. Anyway, it's my fault I got here early. I decided to come with the others. I like to travel by road if I can – I prefer to see things close-up.'

As he spoke, Mara listened for an Australian accent. Leonard was right – you'd never know the actor came from her homeland. He sounded just like an American.

Peter brushed a hand down his shirt. The front looked as dirty as the back. 'We had to change a tyre.'

Mara managed to smile. 'It looks like it! Well . . .' She took a breath, squaring her shoulders. 'Welcome to Raynor Lodge.' She found herself moving sideways, distancing her dress from the matching curtains. She wondered if there was still any powder left on her face, or pink on her lips.

'Thanks. It's beautiful here.' Peter returned to the task of fitting the net frame in place.

'You shouldn't be doing that,' Mara protested. 'You really mustn't.'

'Why not?' Peter asked. 'Aren't I the "big boss actor"? Surely I can do what I like!' He grinned at her, looking suddenly younger, almost mischievous.

Mara glanced around her, at a loss as to what to say or do next. She ran one hand back over her hair, checking that no strands had come loose from her ponytail. Finally, she turned to the hut boys. 'Make sure Mr Heath's luggage is put up on the table,' she said. 'We don't want it eaten by ants. And swap the net for a new one.' She looked quickly back at Peter. 'If you need anything, please let me know.'

She moved briskly outside. As she hurried back towards the lodge she raised her hands to her cheeks, patting away the heat that still burned there.

FIVE

The hut boys sprinted along the runway, shouting and waving their arms to scare off a family of gazelles. The animals fled in alarm, kicking up their heels in the way they always did – as a show of nonchalance, intended to convince predators that they were not easy targets.

Mara stood nearby, looking up at the plane as it circled overhead. It began its descent as soon as the boys reached the end of the runway. Mara scanned the crowd of villagers that had come down to the grassy plain to watch – she hoped they understood the need to keep well away until the plane had stopped. Shifting her attention to the runway, she began to worry that there might still be some stumps or rocks left behind. Then she dragged her gaze away. There was nothing she could do about it now.

She thought, instead, about Lillian Lane – would she be as beautiful in real life as she was onscreen? And what would she be wearing? Mara half-imagined her appearing in a long gown, a stole draping her shoulders. But in reality, she knew Lillian Lane would most likely be outfitted in the same style as the other women who came to stay at the lodge. Almost invariably, they arrived wearing safari suits that had been tailored impractically to show off their figures, and bush hats they'd bought in Nairobi or Dar – the kind that came ready-made with a band of leopard-skin around the crown.

The first glimpse of the famous face appeared in the small round window of the plane as it taxied to a standstill. Even from a distance, and shrouded with the dust thrown up by the wheels, there was no mistaking who it was. Mara felt a flutter of nervous excitement as she waited for the propellers to slow down.

She saw the pilot jump out and open the passenger door. For what felt like a long time, nothing else happened. Then Carlton climbed from the cabin, stretching his limbs as if relieved to have escaped the cramped space. Moments later, a foot appeared, elegantly shod in a yellow suede boot laced to the knee. It hovered in mid-air before coming to rest on the metal step. A second foot followed. Then the rest of Lillian's body came into view as she took Carlton's outstretched hand and stepped down onto the ground. She paused, looking around, before giving the onlookers a small wave. In response, the Africans drew nearer. A child stepped from their midst, holding out a huge bunch of white native lillies.

Mara moved closer as well, trying not to stare. Lillian Lane was dressed, as expected, in a khaki safari suit. But rather than consisting of a pair of tailored trousers and a close-fitting shirt, hers had been made in one piece like a jump suit and was gathered at the waist by a leather belt. She did not wear a hat, and her hair was tied back in a low chignon. Her mouth, painted scarlet, stood out against her fair skin.

Instead of moving away from the plane, Lillian stepped aside, then turned immediately to look into the cabin. It occurred to Mara that she might have brought her boyfriend with her – the one who'd stood with her on the deck of the yacht. Luckily, there were two beds in Lillian's rondavel. They could easily be pushed together and a double net brought in . . .

But the person who climbed out of the aircraft next was an African. From his red beret and green uniform, Mara identified him as the ranger from Arusha. Reaching back into the dim interior, he pulled out a heavy-gauge double-barrelled rifle. While Carlton and Lillian looked on, he broke the breach and took two cartridges from his chest pocket and loaded them. Only then, with the ranger at their side, did they venture from the shadows cast by the wings of the plane.

Carlton kept an arm on the actress's elbow. He steered her towards Mara, his portly body moving awkwardly over the uneven ground, calling out introductions as he approached.

'Lillian – this is Mrs Sutherland. Mrs Sutherland – Miss Lane.'

The actress smiled warmly, her bright lips hugging the line of her teeth. She wore no other make-up yet still managed to look utterly glamorous. The turned-up collar of her suit brushed the tips of a pair of drop pearl earrings.

'Call me Lillian, please,' she said.

'Thank you,' Mara said politely. 'My name's Mara.'

'Mara,' Lillian repeated. 'What a pretty name! I've never heard it before.' There was a look of intense interest on her face.

Mara smiled, feeling pleased, as if she'd chosen the name herself.

Lillian leaned towards her, putting a hand on her arm. 'I'm so glad to be here,' she confided. 'I hate small planes, you know. I have a fear of heights.'

'Oh, poor you,' Mara responded. She was touched by Lillian's friendly manner – it wasn't what she'd expected. 'Why don't you come straight up to the lodge and have a cup of tea?'

'That's very sweet of you,' Lillian said. 'But I don't drink tea. Or coffee.'

'Well, have a lemonade, then,' Carlton broke in. 'You have to drink something in this heat.'

Lillian didn't seem to hear him. She turned towards the little girl with the flowers. Bending to accept the offering, she laid one hand on the child's curly hair and looked straight into her eyes. Mara recognised the same intent gaze that had just been lavished on her. Perhaps this was how famous people behaved, she thought, parcelling out their attention in small, careful pieces.

They set off along the path that had already been worn between the runway and the track that led up to the lodge. As they walked – the ranger hovering nearby, his gun cradled in his hands – Lillian leaned close to Mara again. There was a waft of floral perfume: a light, innocent scent.

'What I'd really like,' she said, 'is a gin and tonic with ice.'

Mara fought an impulse to look down at her watch; it could not be much later than three. 'Of course,' she replied in a confidential tone. 'I'll have the house boy bring one to your room.'

'Thank you,' Lillian responded. 'You're an angel.'

Mara ushered Lillian into the rondavel ahead of her. The actress turned in a slow circle. There was a small smile of pleasure fixed on her lips. Mara had watched it settle there as they'd walked in under the elephant tusks. It had not wavered as they'd crossed the brown lawns and walked down the path beside the half-dug swimming pool hole. Mara watched that smile, now, as Lillian studied her surroundings. Carlton stood in the open doorway, motionless, as if holding his breath. The quiet seemed to stretch out, becoming thin and taut. But then, suddenly, Lillian spoke.

'I just love it – it's gorgeous!'

As tension eased from the air, Mara relaxed and began her hostess speech. 'I'm sure you'll be comfortable here. It's one of our best rooms. As you can see, the floors are made of earth.' She pointed to the ground near her feet; the surface had recently been re-sealed with a shiny film of beeswax and cooking oil. 'It's much better than the wooden floors we have in the tin huts; nothing can get in and live underneath it. The only thing you have to be careful about is white ants. They'll eat anything you leave on the ground, so please keep all your belongings up on the trunk stand or on the spare bed. Then, of course, there are drawers for you to use as well.' She waved her hand towards the dressing table – the one that had been brought here from her own bedroom.

Mara noticed Lillian looking with a puzzled frown at the small jars that had been placed beneath each leg of the two beds. 'They contain kerosene,' she explained, 'which stops anything like ticks or bed bugs crawling up into the bed when the mosquito net's not in place.'

She pointed to the place where Bwana Stimu had modified a

light fitting to create a power point. 'That's for your hairdryer,' she said. 'Don't worry about that wire. It isn't dangerous.'

Carlton entered the space as though drawn by the word. 'What's dangerous?' he demanded. He frowned at the trailing earth wire. 'Don't touch it,' he instructed Lillian. 'I'll get Brendan to check it.'

'That's really not necessary.' Mara felt a flash of indignation on Bwana Stimu's behalf. 'I'll ask our own electricity expert to come and demonstrate it for you later, when the generator's running.' She crossed the room and leaned into the toilet annexe. She could smell the freshly cut grass the hut boys had used to line the four-gallon tin that sat beneath the wooden toilet seat. 'This is the *chow* hut. Sprinkle with ash after use to discourage flies. It will be changed each day.'

Mara's gaze lingered on the set of towels that hung from the hooks. They were – as Carlton had instructed – all in a matching shade of mauve: handtowel, face washer and bath towel. The lodge linen closets did not contain any full sets of towels – these had been a wedding present. Mara's Auntie Ade had hand embroidered them with *His* and *Hers*. She'd given them to Mara in the kitchen – surreptitiously, as if they, like Lorna's wedding dress, were a coded expression of rebellion against the rules of the world the women inhabited. Mara had deliberated over whether or not the towels should be placed in here – they were, after all, meant only for her and John. Now she'd met Lillian she knew she'd made the right decision. If the towels helped the actress feel more comfortable here, Mara was happy to let her use them.

But when she leaned back into the main room, she saw that Lillian's smile had gone, and she was now eyeing her surroundings with alarm. Mara hid her dismay, reminding herself she'd seen this reaction before. What she had to do was add the final piece of her speech – the bit designed to help guests take a positive view of the facilities. She adopted a bright tone. 'Of course, it's not what you're used to. It's not like home. This is Africa. The real Africa!'

She watched the familiar struggle playing out on Lillian's face – the battle between the person a guest knew themselves to be, and the one they wished they could become.

'The real Africa,' Lillian repeated the words. 'At last . . .'

Mara saw Carlton close his eyes with relief as he stepped quietly away, disappearing in the direction of the other huts. With the doorway now clear, the hut boys began bringing in Lillian's luggage. The first boy carried a large battered suitcase in one hand and a bulging tapestry shoulder bag in the other, and the second appeared with three more suitcases – all in matching red leather – piled on top of his head.

'Would you like them to help you unpack?' Mara asked.

'I'd much rather you stayed,' said Lillian. 'If you can spare the time . . .' She was already waving the boys away.

Mara hovered near the cases, ready to receive instructions. But Lillian gestured for her to sit down. Then Lillian opened the first of the cases and took out a bottle of perfume. As she dabbed some of it onto her wrists, the same light floral scent Mara had already smelled on her drifted into the air.

'My favourite perfume,' Lillian said. '*L'Air du Temps.* Don't you just love the bottle?'

She handed it over, so that Mara could see the distinctive frosted glass stopper, cast in the shape of a pair of kissing doves.

Next, Lillian brought out a framed picture and held it at her waist. She stood still, gazing fondly down. Then she showed it to Mara.

Mara's eyes widened in surprise. She'd expected to see a photograph of a man – perhaps the one she'd seen in the magazine picture. Instead she found herself looking at an image of an Alsatian dog.

'That's Theo,' Lillian said. 'I miss him terribly. Usually he travels everywhere with me.' She sighed. 'I seriously considered not taking the part of Maggie because I couldn't bring him here. But it's not every day you get the chance to work with the Miller brothers. They're making such interesting movies compared with the studios.' She flashed a smile at Mara. 'You know, they wrote the part with me in mind.'

Mara smiled back, nodding – unsure what to say. It was not as if she were used to taking part in this kind of conversation. Lillian pulled a pair of satin pyjamas from the case and tossed them behind her onto the bed. Mara knew she should be insisting on doing something to help, but the truth was, she was enjoying just sitting here, listening to Lillian. The women who came to the lodge usually didn't bother to talk much to Mara. In fact, they often seemed disappointed that she was there. It spoiled their romantic view of John, the hunter, to see him with a wife.

Lillian picked up the shoulder bag. The sound of metal clinking against metal came from inside.

'This is my kit,' she said. 'When Katharine Hepburn was on location in the Congo – making *The African Queen* – she always made sure she had her own essentials.' The contents of the bag spilled out onto the bed: a torch with spare batteries, a compass, some bandages.

Mara raised her eyebrows as an enamel pot appeared – the bottom half of a double boiler. 'What's that for?'

Lillian picked it up, turning it around to view it from all angles like an unusual antique. 'That's in case there's no chamber pot, or commode, or whatever you want to call it. Hepburn was very particular about being able to go to the bathroom whenever she needed to. Her father was a urologist, you see.' She waited for Mara to nod, before she continued her unpacking. 'I haven't had to make use of any of these things yet, of course. But now we're way out here – who knows?' She turned to look through the window. The feathery foliage of a thorn tree was framed against a distant background of burnt grass, and a blazing blue sky. 'Are there lions down there?' she asked anxiously.

'There are – but you don't have to worry,' Mara answered in a reassuring tone. 'They very rarely come up off the plains. When you need to leave the lodge grounds, the ranger will always be with you.' Mara was glad to see that the tension was draining from Lillian's face. 'Then you will be quite safe – I promise.'

'Oh, I'm not really worried,' Lillian said. 'I like lions. Did you see that film *Born Free*? The girl was all wrong, of course – the man wasn't much good either. But the lions were adorable.'

Mara tried to find a suitable response. All she could think of were savaged carcasses of zebras and wildebeest, and bloodstains on the oat grass. 'Perhaps you'd like me to help you unpack this,' she said eventually, pointing at the largest suitcase – the odd one out.

'Not yet,' Lillian replied. 'That's the wardrobe. Make-up's in there as well. It depends where the dressing room's going to be . . . I suppose Carlton will speak to you about it. Or Rudi, perhaps. There's no one here from those departments. Peter and I have agreed to do our own dressing. It's a very unusual situation. Everyone's just pitching in – to help save the picture.' She glanced towards the window and lowered her voice before continuing. 'The schedule is shot to pieces. The budget's gone way over.' She turned back to her suitcase and lifted out a silk kimono. 'But the rushes are fabulous. It's a masterpiece in the making. You'll see it one day – and then you'll understand why we all care about it so much.' As she moved to hang the gown on the back of the door, she passed close to Mara. She stopped, and looked straight into her eyes. It was the intense gaze Mara had seen before – like a light being switched on. She felt herself being drawn to its brightness. 'It will be one of those movies you remember for the rest of your life.' The words seemed to linger in the quiet room, as if they held the weight of a promise, or a curse. Then the moment was gone. Lillian smiled at Mara. 'I'd love that gin and tonic, by the way.'

'Yes, of course,' Mara said, jumping to her feet. 'I'll send Kefa over with it straightaway.'

Mara sat near the head of the main dining table, in the place that was always reserved for John. As she glanced around the room, she felt a glow of pride. All the tables had been set ready for the meal. Glittering wine glasses and freshly cleaned silver cutlery were laid out in rows along the ebony tables. Ranks of starched linen napkins, folded into triangles, stood out in contrast to the dark wood. The impressive display was made complete by vases of white, apricot and pink bougainvillea. The whole scene was subtly lit by candles and hurricane lanterns, even though the generator was still running.

Kefa was directing people to their seats, making sweeping gestures with his hands. The hut boys – now outfitted in long white caftans and red skull caps – were helping him. Near the end of Mara's table were the two Nicks – the director of photography and his young assistant – identically attired in white lounge suits. They were too far away for Mara to greet, so she just waved. As she did so, she became aware that Carlton, Leonard and Peter were approaching her table. Kefa pulled out chairs so they could take their places. The seat to Mara's right was reserved for Lillian. The two brothers filled the spaces beside it and Peter sat down to her left. Mara stole a sideways look at him, registering his fine, even features and unusual blue-green eyes. She tried not to think back over their previous encounter. She couldn't imagine, now, how she'd managed to mistake him for a member of the crew.

Suddenly, she realised he was looking at her.

'Is everything all right in your room?' she asked.

'Yes, thanks,' he responded. 'It's a great room.'

'Good.' Mara searched for something more to say – something intelligent, sensible. 'The net's okay?'

'Yes. It hangs beautifully.' There was a hint of a smile on Peter's lips. 'I like sleeping under nets – it reminds me of going to our shack as a kid.'

Mara looked at him with interest. She was about to ask him

where his family shack had been – up in the bush or by the sea. But then she realised Leonard was leaning across the table towards Peter, seeking his attention.

'I've been thinking about that line in scene forty-seven,' he said now. 'The one about Maggie and the phone call. You should be really definite about it. Make it strong.'

Peter gave Mara an apologetic look as he turned to Leonard. Carlton abandoned the cufflink he'd been adjusting, and followed suit, fixing his attention upon his brother. Mara had the impression that this scenario was played out often: when the director spoke, everyone listened.

'The stakes are high,' Leonard was saying. He waved his hands for emphasis, bony fingers outspread. 'I want a serious argument between you and Maggie!'

Peter nodded his agreement, then lifted his water glass to his lips. As he tilted his head back to drink, Mara's eyes were drawn to the curve of his chin, his throat. Lamplight threw a yellow glow over his face. His skin looked darker against the white linen of his shirt; his eyes a paler green. Soft shadows showed up the bones of his cheeks and forehead. He looked like an actor again – larger than life.

Mara knew she should not be staring. Perhaps Peter would be able to feel her gaze, as some people believed elephants could. John taught his clients only to observe their prey from the corners of their eyes – until the moment they were ready to take aim and shoot.

Peter lowered his glass. As he turned towards Mara, she looked quickly away, pretending to watch with interest as Kefa directed

Daudi to the vacant chair beside the red-haired sound recordist, Jamie. Daudi had swapped his brown suit for a simply cut blue shirt with a Mao collar, a style favoured by the president. Mara wondered if he had chosen it specially – a silent rebuke aimed at the gathering of Europeans in their fine suits and ties.

When all the hovering figures had been seated, there was a short hush – then Lillian strolled in. She was draped in a red evening gown that left one shoulder bare. Diamonds shone from her ears and made a sparkling circle around her neck.

She paused in the middle of the room. Suddenly she was the centrepiece, making sense of all the other elements that made up the scene. The flowers seemed to have been placed there just for her; the tables arranged so that everyone could see her arrive. Even the scent of the African night seemed to have crept inside specially to greet her.

Carlton stood up to pull out Lillian's chair. Everyone else remained seated – they were not like the English, who always stood when a lady entered the room and then hovered upright until she asked them to sit down, or did so herself. With a pang of longing, Mara remembered how endearing she'd found this habit in John. How flattering it had been to be treated so courteously. As if she were someone special – someone like Lillian – and not just the middle child of seven, raised in Mole Creek at the edge of the Western Tiers.

'I can't sit there,' Lillian stated.

Mara looked at her in surprise. Leaning sideways she checked the chair to see if there was something wrong with it, but it looked perfectly fine.

Lillian gave a high little laugh. 'I just have this thing, you know – I prefer to have my back to the wall.'

Mara sensed Carlton growing tense beside her. She stood up straightaway and offered her own chair. 'Swap with me.'

'Thank you, Mara,' Lillian said with a grateful smile as she took Mara's place. As soon as she was settled, she called Kefa and asked for a drink. Then she turned towards Peter, laying her hand on his arm. Within a few moments, she was chatting happily to him, and drawing Leonard into the conversation as well.

Carlton watched her for a moment, then he turned his attention to Mara. The expression on his face was friendly, but quite serious.

'So tell me, Mara,' he said. 'How did you come to be a hunter's wife?'

Mara had often been asked this question by guests. She usually briefly explained that she and John had met by chance in Melbourne. But she suspected that wasn't what Carlton wanted to hear. She remembered how he'd asked about the elephant skull, the first time he was here, and how she'd said a lot more than she'd intended to in response.

'When we met,' she said carefully, 'John had decided to give up professional hunting. He didn't want to shoot big game any more. He'd had enough of helping people kill animals just to take home their heads, or their tusks, as trophies.'

'I've heard of that happening,' Carlton said. 'I knew a guy who hunted every season in the Yukon. One year he just came back and sold his gun. He said, "I've shot my last deer." And that was it, for him. He never went back.'

Mara nodded. 'Yes. Well, for us, it didn't turn out to be that simple. John thought people would come here for holidays – just to relax and enjoy watching the game. But it didn't work out.'

'So . . . he had to go back to hunting?' Carlton raised his eyebrows, prompting her to go on.

'Yes.' Mara knew she should not be talking in this way. But putting the predicament she and John had faced into words was such a relief. And it didn't matter, really, what she said to Carlton – it was not like betraying confidences to Helen. In two weeks Carlton would be gone and Mara would never see him again. 'John felt bad about it – he found it difficult. But he did it.' She sighed. 'I had to learn how to be a hostess on a hunting safari. There were lots of tasks for me to help with – not just running the camp, but out hunting as well.' She looked into Carlton's eyes. Now she felt like someone making their confession. 'I tried to get used to the killing. After all, I was a farmer's daughter. Shooting eland or gazelle for the pot was fine. But the big game . . . I could cope with the buffalo, crocodiles – even lions, usually. I always left the kill before the skinners got to work. But I couldn't watch them shoot elephants. I just couldn't.' She bit her lip. Carlton didn't want to hear all this, she told herself. But she couldn't stop. 'An elephant falls so hard that the ground shakes, you can feel the shock travelling inside you. You just know – it's *wrong*.'

'I can imagine,' Carlton said.

'No.' Mara shook her head slowly. 'You can't imagine.' She looked down at her hands, grasping the edge of the tabletop, her knuckles white with tension. 'Anyway, the last straw came when John had to shoot an elephant calf. A client had disobeyed him and killed the mother by mistake. I know the baby wouldn't have survived – shooting it was the right thing to do. But it was so terrible, watching my husband do it . . . After that, I stopped going on safari with John. And that's when everything started to go wrong.' She could feel her throat closing up, her voice becoming thin. 'And, the trouble is, once things start to go wrong they just seem to get worse and worse. You can't go back and change them. There's nothing you can do.'

She broke off, aware she was not even making any sense. But Carlton nodded as though he'd understood every word.

'Believe me, I know,' he said. 'In the movie-making business, we have a saying – if it can go wrong, it will. And it will again. And again. But you know what?' He leaned towards Mara. His round face was warm and kind. 'Nearly always, it works out in the end. You can't see how it will – but something happens when you least expect it. And suddenly, everything's all right again.'

Mara found herself clinging to Carlton's words. There was such a confident, comforting tone in his voice . . . Then she reminded herself he was a film-maker. It was his job to make people believe in fairytales.

The serving of the meal proceeded smoothly, with the hut boys making surprisingly efficient waiters. The only tension arose when Lillian sent her main course back to the kitchen, asking for each portion of it to be served on a separate plate so she could see exactly what she was eating. Mara waited anxiously for a response from Menelik, and was relieved when Kefa appeared with a tray bearing a collection of little sundae bowls, each containing a small serving of a different dish. Now, most of the guests were just finishing their dessert and the hum of contented conversation flowed around the tables. Mara would have felt almost relaxed, except she had one more task to undertake before the evening was over.

When the coffee had been served, she told Carlton that before anyone left the dining room she needed to give a talk about safety. It was something John always did when new guests arrived. As well as being necessary from a practical point of view, it was one of the ways he asserted his authority. He adopted a manner that was very firm, yet kind and calm; his voice was that of a parent – someone to be respected and obeyed. It was vital to establish the right relationship with clients from the beginning or there was no knowing what they might do out on the trail, when faced with danger, or when tempted to a make a kill that was illegal or immoral – or both.

'Are you sure it's necessary?' Carlton glanced at Lillian. 'Can't you just tell me and I'll pass the word around?'

Mara hesitated. She was certainly not looking forward to playing the part of the Bwana. She wasn't sure who she felt more self-conscious about performing in front of – the film people, or her own staff.

But she got to her feet, shaking her head. It had to be done properly.

She positioned herself so that she was looking at everyone, and no one. In a voice that she knew mimicked John's, she delivered her speech.

First, she listed the more serious potential dangers in this part of Africa: getting bitten by malaria-carrying mosquitoes; coming down with dysentery after drinking water straight from the tap; being attacked by a rabid dog or monkey; encountering a lion or leopard or elephant; or stepping on a Green Mamba, the local snake whose bite was always fatal.

She outlined safety precautions in what she hoped was a comforting tone. She reassured her listeners that wild animals normally prefer to leave humans well alone – but made it clear that nonetheless, as a precaution, guests should never leave the lodge grounds without being accompanied by a member of the staff. After all, whereas people accustomed to living in Africa might be able to assess levels of danger, a newcomer could not afford to take any risks. She paused, to let this point sink in. Then she moved on to less serious issues. If guests left food in their rooms, bats and monkeys would find a way to get in – and they were very untidy visitors. If people walked around outside with bare feet they might pick up hookworm or a jigger. If they dropped their watch or wedding ring into the pit latrines, there would be no way of retrieving it.

Mara was conscious of tension growing in the room. She understood that she just didn't have the reassuring presence of the Bwana – the white hunter. She didn't have the belief in herself.

She was glad when at last she was finished. A hush fell over the room as she sat down. She picked up her table napkin, occupying herself in spreading it over her lap. She kept her head bowed, her gaze fixed on the white linen square as she twisted it into a knot.

'How did you remember all that?' Peter's voice came to her softly, kindly. 'You didn't even have notes.'

Now that the quiet had been broken, a murmur of conversation started up.

Mara smiled gratefully at him. 'Oh, I've heard it a few times before.'

'Speaking of safety precautions . . .' Lillian drained her glass, before looking around at her companions. 'Did you know that Bogart drank gin all the time when they were making *The African Queen*? And I mean all the time! Well, it's true.' She stood up, waving to attract Kefa's attention and holding her glass out as he drew near. 'And guess what? He was the one who never got ill. So from now on, I'm going to think of gin as medicine.'

'Medicine,' Kefa repeated. He turned to Mara, repeating the word in Swahili to see if he'd understood correctly. '*Dawa?*'

Mara gave a non-committal shrug. The translation was correct, but she didn't want to seem to be endorsing Lillian's comments. Some people believed the quinine in tonic water helped keep malaria at bay – but she'd not heard of gin protecting against tropical illnesses.

When Kefa returned with her drink, Lillian announced she'd take it to her room. She stifled a yawn, pressing smooth, manicured fingertips over her mouth.

'It's been a long day.' She held out a hand towards Peter. 'Darling, would you be an angel and walk me to my room? It's awfully dark out there.'

Peter got to his feet straightaway, excusing himself to Mara, Carlton and Leonard. 'Of course I will.'

Lillian slipped her arm through Peter's as she led him away. Mara found herself watching them as they moved through the room. At first, she thought she detected a slight reserve in Peter's manner, but then he turned side-on – shepherding Lillian past the other table – and Mara saw him laugh in a relaxed and comfortable way. Lillian rested her head on his shoulder in a brief, yet intimate gesture. For a moment, Mara was surprised – almost shocked. But then, why wouldn't they be close, she asked herself? They'd been living and working together for weeks. Not only that, she realised, they could well be playing the part of lovers, onscreen: the leading lady and the leading man usually did.

The two stepped out onto the verandah. Moths drawn to the light above the doorway fluttered like golden confetti above their heads. As they disappeared into the night, it suddenly occurred to Mara that they might even, in fact, be lovers. Perhaps that's how it was, for people like Lillian Lane and Peter Heath. Each new film brought a new love affair. Then they moved on. They were sophisticated enough – strong enough – not to let anything matter too much . . .

Moonlight shone through the window, adding a cool blue edge to the glow of the kerosene lantern. Mara had hung the lamp high on the wall so that it cast its soft light broadly over the room. She stood by the window in a short nightdress made of plain white cotton. In her hand she held the note she'd been given by the mission radio operator. Smoothing out the scrap of paper, she reread John's message. She knew that radio messages always sounded blunt: they were designed to be clear and brief. But even so, she felt the coolness in the words – a remoteness from her.

Folding the message again, Mara looked out into the night, staring into the distance beyond the dark shapes of the garden.

Somewhere out there – half a country away – lay the Selous Reserve. And somewhere in that ten thousand square miles of wild bushland, was John.

She pictured him sitting by the campfire, resting his elbows on his knees, a tin cup cradled in his hands. He would be quiet, letting the chatter of his companions and the singing of porters on the other side of the camp wash over him. He'd be relaxed in the knowledge that he'd chosen his camp well – in an open space, protected by a few solid trees. Nevertheless, his senses would be constantly focused on the sounds of the bush, listening out for the telltale crack of a tree limb, or the quiet cough of a leopard.

Mara could almost smell the fragrant smoke of the campfire, blending with insect repellent and dried sweat. She could hear the hiss of the Tilley lamp and the faint crackle of insects roasting on the hot glass of the chimney. What had they eaten for the evening meal, she wondered, these foot safari clients.

And who were they?

She tried to cut off the thought – snapping it like a piece of cotton and picking up another thread. But still, she found herself imagining the circle of faces gathered around the fire. The eyes flashing bright in the glow of the flames, cheeks washed with orange. Rugged men's faces, sunburnt and tough. Their voices blending into a low rumble. Then another voice rising above theirs, high and silvery. Slender legs moving past the fire, lit from behind . . .

Women don't take foot safaris into the Selous, Mara told herself. It's tough even for men.

But still, she felt drawn to the idea – like a moth fluttering towards the light, not stopping, even as the heat begins to singe its wings.

Perhaps, there was a woman there – a daughter, perhaps; or a wife who didn't love her husband; or even one of those female zoologists people admired so much. Mara had met a group of them once, on their way to join Jane Goodall – they were tough, independent; interesting and attractive.

Mara told herself to put these thoughts from her mind. Not to give in to them.

Instead, her hands pushed her away from the window. Her feet carried her across the room. The next moment, she was standing by John's chest of drawers, searching blindly amongst the piles of ironed shorts and socks rolled into pairs . . .

And there it was – the old bush vest folded up at the back, no longer used.

From the chest pocket she took out an envelope. Slowly she drew out two pictures, holding them one behind the other, the top one tilted towards the lamp. She tried to view them as items of mild curiosity – the way Carlton had examined the photographs on the wall in the sitting room.

The light played over the matt surface of the first picture, picking out the larger-than-life tones of Kodachrome colour. It was an image of a tall woman with long fair hair, standing beside John. They were close together, their bodies meeting shoulder to shoulder, hip to hip – no dead animal at their feet, coming between them. With matching hair and eyes, they looked like brother and sister. And the way they stood, so relaxed and at ease – they might have been companions for years. There was none of the seductive posing or fake bravado typical of the client and hunter image. The woman's gaze was level and frank.

She looked like someone you would want to meet. She looked nice.

Mara closed her eyes, the ache of jealousy spreading out from the pit of her stomach, invading her body.

But still, she drew out the second photograph.

This one was only of her.

Matilda.

Mara mouthed the name. It sounded light, pretty; yet it carried with it a certain weight and gravity.

Matilda was standing on the steps of the Muthaiga Club, dressed for dinner in a long silver sheath with a matching stole. In the light of the camera's flashbulb, the garments gleamed; Matilda looked like a goddess, wrapped in moonshine. She wore a subtle deep red lipstick and had her hair piled high on her head. Standing there, poised and beautiful, she could have been a film star – like Lillian Lane.

Mara drew a folded sheet of paper from the envelope. Her fingers were poised, ready to open it out. But the truth was, she could recite every word by heart; she already knew the shape of each hand-drawn letter, arranged in long sloping lines across the page.

She'd found the envelope by chance, rifling through John's drawers in search of an old shirt to wear. The task of putting away the Bwana's laundered clothing was the responsibility of the kitchen boy – and when Mara had found the old vest, tightly rolled up and stuffed in behind a pile of khaki shorts, she'd almost called the boy in to explain why it was there, and not hanging in the wardrobe. But then she'd glimpsed the corner of the envelope protruding from the pocket.

The photographs had not immediately concerned her. It was not unusual for clients to send prints of their photographs here – their African safari loomed large in their minds, and they imagined themselves to have held a unique place in the story of the lodge. Usually, the pictures were pinned up on the corkboard behind the bar, for other clients to see. Occasionally, an image was framed and added to the collection on the wall.

But John had hidden these ones away. And the envelope they were in had just two words on the front – *for John*. There was no address or stamp; it had been delivered by hand.

Then Mara had seen the letter. Before the questions even had time to form in her mind, she'd opened out a single sheet of paper printed with the letterhead of Raynor Lodge.

The words had swum before her – phrases appearing in stark clarity, then being swept away in a haze of shock.

One night to treasure forever . . . Though we'll never meet again, I'll always remember your hands on my body, your lips in my hair . . . Let's not say love, for we are strangers still – and yet there will never be anything so precious, so true . . .

She'd stood there, the paper trembling in her hand, the words refusing to stay still – their meaning so huge. She felt the air being squeezed from her lungs. Strength drained from her legs. Pain shafted deep into her soul, like the strike of a sword.

It had been five months ago. Five months, three days and a night.

Countless times since then, Mara had relived each step in the unfolding nightmare. First, she'd hidden behind disbelief. It seemed impossible that John would have broken his golden rule, the one Raynor had taught him mattered most – that you rent out your services as a hunter, but you keep yourself to yourself. There is a line that must never be crossed.

But he had. He had . . .

Then, she'd begun looking back, replaying scenes in her mind, trying to reinterpret them in the light of what she now knew.

She remembered Matilda's arrival at the lodge, in the company of her father. Mara had been able to tell that they were English, even before they offered their opening greetings. *How do you do? How do you do?*

There had been the dinner at the lodge, the night before the safari. Mara had expected Matilda to appear – as guests usually did – in an evening gown. Instead, she'd worn a simple knee-length dress, which had somehow contrived to make her look even more glamorous.

Most of all, Mara remembered the morning Matilda and her father had left with John on safari. It was just after first light. The trees surrounding the lodge were dark cut-out shapes set against a deep pink sky. It was the quiet time, in the moments before the sunrise. Soon the sun would emerge – a ball of gold, shedding light over the plains. The air was filled with the subdued excitement of people preparing to leave on safari. Menelik stood near the Land Rover holding his collection of cooking utensils and looking on while Dudu brought load after load of supplies – bottles, sacks, buckets and tins – from the kitchen. Kefa hovered close by, counting camp beds, tent bags, nets, bedding, lamps and washbasins. The gunbearer worked his way along a line-up of firearms, examining them one by one, then securing them in place on the vehicle's gun racks.

Matilda had wandered into the scene, still eating a hot biscuit from the breakfast buffet. Her father followed. He was fidgeting with the epaulettes on his bush shirt, and in his taut movements, Mara recognised the tension of a man torn between excitement and fear. He was an experienced hunter, and he knew what lay ahead.

Mara had smiled as Matilda approached her. She could smell the clean fragrance of Matilda's soap.

'I don't know how you can bear to stay behind!' Matilda had said. She had the same accent as John, and the same way of shaping each word individually before letting it go. 'Don't you wish you were coming?'

'Well, of course,' Mara had said. 'But I've got a lot to do around here.'

She hoped the question would not be pursued. She couldn't imagine explaining to someone like Matilda – who had described to John the pleasures of stalking deer on the family estate – that she was not prepared to stand behind people holding guns, watching them take aim at an elephant grazing, or a lion yawning at the sunset. That she couldn't be sure she would not shout out a warning. Or how, if she found herself waiting back in the Land Rover while hunters covered the last mandatory yards on foot before making their kill, her hand would be hovering near the horn.

And she couldn't explain that she was still haunted by the screams of a small pale baby, his trunk waving frantically in the air as he tried to wake his mother from her stillness. And by the silence that had enveloped the land, draining the air of oxygen, after John had pressed the barrel of his gun against the little head, and squeezed the trigger . . .

John had appeared, then, neatly dressed to match his freshly washed vehicle. Mara had watched him check the blackened tyres and bend down to look underneath the chassis. Then he was ready to go.

While Matilda and her father climbed into the Land Rover, he'd come to stand in front of Mara.

They'd swapped goodbyes, their smiles edged with tension, an unspoken question hanging between them. Did his wife wish him luck – or a futile safari?

John had leaned to kiss Mara goodbye.

As she'd brushed her lips against his cheek, she'd imagined she could already smell on him the fresh open air of the plains, the herbal tang of wild sage being squashed underfoot. The gun-oil and the blood . . .

She'd met his gaze and seen a flicker of defiance there. Had he known, already, she now asked herself? Had Matilda? Perhaps it had been so inevitable that even Menelik, looking on, had understood what was going to happen?

Mara pushed the letter and the two photographs back into the envelope and carefully replaced them in the vest pocket. She rolled the vest into a ball – exactly as she'd found it that first time – and put it back in its hiding place. She didn't want John to realise it had ever been disturbed.

His secret had become hers.

If John had been away when she'd made her discovery, perhaps Mara might have packed a suitcase and left. But where would she have gone? Even if she'd had the money to return to Australia, she would not have contemplated it. She could not go back and admit to her father that he had been right all along. Nor could she bear to tell Lorna that their shared faith in the power of dreams had proved unfounded. And what kind of life would Mara have as a divorcee? She had never even met anyone whose marriage had ended. In the farming communities of Tasmania, the bonds of matrimony were as solid and reliable as the boundary fence-lines that marked out one farm from another.

As it was, the day Mara found the envelope, John had been right here at the lodge, working outside. After standing motionless in the bedroom, anger building inside her as the meaning of what had happened seeped in, Mara had gone to find him.

There was an air of unreality in the way her feet moved one after another so normally; finding their way through doorways and over steps as though nothing in the world had changed.

She found him at work in the swimming pool hole, digging steadily. At the sight of him, she froze, prickles running up her spine. Part of her wanted to run to him, asking for comfort – as if the pain she felt had been inflicted by an enemy. John would defend her, help her, comfort her.

But it was so much more complicated than that.

Mara retreated behind a frangipani bush, her heart thumping in her chest; the heavy perfume of the pink blooms stirring the sickness inside her. Through the screen of leaves and branches, she watched him.

John was stripped to the waist and grimy with dust. As he swung the shovel, muscles hardened in his arms, his chest, his torso.

She stared at his body – the same body that had been touched by another woman.

The body that was no longer hers . . .

Sweat ran in streams down his face. There was a sense of desperation in his labour, as though everything depended on the hole growing bigger and bigger, the pool being finished. His lips were pressed together in the grim line of someone fighting pain.

Mara stood there, motionless. She'd come to confront him, but now, when she tried to think of how she would begin, words refused to come to her. She felt unnerved by the expression on his face – he was like a stranger to her. She couldn't guess how he would react.

Tears filled her eyes. Her anger dwindled away, becoming thin and useless. Uncertainty and confusion grew up in its place. And a cold thread of fear. The consequences of this moment would go on forever. Time could not be wound back.

It occurred to her, then, that it might be better just to try to forget what had happened. Matilda had said in her letter that she and John would never meet again – everything she'd written had suggested it was a one-night affair. Perhaps Mara should not let it become more important than it was.

She knew that if she were to ask one of the wives in the village what they'd do in her situation, they'd just laugh at her. 'Is he throwing you out of your house?' they would ask. 'Is he giving this other woman babies and depriving you?' They might even suggest Mara demand that her husband marry this second woman – then there would be two Memsahibs to share all the work of running the lodge.

Mara also knew that if she were one of the 'Kenya wives' living in Happy Valley – where singles and couples alike indulged in wild house parties – she might not take John's unfaithfulness too seriously either.

And surely, that was the most practical way to move on.

But 'moving on' had not been that simple. Mara began avoiding any kind of intimate conversation with John, in case the secret might have to be addressed.

And, she kept looking in the mirror, evaluating her appearance. John had been her first lover, and she had been his. On their honeymoon night, they had been equal in their ignorance. Now, Mara was haunted by the realisation that her husband had someone to compare her with.

She tortured herself with questions. She was dark where the English woman was fair. Did John prefer the delicacy of light-coloured hair? Did his wife's body seem blemished, now – crudely marked with black? And what were the secrets of the other woman's body?

If John touched Mara, now – or if he didn't touch her – she couldn't help wondering if he was wishing she were someone else. Someone who looked like an angel and spoke with the voice of a queen . . .

As the weeks lengthened into months, Mara told herself that she understood why her husband had been unfaithful to her. She knew he felt that her refusal to join him on safari was a personal rejection. She was also aware that while it was true he'd expressed a wish to stop trophy hunting, John found his wife's abhorrence of his work deeply hurtful. Hunting big game was the thing he did best in life – his finest skill. And it was tied up with his admiration for his beloved mentor, Raynor. And then, there was the stress of the failing business. The financial pressure. The endless hard work.

So many reasons for a man to be tempted by warmth and laughter and the admiration of a beautiful woman . . .

But however much she might have understood the reasons for the affair, Mara had not been able to counter its effects. She could feel all the unspoken words, the embraces she had held back, forming an invisible wall that enclosed her in a cold and lonely place. With each day that passed, the barrier grew higher.

She could not imagine any way, now, that the wall could be breached – that something could break through, and touch her.

Mara lay on one side of the bed, keeping her arms close to her body – as if John were not hundreds of miles away but there beside her, taking up the empty space. Small sounds punctuated the quiet of the evening: the murmur of voices, the bang of a door, a cough, a laugh. These were not the usual night noises of the bush, but the sounds of a place inhabited by many people. Mara reminded herself that this was what John and she had dreamed of – Raynor Lodge, humming with people, life. But it meant nothing, now. Nothing mattered any more.

She shifted her head on the pillow, trying to ease the tension in her neck. The exhaustion she'd felt earlier on had abandoned her. She lay rigid, kept awake by her thoughts. They circled in her head – whining, angry – like hungry insects hunting in the dark.

SIX

A steady thudding sound worked its way slowly into Mara's consciousness, finally dragging her from her troubled dreams. She lifted her head from the pillow. She could hear a murmur of voices coming from the garden. And from the other side of the bedroom wall came the clatter of plates being washed up in the kitchen. She sat upright, looking across to the window. The light was clear and strong. It was well after dawn.

Throwing back her sheet, she dragged the end of the net from under the mattress and jumped out of bed. Grabbing her watch from the side table she stared in dismay at the tiny hands. Nearly eight o'clock. How could she have slept in, with the lodge full of people to care for?

She ran into the adjoining bathroom. Turning on the hot tap, she held her fingers under the stream of water. When it ran warm, she breathed a sigh of relief: the firewood boy had done his job – even though she had not been there to supervise him.

After washing quickly, Mara pulled on her work clothes and emerged from her room, treading quietly down the hallway. She felt like an intruder. The day had begun without her, and now she had to find a way to enter the activity going on around her. She dreaded walking into the main room and facing all the people gathered there. There was no warm buzz of conversation emanating from behind the door – she feared her guests might be sitting in sullen silence. Breakfast may not have been served. The hut boys may well have forgotten to deliver hot water to the rooms. They may not even have served *chai* to the guests as they lay in their beds preparing to face the day.

She paused near the doorway, unsure how to proceed. Perhaps if she crept round behind the bar, she could make it through the dining area unobserved. In the sitting-room end, she could hide behind the bamboo screen and have a good look at what was happening before she made her presence known. She was already reaching for the handle, when her gaze fell on the hall table nearby. Her hat still lay there, in the place where John always put his.

The Bwana Memsahib's hat.

After a moment's hesitation, she picked it up and placed it on her head, levelling the brim. Next, she buttoned the flap on her chest pocket, before tucking the end of her belt into the loop on her trousers waistband. Lifting her chin, she drew her face into a frown – the look of someone engrossed in an urgent mission. Then she threw open the door and strode into the room.

It took her a few seconds to realise that the place was virtually deserted. A single figure moved in the stillness. She recognised Rudi's blond curls; the props man was bent over an array of books laid out on one of the tables. As she veered towards him, trying to maintain the brisk momentum of her movements, Mara's attention was caught by a splash of colour on the sideboard. A large vase of bright red flowers had been placed there. The leafy branches dotted with trumpet-shaped blooms had been cut from one of the hibiscus bushes that grew alongside the verandah. The striking display held Mara's gaze for a moment, but then she noticed that the space around the vase looked oddly bare. Her step faltered – someone had removed Alice's collection of antique plates. Looking around, Mara saw other changes as well. On the bar lay a pile of folded white cloths and a rifle that she did not recognise. There was a three-legged stool with a zebra-skin seat that did not belong to the lodge. And the bookcase was empty.

'Hi there!' Rudi lifted his head and gave Mara a smile. 'You look busy.'

'Yes, well – so do you,' Mara answered.

Rudi was shuffling through the books.

'I hope it's okay,' he said, without looking up. 'I've packed away a few of your things, including your books. They just didn't make sense at all. *The Collected Poems of Auden. Norse Mythology. Hamlet.* How on earth did they end up here?'

Mara looked around for the books. They were some of John's most prized possessions. The leather-bound editions had been bought for him by Raynor, who had believed it was his responsibility to ensure his young apprentice did not miss out entirely on a proper education. The only book more precious to John than the ones in this collection was the battered copy of *King Solomon's Mines* he kept by his bedside. It had been his companion during the lonely years he'd spent exiled from Africa, in an English boarding school.

'Don't worry, they're safe,' Rudi said, observing Mara's expression. 'I put them in the cupboard near the door.' He began selecting books from the table, reading out their titles as he placed them in the bookshelf. '*The Wanderings of an Elephant Hunter* by Karamojo Bell. *A Hunter's Wanderings* by Frederick Selous.' He flashed a grin at Mara. 'They were sure into wandering, these guys!' He picked up a dark-covered book with an aqua spine, cradling it lovingly in his hands. 'Look at this baby. First edition *Green Hills of Africa*. I've got *Snows of Kilimanjaro* as well. Gotta have lots of Hemingway.'

Mara barely listened to him. She scanned her surroundings, noticing more and more small alterations. The room had been subtly transformed. Mara drew in a sharp breath as she imagined what John would say. Not only had he kept the room unchanged since Raynor's death – Raynor had done the same before him; apparently, the old man had not so much as moved an ornament sideways since Alice had been the memsahib here.

Mara turned back to Rudi. 'What exactly are you doing?' she demanded.

Rudi peered at her over his shoulder. 'I'm making it look more authentic. We're meant to be in a hunting lodge that was built in the thirties. The film is set in the present, when it's all faded and rundown.'

Mara glanced around her in confusion. 'But – that's exactly what it is.' As soon as the words left her mouth, she regretted them. They sounded so . . . simple.

'I have to make it more real than real,' Rudi explained. 'That's my job. I have to create the place the audience expects, taking into account what they already know. Then I add the surprise touches they would never have imagined.' He looked expectantly at Mara, like a performer awaiting applause.

'I see,' Mara said.

'It's pretty good as it is, I agree,' Rudi said. 'Much better than the farmhouse we were going to have to work with, over near that hotel. We were looking at building walls, lowering ceilings and bringing in all the basic furniture as well as the trophies, photographs, firearms —' He broke off and looked earnestly at Mara. 'I have to do a good job, you know – better than good. Working with the Miller brothers is my big break. When this movie gets released I'll be able to give up my day job. No more taxi-driving.'

Mara gave him a tentative smile. 'What else are you planning to do in here?' she asked cautiously.

Rudi was eyeing the mantelpiece as she spoke, running his gaze along the collection of African carvings and Masai beadwork necklaces arranged there. 'Heaps. I've only just begun.'

Mara knew she should tell him he must stop, right now. But she found herself unwilling to speak – and not just because of Rudi's enthusiasm for his job. The truth was, a part of her took a guilty pleasure in what he was doing. Many times, since she'd come to live at Raynor Lodge, she'd felt like making some changes herself.

'Well, you must put it back exactly as it was, when you're finished,' she said finally.

'Sure. No problem. We always do that,' Rudi answered. The words fell easily from his lips, as if they held little meaning for him. 'Great breakfast by the way. Phew,' he blew air out through his lips. 'That omelette was sure fiery. I thought I was back in Mexico.'

Mara raised her eyebrows, hoping she looked politely interested, rather than confused. Menelik only ever prepared English omelettes – light, fluffy and bland. And if breakfast had already been served, why were there no signs of it in here?

'I ordered the Tanzanian omelette,' he said. 'I saw the one they brought out for Daudi – full of green chillies. Really got me going. Fantastic.'

'I'm pleased to hear it,' Mara said. She struggled to hide her surprise. *Tanzanian omelette? Chillies?* Adopting her business-like stance again, she folded her arms. 'Where will I find Carlton?'

'Last I saw him, he was still finishing breakfast.'

'In his room?' Mara asked.

Rudi shook his head, his curls dancing around his face. 'Outside, where we all had breakfast. I couldn't have them all in here, could I – eating in the middle of my set?'

'Of course not,' Mara agreed. She turned smartly on her heels and went out onto the verandah.

Trestle tables covered with white cloths had been set up on the lawn beneath a large open-sided tent. The shelter was still being constructed; two of the Somali crew were at work hammering pegs into the hard earth. Chairs were scattered around, abandoned where their occupants had pushed them back while standing up to leave. Napkins rested in limp heaps at intervals along the tables, and scattered crumbs and red jam stains attested to the recent presence of plates and cutlery. As Mara watched, a crow swooped down on a fragment of toast. Before it had a chance to land, the kitchen boy appeared, waving a fly switch made from a zebra's tail.

'*Jambo*, Bwana Memsahib,' he sang.

'*Jambo*, Dudu,' Mara called after the boy as he chased the bird away. Flapping his arms, he looked like a bird, himself – or a flying insect. The sight brought a smile to her face.

Carlton was seated at the far end of the line of tables. Even in the shade of the tent, his Hawaiian shirt stood out, bright and cheerful. Mara was on her way towards him, when Kefa approached from the direction of the kitchen. She stopped mid-stride, a knot of anxiety tightening inside her.

'You are here!' Kefa said. He was carrying a tray, bearing a tiny cup of steaming black coffee. There was a bread roll as well, and a perfect scroll of butter. 'Menelik has sent me to find you. You are very busy. But you must eat.'

Mara looked into Kefa's eyes. He knew she had been asleep, she felt certain. She would hardly have gone off hunting at a time like this. But this was the African way, she knew – a courteous person always left room for another to retain their dignity. She lowered her gaze, humbled and grateful.

'You have served breakfast,' she stated. Glancing up, she saw Kefa bow his head in assent. 'Are there problems?' She used the Swahili word *shauri* – a broad term that covered anything from a minor difficulty to a complete catastrophe.

'No problems at all. Everyone is satisfied.'

There was no hint of reproach in Kefa's eyes, but still, Mara felt guilty that she'd left him – and Menelik – to face this first morning with the film company, on their own. She opened her mouth to say how sorry she was – then she remembered the advice Bina had given her, when she'd first come here.

Never apologise to your staff. They will not respect you for it. They will become unruly.

'You have done an excellent job,' Mara said simply.

Kefa smiled seriously. 'Thank you, Bwana Memsahib.'

'And . . .' Mara hunted for the words she wanted to add. 'I regret that I remained sleeping and did not shoulder my responsibilities.'

Kefa nodded gravely. He held out the tray towards her.

But Mara did not take it straightaway. Instead she spoke again. *'Pole sana.'* I am very sorry.

Kefa said nothing in reply. He just bowed and handed over the tray. But Mara could see how surprised he was by her words. Surprised and pleased, she hoped – but she could not be sure.

Mara carried her tray towards Carlton. As she walked, she glanced longingly down at the cup of coffee. It was not the percolated coffee Menelik would have served to the Americans. He'd made her some real Ethiopian coffee. Somehow, in the chaotic aftermath of cooking breakfast for all the guests, he'd found time to carry out the elaborate process of roasting the green beans and then grinding them in the pestle and mortar. The brew would be strong and sweet. Mara breathed its aroma. She could already feel how it would enter her body, banishing her tiredness. It was so precisely what she needed right now, she wondered if Menelik knew – somehow – just how little sleep she'd had.

Carlton was engrossed in a thick pile of papers that lay on the table in front of him. Whatever he was reading had brought lines of tension to his face. As she drew close, Mara saw that he was studying long columns of figures. They were marked: *Costs to Date, Estimate to Complete* and *Final Cost.* There were other headings as well. *Hotel and Living. Camera Department. Film Stock.*

As soon as Carlton became aware of her presence, he slid the document sideways, out of sight. He smiled up at her. 'We start shooting in two hours,' he said. 'So far, so good.'

Mara gave him what she hoped was a reassuring smile. 'Is there anything you need? Would you like more coffee?'

'No, thank you,' Carlton said. 'I've had four already – strong ones.' He waved a hand towards Mara's tray. 'You go ahead.'

Mara sipped her coffee, closing her eyes for a moment to savour the smell and taste. When she opened them, Carlton had risen from his seat to a half-standing position, his eyes directed towards the path near the rondavels. Mara turned to see Leonard marching towards them. A megaphone dangled from a strap hooked over his bony wrist.

'What's happened?' Carlton asked.

Leonard called out as he approached. 'Rudi just checked the suitcase. The wardrobe department only packed half of the stuff we need. The rest is on its way back to the States.'

Carlton's mouth dropped open. 'The things for today's shoot?'

'Yep.'

Leonard acknowledged Mara with a mere brush of eye contact. Then he sat down on a nearby chair, one foot tapping a staccato against the ground.

For a few seconds, Carlton sat there, looking around helplessly. Then he seemed to gather himself. Raising his hands, he began making soothing, patting motions in the air.

'It's all right. It's fine. We're beginning a new scene sequence. Those wardrobe items haven't been filmed yet. We can get something else.' He turned to Mara. 'We need some safari clothes – one set for Lillian and another for Peter. Ideally, they'd be a bit old-fashioned. Can you help us out?'

'As a matter of fact, we can.' Mara knew she sounded smug, but she didn't mind – it was nice to be able to solve a problem so easily. 'We just happen to have a whole cupboard full of clothes that were bought in the fifties: bush shirts, trousers; even belts and boots. They've never even been worn.'

Mara stood up, ready to lead the way over to the lodge. Carlton followed suit, but Leonard remained where he was. He suddenly pointed towards Mara's shirt.

'You've taken the pocket off,' he stated. 'I can see where it was stitched.'

Mara eyed him uncertainly. The comment seemed completely irrelevant.

'That's what we do,' she said after a short pause. 'Otherwise the butt of the gun can get caught on the flap or the button.'

'And you've added an extra row of cartridge loops?'

'This is really my husband's shirt,' Mara said. 'He always carries two kinds of cartridge.'

Now Leonard leaned forward, gazing intently at her trousers. Looking down, Mara saw that one leg was marked with a ragged-edged stain of rusty brown blood.

Leonard jumped to his feet with the energy of a puppet on a coiled spring. 'We'll use your clothes, if that's okay. They're even better than what we had! We'll need a set of your husband's as well. Old stuff, well-worn . . .'

Carlton turned to Mara. 'We'd really appreciate it. Do you mind?'

'No, it's fine,' Mara said. How could it not be fine, she asked herself, to lend someone your half worn-out work clothes? She felt uneasy about agreeing on John's behalf, but then she reminded herself that he'd once given his spare shirt to a client out on safari. The man had been planning to go hunting wearing the red and blue checked cowboy shirt that now belonged to Tomba.

'You want to hunt – or be hunted?' John had asked. He'd made his query sound like a joke, but Mara knew he was serious about the dangers of colourful clothing. The client – the chief executive of a mining company – had been both embarrassed and alarmed. He'd meekly put on John's shirt, even though he could barely button it over his protruding belly.

'Just give me a list,' she said. 'I'll bring you whatever you need.'

Carlton looked at his watch. 'Rudi's still dressing the set, so we've got a bit of time on our hands. If you could bring them to me before lunch, that would be fine.'

Mara was about to walk away, when Leonard tapped her shoulder. 'What size is he – your husband? Will Peter fit into his clothes?'

Mara studied the ground, kicking the toe of her boot into the clumps of hardy grass. It was a simple – and obvious – question. But she felt awkward picturing John and the actor side by side, comparing their bodies.

'Well, look at it this way.' It was Carlton's voice, helpful and tactful. 'You said you're wearing an old shirt of his – well, it looks to me like it would be fine on Peter. How tall is your husband?'

Mara looked up. 'Don't worry. The clothes will be fine.'

The hallway smelled of fresh floor polish, faintly overlaid with the smell of frying onions filtering out from the kitchen. Mara paused by the side-table to check her watch. She'd just finished a meeting with Kefa, during which they'd discussed how to deal with the city-bred Somalis, who made too much noise late at night, and with Tomba, who believed that now he was Bwana Boom he should be allowed to eat in the dining room with the rest of the crew. Before that, she'd listened while Menelik recited a lunch menu that could have been prepared for the Prince of Wales. Now it was time for her to find the wardrobe items Carlton had asked for.

On her way to the bedroom, she stopped outside the main room. She eyed the door anxiously, imagining a scenario in which Rudi had painted all the walls and the furniture, covering up forever the precious African timbers. She knew he wouldn't really have done this – but just to ease her mind, she opened the door and peered inside.

Her hand gripped the doorknob as she stared into the stillness of the room. The place was deserted. Faded curtains were drawn across the windows, closing out most of the light. Dust cloths draped the furniture; they were even hung to cover the collection of photographs on the wall. The mantelpiece was bare and the fireplace beneath it boarded up. The skeleton of a dead bird lay in the middle of the floor. A few dried hibiscus petals were scattered nearby.

Mara frowned uneasily. She felt as if she were seeing another vision of the future: the lodge, closed up and abandoned, after she and John were gone. The scene was unnervingly real.

A sudden movement near the far end of the room drew Mara's

attention. It was Leonard, standing near the bamboo screen. He was studying the room, his hands clasped behind his narrow back. He seemed to be murmuring to himself, like a priest chanting prayers. Slowly and quietly, she closed the door and crept away.

Mara walked along the pathway towards Lillian's rondavel. She was wearing a new set of clothes from the store and the fabric felt stiff and scratchy. The trousers and shirt she had been wearing earlier were now folded into a neat bundle that she carried tucked under her arm. Carlton had asked if she would deliver them to Lillian and then stay and help her get dressed – the actress wasn't used to having to manage on her own.

Now, as Mara approached the rondavel, she felt a sense of unreality about the role she was about to play. It was true that Lillian had been more friendly and easier to deal with than many of the other wealthy women who'd come here – so far, there'd only been that fuss about where she would sit, and the matter of the separate bowls. But that didn't change the facts of who she was. In other circumstances, Mara would be lucky if she had the chance even to ask her for an autograph.

Outside the door, Mara paused. She was reminded of the moments before a play was about to begin: the audience waiting, hushed, already aware of the energy of the performers, reaching out from behind the curtain.

She knocked tentatively.

'Who is it?' Lillian called out.

'It's me. Mara.'

The door swung open. As she looked quickly around the little room, Mara found it hard to believe this was the same pretty, tidy rondavel she had prepared so carefully for the actress: clothes were now strewn everywhere and the bed was a tangle of sheets. The mosquito net had not been put up, and a breakfast tray still stood on the table. One of the mauve wedding towels lay wet and crumpled on the floor.

Lillian peered from behind the door, using it as a screen while Mara entered. Her face looked wan – almost bleached. Mara wondered if it was because the curtains were still closed and the light muted, or if it was simply because Lillian was not wearing her usual scarlet lipstick.

As Mara moved further inside, the actress was revealed standing in her underwear. Mara could not help staring at the red silk French knickers edged with lace.

'My lucky knickers,' Lillian said. 'I've only just found them. Thank God. I was about to call Carlton and break the news.'

Mara looked at her in puzzled silence.

'I have to wear them on the first day of each shoot – I just have to.' The earnest tone in Lillian's voice reminded Mara of the way John spoke about the hunters' superstitions. Most of them were linked with the killing of elephants – as if it were understood, somehow, that this was the greatest sin and therefore the one that should be approached most carefully. Before a hunting party left the Land Rover, John always made his clients turn out their pockets to ensure no one was carrying money – an elephant, he explained, cannot be bought. He also warned there would be no hope of locating a good elephant, if anyone picked up porcupine quills found lying on the ground.

'I've had these ones for years, of course,' Lillian said. 'But if I'd thought about it, I'd have bought lots more pairs and worn them every day. They're ideal for Africa – cool, and easy to dry.'

Mara tried not to think of how the hut boys would react to laundering a whole collection of garments like these. They would be convinced that Lillian was a prostitute.

Mara held out the clothes she'd brought. 'Here's your wardrobe.'

Lillian examined the trousers and then the shirt, holding them towards the meagre light filtering through the curtains.

'They're quite good, aren't they? Suzie's very skilled at this kind of thing – staining cloth, fraying cuffs . . .'

Mara didn't like to say that the clothes belonged to her – and that, in fact, she'd only recently taken them off. She would have much preferred to provide clean garments from her drawer for use in the filming, but Carlton had made it clear that Leonard wanted to have the actual shirt and trousers he'd seen Mara wearing.

Lillian seemed not to notice Mara's reticence. 'Suzie was in charge of my wardrobe,' she continued. 'She did a good job – Carlton said she could stay on for second unit. But she went home.' She sounded almost hurt as she said these last words. Mara was reminded, suddenly, of a child, abandoned by her playmate. 'But we don't need her, do we?' Lillian added, smiling over her shoulder.

'No,' Mara agreed, 'we don't.' She smiled back, meeting Lillian's gaze. She felt a warm sense of being included – being wanted.

'Make-up first,' Lillian said. As she reached for her silk kimono, she gestured towards the table near the door. A small black suitcase that looked like a doctor's bag had been placed there.

Mara brought it over to the dressing table, laid it down and unsnapped the catches. A powdery smell escaped as she lifted the lid. Inside was a huge array of make-up, neatly laid out in compartments. There were at least seven bottles of foundation in various tones and the same number of powder compacts. There were brushes, brow combs, sponges, several mascaras, some eyelash curlers, cold cream, half a dozen lipsticks. And some vials of red liquid that looked like blood.

Lillian pulled a notebook from the case. Opening it up, she showed Mara a diagram of a woman's face – cheekbones, fore-head, eyelids, nostrils – shaded in different colours. Each section had been tagged with a note that named the cosmetic to be used there.

Lillian referred to the diagram, then began taking products from the case and lining them up on the dressing table.

'You'd be surprised how much it takes,' she said, 'to create a natural look.' She frowned into the mirror. 'We'll need more light than this.'

Mara pulled back the curtains. Sunlight filled the room, making it look even more chaotic. Lillian was now fossicking in the tapestry bag that had held the double boiler. She drew out a man's shaving mirror and held it up.

'For emergencies,' she said, sounding pleased with herself. She carried it over to the window and perched it on the ledge.

When Lillian sat down, Mara stood beside her, ready to hand over each item as it was required, like a surgical nurse. Lillian began by patting foundation over her face and neck with a small sponge. Watching the steady stroking movements had a mesmerising effect on Mara, as if she were experiencing the soothing touch against her own skin. When Lillian had finished with the foundation, she began to put shadow on her eyelids, first a skin-coloured tone and then a darker shade. The effect was subtle – she didn't look like a glamorous woman wearing make-up. She just looked like a more beautiful version of herself.

It was not until the process was almost complete that Mara noticed the two hut boys, along with Dudu, watching through the window. She frowned at them, to indicate that they should leave. Instead, Dudu took her recognition of their presence as a licence to speak. He pointed to the bottle of light tan foundation Mara had placed on the window ledge.

'She is putting mud on her body,' he stated. He jerked his head towards the hut boys. 'They want to know if you are going to host a dance party.' He used the word *ngoma* – referring to a large gathering of tribespeople that involved feasting and dancing, and sometimes lasted for days. The warriors always wore full traditional dress and plenty of red ochre on their skin.

Before Mara had a chance to reply, Lillian paused in the midst of stroking on mascara.

'What did he say?' she asked.

'He wants to know what you are doing,' Mara answered. 'They are village boys – they haven't worked here before. They've never seen someone putting make-up on.'

Dudu took a step closer. He pointed, again, to the hut boys before speaking to Mara in Swahili. 'They have told me that putting mud on your skin is now forbidden in Tanzania. The president does not like it. He says it is only for savages.'

Mara looked at the hut boys in surprise. 'Who told you this?'

'Bwana Daudi has told us,' one of them replied. 'He has also told us we will not remain as hut boys. The president is going to build a school in every village. We will learn to read and write and stand on our own feet without needing the European bwanas.'

He fixed his eyes on Mara. He seemed to be asking her to verify his statement.

Mara hesitated. It occurred to her that whatever she said might find its way back to Daudi – perhaps even to Kabeya.

'You are excellent hut boys,' she said carefully. 'And you will be excellent students as well.'

Lillian frowned impatiently. 'What are you talking about now?'

'They are hoping to go to school,' Mara said.

Lillian continued applying mascara. 'Talk to Carlton,' she said. 'He arranges everything.' She picked up the mirror and examined her appearance closely before nodding her approval. 'It's exactly how Wanda, the make-up girl, did it.' She glanced at Mara. 'I'm a bit of an artist, you know. I draw.'

'What do you draw?' Mara asked. She went over to the bed and picked up the trousers, holding them towards Lillian. She was aware that time was passing; Carlton had asked her to bring the actress to the set as soon as possible.

'People, mainly,' Lillian said as she shed her kimono, dropping it by her feet, and began putting on the trousers. 'And Theo, of course.' She looked longingly at the framed photograph of her Alsatian. 'He's a better person than plenty I've come across . . .' She paused to look at Mara. 'You must meet all sorts of characters, running a lodge.'

'We do,' Mara said. 'Sometimes we get to know them quite well.'

Quite well . . .

Mara busied herself with unbuttoning the shirt. But still, the pain began – the sickness stirring inside her. She remembered Matilda's voice as she'd chatted during dinner on that first night at the lodge. The simple, ordinary phrases.

Pass the salt please, John. Thank you, John. How kind of you . . .

And the silvery laugh. The head tipped back, the blonde hair falling like a cascade of moonshine.

Mara forced herself to think of someone else. That Canadian, who had insisted on sleeping under the stars. She clung to the memory of his lined face and greying hair. She reminded herself how he'd learned to speak basic Swahili in preparation for his safari. And how, instead of sitting around the fireside swapping yarns with the other clients, he'd gone over to the Africans' fire and asked Menelik to tell him folk stories from Ethiopia. Long afterwards, the camp staff had included him in their night-time songs. The safari chronicler – who was the gunbearer by day – gave him a name. *Rafiki Bilu Ubaguzi.* The European Who Did Not Care Only About European Things.

Mara held up the shirt, ready for Lillian to slip her arms into the sleeves. 'But then they leave, of course,' she said, her tone easy and light. 'And new people arrive.'

'I know what you mean,' Lillian said. 'Film shoots are the same. You become like a family – cast and crew. You mean the world to each other. And then —' She spread her hands and shook her head. 'It's amazing. Suddenly, one day, it's over. And you forget all about them.'

Mara nodded slowly. *Forget all about them.* It sounded so easy. She was reminded of that other phrase she knew so well: forgive and forget. How often she had chanted it to herself, like a spell that could carry power. Such a simple phrase, yet one so hard to live by. Sometimes Mara found it possible to forget, and sometimes to forgive, but holding the two together, at the same time, required a strength she simply did not seem to possess.

The dining end of the main room was crowded with people and equipment. Mara stood to one side, watching as the two Nicks moved a wheeled platform backward and forward along what looked like a tiny train track laid over the floor. Not far from them stood a tripod. A huge camera was attached to the top. The combination looked precarious – the camera too big and solid for the spindly legs to hold up. Tomba stood in front of it. Mara guessed he'd been borrowed from Jamie's department. Clearly, he had been assigned the duty of protecting the camera. He held his arms outstretched and looked around him constantly, as if expecting an imminent attack from any quarter.

Lillian sat in one of three canvas chairs grouped near the door to the verandah. Mara knew that the back of each chair was marked with a name. *Mr Heath. Miss Lane. Mr L Miller.* She guessed there was one for *Mr C Miller* somewhere else – but perhaps Carlton never got the chance to sit down on the set; he was too busy working in the background, solving problems.

Rudi came to stand beside Mara.

'What do you think?' he asked, waving his hand to take in the room.

'It looks extraordinary – so abandoned and lonely,' Mara said. 'But why did you go to so much trouble with the books and other things? They're all hidden.'

A shadow of disappointment showed in Rudi's eyes. Then he shrugged. 'Leonard came to inspect the set, and he got the idea of having all these dust cloths. We were going to use one or two, but he wanted to see the whole place shrouded in them. It's a kind of metaphor for the story – you know, secrets and lies, the truth covered up. Kefa helped out by finding some old sheets.' Rudi's gaze strayed across to the hidden bookcase. 'You never know, though. Leonard might change his mind again before they start shooting. Or, Maggie or Luke might decide to pull off one of the cloths. Anything could happen.'

'Who are Maggie and Luke?' Mara asked. She wondered if more members of the film company had arrived.

For a moment, Rudi looked surprised by her ignorance – then he gave her an understanding smile. 'They're the main characters in the movie,' he said. 'The ones who get to have all the adventures. They're lovers as well, of course – that goes without saying in Hollywood.' He pointed at the room again. 'This is their refuge. They need a place to hide out and Maggie remembers this hunting lodge she used to come to with her parents when she was a kid. They go through a long journey and when they finally get here, they find the place all closed up and abandoned. But it's beautiful, in a way. Have you seen David Lean's latest movie, *Dr Zhivago*?' He laughed dismissively, even before Mara shook her head. 'I guess it wouldn't have made it out here yet! Anyway, Julie Christie and Omar Sharif go to a big mansion out in the wilds of Russia. The place is full of ice and dust and the furniture's all draped with cloths. And they just walk through it. It's one of the great moments in the movie. That's the kind of feeling we're after here.'

Mara listened to him closely, glad to at last hear something about the content of the film. She was about to ask him what else he could tell her, when Brendan – the electricity expert – came towards them unrolling a long cable. Another cable was loosely coiled and lodged under his arm.

'Gangway!' he called.

Rudi jumped aside. Mara followed suit. Just as Brendan reached her, he dropped the coiled cable. It fell in a heap at her feet.

Brendan groaned in frustration. 'I really need an assistant!'

'Let me help for a bit,' Mara said. As she bent to pick it up, she glanced across to check that Lillian didn't need her – the actress was her first responsibility. But Lillian was no longer in her chair. She was standing by the verandah door, talking to someone. Mara straightened up slowly, clutching the cable to her chest. It was a man wearing bush clothes. He still had his hat on his head; a water bottle swung at his hip; and his gun was slung over his shoulder, as though he'd just strolled in here from his safari.

Mara took two steps towards them before her foot caught on a chair and tipped it over. The sound drew attention and people swung round towards her. But she kept on gazing at the man in the hunter's clothes.

Peter Heath.

Before Mara had the chance to turn away, Peter's eyes met

hers. He smiled and nodded in greeting. Mara gestured towards his outfit – as if, by mime, she could explain how she'd imagined he was her husband, inexplicably back from the Selous. She made herself smile politely, hiding how annoyed she was with herself for staring at him. After all, she'd been the one who'd chosen those items from John's wardrobe for the actor to wear.

She was grateful when Brendan appeared next to her, giving her a reason to turn away.

'That will need to be untangled,' he said, pointing at the cable in her arms. 'Someone's wrapped it up wrongly. Best thing would be to take it outside where there's more room.'

Mara hurried to follow his recommendation. As she crossed to the verandah door, she could see Peter talking to Carlton. Viewed from the front, he didn't look like her husband at all. Nor did he look like an actor. He just looked like a man who worked in the bush – one whom Mara had never met before.

By early afternoon, the main room of the lodge was stifling, with the warmth generated by Brendan's lights adding to the normal heat of the day. Carlton had the hut boys posted by the doors to the verandah so that when Leonard called, 'Cut!', they could be opened up to let in some fresh air. The rest of the time, the room was closed in, to keep the daylight at bay.

Mara sat well out of the way of the filming. People seemed to be coming to her constantly, asking for little things – a piece of string, a candle, a penknife. Rudi had explained that each department would normally have several trucks full of equipment, with everything they could possibly need on hand, but they'd all had to travel light for second unit. Light equals cheap, he'd said.

In between fielding the various requests, Mara sat back in her chair, watching the cast and crew at work. She was struck by the slow, steady way in which the process took place. Lillian and Peter had to perform the same small sequences over and over again, until finally Leonard was satisfied. No one seemed to mind, although Mara noticed Carlton surreptitiously checking his watch now and then. All attention was focused on the director. He was easy to pick out: his lean-limbed figure was dressed oddly in a pair of red-dyed workman's overalls. Even when people were chatting to one another, or moving towards the open doorways to breathe the cooler air during the long gaps between filming, they kept one eye on him, always poised to respond to his commands.

As the day wore on, Mara came to understand the rhythm of the shooting. There was the long slow preparation, during which Leonard talked intently with first Lillian and Peter and then Nick. Nick spoke, in turn, to Brendan and Nick Two, while Rudi listened in. Jamie never seemed to be very interested in what was going on – the sound recordist always seemed to be bent over his equipment as he studied the row of dials. But Tomba made up for it by listening intently to everything Leonard said.

When the instructions had been given, a buzz of activity that lasted for anything up to half an hour broke out, and then it gave way to an intent stillness. Leonard would cast his gaze around the room, seeming to gather up all of the energy in the space and hold it in his hand. Cast and crew were statues, waiting for the words that would set them in motion.

Standing by. Quiet please. Roll sound. Roll camera.

Leonard delivered the phrases like the edicts of a priest. And his followers responded.

Rolling. Speed.

Leonard always waited, at this point – it was only for a few seconds, but the time seemed to stretch out – before delivering the final signal for the acting to begin. In that interval, Lillian and Peter began to transform themselves. Mara watched it happen: their expressions changed; they held their bodies differently. By the time Leonard said the word, *Action!*, the process was complete. The two people in front of the camera were no longer Lillian Lane and Peter Heath – they were Maggie and Luke.

In the long succession of scenes that were filmed – all broken down into small pieces – there were moments that stood out in Mara's mind. For example, when Brendan switched on a light he had angled carefully towards Peter's face, and suddenly Peter was movie-star handsome again, soft shadows highlighting the perfect moulding of his features.

Then there was the filming of the first scene in which the characters had to speak. Mara had sat forward in her chair, gripping the armrests in surprise as she discovered that Maggie and Luke had lilting Irish accents.

There was the scene in which Maggie and Luke argued passionately with one another. Mara had been out to the kitchen to check with Menelik and Kefa that the plans for dinner were in order. She'd returned to the main room only moments before the lead-up to filming had begun. There was the usual calm atmosphere as Leonard called for the camera and sound to begin rolling. Then he gave his final signal. Without warning, Maggie exploded into a rage. She shouted at Luke as she strode around the dining room – at one point, catching her foot in a dustsheet and almost unveiling Rudi's bookcase. Luke was calm, at first. But eventually, he raised his voice as well. They were arguing about whether they could stay here together, or if they had to go back to Zanzibar and face what they'd left behind there. The performance was so real – Maggie's face was taut with anger and Luke's whole body seemed to radiate his frustration. Then a mood of despair took over, and Maggie began to cry. Tears ran down her cheeks, her eyes reddened and her lips swelled. Mara stared at the woman's face. She told herself that the emotion was not real – it was just a performance – but she still felt an answering distress rising up inside her. Then Leonard called, 'Cut!', and it was all over. Lillian and Peter reappeared, calm and courteous, preparing quietly for the next take.

As Mara waited for the scene to be played out again, she wondered how it would be possible for the two to make the emotional journey a second time. But to her surprise – and Carlton's obvious pleasure – Leonard said it would not be necessary. He had got exactly what he wanted. He waited for Nick Two to confirm that all was well with the camera, and then he consulted the dog-eared script that he kept tucked in the front of his overalls. After a few moments, he looked up – in Mara's direction. He beckoned her to come over.

Mara trod carefully over Brendan's cables. Then she edged around the tripod and moved on towards Jamie. Tomba lifted his boom to let her pass – the gesture of a warrior wielding a spear.

'What do you need?' Mara asked Leonard.

'You,' he said. He looked towards Rudi, who was setting up a Tilley lamp on the table. 'We've got to get a shot of Maggie lighting that thing.'

Mara nodded. 'You want me to show Lillian how to do it?' She'd known the scene was coming: she had helped the actress sponge foundation carefully over her hands.

'For the wide shot, yes. But for the close-up, I want to use your hands.'

Mara eyed him nervously. He was asking her to do something very simple, but she feared that under the scrutiny of all these people – let alone the big dark eye of the camera – she would become awkward and clumsy.

'Just relax,' Leonard said, as if reading her mind. 'We've got all the time in the world. Forget about all this stuff.' He waved one hand, dismissing their surroundings. 'Pretend you're on your own.'

A short time later, Mara was sitting at the table in front of the lantern and a box of matches. She could feel the heat of Brendan's lights touching her skin. The musty smell of warmed dust cloths entered her lungs. Nick was standing behind her, pointing the camera down over her shoulder at her hands.

Glancing up, she saw Lillian sitting in a chair that had been carefully placed so the actress would be able to study Mara's movements and replicate them for the wide shot. Peter stood not far from her. He met Mara's gaze, giving her a brief, encouraging smile – and then turned tactfully away, picking up a book and bending his head over the pages. He understood, Mara felt sure, that if he watched as well it would only make her more nervous. But there was something about the way he stood – the angle of his face – that suggested his attention was still focused on her . . .

Mara swallowed on a dry throat, a mixture of anxiety and tension flowing through her as she waited for Leonard to direct her. In the brief pause after the camera started rolling, and before she was to light her match, she reminded herself she'd been told to pretend she was alone. But then it came to her, suddenly, that she didn't want to think of this moment in that way. She wanted, instead, to savour the experience of being at the centre of all this activity. It was a tiny contribution she was making, Mara knew, and it would soon be over. But for now, she was a part of Leonard's team. She was no longer the safari hostess – the person who wore a dress but was not to be treated like a woman; the one who was a European but not in the same league as the clients; or the wife who had to act as if she were no more than the manager of her husband's camp and his lodge.

She was Maggie.

When Leonard gave the signal, she struck the match, waiting for a few seconds to let the flame take hold. Then, lodging the match-stick expertly between two fingers, she lifted the glass chimney to expose the mantle. As she touched it with the flame, the mesh globe glowed – first red, then blue. When the light burned steady, she lowered the glass and blew out the match.

'And – *Cut!*' Leonard called. 'That's excellent. Let's just do it again. Move in closer, Nick.'

After the third take, Leonard was satisfied. 'That's it, Maggie,' he said. He came up to Mara and rested his hand on her shoulder. 'Thank you,' he said. 'Some people just freeze in front of the camera

and every little thing they do looks awkward. But you were great!'
He smiled and turned away.

Mara bowed her head. As she pushed the used matches back inside the matchbox, she could still feel the warmth of Leonard's praise, poured over her like sunshine from above.

SEVEN

Iceblocks chinked gently in the six glasses of water Mara carried on a tray. The sound rose above the constant low rumble of Brendan's generator. Mara was struck by how strange it was to hear the noise now, in daylight, when it was usually heard only after dark. She walked along the verandah, approaching the cane sofa where Lillian was sitting. The actress had kicked off the boots she'd been wearing – Mara's spare pair – and folded her legs underneath her. Her head was bent over a sketchpad. Jamie sat nearby on a chair. Tomba squatted comfortably on the ground beside him, his elbows resting on his knees. As Mara came near, Tomba jumped to his feet.

'We are not needed inside.' He spoke hurriedly as if Mara had reproached him for abandoning his post. 'They are filming but it is pictures of furniture only. There is no sound to be recorded.' He turned to Jamie, seeking confirmation.

'That's right,' Jamie said. He studied the freckly skin of his arms as he spoke. 'You've got it. It's called a mute take.'

Mara nodded approvingly at Tomba. This was his second day as boom operator and he seemed to be managing well. She turned to Lillian, greeting her with a smile. 'Kefa told me you were sitting out here.' She looked around for the actor. 'I thought he said Peter was here, as well.'

'He went for a walk,' Lillian said. 'He won't be needed for a while. There are some set-ups with just me.'

'Where did he go?' Mara asked with a frown. She hoped he'd remembered her warnings about not leaving the grounds.

'Somewhere in the garden, I think. Not far away,' Lillian said. She lifted up her sketchpad.

Mara caught a fleeting impression of a human figure drawn in dark strong lines. But before she was able to see the drawing properly, Lillian returned the pad to her lap and signed the corner of the picture with the confident flourish of someone practiced at giving autographs. Then she tore off the page, handing it to Jamie.

'It's for you!' Lillian said.

Jamie looked at the drawing, his face unreadable. Then he smiled enthusiastically. 'Thank you so much. I'll treasure that.'

Lillian received his words with a graceful inclination of her head. Then, taking a glass of water from Mara's tray, she continued to watch Jamie over the rim of her glass as she sipped.

Jamie fiddled with the drawing, clearly aware of Lillian's gaze still fixed on him. He smiled again. 'It's a great drawing.'

Lillian relaxed in her chair. 'Thanks. I think I've really captured something about you.'

'You sure have.' Jamie held the picture up to Mara. 'Look at that! Isn't she amazing?'

Mara moved closer to the drawing and was surprised to see that the proportions of the body were all wrong and the expression on the face was wooden. The drawing bore only the faintest resemblance to Jamie.

'The lines are certainly very . . . dramatic,' she said. She looked from Jamie to the drawing and back. 'You're right – it's amazing.'

Tomba shifted closer to see what the exchange had been about. He picked up the drawing – carefully, using two hands – and studied it intently. Mara could see a puzzled look growing in his eyes. She moved quickly to stand in front of him, shielding him from Lillian's view as he turned the picture upside-down, and looked at it again.

'When you've finished, Tomba,' she said, reaching a hand towards the paper, 'I'll put it away somewhere safe.'

At that moment, Carlton emerged from the dining room. His face was gleaming with sweat.

He addressed Jamie first. 'You're needed for the next shot.' Then he turned to Lillian, smiling encouragingly. 'Leonard's ready for you, now.'

'Already?' Lillian screwed up her nose as she laid down her sketchpad. She frowned as she pulled on her boots. But then, when she stood up, turning towards the dining room, her expression began to change. Her eyes brightened and a look of anticipation crept onto her face. Mara could see her picturing the director and crew gathered in there, awaiting her presence. The prospect of becoming, once again, the centre of their attention seemed to breathe life into her soul.

Mara could find no sign of Peter anywhere in the garden. Aware that it was her responsibility to check on his whereabouts, she headed for his rondavel and knocked on the door. In the lengthening silence, she could feel emptiness emanating from the room. She was about to leave, when it occurred to her that she might as well go inside and check that the hut boys had made the bed and changed the straw in the *chow* pot.

The rondavel looked almost unchanged from how it had been when Mara had first discovered Peter standing by the bed. There were just a few personal items set out on the desk by the window. Out of respect for the actor's privacy, Mara tried not to look closely at anything as she crossed the room to the adjoining *chow* hut. But as she passed the bed, something caught her eye. A picture frame of red leather lay facedown in the space between the pillow and the bedside table. Mara guessed that Peter, like Lillian, travelled with an image of his loved one. Only he kept his picture in a place where he could see it as he prepared for sleep.

Glancing behind her to make certain that she was still alone, Mara picked up the leather frame. She turned it over, expecting to see someone glamorous and beautiful, a woman with features as perfect as his.

Instead, she saw a family photograph: two adults and four kids, all smiling at the camera. They were grouped in front of a smog-stained marble statue with tall buildings rising behind them. Mara tilted the picture towards the light. Peter had one arm round the shoulders of a woman she guessed was his wife. Even in this informal snapshot, Mara could see how beautiful she was – her creamy skin contrasted with the red of her long curly hair; her eyes were a vivid blue. She held a toddler on her hip. She was shorter than Peter and she leaned slightly towards him, as if drawn by the strength of his presence. The other three children stood in front of the adults. There were two fair-haired boys, who looked about three and five, and a slightly older girl with red curly hair. The mother's hand was cupped over the girl's shoulder and Peter's arm draped over the younger boy's chest, his hand resting over the child's heart.

The world was full of images like these, Mara knew, yet there was something striking about this one. There was a sense of completeness about the little group; the bond between them was almost tangible. Mara smiled longingly at the photograph. It reminded her of the family of her school friend, Sally McPhee. Sally and her parents and brother had shared a passion for horses and used to spend every Saturday riding together. Mara had envied her deeply. Her own family rarely seemed to have time for anything other than working on the farm. And even when they did attempt a family outing – the occasional fishing trip, or a visit to the beach – the tensions between Mara's parents made it hard for any of them to relax and enjoy it. Growing up, Mara had dreamed of one day being part of a family like Sally's. With a twist of pain, she thought of how she and John had planned to have children: at least two or three. That was in the days when the future had stretched out ahead of them, clear and bright and certain.

Carefully, Mara put the picture back where she had found it, her fingertips lingering for a moment on the smooth soft leather of the frame. Then she quickly checked the *chow* pot, before hurrying from the room.

She headed for the car park next, in case Peter had gone to get something from one of the vehicles. As she passed under the archway of tusks, she scanned the area – peering into each of the two zebra-striped Land Rovers, still on hire from the Manyala Hotel, and then the truck and even her own old vehicle. But there was no one to be seen. She was about to turn back when she noticed a line of footprints in the fine surface of the gravel. The size, shape and the tread of the sole were immediately familiar to her: the prints had been made by a pair of John's boots – the ones she had given to Carlton for Peter.

She followed the tracks along the driveway, picking up her pace. Anxiety grew inside her, quickly turning to anger. She had given clear instructions to the guests about not leaving the lodge grounds alone. Peter had seemed so normal and nice – and the photograph she'd just seen only added to that image of him. But, she reminded herself, he was still a famous actor. Spoiled, no doubt. Used to doing exactly what he liked, when he liked.

She was about to turn back and get the Land Rover and her rifle when she caught sight of Peter up ahead. He was standing on top of a large rock, a little to one side of the track. The place was a favourite vantage point of Mara's. The rock formed a wide flat ledge, which offered a clear view over the treetops, down to the plains. An old fig tree grew nearby and one thick twisted limb stretched across the front of the rock at waist height, forming a natural railing. Mara often stopped there on her way to shoot guinea fowl or quail for the kitchen. She liked to rest her elbows on the branch of the fig tree and take a few moments to look down at the grasslands – as if she were a god, up in heaven – before going on to take her own small place in the world spread before her.

Mara walked towards the rock, shaking her head. Peter had no rifle to protect himself with and probably no understanding of how to check an area before entering it. He was standing there with his hands in his pockets, clearly relaxed and enjoying the scenery, oblivious to the fact that there could be a leopard or a lion crouching on the limb of a tree, only a yard away from his head.

Mara took a deep breath, preparing her words. She knew it was important to remain courteous. But she had to be firm as well.

You seem to have forgotten my advice. You must understand, I am only concerned about your safety. I'm afraid I must insist . . .

She was almost at the base of the rock when a figure stepped into her path – an African, armed with a heavy-gauge shotgun. She felt a rush of panic, but then she recognised the ranger from Arusha. She'd barely seen him – as they'd been filming inside the lodge, he'd not been needed yet. She'd forgotten all about him.

'I am here,' he stated. 'I am guarding this American.'

'Very good,' Mara responded, gathering her composure. 'I can see that all is well.'

Their exchange drew Peter's attention. He turned round, beckoning Mara to join him. 'Hey, come on up here. What a view!'

She hesitated, feeling nervous. What if she couldn't think of anything interesting to say? She glanced at her watch, to suggest that she was short of time. Then she picked her way through the low scrub and climbed up onto the rock.

Peter offered her his hand, to pull her up.

'I'm fine, thanks,' she said.

Soon they were standing side by side on the ledge. Beneath the green-leaf smell of the woodland Mara could just pick out a trace of his aftershave – a spicy cinnamon fragrance.

They were both quiet for a time, looking out at the view. The plains were dotted with mingled herds of zebras and wildebeests, the animals all grazing peacefully. White birds wheeled and soared against a clear blue sky.

Peter pointed at a large rocky outcrop that rose up beyond the waterhole. The pile of rounded shapes was formed from reddish stone. Dark purple gullies scored its sides and bushes clustered at its base. 'Does that have a name?' he asked.

'We call it Lion Rock,' Mara said, tracing the shape of a crouching lion in the air. 'But the Africans call it – in Swahili – *The rocks that were put here by giants.*'

'There must be a story to go with that,' Peter said.

'There is.' Mara looked sideways, trying to guess whether he wanted to hear what it was – visitors often gave the impression of being more interested in such things than they really were. Peter was studying the shape of the rock formation, his eyes narrowed with concentration. 'Apparently,' she said, 'there were some giants who were preparing for a great battle. They collected up boulders ready to throw at their enemies. But then a great rain came and washed all the giants away. Only the pile of stones was left.'

Peter tilted his head to one side, his eyes fixed thoughtfully on the rock. 'Now that you've told me that story, it doesn't look at all like a lion any more.'

Mara's lips parted in surprise. She'd had exactly the same response, the first time she'd come here after Kefa had told her the story.

'I know,' she said simply.

They stood there, looking down over the plain. Peter leaned forward, resting his arms on the fig branch. His hands, Mara noticed, looked surprisingly strong, even calloused in places. And the cuffs of his shirt-sleeves were worn through. It would almost be possible to mistake him for an ordinary person.

Silence fell over them – a quiet that seemed undisturbed by the distant whine of the generator, or the calls of the weaverbirds. Mara enjoyed the peace for a while, but then felt she should make conversation.

'Do you enjoy travelling?' she asked. 'I suppose you do it quite a lot.'

'I love it,' Peter replied, turning to face Mara, 'except I miss my four kids – and my wife, Paula, of course. I keep wondering what they're all doing, back home.'

'You must wish they'd been able to come with you,' Mara said, remembering the closeness of the little group in the photograph.

Peter took a breath, letting it out in a faint sigh. 'Well, I do – except that Paula would hate it here. She'd be terrified of the kids getting sick or being bitten by snakes. She's a real city girl. She prefers sidewalks to bush tracks, any day. It's a pity, because I love nothing better than getting off the beaten track, away from the crowds.' A wistful tone entered his voice, but he banished it with a smile and his face took on the fond look of a parent describing the idiosyncracies of a child. 'She's always been like that. It's just who she is.'

'Well, she must be very busy, anyway, with four children to care for,' Mara commented. But she was not really concentrating on what she was saying. A single, envious thought filled her head: Paula's husband accepted her for who she was. He didn't ask her to be someone she was not. He didn't ask her to go to places she didn't want to be.

Where bloodied tusks lie on the ground. And severed feet – huge and grey – dangle from ropes tied to the limbs of a tree.

Peter stirred, pulling back the sleeve of his shirt. 'Time to go,' he said. 'I'm due back on set before much longer.'

He waited for Mara to climb down the face of the rock ahead of him. Then he slid down behind her. The ranger stood ready to greet them, his shotgun poised on his arm.

The last of the daylight reached in through the crack between the blue *kitenge* curtains of Lillian's rondavel. They were drawn firmly shut and the door was closed. The space was lit by the yellow glow of a single electric globe, which cast soft shadows over Lillian's face and body. Clad only in her silk petticoat, she looked like a Greek goddess, formed in stone by a master sculptor. She was leaning over a deep enamel basin, the long dark mass of her hair falling forward, hiding her face. Mara stood behind her, ready to offer more hot water. Lillian's hair drifted in the foamy water like seaweed strands in the ocean. It looked strangely sinister to Mara, as if Lillian were drowning.

Mara shifted her gaze to the jug of water she held in her hands. Steam rose up to her, adding heat to air that was already warm. She breathed the smell of expensive shampoo, blended with the sharp flowery scent of the glasses of gin and tonic Lillian had asked Kefa to bring to her rondavel.

'I deserve a sundowner,' she'd said to Mara. 'And so do you.'

When Lillian's hair was finally rinsed to her satisfaction, Mara wrapped the mauve towel around her head, making a turban. She wanted to be as helpful as possible, well aware these were not the bathroom facilities Lillian was accustomed to. Mara had considered inviting the actress to use her and John's bathroom. It was the one place in the lodge (aside from the kitchen) where there was hot and cold running water. But there were clear divisions between private and public spaces at Raynor Lodge. John had explained to Mara that respecting them was a vital part of keeping a professional distance from clients. Once the physical boundaries became blurred, relationships became negotiable as well. This was considered a normal situation in some lodges; there were places – here in Tanzania as well as in other parts of Safariland – where guests could expect to find the kind of establishment they recognised from Hemingway novels, or from the Hollywood films of his work. In these settings, it was taken for granted that the white hunter was as expert in hunting women as he was big game. Female clients felt the safari had not been a success unless they'd had an affair with someone – and the professional hunter was always their first choice. Raynor had despised this kind of behaviour. According to John, the old hunter had never compromised himself in this way, and he'd made it clear he expected the same from his apprentice.

Mara's lips tightened as she imagined what Raynor would have said about John and Matilda.

'What are you thinking about?' Lillian asked. She held her head on one side as she sipped her drink. 'You look unhappy.'

Mara forced a smile. 'Oh, no – I was thinking of the film. I was wondering about the story, what happens in it.'

A shadow of disappointment crossed Lillian's face. Then she adopted a look of measured enthusiasm. 'It's a thriller – the kind of thing that would normally be set in a city. Paris or New York. That's one of the things Leonard's interested in, you see – the surprise of it being filmed in Africa. It's a wonderful script.'

'I like your character – Maggie. The way she speaks. She's so strong and brave.'

Lillian snorted into her glass. 'She's an idiot.'

Mara frowned, surprised and confused. In her mind, she replayed the scene of the argument between Maggie and Luke: the passion, the certainty, the belief in doing what was right. 'You mean, you don't agree with the things Maggie said?'

'Not at all – carrying on about doing the right thing! She'd be better off watching out for herself,' Lillian said. 'That's what everyone else is doing. That's how the world works.'

'But you sounded so . . . real.'

Lillian laughed. 'Mara, it's called acting. I'm an actress. That's what I do.'

'But how do you manage it? How can you cry real tears if you don't feel anything?'

'Well, I don't know what other people do, but I just look back into my life and find something that goes with the emotion I want to feel. That's what I draw on. I bring the memory and the performance together. It always works.'

Lillian picked up a nailfile and began to pick nonchalantly at one of her nails. There was a smudge of make-up trapped underneath it, but still, the action looked oddly forced. Watching her, Mara tried to imagine what wellspring of pain and anger Lillian had tapped into when Maggie had wept in front of Luke. In the stillness that surrounded them, Mara felt she could almost ask the question – there was something about the warmth of the air, the intimacy of hair-washing, the talk of tears. But then she reminded herself whom it was she was with.

Lillian dropped the nailfile and reached for a tortoiseshell hair-brush. She handed it to Mara. 'Could you do my hair?' Instead of the usual demanding edge of someone accustomed to being served, there was a pleading note in her voice.

Mara picked up a long strand and brushed it out, using slow, steady strokes.

'My momma used to do this for me,' Lillian murmured. She closed her eyes, letting her arms fall at her sides. But she did not seem relaxed. The muscles around her eyes tightened and a line appeared on her forehead. 'Don't stop,' she said. 'Just keep brushing.'

Mara eased the brush smoothly through Lillian's hair. Gradually, the woman's face grew softer and the lines of tension disappeared.

'Tell me about you,' Lillian said. Her voice was dreamy, like that of a little girl asking for a bedtime story. 'How long have you been married?'

'Three years.'

'And are you happy?'

Mara's hand faltered in the middle of a brushstroke. Though the question took her by surprise, it didn't seem out of place. She was struck, again, by the sense of intimacy that surrounded them. The rondavel, with its soft-moulded mud walls, seemed like their own private world; and they were just two ordinary people held together in its embrace. Two friends. For just a moment, Mara imagined telling Lillian everything – not only about the financial problems with the lodge, or her inability to be a proper hunter's wife, like Alice, or even about how she could not picture the future any more. She imagined telling her about Matilda.

Instead, she forced another smile. 'Of course I'm happy,' she said lightly. She tried to make her tone easy, yet definite. She glanced at Lillian's face to see if she had succeeded.

'I'll never marry,' Lillian said. 'I don't understand why you'd want to settle for just one man when there's a whole world of them out there.' She opened her eyes and shifted so that she could meet Mara's gaze. 'And besides . . .' A briskness entered her voice. 'You can't have a career and a husband. Not in this business.'

Mara picked up another length of glossy dark hair and began to brush. 'Is it different, then, for an actor?' she asked.

Lillian nodded vehemently. 'Of course. What do you think? Everything's different for a man!'

'I guess so,' Mara agreed. It was certainly true in Africa – for Europeans as well as Africans. Bina was one of the few women whose circumstances suggested a different status quo. 'Peter is married, after all.'

'He sure is,' Lillian said. 'He's famous for being married.'

'What do you mean?' Mara asked.

'He's worked with some of the most beautiful women in Hollywood, and in all these years, there's never been gossip, never a moment of scandal.' Lillian's eyes widened, as if she felt surprised by this fact all over again. 'He just never crosses the line. If he did, believe me, everyone would know – there are no secrets in Hollywood.'

Mara studied the hairbrush – the whorls and scrolls of yellow-amber in the dark tortoiseshell. She sensed Lillian waiting for her to comment. But she feared that whatever she said, her voice would betray her, and that her whole story would be read in her response. She was certain, now, that she didn't want this to happen. She never wanted anyone to know what John had done to her – to have her unhealed wound laid bare for another to see. The shameful mark of a woman whose husband did not love her enough.

EIGHT

The place Leonard had chosen was marked by a small chunk of crumbly orange rock. It rested on a patch of hard-baked earth dotted sparsely with dry grass.

'Stand right here,' he instructed Mara. 'This is your first position. When I call *action*, I want you to pause for about six seconds, looking out that way.' He waved an arm to take in the valley that stretched out below them. 'Then walk slowly along the side of the hill to that big old tree. You're in no hurry; you're lost in thought. When you step into the shade, wait for a moment, then take off your hat and shake out your hair. You've got that?'

Mara nodded. 'I think so.'

'Well, don't worry, it's a mute shot – I'll talk you through it.' He held up his battered megaphone. 'Okay. Let's do it.'

Mara watched him – a tall red shape, in his overalls – as he scrambled down the hill to a dry stream bed. He leapt over it in a single bound, and then ran up the other side of the gully towards his crew, who were gathered around the camera and tripod. They looked like a strange little herd of animals – mismatched in size and colour, yet drawn to stand closely together.

About halfway between them and the spot where Mara stood, the khaki-clad figure of the ranger was crouching under a bush. He'd left John's gunbearer to protect the crew and was focusing all his attention on her. He held his body awkwardly, keeping his head down while turning his face constantly from side to side, scanning the surroundings. He was checking for signs of danger, Mara knew – even though, with his shotgun held at the ready, he looked exactly like a hunter assessing his prey. Earlier on in the day, a lion had appeared on the top of the ridge behind Mara. The ranger had let out a low warning whistle to attract her attention, then signalled to her not to move. Although he'd raised the twin barrels of his gun, something about his posture suggested to Mara that he was not unduly alarmed. When the lion moved into her view she saw why – the animal's mouth and neck were stained pink from a recent feed and it was ambling along with a relaxed, loose-pawed gait. Mara watched, unmoving, until the lion disappeared out of sight. Then she turned back to the ranger, in time to see him waving at Leonard, letting him know that the danger was over. Leonard wasn't watching, though – he'd taken Nick's place behind the camera and still had his eye pressed to the viewfinder. When he'd finally lifted his head, he'd looked towards Mara and raised one hand in a thumbs-up sign. Mara had smiled and waved in reply. She felt a warm sense of achievement. He had one of the shots he wanted most, she knew – Maggie in the same frame as a lion.

Lillian Lane, really there, in the wilds of Africa . . .

Now, the only animals in view were a couple of zebras. They grazed on a stretch of grass not far from the place where one of the black and white striped Land Rovers was parked. Now and then, they lifted their heads and looked towards the vehicle, as if intrigued by the presence of something that mimicked their colouring, and yet was so huge and hard-edged and shiny.

Mara edged backward until the heel of her boot just touched the marker stone, and then turned to gaze out over the landscape as Leonard had instructed. She knew the setting well. A sloping grassland ran down to a stand of fever trees, eye-catching with their tall trunks and spreading limbs sheathed in yellow-green bark. Here and there a euphorbia could be seen. They always looked out of place, like giant, overgrown cacti. Beyond the trees it was just possible to see the silver flash of a lake.

As she stood there, Mara was conscious that she was wearing Maggie's shirt and trousers and hat. Their touch against her skin was familiar, but they were faintly infused with Lillian's French perfume, blended with insect repellent and sweat. As she waited for Leonard's command, she picked nervously at a loose thread in one of the shirt-sleeves. She was glad neither Lillian nor Peter were here to watch her. Lillian had developed a headache in the heat and had just set out with a driver on the hour-long journey back to the lodge. Peter wasn't due until later in the day.

Thinking of Peter, still back at the lodge, reminded Mara that she should be there as well. It wasn't fair to leave the staff unsupervised with so many guests. But after the scenes in the dining room had been finished, Leonard had moved his crew out here into the bush – and for the second day in a row, Mara had been instructed to join them. She had no choice but to trust that Kefa and Menelik would be able to manage without her.

Mara bent to retie her shoelace. As her hair fell forward around her face, its colour took her by surprise. In preparation for these scenes, Rudi had dyed it a shade darker.

'You could almost get away with your colour as it is,' he'd said as he painted a thick crème onto Mara's wet hair, 'but best to be on the safe side.'

Mara had felt awkward, at first, sitting in her bathroom with this man she barely knew. He'd worked on her hair in silence. With gentle pressure of his hands he'd guided her head into different positions. He'd smoothed strands of her hair and wiped drops of water from her eyes with the corner of a towel. His gestures might have been intimate – almost tender – in another setting. But there was a look of intense concentration on his face that Mara recognised: it was the same one she'd seen when he was preparing the main room at the lodge for filming. When he'd finished, he'd stood back, assessing his handiwork with narrowed eyes. Mara had realised, then, that the task of dyeing her hair was completely impersonal for Rudi. She was just another of his props. It had been strangely liberating to be viewed this way. Somehow, the sense of being unimportant seemed to diminish the scale of all her fears and concerns.

Mara lifted her hand to shield her eyes from the sun, and peered across the gully. The two Nicks were still adjusting the camera equipment, while Leonard waited patiently. Jamie was sheltering under a black umbrella, his head bent over a newspaper. Tomba was a tall dark statue beside him, standing on one leg like a herdsman, the boom pole resting over his shoulder.

There was some shade over where they were, but on the hillside Mara was sweltering. The sun's rays pressed like a hot iron onto her shoulders. Sweat trickled in slow steady lines down her back and in between her breasts. A fly settled on her cheek. She felt its feet printing a track over her skin and the lick-lick of its mouth as it sucked at her sweat. She didn't bother to brush the fly away. Instead, she pretended that the skin, and the sweat, did not belong to her. Why should she care if her body was hot and uncomfortable and dirty? It was just a lump of flesh she had abandoned to its own discomforts, while she, Mara, took refuge in a cool faraway place, empty of all feeling.

It was a skill she'd acquired while out hunting with John, when she'd found herself waiting interminably, forbidden to move a muscle until the tracker gave the signal. She'd learned that by consciously separating herself from her body she could escape from the cramped muscles, the thirst, the heat, the itchy bites of insects.

And then she'd discovered she could hold on to this sense of remoteness. When the tracking of the game continued, and even when the fatal shots were eventually fired, she was still able to view herself from a distance. It was not Mara who stood there watching the animals falter and crash to the ground. It was a stranger who witnessed it all.

The great belly of a fallen elephant rising up from the earth like a small mountain.

Black-skinned arms wielding long knives, reaching high up its side. Blades plunging into the abdomen, rupturing the wall. A mass of intestines bursting out – the long sausage shapes unimaginably huge, each one a foot in diameter. A mounting pile, writhing like something still alive. Pale membranes gleaming opal colours in the sun.

To one side of the grey mountain, the long pink-tinged trunk sprawled in the dust. Limp. Breathless.

The air filling with African voices, singing the joys of meat, red meat, as much as you could eat.

And all the while, as the stranger watched, the hunter's wife observed herself from afar – cut off, safe. Innocent.

Looking back, Mara felt it was almost as if she'd known, somehow, that this skill would one day prove as vital to her survival as the knowledge of how to avoid snakebite, or how to move past a prowling lion without looking into its eyes. How else would she have lived through the agony that followed her discovery of Matilda's envelope? As the days turned into weeks, and then months, she'd taken refuge from her despair by distancing herself, all the time pretending to John that nothing was wrong. But every cure, she had discovered, has its cost. The body she had learned to abandon now seemed permanently lost to her. When John touched her – with hands that had made love to another woman – she felt like a puppet made of wood. Dried up and dead.

Mara tensed suddenly as a memory came to her of the night before John left for Dar. She had gone to bed early, as usual, but when John came in, he'd ignored her pretence at sleep. Reaching for her hunched shoulder, he'd pulled her round to face him. Then he'd moved on top of her, his knee parting her legs. No words passed between them, no kisses. He pressed his face into the pillow as he pushed up inside her. It felt to Mara like an act of possession, not love; and it was over quickly. Afterwards, they did not speak, or touch.

Mara cut off the memory, fixing her gaze on Leonard's red-suited figure. At last, his voice cut through the air, sounding flat and mechanical through the megaphone. She focused all her attention on following his orders. She walked back and forth as he instructed – stopping, starting, waiting; then doing it all again. Eventually she escaped from her own thoughts and emotions and was able to view the scene as an interested observer.

She was struck, once again, by the repetitive nature of filming. When they'd been here the previous day, Maggie had been doing much the same things as now, only the camera had been set up right beside the spot marked by the red stone. Mara's task had been to stand in for Lillian, doing dummy runs of the scene so the crew could see exactly what the actress would do when the real performance began. They had gathered in close around Mara, Nick Two using a measuring tape to take what he called focus readings. And Tomba practising the skill of tracking her movements with the microphone, while Jamie offered grunts of approval or criticism.

Lillian, meanwhile, had rested in the shade of a beach umbrella that had been draped with a piece of old khaki tent. Mara had insisted Rudi cover up the red and blue stripes, pointing out it was risky enough that half of the crew were dressed in bright colours. On the small table beside Lillian were her sketchpad and pencil, some insect repellent and a thermos flask. During the morning tea break, Mara had overheard Lillian telling Carlton the flask contained iced water, but she felt pretty sure it did not. Since arriving at Raynor Lodge, Lillian had taken pains to ensure Kefa understood how much she depended on her *dawa* – she didn't even call it 'gin and tonic' any more. Mara had wondered if Carlton knew exactly how much Lillian was drinking – and whether or not it was the safari hostess's responsibility to discuss it with him. But to do that would surely be a betrayal of Lillian. And anyway, the drinking didn't seem to affect the actress's ability to do her job. When the time had finally come for her to swap places with Mara, she'd performed with flawless precision.

Mara had taken up Lillian's position in the chair under the umbrella to watch. It had been strange, at first, to see someone dressed in her own clothes, moving through a landscape so well known to her, and recreating a sequence of actions she had just played out. After a while, Mara saw that there was another component to this impression of familiarity as well. She began to recognise her own little habits: the way Lillian lifted her hat, now and then, to let air in under the brim; the way she used the inside of her shirt-sleeve to wipe the sweat from her skin, so the dirt would not show. (In Lillian's case, of course, it was not real sweat, but droplets of some special liquid Rudi sprayed onto her face, just before she took her place in front of the camera.) Mara found it disconcerting to be used this way as a model for Maggie – but flattering as well.

Before long, the pattern of changing places had become familiar. Sometimes Lillian seemed to take it for granted that it was Mara's job to offer her a respite from the sun – but often she seemed genuinely grateful. In these instances, Mara felt noble and strong, like someone involved in a rescue. Even after Lillian returned to the set, reclaiming her place in front of the camera, the feeling lingered. Mara settled back confidently into Lillian's chair – the one with *Miss Lane* printed across its back. She'd even found herself touching the actress's possessions – the sketchbook, thermos, a handkerchief, a hairbrush – as if they were her own.

Mara finished her walk along the side of the hill and entered the welcome shade of the old thorn tree. She looked up, pretending to check for lurking animals in the gnarled old limbs that spread above her. Then she took off her hat and let the cool air flow over her head. On cue, Leonard's command came from across the gully.

'*Cut!*'

Mara watched a flurry of movement stir through the crew like a gust of wind. After a few moments Leonard lifted the megaphone to his mouth again. 'Thank you, Maggie. We're done here. We're moving to a new set-up now.'

Mara's impulse was to hurry across to the crew and help with packing up the equipment. But then Leonard called to her again. 'Rudi's coming to get you.'

Mara hovered there, feeling awkward. Even though the filming was finished for the moment, it seemed she was still expected to play the part of an actress: helpless and in need of assistance. She watched Rudi cautiously making his way towards her, taking small steps as though he did not trust the ground beneath his feet.

When he reached Mara he was panting. His sweat-damp curls had turned into tight ringlets. He jerked his head towards the southern end of the plains. 'We're going to the lake.'

Maggie and Luke stood side by side at the water's edge, the camera set up at a distance behind them.

Mara was no longer wearing her hat. Now she had a pale green scarf tied over her hair. It was a different day, Rudi had explained, from the one when Maggie had walked across the hillside alone.

Peter looked exactly as he had in the scene that had been filmed in the dining room, wearing the clothes Mara had chosen from John's drawers. He had the rifle as well, slung across his back, and the water bottle at his hip.

Mara stood stiffly beside him. The space between them felt dense, as if it held a shape of its own. She found herself breathing too fast. She licked her lips.

'Don't worry,' Peter said quietly. 'Think of it like a dance – just follow the steps. And remember, it's a wide shot. They can't see much detail.'

Mara nodded. 'Okay.'

Leonard's voice came to them faintly, as he gave instructions to Nick and Jamie.

There was the sound of Nick Two's garbled identification of the shot, and the snap of his clapperboard. 'Three-ninety-eight. Take one.'

'And – *action!*' Leonard called through his megaphone.

Maggie and Luke stepped off the grassy bank onto a muddy shore. The surface was paved with dried-up plates of grey clay. The curled edges crunched underfoot as the two walked towards the edge of the lake. Mara fixed her gaze straight ahead, focusing on a flock of pink-legged flamingos clustered in the shallows.

'Walk closer,' Leonard instructed. Peter veered casually towards Mara until they were virtually shoulder to shoulder. 'Maggie, put your hand on his arm for balance. Then bend down and re-tie your shoe. Or, pick out a thorn from your sock. Something like that.'

Mara put her hand on Peter's forearm. She felt his muscles tense beneath the soft cloth of the shirt. Lifting one foot, she pulled at the back of her boot.

'That's good. Now wobble a bit. Luke, catch hold of her.'

Peter's arm encircled her waist, catching Mara by surprise. She tightened her grip on his arm as her show of losing her balance suddenly became real. Peter kept his arm around her waist, holding her close. She could smell his cinnamon fragrance overlaying the taint of fresh sweat.

'Just stay like that,' called Leonard. 'Now start chatting. Relax together. Maggie, tell him all about this place you love so much.'

Mara stared at the lake, her body rigid. She couldn't think of anything to say.

Peter lifted his free arm, pointing along the shoreline to an outcrop of rocks surrounded by a small beach of pebbles. 'Let's go and sit over there – take it easy.'

Mara eyed him uncertainly. 'But Leonard said to stay here . . .'

Peter grinned. 'We don't have to do everything he says. I know what he's after – he wants to see us enjoying ourselves, settling into the place. Let's just do it our own way.'

He put his arm around her shoulders, steering her towards the rocks, where they sat side by side. Peter gestured towards the flamingos. 'Tell me something about these birds.'

'Well, they get their pink colour from the algae they eat,' Mara said. 'If you keep a flamingo in captivity it goes all pale. And the young birds are plain white, until they start feeding for themselves.' She pointed to the nearest of the birds, which had lowered its head to the water, to feed. 'See how they eat? They put their heads right upside down, the upper beak resting on the water so that it can filter out the algae.'

Peter looked impressed. 'How do you know all this?' he asked.

'From my husband,' Mara answered. 'John knows everything about this place – the plants, insects, animals . . .' She let her voice trail off, suddenly uneasy. She wondered what John would think if he were here. He'd understand why Mara had agreed to let the film people come to Raynor Lodge, and why she had to do everything she could to help them complete their work successfully, of course he would. But she found it hard to imagine him being happy about another man touching her in this way – or about her letting it happen.

Yet, how could he object? After all, he had done much, much more.

'Yes, it's a real pity he's not here,' Peter said. 'I'd like to meet him. I saw some photos of him in the dining room.'

Mara glanced at his face. He looked completely relaxed. And the way he mentioned her husband was so calm and matter-of-fact – it was clear that he didn't think he had anything to hide. Mara found herself reconsidering how John might react to this scene. Her ideas began to change – breaking up like a kaleidoscope image and reforming in a new shape. John would *approve* of what was happening here, she realised, just like everyone did: Carlton, Daudi, Leonard, Kabeya; even the president himself.

Peter picked up a handful of pebbles and gave them to Mara. Then he collected a small pile for himself.

'See that dead log?' He gestured towards a sun-bleached trunk that stuck up out of the water, well away from where the birds were gathered. He hurled a stone towards it. 'Whoever hits it first gets a prize.'

Mara watched as he threw a second stone, and smiled to herself.

Peter didn't know that she was the sister of six brothers. She'd spent hours throwing rocks at targets on the farm and her aim was as good as theirs. It was why she'd been able to learn to shoot so accurately, so quickly. She stood up so that she could take a better aim.

Each stone she threw moved steadily closer to its target.

'Hey, you've done this before,' Peter said.

She could hear a note of surprise in his voice. 'Oh, yes,' she told him, sending another stone in an arc across the water. 'Quite a few times.' From the corner of her eye, she could see Peter watching her.

'Well, so have I,' he said. He crouched over, hooking his arm sideways and throwing low. There was a look of serious intent on his face.

Mara laughed. 'I'm going to win,' she taunted him. Even as she spoke, the stone she'd just thrown landed with a distant thud on the middle of the log.

Peter threw up his hands with mock despair, and shook his head wonderingly. 'You've sure got a straight eye!'

Mara grinned triumphantly at him. 'What's my prize?' she asked. She met his laughing gaze. His admiration stirred something inside her, making her feel lightheaded and careless.

'I'm not sure,' Peter said. 'I'll have to give it some thought.'

Just then, Leonard's voice broke in – a jolting reminder of reality. 'And, *cut*! Fantastic, guys. That was great – wonderful stuff.'

Mara peered intently ahead as she steered the old Land Rover over the trackless terrain, avoiding honey-badger holes and termite hills. The two Manyala Land Rovers had set off a little earlier and were now out of sight in the next valley, but there were small clues to the route they had taken: the occasional crushed bush or flattened pile of dung.

Her only passenger was Peter. He'd lingered by the lake taking photographs and, since the others were keen to get back and tackle the equipment maintenance and paperwork that followed each day's shooting, she'd offered to wait for him. Now he was leaning out through the passenger-side window, assessing the way ahead, lifting one hand, at intervals, and saying simply, 'This way,' or 'That way.' He seemed to understand instinctively that driving cross-country like this was an activity that involved everyone on board. Mara guessed that if the conditions had been more demanding, he'd have been quite happy to sit on the spare tyre on the bonnet, or even stand on the front bumper bar, to assess the ground ahead.

The late-afternoon light brewed strong colours in the land – the sky was purple, the earth a deep red, overlaid with a thin covering of spun gold grass. Trees and bushes were beginning to flatten into silhouettes. The birds resting in their branches were splashes of white that blazed as though lit from within. Mara glanced at Peter. She could see he was struck by the beauty of the landscape as well, and she felt a burst of pride, as if she were somehow responsible for it all.

'This reminds me of home,' Peter commented. 'Australia, I mean . . .'

Mara nodded, feeling a wave of longing at his words. The landscapes of Tanzania often evoked in her memories of Tasmania – especially the area around Coal River. Even the names of the two places were linked. Tanzania and Tasmania sounded so similar, many people in the world thought they were the same place.

In her early days in Africa, Mara had savoured this connection; it had helped her feel a sense of belonging. But now she found it increasingly painful to think about her old home – how she'd left there with such high hopes for her future. Her letters to her mother were becoming shorter and less frequent. The truth about her life here was no longer something she wanted to share.

'How long have you been here?' Peter asked her.

'A bit over three years now.'

'Have you been back for a visit?'

Mara shook her head.

'You must miss seeing your family. Do you have brothers and sisters?'

'Just brothers,' Mara said. 'But lots of them!' She paused, an aching lump in her throat. She wanted to tell Peter that though she'd often wanted to escape from them, in the past, she now missed them terribly.

'I was an only child,' Peter said. 'That's why I always wanted to have a big family of my own. But I had a happy childhood. We had a house right on the beach at Bondi. I lived in the surf – before school, after school, during school. That's why I had to become an actor. I couldn't get a real job.' He smiled, but then grew serious. 'I'd love to move back to Australia, actually. I'd prefer to bring the kids up there. But Paula doesn't want to leave America and I guess it's more important for her to be where she wants to be. I'm away now and then, after all.'

Mara was unsure how to reply – the conversation seemed to have grown suddenly personal. Being alone together in the Land Rover, after the day's filming, had made them seem like old friends.

But they weren't, Mara reminded herself. He was Peter Heath and she was just the safari hostess, driving him home from location.

She slowed and swerved to avoid a dried-out riverbed. A narrow ribbon of dark earth was the only clue to its presence, but she knew that beneath the dry surface of the ground that bordered it, was a layer of deep wet mud. The Land Rover would break through the firm crust, and sink to its axles. She hauled at the steering wheel, aiming towards higher ground.

'Wait! Stop!' Peter called.

Responding to the urgency in his voice, Mara slammed on the brakes.

'What's that over there?' Peter pointed along the riverbed to the place where it opened onto a wide pan of dark mud – all that remained of a rainy-season lake – and raised a pair of binoculars to his eyes. 'It's an animal – stuck in the mud. It looks like a young buffalo.' There was a brief silence as Peter leaned further out of the window, still peering through the binoculars. 'It moved its head!' he called back into the cab. 'It's alive! We have to do something.' He swung one arm in an arc. 'If you drive round that way we can get right up to it. The ground looks fine.'

Mara kept the engine idling. She knew the rule: in a situation like this, a wild animal should be left to its own fate.

Peter lowered the glasses, turning to Mara. 'There must be a way to get it out of there.'

Mara's hand hovered over the gearstick as she scanned the open grassland. The only animals in sight were a few Thomson's gazelles, grazing in a relaxed manner, tails flicking constantly from side to side. There was no sign of buffalo. She felt a wave of relief. Buffalo were some of the most dangerous animals in the bush. A herd could materialise soundlessly, encircling a hunting party or group of sightseers. Usually they just stood in menacing stillness, but if stirred to anger for some reason, they became murderous – and the hard shell of a Land Rover offered only temporary protection from their attack.

'The herd has gone,' Peter said, as if reading her thoughts. 'They've left it behind.'

Mara nodded. 'There wouldn't have been much they could do by staying. They haven't got trunks, like elephants, to try to pull it out.'

'Come on, then,' Peter said impatiently. 'Let's go.'

Mara looked away. Inside her head, she could hear John's voice – calm and sure and reasonable. *Leave it alone. The herd is gone. It'll die anyway.*

Glancing sideways, she saw Peter guessing the meaning of her hesitation. Shock and outrage gathered in his eyes. Again, Mara knew exactly what John would have said. *You have to be able to make the tough decisions. Africa is not for the faint-hearted.*

Mara looked at Peter's face. His eyes were screwed up at the corners like someone wincing in pain. She knew just how it felt, to look like that – the way each muscle tightened, pulling the skin into lines. It was so familiar to her that she might have been watching her own reflection.

Suddenly, she made her decision. Without saying anything, she reached down to select low ratio and then let out the clutch. The vehicle lurched off slowly in the direction of the dried-up lake.

At a safe distance from the edge, she stopped the Land Rover.

The two climbed out of the vehicle. Mara took the heavy-gauge shotgun from the rack, then loaded it and flicked on the safety catch. Slinging it over her shoulder, she walked with Peter to the edge of the mud-pan.

The stranded animal was very young, and only about the size of a newborn foal. It was so plastered with mud that if it had not been for the horns – only half-grown, yet showing the distinctive blunt shape – Mara would barely have recognised it as a buffalo. It stared at them with its head tilted to one side, looking cute and almost comical, like something from a children's storybook.

Mara measured with her eye the distance they'd have to plough through the mud to reach the little calf. They would have to be careful not to get stuck themselves. She looked warily at the dark mud, considering other dangers. She was glad there were no reeds growing here to harbour the snails that carried the bilharzia parasite.

Peter pointed to the lines of hoof prints that pocked the surface of the mud. 'You can guess what happened,' he said. 'The herd came galloping down here, looking for water and they were in the mud before they knew it. The adults were strong enough to get back out – but this little one was trapped.'

Mara eyed him curiously. There was a commonsense practicality about him, as if he'd grown up on a farm, like she had, and not at the beach. It occurred to her that perhaps the sea taught the same kind of lessons as the land . . .

Peter was still gazing at the calf. 'I reckon if we get on each side of it,' he said, 'we might be able to dig it free with our hands. But we've got to get out there, first.' He looked down at his clothes and boots. 'Lucky Rudi made us change out of our wardrobe,' he commented. 'We sure wouldn't be popular if we came back with that stuff all covered in mud!'

Mara stared at him, shocked at the very idea of letting such a thing happen. Rudi had told her more than once that the wardrobe clothes were very precious – irreplaceable, in fact – now they'd been filmed. Even though everything was safely back in his hands, the disturbing thought only added to Mara's sense of unease about what she'd agreed to do.

Peter began walking towards the calf. Mara took a couple of steps after him, but then hesitated. She could feel the hard metal of the gun barrel resting across her back. She felt she should keep the gun with her, but allowing it to get muddy would be as bad as damaging Rudi's clothes. No matter how carefully she cleaned it when she got home, she knew there would be telltale remnants of grit for John to discover later on. She checked their surroundings again. She could still see no sign of danger – so she pulled the strap over her head and left the gun behind on the ground.

At first, they made easy progress, but then Peter's boot crunched through the dry surface and sank into the mud. Moments later, the same thing happened to Mara. She stifled a cry as her leg disappeared almost to the knee in thick, squelching mud. A rank, rotting smell rose up. Struggling to keep her balance, she took another step. When she dragged out her first leg, it emerged painted black with the tarry mud.

'Are you okay?' Peter called back to her.

'Fine,' Mara replied.

At the sound of their voices, the calf rolled its eyes and let out a low, desperate moan; it began to struggle weakly. Mara knew the poor creature was afraid, and would fight them in panic when they tried to set it free.

Mara made her way to one side of the calf and Peter took the other. They tried to dig down around the buffalo's spindly legs, scooping away the mud with their hands. Soon, they were both black to their shoulders, their clothes glued to their skin.

They struggled in silence. Mara felt sweat breaking out over her body, beneath the clammy mud.

'It's no good,' Peter said finally. 'We're making no progress at all.'

The calf lowed mournfully. It looked thirsty, as well as exhausted, its limp grey tongue protruding from its mouth. Mara looked across to her gun, lying on the shore. She didn't think she could bear to stand at the animal's shoulder, placing the gun barrel against the side of its head. On the other hand, it would be even worse to leave the calf here alive, trapped beneath the blazing heat of the sun. She pictured it suffering through all the next day and perhaps the one after. Until it finally laid down its little head and died here, all alone.

'It's just a baby . . .' An idea came to Mara. 'It can't weigh all that much. Let's try and lift it out. We could join hands underneath it.'

Peter nodded, and without wasting any time, began burrowing into the mud under the calf's belly.

Mara followed his example. Pressing her head against the calf's shoulder, she could feel the heat of its body through her hair.

Before long, her hands – grasping blindly – met Peter's. They entwined gritty fingers, and tightened their grip.

'Okay, on the count of three,' Peter said. 'One – two – three.'

Using the weight of their bodies to lean back, they struggled to raise up the calf. Meanwhile, it grunted and twisted in fear, craning its neck, wanting to reach them with its horns. Mara and Peter kept pulling and lifting. Their eyes met over the animal's back, each willing the other to maintain the effort. But the calf did not budge.

After a while, they gave up and took a rest, keeping their hands locked, but easing their muscles.

'Perhaps we should try a rope?' Mara suggested. 'We might be able to pull it out with the Land Rover.'

'Let's give this one more shot first,' Peter said. 'Okay, again,' he panted. 'One – two – three.'

This time, when they lifted, there was a faint sucking sound and the buffalo's body rose slightly. They tried again. Before long, there was another small shift. Then there was a slow hissing sound, and the body rose up above the surface. The calf fell onto its side, legs sprawling as it struggled weakly.

For a few seconds Mara and Peter just stared at one another in relief. Then Peter shifted his attention to the calf, running his eyes over the mud-plastered hide. 'You little beauty!' he said quietly.

Mara looked at him. For the first time, he'd spoken as an Australian – not just in his choice of expression, but in his accent as well. She smiled as she watched him bend over the calf, patting its heaving side.

The buffalo began to bleat frantically, as though it sensed rescue was imminent. The desperate noise seemed too loud for the weakened body. It echoed through the still, hot air. There was a flapping of wings as birds flew from the branches of a dead tree that stood behind the Land Rover. Mara looked up, following their flight. With a thud of horror she realised they were vultures. The birds had probably been sitting there for hours, watching and waiting . . .

'Come on,' Mara said to Peter. There was a fresh note of urgency in her voice. 'Let's keep moving.'

They took up their positions on each side of the buffalo, preparing to join forces again and move it back to solid ground.

It was an exhausting process, holding the calf up out of the mud and dragging it along, while battling their own way through the quagmire towards the shore.

Finally, they stumbled onto the hard ground and stood there breathing heavily, rubbing stretched muscles. The calf lay on the ground between them, its legs folded underneath its body.

'Let's get it up on its feet,' Peter said.

Mara grasped one of the animal's forelegs, ready to help lift. But then she froze, as something caught her eye: grey shapes and a cloud of dust, moving at the edge of her vision.

She yelled in alarm. 'Buffalo! Quick!'

Peter jolted into action, lunging towards the Land Rover. Mara was right behind him. She snatched up the gun without breaking her stride and ran on, holding it with the barrel pointed to the sky.

Peter reached the Land Rover and jumped into the front passenger seat. Leaning across, he opened the driver's side door.

Mara angled the gun over the back of the seat, then leapt in and started the engine. In the rear-vision mirror, she could see the approaching herd. The animals were jogging towards them over the plain – heads lowered, solid bodies bunched with muscle. She could hear the sound of their hooves drumming against the dry ground. They were only a few hundred yards away.

She steered wildly, half-standing to get a better look at the ground ahead. Beside her, Peter braced himself against the lurching motion. He called out information about what he could see, but his voice was almost lost beneath the rattle of the Land Rover as it bounced over the rough terrain.

Mara's stomach tightened with fear. She knew buffalo were fast-moving animals, in spite of their bulk, and she could see the herd was already nearing the calf. Within moments, they would storm past it in pursuit of the Land Rover. Everything Mara had ever heard about buffalo attacks came back to her – accounts of vehicles torn to pieces, the occupants lucky to survive their wounds; and hunters on foot being trampled until they were just red pulp on the savannah.

'They're stopping!' Peter yelled.

A glance in the mirror told Mara that he was right. The buffalo were milling around the edge of the mud-pan. Not a single animal in the herd so much as lifted its head in the direction of the Land Rover. Mara stared in surprise. The buffalo seemed only to be concerned with the fate of the calf.

She sat back down in her seat so that she could steer more smoothly. When they were a good distance from the mud-pan, she slowed the Land Rover to a safer speed. As the jolting subsided, she turned to Peter, giving him what she hoped was a reassuring smile. 'Are you okay?'

'Yes – are you?' he asked.

Mara nodded silently. As fear ebbed from her body, relief flooded through her. But that emotion was soon displaced by a sense of dismay. She had put a client's life at risk. What had she been thinking?

She leaned over the wheel, her muddy hair falling forward to hide her face. The Land Rover was moving at a steady pace now, following a marked, though bumpy, track. Her knee banged against the door, but she made no move to protect it.

Beside her, Peter let out a long breath.

'Well done,' he said.

The warmth in his voice drew Mara's gaze. She saw that he was smiling proudly at her. His eyes, sparkling with excitement, blazed a clear blue-green. Mara felt herself caught in their power – transfixed like a night animal in a spotlight. She had to force herself to look away.

From the corner of her eye, she saw him studying her, his eyes travelling up and down her body. 'You look . . .' he began, then his voice trailed off and he shook his head, smiling.

Mara did not need to glance down at herself to imagine how she appeared, sitting there at the wheel – clothes caked in mud, skin blackened. She scanned Peter's body instead.

'So do you.' She grinned back.

Suddenly, it was as if they were just kids, stopping at the end of a day's play and only then discovering how dirty they'd become. They both broke into laughter. The sound seemed to bounce back and forth between them, growing louder and longer, being fed from both sides. Several times, it faded away, only to burst out again.

Eventually, they became quiet. They sat, side by side, their bodies jostled by the movement of the Land Rover, the hum of the engine the only sound. Mara drove easily now, one elbow resting out through the open window. Before long, they left the plains behind and began climbing to higher ground. A mood of peacefulness grew between them, mirrored by the calm beauty of the land through which they passed. The sun was low in the sky, casting golden rays over the grass.

As the journey wound on, the sunlight turned rosy and the sky became a deep shade of mauve. In the lower branches of the thorn trees, guineafowl began roosting, seeking safety above the ground from the predators of the night. Mara switched on the headlights and had to concentrate, again, on following the track. But every nerve in her body was attuned to the presence of the man sitting next to her. And his attention was focused on her, too, she could tell – now and then, he turned away from the view, and watched her.

Finally, he spoke. 'That was amazing. Something I'll never forget.'

Mara smiled. 'Me, too.'

She could feel the sense of closeness again. She told herself it was not surprising. They were both Australians, far from their homeland. They'd been working side by side on the film. And now, they'd just saved the life of a baby buffalo. She felt a warm glow spreading inside her at the thought of what they'd done. Together, they had defied the laws of the strong-hearted – and won.

NINE

It was dusk by the time they drew into the lodge. In the half-light the tusks that formed the entrance archway were two white slashes standing out against a backdrop of grey leaves and branches. The smoke of village cooking fires drifted on the air.

Mara switched off the ignition and the engine shuddered to a stop but she remained in the driver's seat, reluctant to let the journey come to an end. She turned to Peter. He had not moved either, as if he, too, were savouring these last moments. His face was shadowy, but she could see the shine of his eyes. Neither of them spoke – the peace of the journey was still wrapped around them, warm and close.

Finally, Mara stirred, opening her door. Climbing down from her seat, she picked up the gun then waited for Peter to join her. They walked side by side under the tusks and on along the stone-paved path. The foliage seemed to press in around them, as if to keep them hidden for as long as possible. But soon, the lodge building came into view.

Mara's step faltered as she caught sight of Carlton pacing the verandah. He moved in quick, tense bursts. His left shirt-sleeve was pulled up to expose his watch.

Mara glanced nervously at Peter, trying to decide whether she could ask him to be the first to speak. But just then she stepped on a fallen twig. The faint cracking sound caught Carlton's attention. As he looked up the path his face became transfixed with alarm.

'What's happened?' he demanded. His gaze jerked from Peter to Mara and back. 'Are you hurt?'

Peter spread his hands in a calming gesture. 'We're fine. Don't worry.'

Carlton was speechless for a moment. 'Don't worry?' he spluttered eventually. 'Don't worry that it's nearly dark and you weren't back? I was about to send out a search party! They'd have left already, except Brendan went off somewhere with both sets of keys . . .' His voice trailed off as he stared at Peter, his eyes moving over the actor's mud-caked body. When he spoke again, his voice was hushed. 'What have you been doing?'

'We had to rescue a baby buffalo,' Peter answered him. 'We waded out to it through some mud.'

Carlton shook his head like someone wanting to wake up from a bad dream.

Peter glanced at Mara. 'I was the one who saw it. I asked her to stop.'

Carlton shifted his attention to Mara. 'Well, you shouldn't have agreed,' he said bluntly. 'What if there had been an accident?' Without waiting for a reply, he swung back to Peter. 'You know as well as I do that even a minor accident would be a disaster for us. We can't accommodate any delays at all.' A note of panic entered his voice, as though the danger had not already been averted. 'The picture would fold, simple as that. We'd be finished!'

'But there *wasn't* an accident,' Peter said soothingly.

Carlton frowned at Mara. 'That's not the point.'

'It really wasn't her fault,' Peter said.

But Mara shook her head. 'It was my responsibility. I'm really sorry, Carlton.' She moved instinctively towards him. 'I won't let anything like this happen again.'

Carlton stepped backwards. Mara guessed he was so angry with her that he could no longer bear being near her. But then his nose wrinkled up. 'Boy, you smell bad! You'd better take a bath – both of you.'

Peter caught Mara's eye as she retreated. Suddenly, she saw the funny side of the scene. She felt laughter rising inside her. She almost forgot Carlton was still standing there, frowning.

'Peter will need hot water in his rondavel,' he said stiffly.

'Yes, of course.' Gathering herself, Mara turned to Peter. 'I'll get the hut boys to bring you some straightaway.' She noticed that the mud had dried into a pale coating on the bare skin of his forearms; it was cracking away at the joints of his hands and elbows. 'It might be best to take a shower first – the water will be cold, but it'll wash away the mud more easily.'

'Thanks, I'll do that,' Peter replied. He looked pointedly at Mara's muddy hair and face. 'You could do with a hose-down yourself.'

Mara smiled. The way he spoke now was *so* Australian – the mock-seriousness, combined with the words and the accent – that she glanced at Carlton to see if it had caught his attention. Carlton was looking at Peter, a thoughtful frown on his face, but what he was thinking about, Mara could not tell.

Peter turned away, heading towards the line of rondavels.

Mara expected Carlton to go with him, but he hovered beside her. Anticipating another reprimand, she waited anxiously for him to speak. When he finally did, he surprised her.

'All this trouble aside,' he said, 'I hear it's been a great day's work. Leonard's very pleased – everyone is. Thank you for your help.'

'Not at all,' Mara said. 'It was my pleasure.' She smiled warmly at him.

Carlton nodded in reply. 'See you at dinner.'

At the mention of the evening meal, Mara sobered instantly. It dawned on her that she would have to hurry straight to the kitchen and see what was being prepared.

'It's going to be a special Tanzanian feast,' Carlton announced. 'Daudi and Kefa discussed it with me this morning, since you were out on location.' His tone was bright, now, clearly buoyed by relief that the crisis was over. 'I said it was a fine idea – much more interesting than just having English food every day. They promised not to put chilli in everything.'

Mara tried to mask her surprise. As far as she knew, a Tanzanian feast consisted simply of slaughtering a goat and roasting the meat on the fire.

'Did they mention any particular dishes?' she asked cautiously.

'*Kilimanjaro chicken* – that's one, I remember,' Carlton responded. 'Then they talked about spinach cooked with peanuts. And something made from green bananas for desert. It all sounded great.'

'Oh yes, delicious,' Mara said. She tried to sound knowledgeable, as though the things he'd mentioned were specialties of Raynor Lodge, when the truth was that in the years she'd been here Menelik had never served up such fare before. She suspected the idea of offering a national cuisine had come from Daudi, as a part of his mission to promote the new Tanzania.

Mara hovered politely until Carlton turned to go. Then she half-ran in the direction of the compound, heading for the kitchen. Even though she dreaded facing Menelik, she knew she could not postpone letting him know she was back. She'd have to call out to him from the kitchen doorway – all dirty and smelly, like a village outcast. She shook her head helplessly. She didn't even want to think about how the old man would react when he saw her. She was painfully aware that if she had deliberately set out to prove she was an incompetent memsahib, she could hardly have done better than this.

Mara lay back in the bathtub, wet hair swirling around her shoulders. She'd washed off most of the mud at an outside tap, but still, the bathwater was grey. The smell of the mud-pan was gone, however, replaced by *L'Air du Temps*. The fragrance had come from a special bar of soap Lillian had insisted Mara use. The actress had been fascinated by Mara and Peter's adventure. She'd relived with them every moment of the rescue in such detail, it had begun to seem as though the experience had somehow included her as well. Mara sensed that the sharing of the soap – as well as being a thoughtful gesture – was a part of that illusion.

Mara moved her hands slowly over her breasts and belly, massaging the soap into her skin. Her whole body tingled from being scrubbed in gritty water. She felt strangely alive, even while the smooth circular movements evoked a languorous sense of indulgence.

Closing her eyes, she drew the fragrance deeply into her lungs. She let herself imagine – just for a few moments – that she was no longer Mara Sutherland, the hunter's wife. She was, instead, a pampered creature who lived in a world of luxury and romance. Someone like Lillian. Free to go where she liked and do whatever she chose. Free to fall in love with a handsome stranger.

Not a married man, like Peter Heath. No.

Not Peter. But someone like him . . .

Mara rubbed her hands over her face as though to wash the vision away. She reminded herself of who she really was. The Memsahib of Raynor Lodge. The thought brought a wry smile to her face as she recalled the encounter she'd just had with Menelik. It had not gone as badly as she'd feared. Instead of being cold and disapproving, he'd stared at Mara in disbelief – then broken down into laughter. The kitchen boy and the firewood boy, who'd been standing nearby, rigid with shock, had soon followed suit. Mara knew that Africans sometimes laughed out of embarrassment, or even as an expression of sympathy, so she had not been quite sure how to read the scene. But in the end she'd joined in as well. The sound of the blended laughter seemed to fill the air, driving out tension. And as Mara had glanced beyond Menelik into the kitchen, her relief grew even greater because she could see without having to ask that preparations for the evening meal were well in hand. Even Lillian's little dishes were already set out, ready to receive her separate portions. Clearly, everything was organised and calm.

Mara waved her hands under the water, sending eddies over her skin. She breathed out slowly, letting her body relax. For now, there was nothing she needed to worry about. The interlude of peace was hers to enjoy.

Mara walked towards the rondavels with the bar of special soap in her hand. She wasn't sure if it had been a loan or a gift – but she planned to return it to Lillian anyway. It might be the only bar she had brought with her. And now that Mara had used the soft, creamy soap, she knew neither Palmolive nor Lifebuoy were suitable alternatives.

Kerosene lanterns hung along the pathway, adding to the electric light that flowed from the main lodge building. As she walked, Mara glanced down at her unfamiliar blouse and skirt – the new outfit she'd ordered from Bina. Tonight, when she'd climbed out of her bath – clean and refreshed, with exotic perfume clinging to her skin – she'd suddenly decided to wear her new clothes to dinner. After all, it was a special occasion. A Tanzanian feast was being served at Raynor Lodge for the first time ever.

Mara regretted the absence of her dressing table. To see how she looked in the new clothes, she'd had to make use of the hand-mirror again, moving it around her body like a small camera. Judging by the fractured images she collected, the outfit was a success. The style suited her, and the fabric – printed with a dappled pattern of sunny, tawny colours – was even more beautiful than she'd remembered. Clad in the skirt and top, she imagined she looked like a character out of a child's fairytale: the *Spirit of the Savannah*. It was not the dry-season landscape she evoked, but the one that emerged after the first short rains, when a flush of green crept over the plains promising new life to all.

She was also wearing high heels – the ones she'd brought to Africa for her wedding. She'd had them re-dyed by the leather merchant to a light creamy tan, and now they went perfectly with her new clothes.

Mara walked slowly along the path, the soft folds of the skirt caressing her legs, her freshly washed hair sweeping her shoulder-blades. She glanced up at the night sky. The curtain of velvet was already punctured with stars and she paused to identify the one con-stellation whose African name she knew. *Mapacha* – the Twins.

It was impossible to pick the moment at which she first sensed she was being watched – the realisation crept up on her impercep-tibly, the way the sky lightens before dawn. But as the knowledge settled inside her, she stopped. Then, as if pulled by an invis-ible cord, she turned slowly towards the second of the rondavels. Standing in the doorway was Peter.

A pool of lantern light fell over him, settling in soft shadows around the finely sculpted lines of his face. He was looking straight at Mara. He did not nod his head in greeting, or smile. He seemed frozen – stunned. Mara returned his gaze in silence. She tried to read his expression. He was struck by her changed appearance, she could see that much. He admired her.

But there was another emotion there, as well, one that was less easy to identify. She caught her breath. Was it was fear, or longing – or both?

Then Peter smiled, breaking the spell. He gestured towards her skirt and top. 'You look beautiful.' His voice was deep and soft, floating across to her.

'Thank you,' Mara replied. 'It's new.'

She stepped closer to him. Their eyes met again. Mara knew that the lingering gaze held a meaning that was potent and dangerous – but still, she let a long moment pass. Then she began to turn away. In the same instant, she saw Peter lower his head, hiding his face from view.

She could feel him there behind her as she walked back along the path. Her heart beat fast in her chest, and her stomach fluttered. Her senses seemed distorted – his presence reaching out to her, while at the same time, pulling away. She felt he was as close to her as the moths that circled nearby in the lamplight; and as distant as the stars.

As she neared Lillian's rondavel, Mara paused in the shadow of a frangipani tree, willing herself to become calm. When she felt she was ready, she approached the hut with the bar of soap held out in her hand.

She was about to pass the window, when she heard a man's voice coming from inside the room. She stopped and backed into the shadows again, hoping she had not already been seen – she knew how important it was for guests to have privacy in their rooms. Then the man spoke again, more loudly this time. Mara recognised Carlton's voice.

'That's not the point, Lillian,' he was saying. 'I agree you're doing fine on set. But I know – and you know – that you're drinking way too much.'

'Oh come on, Carlton,' Lillian said. 'Just a few nips of gin, now and then – it's no big deal.'

'It's more than just a few, Lillian,' Carlton said patiently. 'You think you're hiding it, but you don't fool me.'

There was a short silence. When Lillian spoke again, Mara

recognised the pleading tone she'd heard before. 'I'm just trying to get through this, you see. Being in Africa's harder than I thought it would be – all the germs and diseases, insects and wild animals. Zanzibar was a *nightmare* . . .' There was another brief quiet. Mara pictured Lillian putting on a sweet, winning smile. 'Don't be hard on me, Carlton. Please.' A calculating note entered her voice. 'The way I see it, it's best for the movie if I keep going as I am, just until the shoot is over. We've got some of the most important scenes still to do. I'll cut down when I get back home.'

Carlton let out a loud, exasperated sigh. 'Lillian. This isn't just about finishing the movie. I care about you. You'll end up back in that clinic – and then no one will work with you again. One break-down can be explained away, but two is a pattern.'

Mara caught her breath, torn between disbelief and mounting concern as she struggled to take in the meaning of Carlton's words. *Clinic. Breakdown. No one will work with you again.*

'Listen, Lillian,' Carlton continued. 'I had to do some hard talk-ing to get insurance for you on this picture – and even then, they insisted on some exclusions. You can't afford to take any risks.'

'You're completely overreacting,' stated Lillian. 'I've got every-thing under control.'

There was the sound of footsteps, then – brisk, and heavy with intent. Lillian uttered a short, sharp cry of protest. A moment later the door flew open. Mara pressed herself into a bush to make sure she was out of sight. Carlton emerged from the rondavel clutching two green gin bottles against his chest.

'Give them back!' Lillian's voice was shrill with alarm. 'What do you think you're doing?'

Mara watched as Carlton removed the tops from the bottles.

'No!' Lillian cried. 'Don't do that. Please.'

Carlton held out the bottles, one in each hand. Then he upended them simultaneously – and stood motionless as the contents glugged out in a steady silver stream. There was a look of surprise on his face, as if he couldn't quite believe he was acting so boldly. A strong smell of juniper and alcohol rose in the air. When the two bottles were empty, Carlton gave Lillian a long, silent look – before placing them on the ground and striding away without a backward glance.

The door to Lillian's hut slammed shut.

Mara stayed where she was, waiting for Carlton to disappear from view. Her whole body was rigid with shock. Of course, she knew Lillian drank, but she had never imagined the actress might be an alcoholic. In Mara's mind the word went with burnt-out people trapped in failed lives. It didn't fit with someone successful and talented. Peering in the direction of the rondavel, Mara felt an impulse to go to Lillian and make sure she was all right. But that would mean letting her know Mara had witnessed the humiliating scene, which could only make her feel worse. It would be much better, Mara realised, just to leave everything in Carlton's hands. He was a film producer, after all – he knew what to do when things went wrong.

Crouching in the shadows, Mara tightened her fingers around the bar of soap. It felt reassuringly firm: a solid point in a world that seemed suddenly unreliable. If Lillian Lane could be revealed as a woman whose career was threatened by disaster, who could say what else might happen?

Mara felt a shiver of confusion travel through her body. But even that emotion was not all that it first appeared to be; it was entwined with something else – a sense that in a place of secrets and contradictions the normal rules of life might be suspended.

Anything could happen.

An image of Peter's face floated into her mind. A thrill of excitement stirred inside her, quickening the blood in her veins.

TEN

Lillian lay stretched out on a cane lounge in the dappled shade of the jacaranda tree. Her hair was wrapped in a silk scarf that perfectly matched the pink of the flowers on the bougainvillea bush nearby, as did the floral print of her dress. As Mara crossed the brown lawn towards her, she couldn't help wondering if this colour coordination might be deliberate. Perhaps Lillian had spent so much time seeing herself as a part of a carefully arranged film set, she couldn't help ordering the real world in the same way.

The tea tray Mara had come to collect was on the ground beside the lounge. She approached it quietly; Lillian was fast asleep, breathing deeply and evenly through parted lips. There were faint shadows under her eyes, but other than that, she looked fine. Beautiful, in fact. It was hard to believe this was the same person Carlton had confronted last night.

Mara lifted the tray carefully, making sure not to rattle the crockery. She was about to turn away, when she noticed Lillian's sketchbook lying abandoned on the grass. As she watched, a beetle crawled up onto the paper, beginning a slow, trackless journey over a painstaking drawing of a man sitting in a chair. Mara guessed it was meant to be Peter – she recognised the hip flask and rifle. Mara wondered if Lillian would give the finished drawing to Peter, and if she did, whether he would lie and say it was good, like everyone else seemed to. Mara felt a rush of anger on Lillian's behalf. It didn't seem fair that she put so much effort into her drawing and yet had no idea if she was talented or otherwise, all because no one gave her an honest opinion of her work.

Looking at Lillian lying there, Mara wondered about the other drawbacks of fame – the more serious ones, that might have led Lillian to where she was now. Then her thoughts turned to Peter. He was equally famous, yet there was something solid and grounded about him. She felt sure it was not a façade. She could not say whether it was due to who he was, or where he had come from, or the choices he had made in his life – but he seemed to have survived his success unscathed.

Mara glanced around the lodge grounds. It was already midmorning, but in place of the usual frenetic activity there was an atmosphere of calm. Carlton had announced that there would be no filming this morning – he was giving everyone the opportunity to renew their energy for the second half of the shoot. Several members of the film company had joined Lillian, relaxing outside. Brendan had abandoned his lights and coils of electric leads, and was reading an old newspaper on the front verandah. Rudi was sitting on a rug near the mango tree talking to the hut boys, who were responding with a mixture of words and laughter. Their high, childish voices seemed to brighten the air. Although Mara suspected there was work they should be doing elsewhere, she didn't interrupt the pleasant scene.

It was a pity John wasn't here to see the lodge full of contented guests, she thought. It was something he'd so longed for. But then another thought came to her: if John were here, everything would be different. He would be in charge. There would be tension as the staff struggled to meet his instructions, whether they agreed with the Bwana's decisions or not. And Mara, surely, would not have taken part in the filming. With John looking on, she realised, she simply would never have found the courage.

Pushing the thought aside, she crossed to where Jamie was sitting in a deckchair, idly stripping the rows of tiny leaves from a broken frond of jacaranda. Tomba stood close by, a large set of earphones clamped onto his head, holding a microphone mounted in a handgrip that made it look like a pistol. Two long black leads tethered him to the sound-recording deck set up on a card table nearby. As Mara watched, Tomba pointed his microphone towards the noisy hut boys and then swung it away. He repeated the action again and again, a look of rapt attention on his face.

Jamie shook his head at Mara as she came near. 'I think he's after my job.' His tone was mocking, but there was a note of admiration there as well. 'He's quick, you know. Very smart.'

The microphone jerked towards him, holding him in its sights. 'What did you say?' Tomba asked.

'It doesn't matter,' said Jamie. 'The point is, you missed it, because you weren't on me. That's how it is, with the 416. It's a very directional mike.'

Tomba's eyes narrowed with concentration. Mara saw his lips moving as he committed the words to memory.

'Do you know where Carlton is?' Jamie asked Mara.

'In the dining room,' Mara answered. She'd just seen him there with documents strewn around him and an adding machine in his hand. It may have been a half-day's break from filming, but the producer was clearly far from relaxed. From the way he kept adding up figures, Mara guessed he was worrying about money; she felt selfishly pleased she'd already been paid a second large instalment of cash. 'He looks very busy.'

Jamie snorted a brief laugh. 'I'll bet Leonard's hard at work, too, rewriting the script, trying to make us all crazy.' He stretched lazily. 'Well, you know what they say – it's tough at the top. Hey, Tomba, I'll give you some advice. Whatever you do, don't ever be the boss.'

Tomba stared at him for a second, and looked uncertainly at Mara for confirmation. 'Do not be the *Bwana Mkuu*?'

Mara nodded. 'That's what he said: do not choose to be the big man.'

As she turned to go, she saw Tomba looking at Jamie with mixed scepticism and confusion.

Instead of heading straight for the kitchen, Mara set down the tray near the front door. She told herself that she should check to see if the hut boys had carried out their duties in the rondavels. If she found Peter in his room, she could use the opportunity to make sure he'd been offered morning tea.

She could talk to him. She could watch how the sun shone in through the window, onto his face . . .

Rounding the corner, she glanced across to the dining-room window. She could see Carlton still sitting at the table, now surrounded by at least three coffee cups. Scanning the rest of the room, she could see no sign of anyone else, but something caught her eye further along the verandah. Through the open French windows that led to the sitting room she could see a patch of colour: a distinctive shade of blue she recognised as Peter's linen shirt. He was bending down, looking at something on the floor.

She hurried towards him, hoping it was not a squashed lizard or a dead rat or a trail of marching safari ants that had attracted his attention. When she drew close, she saw he was examining some objects laid out on a *kitenge* spread over the grass matting. Kefa was hovering at his shoulder.

Both men turned around as Mara entered the room.

Peter smiled in greeting.

'Good morning,' Mara said.

Kefa threw her a quick, nervous look, as he swung one arm to take in a display of woodcarvings: animals, people, bowls and implements.

'The village carver has brought these things . . .' He began in a tentative tone but then lifted his chin and spoke more boldly. 'It is a gift shop. Daudi advised that our lodge should have one.'

Mara raised her eyebrows – not because he'd arranged for the carvings to be brought here without asking her, but because of the phrase he had used. *Our* lodge. Mara pictured Bina's outrage at a house boy speaking this way. John would be pretty shocked as well. But as she considered Kefa's choice of words, Mara felt a sense of relief. She didn't have to feel negligent about leaving Kefa and Menelik to make their own decisions while she was preoccupied with the demands of the film company. They were all in this together. They were all the bosses. Or, perhaps none of them were.

Kefa was watching her in silence, waiting for her response.

'I think it's a good idea,' Mara said, and it was the truth. She could see no reason why the villagers shouldn't make the most of this opportunity to acquire some cash. After all, it might be a long time before they had another chance like this.

A smile broke over Kefa's face, his body settling into a more relaxed posture.

Peter leaned to pick up a zebra. It had been carved from a golden yellow wood; burn marks had been used to create black stripes and a dark muzzle and mane. He handed it to Mara. 'Isn't it beautiful?'

Mara viewed it from all angles. She'd seen the carver's work before. His wooden animals looked as if they could gallop across the plains, kicking their hind legs up in the air.

'This carver was a cattle boy when he was young,' Kefa commented. 'He spent a long time watching animals. He is an expert.'

Peter picked up another carving made of black timber. 'Looks like ebony,' he said, stroking the satiny surface with his fingers. After a few seconds, he glanced up at Mara, peering almost shyly through the hair that fell forward over his brow. 'I work with wood, a bit.'

Mara met his gaze. 'That's why you have strong hands.' She bit her lip, regretting the words as soon as she'd uttered them. They sounded too personal, as if she'd been studying him.

'I'm more of a cabinet-maker than a whittler,' Peter said. 'I've made the odd piece of furniture. When I see work like this, though, I think maybe I should give it a try – if I had more time, I mean.' He gave Mara a rueful smile, before turning back to the display of carvings. 'I'm trying to choose presents for my kids. I can't make up my mind. What do you think?'

Mara bent her head to hide her face. Her eyes ranged over a giraffe with blackened spots and a pair of savage-looking lions with open jaws. But she barely saw them. She thought, instead, of Peter's children – the faces she'd seen in the photograph. She tried to connect each of them with one of the carvings, but she found it impossible. She was distracted by a sinking feeling in her stomach, and a disturbing sense that her centre of gravity was shifting – that she was falling and did not know where she would end up.

What was the matter with her, she wondered? She struggled to concentrate on the carvings.

Begin with the boys. What do little boys like best?

She stared blankly at the display, then stiffened suddenly. With a shocking clarity, she realised what it was that had so unnerved her – thinking of Peter's children made her feel guilty.

She felt guilty because while they were waiting at home with their mother, looking forward to his return, she wanted to keep him here.

I want him for myself.

Catching her breath, Mara recoiled from the thought. But she could not deny it. She gazed numbly down at her shoes, placed together side by side, their toes lightly scuffed.

'Look at this.' Peter's voice came to her, and then a wooden plaque swung into her view. It was about the size of a large envelope. The edges were decorated with a frieze of baobab trees and animals; the centre contained a single word carved in rounded letters: *Karibu*. 'What does it mean?'

Mara forced herself to focus on it. 'It's a kind of greeting,' she explained. 'When people arrive at someone's hut, they call out *Hodi!*

It means, I am here! The reply is *Karibu*! The closest translation is something like: *Come near. You are welcome*.' Mara thought her voice sounded thin and strained, but Peter seemed not to have noticed. 'Europeans buy them to hang by their front doors.'

Kefa picked up another plaque, which bore the word *Nyumbani*. 'This one means "our home",' he said. 'But you can order words of your own choosing. The carver will produce whatever you like.'

'I'll buy one for the door of the children's playroom,' Peter said. 'With birds and animals around the edges.' He turned to Mara. 'What do you think?'

Mara nodded mutely, avoiding Peter's eyes. His words made her feel cold inside. She realised she'd misread his feelings. She'd thought he was attracted to her. But now it seemed that what he felt about her was so uncomplicated – so innocent – that he wanted to involve her in his relationship with his family.

She tried to answer as if she felt the same way about him. 'You could buy one for each of the children's bedrooms, with their names carved on them.'

She attempted a light-hearted smile, but it wavered on her lips. She couldn't help remembering how he'd looked at her last night outside the rondavel, and during the Tanzanian feast that had followed. They'd barely spoken the whole evening – Lillian had dominated the conversation at their table – but their eyes had met constantly, and for long moments neither had seemed able to look away.

Suddenly, a new thought struck Mara – one that felt immediately solid and true. This was no casual interchange for Peter, she realised, any more than it was for her. He was deliberately trying to connect her with his real life, back home. Because he wanted to show her how much he cared about his family. He wanted to force a distance between himself and Mara.

Because in the same way she wanted him – he wanted her.

Mara searched Peter's face, trying to see if she was right. She felt a wave of sympathy for him. Didn't he already know his plan could not work? It was impossible to evoke the presence of his wife and children here at Raynor Lodge – trying to do so only made them feel more distant, and less real. Like John – far away in the Selous – they existed in a completely separate reality.

Mara reached towards the back of the *kitenge* for a set of four elephants, ranging in size from large to small. They each had a pair of tiny tusks, shaped from bone and embedded in the dark wood. 'Choose these,' she said, gathering them up. 'It's a family.'

Peter smiled as he took the elephants from her. Mara let her gaze travel over his face. He had a touch of sunburn on his forehead and nose. One cheek had been lightly scratched by a thorn bush and she could still see a faint yellow stain from the iodine she'd dabbed there. Near his temple was the small red mound of a mosquito bite. As he bent his head to search in his pocket for some money, she leaned towards him, breathing in the smell of cinnamon aftershave overlaid with Lifebuoy soap.

She took in all these little details; the marks of a world in which they existed together in the moment, cut off from the past and the future.

Floating free.

ELEVEN

It was only five in the morning, but Bwana Stimu had already started up the generator. Electric light shone from the kitchen windows and the peace and stillness of the early hour was broken by the drone of the engine filtering through the walls of the shed.

Mara walked briskly across the compound, arms swinging. Restless energy coursed through her body as she ran through her pre-breakfast tasks, lining them up in her mind like a series of obstacles. When they were all done, she would enter the dining room to sit down with her guests.

And there he'd be, in his place at her table. Right beside her. Looking up as she came near, his expression brightening at the sight of her.

She took a deep breath of the fresh morning air, her eyes closing briefly, and smiled. Then she glanced around in search of Dudu. Had he polished the shoes she'd given him the previous day and returned them to the rondavels? Her second mission was to ask Menelik to boil up some rice – not because someone was hungry, but because she needed the cooking water.

After yesterday's filming, Rudi had come to her, complaining that the rim of Maggie's hat had begun to sag.

'That always happens,' Mara explained. 'They stiffen up when you wash them and get softer through being worn.' She turned the hat over in her hand. They'd been filming for ten days now, and in that time it had been worn almost constantly, either by her or Lillian, and spent the rest of its time squashed into a sack with the other wardrobe items, all dirty and sweaty. No wonder the brim was sagging.

'Well, it's no good for continuity,' Rudi said. 'Think what will happen when bits of film shot on different days get cut together. We'll end up with a brim that flaps up and down like the wings of an aircraft!'

Mara had smiled at the joke, but it had taken her some time to make sense of Rudi's words. The process of making a film kept surprising her. Sometimes the camera seemed able to cope with gross deceptions – like Mara pretending to be Lillian – yet at other times, tiny inconsistencies were unacceptable. Leonard explained that everything could be understood in terms of camera angles, framing, lenses and lighting. But it was all still a mystery to her – a magical world in which the usual rules did not apply.

Rudi had left Maggie's hat with Mara, asking if she could arrange for the brim to be soaked in rice water and pressed flat while it dried. Mara had agreed, knowing Rudi was doing the work of several people and needed all the help he could get. But now, as she approached the kitchen, picking her way between the hens that wandered around looking for food scraps, she half-regretted her words. She wasn't looking forward to explaining her request to

Menelik. It would be so much simpler to be someone like Bina – she wouldn't bother with explanations; she'd just issue demands.

Just as Mara neared the kitchen door, it flew open, banging back on its hinges. Dudu emerged holding a filthy tea towel in one hand. Wheeling round, he flapped it against the wall near the door. Fragments of black soot scattered into the air.

When he saw Mara, he held out the grimy cloth for her to see. '*Haribika kabisa!*' Everything is very dirty. He gestured towards the kitchen. 'Bwana Cook is very angry.'

Mara moved towards the door, quickening her step, but as she entered the room, she came to a sudden standstill. The whole place was smattered with black soot and a strong smell of burnt kerosene filled the air. Menelik was wiping the pantry shelves with a sponge.

When he saw Mara, he pressed his lips together, as if he didn't trust himself to speak.

'What's happened?' Mara's attention was drawn towards the fridge, which seemed to be the source of the soot; on the wall above it was a solid patch of black.

'Someone has entered the kitchen and turned up the fridge,' Menelik stated. 'She has done this late at night while I was sleeping. Now, the flame has been burning too high and making smoke for many hours.'

'She?' queried Mara. 'Do you know who it was?'

Menelik kept rubbing at the shelf. 'The other memsahib came in here last night, after dinner. She complained her tonic was not cold enough. I told her we cannot make all the drinks very cold because our fridge is not big. I offered her ice, made with boiled water. But she was not satisfied. Therefore, I believe it was her.'

Mara was about to say that the evidence was slim, when she noticed that an empty tumbler had been left behind on the table. It was the kind Kefa used for serving gin and tonic and there was a slice of lemon left in the bottom. Its rim was clearly marked with red lipstick.

As Menelik met her gaze, Mara nodded. 'I think you are right.'

The man made a small spitting sound with his lips as he returned to his cleaning. Mara could understand his frustration: the kitchen would take hours to clean. She shook her head in dismay. 'Has this ever happened before?'

Menelik seemed not to have heard her question at first. He moved to a new shelf and began wiping the top of a tin flour canister. 'Only once,' he said finally.

Something about his manner made Mara want to know more. 'Who did it that time?'

Menelik was quiet for a moment. 'It was the first memsahib.'

It took Mara a few seconds to grasp the meaning of his words. Then her eyes widened. 'You mean Alice?'

'Yes,' Menelik confirmed. 'She admitted doing it. But she did not apologise.'

Mara tried not to look pleased at the thought that Alice had also attracted criticism from the cook.

'You are too busy to clean up this mess,' she said generously. 'I'll send the hut boys to help you.'

Menelik acknowledged her offer by bowing his head. Then he dropped the tea towel onto the table. 'Let them come quickly. I must prepare breakfast and it is not possible to cook in such a kitchen. Even the air is bad.'

Wrinkling his nose in distaste, he crossed to the stove and opened the door. With a pair of tongs he removed a glowing piece of charcoal. He placed it in the little brass burner that stood by the back door, then took down a leather bag that hung from a nail on the wall. Fumbling inside it, he removed a small chunk of frankincense. Mara moved closer to watch as he dropped it onto the charcoal. The knob of resin began to fizzle and melt into tiny golden bubbles. Then a thin plume of fragrant smoke rose into the air. Mara closed her eyes as she breathed it in. She'd smelled frankincense before in Menelik's kitchen – it was an Ethiopian tradition to burn it while serving coffee – but the aroma still conjured for her images of ancient camel caravans, palm-tree oases and mysterious figures draped in billowing robes.

Menelik carried the burner slowly around the kitchen, letting the incense banish the taint of burnt kerosene. There was a serious look on his face, as if the smell and the soot represented a violation of his territory that was more than just physical. When he was finished, he set the burner down on the table. Then he picked up Lillian's glass and put it in the sink, before washing his hands.

Mara watched as he cleaned a section of the table and then began chopping pieces of tinned ham. She guessed he was going to put some in his English-style omelette. It was not really a replacement for bacon, as guests had often pointed out. But the bacon here was imported from Kenya, where pigs were sometimes infected with a nasty variety of tapeworm. People who ate the meat risked getting cysts in their brains.

Mara lingered in the kitchen. Now the subject had come up, she couldn't resist asking more about her predecessor. 'What was Alice like? What kind of person was she?'

Menelik didn't answer straightaway. He seemed to be weighing his words carefully; there was a stony edge to his gaze and a curl at the corners of his lips. 'She was . . . a *kali* memsahib.'

Mara stared at him. The word *kali* could be applied to many things. Not all of them were negative – *kali* medicine was powerful and effective; a *kali* teacher was strict and commanded respect; food could be *kali* if it was flavoured strongly with chillies. But in most cases when the word was used to describe a person, it meant hard, tough, uncaring. Certainly, no one would want to work for a *kali* memsahib.

Mara looked down at her hands, blackened by the sooty coating on the table. She did not know what to say.

'You are not like her,' Menelik went on. There was a lilt of surprise in his voice, suggesting the thought had only just occurred to him. 'You are a kind memsahib. You are good.'

Mara lifted her face. She made no attempt to hide her astonishment at his words. She knew she should accept his compliments graciously, with dignity. But instead, she just looked at him, a broad smile spreading over her face.

An answering smile tugged at the corners of the old man's lips.

Mara unfolded a map and spread it out on the dining table.

Leonard peered over her shoulder. 'You know what I'm looking for, don't you?'

'A cave or a rocky overhang,' Mara repeated obediently. 'With a fabulous view, looking down over a plain.' Her eye moved to a section of the map that covered an area near the edge of the escarpment. She knew a place there that offered everything Leonard required – but she had no intention of mentioning it. The cave was John's special place. And it held too many memories for her.

She began moving her finger over the map, pausing from time to time as if an area might be promising. Then she shook her head. 'It's hard to think of anywhere exactly like that.'

Carlton appeared at her other shoulder. 'We may have to compromise here. What about a place with a cave but no view? We can't afford to waste any more time.'

'No way,' Leonard said indignantly. 'We need both things. It's where Maggie and Luke really come together – it's a key scene. You *know* that, Carlton.'

Mara was aware of Carlton growing very still beside her. She'd never seen him disagree with his brother in any way, but suspected he was about to. She lowered her head, pretending to look more closely at the map.

'I'll tell you what I know, Leonard.' Carlton sounded calm, but Mara could feel the tension emanating from his body. 'I know we're almost out of time, and almost out of money. And that the main reason we're in this mess is that you will never agree to compromise.' He paused, drawing a slow, deep breath. Mara recognised the gesture – it was one she resorted to herself when trying to keep her temper with an unreasonable guest.

'I also know we're in big trouble,' Carlton went on. 'When we were in Zanzibar, the production was almost taken over by the guarantors.'

Leonard waved one hand dismissively. 'They wouldn't do that.'

'Oh yes, they would! I didn't want to worry you at the time, but they sent an assessor to the set. I only just managed to talk him into letting us do second unit. He'd still be here, looking over our shoulders – except he doesn't know exactly where to find us.'

Leonard clapped Carlton on the shoulder. 'You got around him! Good for you!' he chuckled.

'It's no laughing matter,' Carlton said. 'I've done my best to juggle the figures but the production reports are a nightmare. If I was the guarantor I'd be closing us down as well.'

'Oh, come on,' Leonard said. 'You always make things sound worse than they are.' He leaned over the map, studying it intently. 'What about that ranger?' he said to Mara. 'Could he find what I'm after?'

Suddenly Carlton slapped his hand onto the table. 'Okay. I give up.'

Leonard threw Mara a triumphant smile. 'Good.'

'We go to Plan B,' Carlton added. 'The film gets finished back home. In the Los Angeles Zoo.'

Leonard laughed again, but when Carlton remained still, his stare unwavering, Leonard looked puzzled. 'Say that again?'

'The film gets finished back home. In the Los Angeles Zoo.'

'You'd never film in a zoo!'

'No, I wouldn't,' Carlton agreed calmly. 'But then, it won't concern me. The guarantors will be in charge. You know how it goes. They appoint a new producer. And a new director.'

Leonard's lips moved silently as he tried to absorb his brother's words.

Carlton ignored him, turning to Mara. 'Don't worry. I'll still pay for the time that was booked. '

'You're leaving *now*?' Mara asked, dismayed.

Leonard put his hand on her arm. 'Of course we're not,' he said. 'Carlton, be reasonable.'

'Don't tell me to be reasonable!' Carlton exploded. 'I've spent my life being reasonable.' He began pacing back and forth as though his emotions could no longer be contained by stillness. 'Ever since Mom and Dad died it's been "Look after your little brother", "Take care of Leonard". At film school it was "the Miller brothers – the great creative partnership". People still say that. But it's not really like that, is it?' He stopped to take a breath. His eyes were wide; he seemed surprised by his own words. 'You do the real work, the stuff that matters. I'm left to solve all the problems – and you don't even want to know what they are! Well, I've had enough. I quit.'

In the tense silence that followed, the hut boys could be heard in the distance, singing while they worked.

Mara sank even lower in her chair. The movement drew Carlton's attention. He looked at her, as if he'd forgotten she was there.

'You can't quit.' Leonard sounded like a bewildered child.

'Watch me,' Carlton said. 'I'm going to pack.'

Mara peered at Leonard from the corner of her eye. He looked smaller, somehow, shrunk into himself – nothing like the man who spent his days calling out directions to his cast and crew.

'Please, Carlton. Don't,' he said quietly. 'We'll change the way we work. I'll do whatever you say.'

Carlton studied his brother's face. 'Will you?' he demanded.

Leonard nodded vigorously, his curls shaking. 'Yes, I promise.'

'Then start behaving like an adult. Take some responsibility for the situation we're in.' Carlton returned to the table and pointed at the map. 'I'll give you ten minutes to find a location where you're prepared to film. Or we pack up and leave. Simple as that.'

He sounded calm, but Mara saw that his hand was shaking.

Leonard was still for a few seconds, as if stunned. Then he sat up straight in his chair, turning eagerly to Mara. 'Do you know of a cave – anywhere at all? Or just some kind of rock shelter.'

Mara eyed the place on the map where she knew the perfect setting could be found. But still, she said nothing. A long moment passed. Carlton stood looking at his watch. His lips were pressed together in a determined line. He was only minutes away, Mara could see, from telling everyone to pack up their things. They could be gone by midday. All of them.

Almost before she'd made her decision, her finger was sliding across the map.

'I've just remembered,' she said. 'This place might do.'

The two men looked at her. Though everything else about their appearance was so different, they had the same brown eyes. Tension began to fade from the air. Mara could see how relieved the brothers were, that the impasse had been broken. When they spoke it was almost in unison.

'Let's go!'

The cave was made of sandstone layered in tones of pink, yellow and brown. From a wide opening it curved backwards into a half-moon shape, forming a perfect haven. Mara rested her hand on the wall as she stepped inside, feeling its soft grainy surface. She had only a short time alone here before the others arrived, a brief interlude in which to remind herself that it was just a cave, a feature of the landscape. And that bringing people here – bringing Peter here – was no different to sharing with them the lodge, the gardens, the plains, or the hillsides.

Mara cast her eyes over the contours of the walls, following them up to the cave roof, which was blackened in the middle from all the fires that had burned in here over countless generations. She scanned the earthen floor, dotted with small chunks of rock and a few bleached bones. Her gaze came to rest on a small mound of mixed charcoal, wood and ash surrounded by stones: the fireplace. Stepping towards it, she picked up a piece of charred wood, turning it over in her hands. Was this the remains of one of their own fires, she wondered? It must have been nearly two years since she and John last camped in the cave, but this was an isolated spot – it was quite possible that in that time not even a herd boy had come here.

Dropping the wood, Mara turned back to the entrance. She tried to fix her thoughts on the day ahead, but it was no good. She could feel the memories poised to crowd in upon her. It was as if they had been roosting here, like bats, just waiting for her return.

She'd come here several times with John, but it was the scene of her first arrival – only three nights after her wedding – that returned to her now. It came in snatches: first, the mouldy canvas smell of her army rucksack; then the taste of sweat on her lips. The touch of cool air followed, washing over her back as she shucked off her load, its solid weight landing with a thud at her feet. And then there was John, standing beside her, panting from the climb.

They'd reached the cave at dusk, on foot, carrying on their backs all they would need for a week-long safari. They had no tent – just a mat to lie on, two sleeping bags that could be zipped together, and a mosquito net. John had packed a supply of simple foods, to be supplemented by fresh fish and game. And for that first night of their honeymoon safari, there was a bottle of Dom Perignon champagne. Mara glanced around her. Perhaps, somewhere here, there was still a fragment of the foil she'd peeled from the top of the bottle, or perhaps the wire casing of the cork . . .

It was time to leave, she knew; to turn around and walk back out into the sunshine and wait for the others to appear. But instead she found herself drawn towards the shadows at the rear of the cave, and a patch of deeper blackness.

When she reached it, she crouched down, straining her eyes into the gloom. It was too dark to see anything.

But she knew what was there.

As soon as she and John had set down their rucksacks, and stretched the tired muscles of their shoulders, John had taken her on a tour of the cave, showing off the high ceiling, the uncluttered floor that was large enough for a whole family to stretch out on, and the convenient natural shelves and cupboard-like alcoves that lined the walls.

'It reminds me of a book I read as a child,' Mara had said. *They Found a Cave*. It was set in Tasmania, but the cave was just like this.'

'Did it have a secret room?' John had crossed to the back of the cave and knelt down. 'Look in there.' He handed Mara the small torch he kept in the pocket of his bush jacket.

216

Scrambling close on hands and knees, Mara leaned inside, sweeping the torchlight around the space. It was only just large enough for a person to stand in. As the circle of light travelled over the wall, she glimpsed something. Holding the torch still, she caught her breath. It was a painting, done in brushstrokes of red ochre: an image of an elephant. It had large, curved tusks like a mammoth.

'Does anyone else know it's here?' she asked John.

'Only me. And now you.'

Mara moved the torch closer to the painting. 'Maybe you should tell someone about it? It looks like it might be very old.'

'Oh, it is.' John said. 'I was only sixteen and a half when I painted that.'

Mara turned to look at him. 'You're pulling my leg, aren't you?'

John shook his head. 'If you look on the shelf above you'll see my paintbrush.'

It was true. Lifting her gaze, Mara could just make out the green handle of an artist's brush.

'But it looks just like an ancient rock painting,' she protested. 'I worked in a museum, remember? I know what they look like.'

John grinned at her. 'I knew as well. I saw one just like it in a *National Geographic*.'

Mara laughed. 'You did it as a joke?'

A look of uncertainty crossed John's face, as if he felt suddenly exposed. 'Not really. I just thought it should be there. It made the place feel . . . inhabited.' He half-turned away. The fading daylight touched the side of his face, gently shadowing his cheekbones.

'Did you come here often?' Mara asked.

John nodded. 'Whenever I got some time off and Raynor let me take the Land Rover.'

'Were you always on your own?'

'No one else had time to spend wandering around for fun,' John responded. 'There were probably things I should have been doing as well.'

Mara studied the painting again. She pictured John out here as a teenager, working away on his painting, all by himself. A sudden tenderness swept through her, making her feel sad and warm at the same time. She went to John and wrapped her arms around him. She was almost as tall as he was, and her face met his, cheek to cheek.

The gesture was new and strange to them both. When Mara had arrived in Tanzania, she and John had greeted one another with excitement. But very soon, an awkwardness arose between them, fuelled by the knowledge they were under constant observation – in Kikuyu, and at the lodge. Even in the privacy of John's bedroom, Mara sensed they were not alone. The spirit of the Raynors seemed strong and near.

Mara tightened her arms across John's back, as though by pulling him closer she could recover the warmth they'd shared through their letters, the friendship that had bloomed into love through the months of writing. Perhaps, she thought, out here they could regain that ease. And take it further.

'Didn't you get lonely?' she asked. 'Spending so much time on your own.'

John's body grew tense in her arms. Leaning back to see his face, she saw the small movements in his neck as he swallowed hard.

'Well, I was used to that – from boarding school.'

'Why did your parents send you so far away?' Mara asked. John had told her in one of his letters that he'd been sent away to boarding school in England when he was ten. 'Weren't there any schools for Europeans in East Africa?'

'There were several.' John moved away from her, turning towards the mouth of the cave. Following his gaze, Mara looked beyond the ledge outside, into the deep purple haze of the valley. The vista was still shrouded in mist, as it had been when they'd approached the cave. But in the morning, according to John, it would be a sight to remember forever.

As the silence in the cave lengthened, the sounds outside seemed loud. Birds called to one another from the treetops, and the flapping of wings could be heard as newcomers arrived, seeking places of safety for the night. Then came the strangled laugh of a hyena, not far off.

'Please talk to me, John,' Mara said. 'I want to know more about you.'

John looked back over his shoulder at her, his eyes narrowed with uncertainty.

'I want to know everything about you.' Mara smiled at him as she waited. She could see in the expressions that crossed his face, his slow cautious steps towards the decision to speak.

'When I was ten, my mother had an affair with a British army officer. There was a big scandal. He was transferred to India. She went with him. One morning she packed a suitcase, kissed me on the forehead, said goodbye. Then she just drove away. I ran after her car, but she wouldn't stop.' John spoke in short sentences, as if the fewer words he used, the less painful their meaning would be. 'My father couldn't face the shame. He took a remote service posting. It was up in the border country where it wasn't possible to take a child. So, you see – it didn't matter where they sent me to school. I had no home to come back to anyway. I spent all my holidays in England – I just stayed on at Harnbrook Hall. Even at Christmas. The headmaster's wife used to ask me for afternoon tea.' A short bitter laugh broke from his throat. 'She was always afraid I'd break something.'

Mara stared at John in dismay. Images of her family Christmases came to her: the chaotic gatherings of relatives in a sweltering house; roast turkey served on tables of different heights pushed together; the all-age cricket game that followed the afternoon nap. At Christmas time, even Mara's father was swept up in the mood of celebration; and her mother, surrounded by guests, seemed happy and content. Mara could almost feel the chill of a wintry English Christmas in the echoing emptiness of an abandoned school. The thought of John being left there all alone as a little boy brought a lump to her throat.

'When I turned sixteen,' John continued, 'my mother sent me some money so I could go to India and see her. I went to the travel agency to buy a ticket to Bombay. But then I changed my mind. I went to Kenya instead.' Squatting down beside the fireplace, John began breaking up some pieces of kindling he'd gathered on the way to the cave. 'I got a job at the Muthaiga Club in Nairobi, welcoming guests and generally helping out.' He gave Mara a wry smile. 'One thing they'd taught me at Harnbrook Hall was how to speak and act like a gentleman. They liked that, at the club.'

John piled the kindling into a small pyramid in the middle of the fireplace. Then he took out a box of matches and lit some dry grass that had been placed under the twigs. Leaning close, he blew steadily until a blue-edged flame rose up.

'How did you come to work for Raynor?' Mara asked as she joined him sitting by the fire.

'I met him at the club. He was sitting out on the verandah, waiting for a client. In those days, professional hunters weren't allowed to come inside. When I saw him there, I guessed what he did for a living. I could tell, even though he was wearing a suit and tie. There was just something about him. He was very still, watchful. I went up to and asked him, straight out, "Are you a hunter?" He said, "Yes, I am." I asked if I could be his apprentice.' John looked at Mara, his gaze now open and warm. 'He said he'd give me a try. I remember his words. "If you've got good eyesight I can teach you to shoot. But the things that matter – a brave heart, clear instincts, a love of the bush – they must be born in a man. Only time will tell if you have what it takes." He took me back to Tanzania with him and I never left.'

Mara thought of the photographs on the lodge wall of John receiving his two Shaw and Hunter trophies. 'He must have been very proud of you.'

'He was.' John looked down at his hands. 'He was like a father to me.'

Mara was silent for a moment. She didn't want to push the conversation too far, but she wanted to make the most of this time, this place, and the openness that seemed possible here.

'What about your real father?' she asked gently. In the firelight she saw a small muscle flicker in John's cheek.

'I never saw him again,' John replied. 'He died of cholera not long after I joined up with Raynor, though it was a long time before I knew anything about it. I lost touch with my mother. She didn't answer my letters after I failed to appear in Bombay. Raynor was all the family I had.'

In the quiet that followed, twigs crackled as the fire took hold.

'And now you've got me,' Mara said.

'And now I've got you.' As John repeated her words, a look of wonder appeared on his face, as if the reality of his marriage had only just dawned upon him.

'We'll make a new family,' Mara said. 'We'll have children together.'

'Yes,' John nodded, with a look of mixed joy and disbelief. 'I'd love that.'

'We'll have at least three,' Mara said.

John looked at her for a moment. Then he took in a deep ragged breath. When he let it out, his whole body seemed to relax; some kind of fear or danger seemed finally to have been dispelled.

'I'm so glad I found you, Mara,' he said. 'It means everything to me.'

He leaned towards her, kissing her cheek. Then his lips travelled to meet hers, probing them gently at first, then pressing harder. Suddenly he was reaching for her, his hands wrapping themselves in her hair as he pulled her face towards him.

As he kissed her, he undid the buttons of her shirt, and pulled it down off her shoulders. He slid one hand over her breast, his roughened skin lightly snagging the lace of her bra. He paused, then, as though waiting for some signal from Mara. Reaching behind her, she unclasped her bra, letting it fall.

He pulled back, looking at her breasts, painted rosy pink by the glow of the fire.

'You are so beautiful,' he said. His tone was almost reverent, and edged with surprise, as though he could not believe she really belonged to him.

Mara felt her body reaching out for him. It felt so right for them to make love here in the cave. Not like their first night, spent at the Kikuyu Hotel, where the mattress had creaked with every movement they made and the murmur of voices filtered up from the bar below. They had been strangers, then, and both so tentative, not wanting to hurt or be hurt. Nor would it be like the two nights they'd spent at the lodge, where they'd made love more easily, but under the cover of sheets, with that sense of being watched.

Here, in the cave, their bare skin at once warmed by the fire and stroked by the cool air of the night air, they would truly begin their marriage.

The memory brought an ache to Mara's throat. She tightened her hand on the piece of charred firewood. Looking down at the ground, she could see exactly where they had lain together that night – so happy, so hopeful. So unaware of all that was to come.

Dropping the wood onto the ashes, she wrapped her arms around her body, to comfort herself. She took a last look around the cave, then moved towards the entrance. She kept her eyes lowered until she reached the open air. Then she looked up slowly, letting the vista come to her afresh.

She remembered how John had led her out here at dawn, after

that first night in the cave, to show her the view she would remember forever. She'd stood beside him, gazing in awed silence.

'Look out there . . .' John swept his arm wide in a gesture that took in the plains below them, dotted with game, and the ranks of hills, plateaus and mountains, the branching rivers and jewel lakes, that stretched away to the horizon. In the golden dawn, it was like a vision of heaven. 'That's the rest of Africa.' There was pride in John's voice, as if the scene before them was his own possession: one he'd spread out in all its vast beauty and fine detail as a gift for his bride.

They stayed side by side, not speaking, just looking at the view. Then John turned to Mara. She saw that the uncertainty had crept back into his eyes. 'Being here, with you. It seems too good to be true.'

Mara smiled at him. 'You don't need to be afraid. I love you.'

As John searched her face, his eyes became shiny with tears. 'Don't ever leave me, Mara,' he said. 'Promise you never will.' He held out his hand.

Mara looked into his eyes as she pressed his fingers firmly with her own. 'I'll never leave you. You can trust me. I promise.'

As she said the words, they felt more solemn and binding than anything either of them had said in the registrar's office. This new vow was being made with the land as their witness.

The rest of Africa.

It was only just over three years since that day, yet it felt like another era to Mara. She could hardly remember feeling such hope and belief in the future. It was all lost to her now: walled over by pain and anger and failure. She closed her eyes, focusing on the cold silence of the cave behind her, willing herself to become numb. She remained there, motionless, unaware of time passing, until at last the drone of Land Rover engines ground its way into her consciousness.

The sound grew steadily louder. As Mara pictured the scene that was about to unfold, she felt a sense of relief. Soon, the place would be invaded by people. The quiet air would be filled with their voices, the space taken up with shiny boxes and lumpy bags of gear. Mara would be kept busy, following Leonard's directions. There would be no more time to think.

She headed for the break in the rocks that gave access to the hillside and began making her way down, dodging boulders and thorn bushes. Below her, only a short distance away, she could see the two zebra-striped Land Rovers drawing to a halt beside hers. Leonard climbed out, followed by Carlton and Rudi. Then Lillian appeared, dressed in Maggie's outfit but wearing a pink sombrero and sunglasses. Her voice carried clearly; she was complaining to Carlton about the dust she could feel in her hair.

Mara shifted her attention to the second vehicle. Tomba, Jamie and Brendan were milling at the back door. And the ranger could be seen sitting in the driver's seat. She peered past him into the interior, searching for another figure, clad in the familiar khaki clothing.

Then the rear door opened. Mara's step slowed as she watched Peter jump to the ground and quickly scan his surroundings. Reaching back into the Land Rover, he brought out Luke's rifle and leaned it carefully against the side of the vehicle. Then he took a drink from his water bottle, tipping back his head and squinting up at the sky. When he was finished he wiped his mouth with the back of his hand. Brendan said something, then, that Mara didn't catch. Peter shook his head and laughed, his teeth standing out white against his sunburnt skin. Mara stood still, her foot poised over a tree root. She felt her gaze trapped by his lingering smile. He seemed larger than life, somehow – more vibrant than the people around him.

He retrieved the rifle, slinging it across his back. Then, shading his eyes with his hand, he began to search the hillside. Mara caught her breath, waiting for him to see her.

After only a few moments, he waved. Then he picked up a camera case and a shoulder bag, and started walking towards her.

Mara remained where she was, her feet still set to each side of the tree root. Peter climbed quickly, leaning into the incline. As his eyes met Mara's, a shiver ran through her body. She managed to nod and murmur a friendly greeting, but inside, she was torn with confusion. Though the cave was hidden from view, she could feel it there – a presence – waiting to see what she would do.

As Peter came to a standstill beside her, a single thought emerged from the turmoil. She could not return there. She could not be there with Peter.

Before he had the chance to speak, she pointed behind her, up the hill. 'You just head for those two boulders at the top. Then the cave's to the right.' She gave him a faint smile. She didn't want to appear abrupt or rude – they were friends, after all. 'I hope everything goes smoothly. I'll see you at dinner.'

Peter frowned in surprise. 'I thought you were standing in for Lillian.'

'Well, I was . . .' Mara gave what she hoped was a casual shrug, but she was aware she'd let the silence lengthen for a beat too long. When she spoke her voice sounded strained. 'There's been a change of plan. I think I should be back at the lodge. I'm just on my way down to tell Carlton now.' She forced another smile. 'Lillian can manage without me today – it's very safe in the cave, and sheltered from the sun.'

She gave a quick wave and turned away, but not before she saw the expression on Peter's face. He was puzzled, and disappointed, she knew. But that wasn't all. She could tell from the look in his eyes that he realised something had happened. Something had changed. As she made herself walk on down the hillside, she could feel him still standing there, watching her.

TWELVE

Two old cane chairs had been placed near the edge of the lawn in the best position for viewing the animals that came to drink at the waterhole. Resting her hand on the woven-string back of the chair closest to her, Mara looked down over the scene below. At the water's edge, she could see Carlton and the two Nicks standing beside the tripod. Jamie, Tomba and Brendan were nearby. At a little distance from them, sitting in their special chairs and shaded by the canopy of a thorn tree, were Leonard, Lillian and Peter. Mara tried to imagine that these people were nothing to her; just strangers milling around, tourists perhaps. But her eyes kept returning to Peter, watching the way he leaned towards Leonard, his hands resting on his knees. The way he tilted his head while he listened to Lillian. He was not very far away. If Mara were to shout his name, he'd hear; and though she couldn't read the expression on his face, she could see exactly what he was doing. Yet she felt cut off, up here, as if she'd been abandoned or sent into exile. She had to remind herself that she had been the one who told Carlton, out at the cave location yesterday, that she was too busy to stay and help with the filming. Today he'd simply assumed she'd prefer to stay at the lodge.

'I've checked with the ranger,' he'd said at breakfast that morning. 'He reckons the area around the waterhole is quite safe during
the day. And if Lillian gets tired she can be driven back here for a
break.' He'd grinned at her. 'So you're free of us. In fact, I don't think
we'll need to trouble you again. I've discussed it with Leonard, and
we think we can manage without you from here on.'

Mara had stared, frozen, as his meaning sank in. She would not
be playing the part of Maggie any more.

She would no longer be working with Peter.

'You've been a great help, Mara.' Carlton spoke seriously, an
earnest look in his eyes. 'You really have.'

Mara lifted her hand, ready to protest. She was aware, suddenly,
that her resolve of yesterday, to keep a distance from Peter, had
vanished. She desperately wanted to tell Carlton there had been
a misunderstanding. The decision she'd made to leave the cave
location was only because the place held special significance for
her. In another setting, she'd be happy to go on being Maggie. But
before she had the chance to speak, Rudi called Carlton away.

While the crew prepared to go down to the waterhole, Mara
hovered in the background, trying to look busy. There was no sign
of Peter. She guessed he was waiting in his rondavel until it was
time to depart. When he did finally appear, he kept a tactful distance from Mara. It had been the same during dinner the evening
before: he'd been friendly and courteous, but Mara could feel a
barrier between them. As she'd pushed her roast guinea fowl around
on her plate – her stomach too knotted to eat – she'd replayed the
scene on the hillside below the cave. She felt sure Peter had read
her departure as a sign that she was stepping back from him – and

he was determined to respect her decision. Had he guessed it was something to do with the cave, she wondered? Or did he think she'd suddenly decided their relationship had become too close? Too dangerous?

She'd gripped her cutlery tight in her hands. She didn't know herself exactly what she had been doing. Or what she really wanted.

On the pretext of helping to carry the equipment, she had followed them all out to the car park. As she'd moved between the members of the crew, she'd felt Peter's presence drawing her like a magnet. At the last minute when he was about to climb into one of the Land Rovers, he'd turned towards Mara. Their eyes locked together, holding tight, as though neither had the power to look away. Mara was tempted, again, to run to Carlton and demand to come with them. To tell him that nothing in the world mattered more to her than having the chance to go on being Maggie.

But Carlton had made himself quite clear. Mara was not needed any more.

As the first of the two Land Rovers had pulled out of the car park, Peter had waved to Mara. She'd returned the gesture, her arm and hand rigid, as though they belonged to a puppet carved from wood.

Now, from her place between the two chairs, Mara stared down at Peter, sitting under the thorn tree. She felt a hollow ache inside her. She longed to reach across the gap that separated them, and feel him close to her again. Shutting her eyes, she drew in a deep breath, as if the weight of the air in her lungs might calm her.

'Hello! Hello!'

A familiar sing-song voice came from inside the sitting room.

It was followed by slow, heavy footsteps, moving towards the verandah.

Mara turned to see Bina emerging from the open doorway in a swirl of gold-embroidered, hot-pink silk. Her lips were painted to match her sari and her hair gleamed with freshly applied oil. She carried a basket in one hand.

'Ah! I have found you!' As Bina walked towards Mara, dozens of sparkly bangles jiggled on her arms. She had never been to Raynor Lodge before, and her eyes darted about taking in all the details of her surroundings.

Mara struggled to form words of greeting – her head felt muddled by all the thoughts and emotions jostling inside her. But Bina didn't seem to notice. She clasped her hands together in excitement.

'Well, where is she?' she demanded. 'Where is the famous actress?'

'She's not here – none of them are. They're away filming.'

'Away?' Bina eyes widened. 'You mean I cannot see her?'

Mara considered her reply. She didn't think Leonard would be pleased if Bina appeared during filming. On the other hand, Mara didn't want to disappoint her visitor. Finally, she gestured towards the waterhole. 'They're down on the plains. You can see them if you come over here.'

Mara stood beside Bina, pointing out Lillian and Peter, and explaining who all the other people were. As she described how the filming was done, she was struck by how much she had learned in just two weeks.

Bina watched avidly for a long time, so engrossed in the scene that she barely spoke a word. Then she shifted her attention to Mara. 'I have not come here just to see the film star, you know,' she said. 'My main purpose is to personally deliver the spices for your chef.' She pointed towards the basket. 'Everything is there.' She nodded knowingly at Mara. 'I see you have taken my advice.'

Mara had no idea what Bina was talking about.

'Since I cannot meet the actress in person,' Bina added, 'I would like to see him instead. Is he the one I recommended?'

Mara frowned, still puzzled. 'I'm not sure exactly what . . .'

'The Gujarati fellow from Arusha?' Bina prompted. She shook her head admiringly. 'He must be preparing for a real Indian feast – he has ordered every spice in my shop!'

Mara remembered, now, Bina's suggestion that she take on an Indian chef to cater for the film crew. Bina would be very surprised, she suspected, to learn how impressed the Americans were with Menelik's cooking.

Mara gestured towards the sitting room. 'Come inside and have some tea. I'll ask the chef to present himself.'

Bina looked pleased. 'Thank you. I would be very happy to have some refreshments.'

Within a short time, Bina was settled comfortably in the middle of the sofa eating a thick slice of teacake spread with butter. Her basket was on the seat beside her.

Mara sat in a chair opposite the sofa sipping her tea while she listened to all the latest news from Kikuyu. Bina told her how a thief had been caught at the market. The crowd had punished him harshly and now he was in the mission hospital. A lion had walked through the main street a week ago, but it had run away before the game warden had arrived with his gun. There had been transport problems and some businesses were experiencing short-ages – though not the New Tanzania Emporium, of course. When Menelik entered the room Bina frowned at him impatiently and kept talking.

Mara saw a wary look in Menelik's eyes, and she smiled reas-suringly as she addressed him in English.

'Mrs Chakraburti has brought some packages for you.' She waited for Bina to absorb her words before she continued. 'She has all the spices you asked Kefa to order for you.'

Bina looked confused. 'There is no Indian chef? But who else would want so many spices?'

Watching Bina's face, Mara felt a flicker of guilt – but she wanted to give Menelik the chance to gain the Indian woman's respect. 'Menelik's menus are not limited to English dishes, you know,' she said.

Bina shook a finger at Menelik, setting her bangles moving again. 'It is not simple to make Indian food, you know. You must understand everything about it. You must be Indian, in fact.'

'I am not planning to serve Indian food,' Menelik said. His voice was quiet, yet clear. 'I am going to cook the food of my homeland, Ethiopia. First, I must prepare *beri beri* – for that I must use twelve different spices. Then, I am making two stews – *sik sik wat* and *doro wat*. I will put *beri beri* in them also, but I must add other spices. It is very difficult.'

'I have never heard of Ethiopian cooking!' Bina exclaimed, as if people had conspired to keep her in ignorance of something she now suspected to be important.

Menelik gave just the hint of a superior smile. 'Our recipes are very old. Our food is very fine.' He squared his shoulders and lifted his chin. 'And I was trained as a chef in the royal kitchens of His Imperial Majesty Haile Selassie, Conquering Lion of Judah.' He held out his hand towards the basket. 'Please. I am very busy.'

Bina handed many small parcels wrapped in brown paper to Menelik. When he had them all, she offered him a small smile. 'I understand these things, you know. My relatives in Udaipur work at the palace of the Maharana.'

Menelik nodded gravely. 'It is a difficult job, working in a palace. The standards are very high.'

'Yes,' agreed Bina. 'My relatives have told me this.'

'And of course,' Mara threw in. 'Menelik insists on the same high standards here at Raynor Lodge.'

Bina looked even more impressed. She raised her eyebrows approvingly.

As Menelik turned to go, he flashed a look of triumph at Mara. There was a glimmer of amusement there as well. Mara bent her head, hiding her face, until the impulse to smile had passed. She looked down at Bina's feet planted in front of her. They were crammed into a pair of gold sandals decorated with glass jewels. The heels were bare, their skin brown-grey and leathery, and marked at intervals with deep cracks, showing baby-pink flesh.

'And what about the skirt and blouse I sewed for you,' she heard Bina say, as if they'd been discussing the garments only moments earlier. 'Do they fit well?'

Mara looked up. 'Oh, yes! I'm sorry, I should have said something before. I'm delighted with them. They fit perfectly.'

Mara remembered when she'd first tried on the new outfit – how she'd used the hand-mirror to see how it looked. She saw herself walking out into the garden, her hair still damp from her bath, her skin perfumed with *L'Air du Temps*, the soft fabric of the skirt rustling at her knees.

She remembered how Peter had looked at her. She heard his words, floating across to her on the warm night air. *You look beautiful . . .*

Mara smiled at Bina. 'Thank you.'

Bina waved one hand dismissively. 'The colours are very dull, but if you are happy, so am I.' She leaned forward, giving Mara a searching look. 'Of course, you have not been able to show your husband yet. He is still away on safari, yes?'

Mara drew back in her chair. She had a sense that Bina knew everything that had been happening at Raynor Lodge and it made Mara feel anxious – even though she had done nothing wrong. But then it occurred to her that Bina was simply preparing to continue the last conversation they'd had – the one about Mara's marriage, and why she had not yet fallen pregnant. The talk had taken place quite recently, yet as Mara thought back to it, the issues that had been raised felt distant to her. She could remember the agony she'd felt, but it was as though the emotion had been experienced by someone else. She stared into her teacup, wanting, yet not wanting, to let the next thought into her head.

Matilda. The blonde curls, the sky-blue eyes. The silvery laugh.

Mara waited for the familiar stab of pain. But when it came, it was a surprisingly faint version of what it had been. So much had happened to her recently, she realised. So much had changed.

She became aware of Bina watching her with an odd expression, still waiting for her to say something. She picked up her teacup, rattling it against the saucer. 'He's in the Selous for another two weeks.'

Bina whistled through her teeth. 'A very long safari,' she said. 'You will be glad when he comes home.'

'Yes, of course,' Mara answered. She tried to picture John walking back into the lodge, resuming his place as the Bwana. The film company would have packed up and gone by then. It would all be over . . .

Suddenly Mara knew she could not continue the conversation. She looked around her distractedly to suggest there were things she should be doing. 'I'm afraid you've come at rather a busy time, Bina.'

'I understand,' Bina said. 'Life is always hectic for professional women like us.'

As Bina heaved herself to her feet, Mara smiled apologetically. Despite her emotional turmoil, she was conscious of the simple warmth of Bina's presence. She touched Bina's arm. 'Thank you for the spices. Come back and visit me again, sometime.'

Bina's eyes shone. 'Next time, I shall bring *samosas*. And some special *chevda* – spiced cornflakes. You can enjoy them with your – what do you call it, the end-of-the-day drink?'

'Sundowner,' Mara said. She followed Bina onto the verandah. When they stepped out into the sunshine, the hut boys emerged from behind a lattice screen as if they had been waiting there. One of them held a bucket and a sponge.

'Your car is ready,' he said to Bina. 'It is very clean.'

Bina inclined her head. 'I shall inspect it.' She looked at Mara. 'A Mercedes-Benz must be black – of course it must – but it shows every speck of dust. I did not want the Americans to think this car was owned by someone from the bush!'

'No,' agreed Mara. She didn't point out that the car would be dusty again the moment Bina drove away. She turned to the hut boys. 'Would you please take Mrs Chakraburti to her car?'

'Yes, Bwana Memsahib,' they replied.

Bina turned to Mara, her eyes widening admiringly. 'This is your title?'

'It's just until John comes home,' Mara explained. *Until John comes home.*

The words sounded strange and hollow – they might have been plucked at random from another conversation.

Bina gave her a sharp look. 'It is a good name. You should hang onto it. That's my advice.'

Mara smiled wryly. 'The funny thing is, we haven't really had a Bwana at all. Everyone's just done their own job.'

Bina shook her head. Her face bore an expression of mixed impatience and fondness – as though Mara were a wayward yet engaging child.

The two exchanged farewells. As the boys led Bina away, Mara heard them break into their usual childish chatter. She expected Bina to silence them impatiently, but instead she began questioning them in her crude Swahili. Mara guessed Bina was eager to glean some gossip about the film that she could pass around Kikuyu.

Back at her vantage point, Mara saw that everyone was now gathered near the waterhole. Lillian stood beside Peter, right in front of the camera. She'd taken off her hat, and her hair hung long and dark around her shoulders. For Mara, it was like seeing herself from a distance. It was so easy to imagine she was in Lillian's place – she knew exactly how the small lines around Peter's eyes deepened when he smiled, and she knew how – when you looked at it close up – the brown of his hair was made up of different tones. Shutting her eyes, she could almost detect the scent of his closeness: the African smells of sweat and dust, backed by his own cinnamon fragrance . . .

When she looked again, Peter was leaning towards Lillian. Mara felt a jolt run through her as she realised what was about to happen. Her hand tightened on the back of the chair, the rough-knotted string pressing into her skin.

She caught her breath, every fibre in her body stretching towards the scene below her, waiting for it to happen. For Luke to take Maggie into his arms, and kiss her.

Mara shook her head, tearing her gaze away. She stared towards the deep still water that lay further out from the shore. As she scanned the silver surface, she tried to focus on the birds, the reeds, the reflections – anything but the people in the foreground – but all the while, potent emotions bubbled up inside her, demanding attention, yet refusing to be named.

Her thoughts came in fragments, half-formed.

They're actors. Professionals. They do this all the time. It doesn't mean anything . . .

At the edge of her vision, she could see them. Their lips pressed together. Lillian's hand on Peter's neck. Mara felt betrayed, as if it were her place to be down there with Peter. As if she were the only one who could be Maggie. As if Luke belonged to her.

Mara rubbed her hands over her face, wanting to erase her thoughts. Crazy thoughts. The truth was, this had nothing to do with her. She was never going to be Maggie again. She was no longer a part of the film company. And it was just as well: the way she felt right now proved it. Carlton had rescued her, whether he knew it or not. The boundaries had become well and truly blurred, but he'd helped pull her back over the line. Now she was just the hunter's wife again. The safari hostess.

All was back as it should be.

As she watched a spur-winged goose land on the water, sending ripples over the surface, Mara waited for the sense of relief she knew she should feel. But it did not come. She only felt empty, as though some vital essence had been drained from her body.

Her eyes ranged restlessly over the landscape, avoiding the place where Maggie and Luke still stood. Finally, she fixed her gaze on the little hut that had been built by the Somali construction workers over near the edge of the woodland. They'd made it from woven grass and sticks instead of the mud-brick the local people would have used, yet it looked at home in the setting – as if it had always been there. It was standing ready for the filming of the final scenes. The day Brendan began setting up his lights to shine in through the doorway, Mara told herself, the shoot would be almost over. And that time would not be long in coming.

All she had to do until then was to remember who she was – and where, and to whom, she belonged.

THIRTEEN

The door of the rondavel was shut and the curtains closed. Mara knocked lightly. She pictured Lillian lying inside, her body clad in a lacy nightdress, her long hair tumbling over the satin pillowslip her beautician had recommended to protect her skin from being dragged into creases while she slept. After waiting a few moments, Mara knocked again, more loudly. She had no choice but to wake Lillian – everyone else had eaten breakfast some time ago and the crew was already preparing for the day's work.

When there was still no response, she pushed the door gently open. The usual scene of chaos was revealed – the scattered socks; an evening dress draped over the lamp-stand; shoes lying on the floor, tempting white ants. But the bed was empty. The sheets were spread out smoothly over the mattress and tucked under the edges. The mosquito net was tied up in its daytime knot. Mara frowned. It made no sense – the hut boys had not yet been in here this morning, and Lillian would never have made her own bed.

Fighting off a sense of foreboding, Mara forced herself to think calmly. Scanning the room, she saw that Lillian's shoulder bag was missing. Her boots were gone, as well.

She hurried from the rondavel, shutting the door behind her. Then, breaking into a half-run, she headed along the path in search of Kefa. She clung to the idea that he would know something, that there would be a simple explanation for the fact that Lillian had not slept in her room.

When she reached the compound she saw Kefa's tall figure over by Bwana Stimu's shed. As she crossed towards him, she faltered briefly. He was wearing a shirt made from the same blue *kitenge* cloth as her safari hostess dress and the lodge curtains. The short sleeves – made of new cloth, crisply pressed – stood out from his arms.

'Kefa!' she called breathlessly as she came near.

Kefa turned towards her, squaring his shoulders and looking slightly defensive. Mara glanced down at her own dress – a gesture of acknowledgement that they were now clad in matching clothes.

'You have a new shirt,' she said quickly. 'It looks very fine.'

'I ordered it from Mrs Chakraburti. It was made for me personally,' Kefa said proudly. Then a look of concern came over his face. 'Something has happened.'

'Lillian is not in her rondavel. She has not slept in her bed.'

Kefa lowered his gaze. 'Perhaps she has stayed in another room.'

Mara stared at him. A vision of Maggie and Luke, kissing by the waterhole, flashed into her head. But everything she knew about Peter made her certain he had nothing more than a professional involvement with Lillian. And she had shown no special interest in any other member of the company. 'I don't think so. Anyway, her bag and her boots are gone.'

Kefa nodded slowly, frowning. 'She went to her rondavel early last night. She was angry.'

Mara looked at him in surprise. She hadn't noticed any tension during the previous evening. But then, she'd been talking to Peter. Somehow, they'd ended up swapping memories of life in Australia. It had begun with a comment he'd made about his mother's cooking, and before long the awkwardness that had arisen between them in recent days had ebbed away. Peter had told her about places he'd love to revisit back in New South Wales, if only Paula could manage without five-star accommodation. Mara had told Peter about Bicheno, the fishing village where she'd camped as a child. It was named after a French explorer, and he'd made her spell its unusual name. There were tiny penguins there, she'd said, that lived in burrows on a diamond-shaped island. Peter talked about places where he'd gone filming, admitting that sometimes he felt it was only on location that he could truly be himself. But then, at the end of each shoot, he always longed to get back to his family.

Mara had experienced each sentence, each smile, as a step in a complex dance. It had been the same for Peter, she could tell. They had let themselves move towards one another, drawn by what they were sharing, and the sheer pleasure of being together. But at the same time they'd kept feeling for that line that kept them apart – kept them safe. And always, lying beneath the warmth that glowed from their eyes, had been the shadow of regret and an unspoken refrain: *This is all we can share. This is all we can be.*

Mara shook off the memory, focusing again on what Kefa had said about Lillian. 'What happened?'

'Bwana Carlton instructed me not to accept her orders from

the bar.' There was a note of outrage in Kefa's voice. The staff at
Raynor Lodge were trained never to question a client's behaviour, especially where alcohol was concerned. John had explained
that a guest should not even be asked if they would like *another*
drink – 'another' suggested that the person making the offer was
aware that one drink (or a dozen for that matter) had already been
consumed, which was none of their business. 'I thought she might
have had her own bottle of gin in her rondavel,' Kefa continued. 'It
is her *dawa*. She has to have it.'

'Yes, she does,' Mara agreed, 'but too much *dawa* is a bad thing.
Anyway, she did have a couple of bottles but Carlton tipped them
out.'

There was a moment of silence as they looked at one another.
Then they both turned towards the car park.

It took only a few moments to discover one of the Manyala
Land Rovers was missing.

'She went to Kikuyu last night.' Mara's voice was filled with
dismay. Even those Europeans who lived here and were familiar
with the roads tried not to be out after dark – especially in these
uncertain times since Independence. And if they had to drive at
night, they never travelled alone. For a woman to be out on her
own was unthinkable.

'She is probably at the hotel,' Kefa said. He sounded calm, but
his face was taut with anxiety. Even at the hotel, a single woman
was not safe – especially if she'd been drinking.

Mara covered her face with her hand, desperately trying to
think. If the radio was working she could contact the police station in Kikuyu and ask for help. But she'd complied with Carlton's

request that it remain out of order. She reproached herself bitterly, aware that she should have overruled him. She was the one responsible for the lodge and all the people in it. She was the one who should have been prepared for any emergency . . . But thinking this way was no help to her now. She gathered herself. 'I'll find Carlton. Then, let us go straightaway.'

Kefa gestured towards the striped Land Rover. 'I will get the keys.'

Mara shook her head. She preferred to drive her own vehicle, especially if she was in a hurry.

'But we are not only three people,' Kefa said. 'We must take the tracker with us.' Mara's eyes widened with alarm. He spread his hands. 'We must be prepared.'

Mara nodded. She knew he was right. It was one of the first rules of the safari. Be prepared. Another thought came to her. 'Should we take Daudi?'

'No,' Kefa said firmly. 'It is our business.' He paused. 'And if there is a problem, he will be very angry.'

'You're right,' Mara agreed. 'We'll deal with it ourselves.'

The tracker half-knelt on the front seat next to Mara, looking out through the windscreen. Now and then he jabbed a gnarled old finger towards the edge of the road, where occasional patches of sand lay over the hard-baked *murrum*.

'I see them again,' he would say. He'd had no trouble identifying the tracks of the Manyala Land Rover: they were sharp and clean, made by brand-new tyres.

'She is driving very badly,' he commented. He moved his hand in a wavy path through the air.

'It was dark,' Mara said.

The tracker shook his head. 'No, it was light. The moon was big. She could see.'

'But she is not accustomed to roads like this,' Mara answered, welcoming the excuse to talk: it seemed to release some of the tension in the air. 'In the city where she lives, the roads are made of concrete. And at night there are lights on tall sticks.'

As the tracker puzzled over her words, Mara glanced in the rear-vision mirror at Carlton, sitting next to Kefa in the back seat. He had barely spoken during the half hour they'd been driving, but his lips, pressed tightly together, conveyed his anxiety. Mara knew he really cared about Lillian. And he felt responsible for her safety. As if he could feel Mara watching him, Carlton looked up, meeting her gaze in the mirror. She tried to smile reassuringly. The most likely scenario, she told herself, was that they would find Lillian safe and well at the Kikuyu Hotel, sitting in the dining room reading a fresh copy of the *East African Standard*. Mara recalled the breakfast she'd eaten there with John the morning after their wedding – the dried-out toast, served with a choice of red or yellow jam, neither of which could be identified as containing any particular fruit; the melting pool of butter and the clammy over-cooked eggs. There was a new hotelier, now – an African businessman from Dar es Salaam had taken over from the previous owner, who'd chosen not to stay on after the end of colonial rule – but that did not necessarily mean that the standard of cooking would have improved. Mara suspected Lillian would soon have discovered how lucky she'd been to have her meals prepared by Menelik.

A sudden jolting of the Land Rover drew her attention back to her driving. They were on a stretch of badly corrugated road. She accelerated, meeting the bumps head-on and gripping the steering wheel as the vehicle rattled and shook. Normally she would have explained to her passengers that the effect was worse if you took it slowly, but now she just drove, saying nothing. Reaching a corner, she hauled the heavy vehicle round to the right, a new length of road unfolding in front of her. Suddenly, her whole body stiffened as her foot clamped onto the brakes.

An impression of black and white stripes bore into her consciousness. Hard, painted lines that could never have belonged to a zebra.

'Oh my God,' Carlton said.

The Manyala Land Rover was half off the road, facing in their direction, its front bumper jammed against the trunk of a baobab tree.

Mara brought her own vehicle to a halt beside it. She leaned out of her window to peer into the interior. With a thud of panic she saw that the driver's seat was empty.

'She's gone.' Carlton's voice came from behind her.

Mara felt sick. She had a flash image of Lillian swerving desperately to avoid an illegal roadblock: a line of fuel drums flaming in the dark. Mara pictured her crashing into the tree, then waiting helplessly as black figures emerged from the darkness, crowding around their victim, their breath laced with homemade liquor. Bloodshot eyes travelling over the woman's pale body – their prize . . .

Mara jumped down onto the road. In a few strides, she was at the baobab tree. Pressing one hand against the purple-skinned trunk, she pushed herself up onto the bonnet of the damaged Land Rover. Then she climbed over the spare tyre and leaned to look in through the windscreen. Her eye went straight to a bundle of blue cloth lodged on the middle seat. Lillian's cardigan. She scanned the rest of the visible space. The shoulder bag was gone, and there were no other personal items. She was about to turn away, when she saw – faintly visible on the dark upholstery – a pool of blood. She stared at it, shock coursing through her body. Lillian had been injured; she was bleeding. Mara told herself it was not surprising – the tree had obviously been hit at speed. But somehow, in spite of the faults and human weaknesses she had seen exposed in Lillian it still seemed impossible that the ordinary rules of flesh and bone meeting metal and wood would apply to her.

Mara dropped to the ground. Meeting Carlton's questioning gaze, she spread her hands and shook her head – there seemed little point in alarming him further by mentioning the blood on the seat. She turned her attention to the tracker, who was crouched studying the road, the maroon army beret he wore almost touching the ground. He brushed his fingers over the earth like a blind man reading braille, turning his head as if to listen as well as look. Kefa stood nearby, watching closely, staying well clear of the tyre-marks.

Finally, the old man straightened up.

'A truck has been here.' He pointed at the disturbed earth as he spoke. 'It has stopped and people have walked to the Land Rover. You can see their footyprints.'

Even in the midst of the tension, Mara noticed how the tracker used his own version of 'footprint'. She'd heard John correct him, several times, but the tracker refused to change.

He pointed at a mess of small marks in the crumbly surface of the road. 'These footyprints are deeper, now. People are carrying her to the truck. Some have shoes, but others have none.' Mara stared at him, wanting him to continue, but dreading what he might say. He bent down and touched a tiny bird dropping that lay in the middle of a footprint. 'It has taken place today, after the sun has come up.'

Mara looked along the road, in one direction and then the other. 'Can you follow the truck?'

The tracker made a dismissive gesture with his hand. 'I know this truck. It has three different tyres. Only one of them is new. And this —' he poked his foot towards the print of a shoe. 'This belongs to Joseph.'

'Joseph,' Mara repeated the name. 'Right, let's go.'

'Who's Joseph?' Carlton asked.

Mara was already heading for her Land Rover and beckoning the others to follow. 'He works at the mission hospital.'

Mara hurried across the compound, ignoring the crowd of curious outpatients, and aiming for the only nurse that she could see: a young African dressed in a pink and white striped uniform, who was standing over a wood-burning stove. She was using two pairs of forceps to lift a tangle of surgical instruments from a pot of boiling water. As Mara came near, she set them down with a clatter on a cloth spread over a tray.

'Did they bring an *mzungu* here?' Mara asked urgently.

'A European woman is here,' the nurse answered in Swahili. 'The doctor is saving her.'

Mara stared at her for a moment, trying to guess exactly what she meant. Could 'saving' be translated as 'treating'? Or did the woman truly mean 'rescuing'? 'Where are they?'

The nurse pointed a pair of dripping forceps towards the main hospital building.

Mara paused to beckon Carlton, who was waiting by the Land Rover with Kefa and the tracker, before running towards the entrance. She mounted a set of stone steps and pushed open a heavy green door. Just as Carlton caught up with her, she stepped inside.

The air was dense with closed-in heat. There was a strong smell of disinfectant blended with fresh cement – one that almost, but not quite, masked more pungent human odours. Whitewashed corridors stretched in both directions. Mara was unsure which way to go; she'd been to the emergency room once before, when a client had needed stitches for a cut hand, but that had been more than a year ago. Taking a punt, she turned left, Carlton following on her heels, but after only a few steps, she stopped. She could hear a male voice coming from somewhere behind her. The English cadence was immediately identifiable, even though the words could not be heard. She spun round. 'This way.'

The voice grew louder and clearer as they approached the room from which it came. Mara recognised the confident tone of Helen's husband, Tony Hemden, the mission doctor. Soon, they reached an open doorway.

Mara paused briefly on the threshold. Dr Hemden, dressed in a white coat, was standing beside a bed at the end of a small ward. An African nurse hovered at his shoulder, her white uniform and cap in stark contrast to her skin and hair. Together the two figures hid most of the bed from view, but Mara glimpsed a thin white arm draped across a blue blanket.

'She's here,' she said to Carlton.

Dr Hemden turned around, nodding in recognition as he met Mara's gaze. She crossed the room towards him, dimly aware that all the beds she passed were unoccupied. Most did not even have mattresses; the bare metal frames with their barred ends looked oddly menacing, like cages.

'Is she all right?' Mara said as she came near. 'We found the Land Rover.'

Dr Hemden stood aside from the bed. Mara's step faltered. For a moment, she did not recognise the face resting on the pillow. One eye was swollen shut, the socket a dark purple from eyebrow to cheekbone. The lower lip was split in the middle. And the fine, flawless skin was marked with several small cuts that had been daubed with red antiseptic. A section of the patient's head had been shaved and a long cut stitched, the black sutures looking like a line of flies feasting at a thin trough of blood. The rest of the hair had been woven into two neat plaits.

Mara focused on the one undamaged eye: the closed eyelid faintly tinged with mauve. It was the only part of the face that looked as if it belonged to Lillian. She held her hand to her mouth. 'What's happened to her?'

'She has two cracked ribs,' said Dr Hemden. 'And a badly bruised knee. It was full of blood; I put a needle in and managed to draw some off, but there's more. I've got her sedated now, because of the pain. As you can see there are quite a few cuts and bruises, but they're minor. The only scar she'll have will be the one on her head – well under the hairline. Her teeth are fine, too. She kept asking me about that.'

Mara glanced at him wondering if he knew the identity of his patient, or if he simply took it as a matter of course that any woman would be concerned about injuries to her face.

'She's got a headache, as well,' he added. 'It's probably concussion. But it's hard to tell, under the circumstances. It might simply be a hangover.' He looked from Mara to Carlton, his eyes narrowed with disapproval. 'She admitted she'd been drinking at the hotel – quite heavily, I'd say. She must have had the accident some time last night. Joseph came across her at first light this morning on his way to Kikuyu in the truck.' He glanced down at the motionless figure on the bed. 'She was very lucky. It could have been a lot worse.'

'So, will she be okay?' Carlton demanded.

'She'll mend,' said Dr Hemden.

Carlton closed his eyes. 'Thank God.'

Mara's eyes were drawn to the end of Lillian's bed, where she saw what looked like a neatly folded shirt made from a leopard-print fabric – the kind of thing women often chose for a safari holiday. Then she realised it was Lillian's yellow silk blouse, spotted with dark blood. She'd seen that blouse hanging in the actress's rondavel; in secret, she'd run her fingers over the Christian Dior monogram embroidered on the pocket. That had been back in the time when she'd envied Lillian, imagining that she possessed all one might need in order to be truly happy . . .

There was silence in the room, broken only by the faint

scratching of the African nurse's pencil as she recorded notes on her clipboard. The doctor watched over her shoulder. Carlton, meanwhile, was leaning close to Lillian, squinting in distress as he studied her face.

Following his gaze, Mara felt her own heart tighten with sympathy. The vulnerability she'd noticed before in Lillian seemed concentrated in this image of her in the white room, framed by the metal-barred bed. She looked like a battered child, neglected and unloved.

'What's going to happen now?' Carlton asked.

'Fortunately we were able to put her in here on her own. It would have been impossible to put her in the women's ward. This is going to be the new children's ward. It's only just been finished.' The doctor gestured towards a plaque mounted on the end wall. The piece of polished timber bore words in gold paint: *Gift of the people of Bexhill-on-Sea*. 'She can stay here until we arrange the evacuation.'

'Evacuation?' Mara repeated in surprise. 'Where to?'

'The Princess Elizabeth Hospital in Nairobi would be the best option. Joseph's putting a call through to MAF.' Dr Hemden turned to Carlton. 'That's the Missionary Aviation Fellowship. They might even be able to get a plane here later today. You'll have to pay. I assume you're happy with the plan?'

'Yes, of course,' Carlton said. 'Whatever you recommend.'

In spite of his words of agreement, Mara could hear the ambivalence in Carlton's voice. She didn't need to look at his face to guess what he was thinking. If Lillian were to arrive at Nairobi airport – or any airport for that matter – news of her presence would quickly get out. There would be photographers and reporters swarming for a scoop. They'd have no difficulty tracing the story back to events at the Kikuyu Hotel. Mara could see it now. *Hollywood Star Injured In Drunken Accident.* How the public would love to see a shot of the famous face looking as it did now . . .

Mara felt a surge of protectiveness. 'Does she have to be moved?' she asked. 'Can't you look after her here?' She knew Dr Hemden was highly experienced both as a surgeon and a general practitioner.

Before he had the chance to respond, Carlton spoke. 'Her safety is paramount, of course. But I'm sure she'd rather stay here. Privacy is important to her. I don't know if you realise it, but she's very well known. Famous, in fact.'

'I know who she is,' Dr Hemden said bluntly. 'And that's why I want her moved out. I've treated plenty of patients in a more serious state than this, but my hospital is no place for a film star.' He paused, looking across the room towards the open window. The sound of a child crying drifted in from the compound; it was not the lusty protest of a robust child fallen ill, but the defeated whine of one who was chronically weak. Following his gaze, Mara glimpsed Helen moving between the numerous people waiting for the outpatients' clinic. Mara guessed she might be explaining that the doctor had been delayed by an emergency. As always, Helen looked neat and calm and efficient.

'For a start, who'd cook her meals and do her laundry?' Dr Hemden asked Mara.

Carlton looked at her, puzzled.

'They don't provide food in bush hospitals like this,' she explained. 'The patients' relatives do it.' She turned back to the doctor. 'If I can arrange all the help she needs, would you let her stay?'.

Dr Hemden was silent for a moment, as though listening to an inner debate. Then he nodded. 'Very well. But I want to be clear – my staff cannot offer any special treatment.'

'Thank you. We're all very grateful.' Even as she spoke, Mara was considering whom she could send here from the village. Perhaps Kefa's wife? She tried to picture Edina sitting in the passenger seat of the Land Rover, balancing Lillian's collection of little dishes on her knees. She would think it absurd. And anyway, her English was too minimal. Mara chewed tensely at her lip, trying to think of an alternative. Then her eyes returned to the window. 'Wait a minute.'

She ran from the ward, out of the main building, and across to where Helen stood near the old fig tree.

Helen turned in surprise. 'You got here quickly! Joseph only left an hour ago.'

'We haven't come from the lodge, we were already out looking for her,' Mara said. 'The tracker brought us here.'

Helen shook her head. 'Poor thing. I was there when they carried her in. I just hope they can send that plane for her. This is hardly the kind of place she's used to.' She glanced around her as if viewing her surroundings through the eyes of their glamorous patient.

'She wants to stay here.' Mara spoke decisively. She reminded herself that even though Lillian hadn't expressed this opinion, it *was* what she would want. After all, the future of her career depended upon keeping the accident a secret.

'Are you sure?' Helen asked. 'I don't think —'

'Listen,' Mara broke in, putting her hand on Helen's shoulder to draw her attention. 'How much more money do you need to find for those air tickets? To take the children back to England?'

Helen looked mystified by the question; she eyed Mara in silence. 'A lot,' she said finally. 'Five hundred pounds. We've given up the idea. The girls were disappointed, but they understand. It was a silly dream in the first place. There's no hope of finding that kind of money.'

'Yes, there is,' Mara said. 'Lillian needs someone to send meals in and fix her laundry and perhaps do a few other things. She'd be happy to pay you to do it.'

Helen frowned. 'I couldn't take money for doing that.'

'Yes, you could,' Mara said firmly. 'She's a very wealthy person. Believe me, it's worth a lot more than five hundred pounds to her to be able to stay here.'

Helen's eyes widened. 'Are you sure?'

'Yes, I'm sure.'

'I still don't think I could ask for so much,' Helen said doubtfully.

Mara waved her words aside. 'You don't have to ask – I will. As long as you think you can find the time?'

A gleam of excitement appeared in Helen's eyes. 'I can. Of course I can.'

Mara smiled. 'Then it's a deal.'

When Mara returned to the ward, she found that Lillian had been roused from her sleep and Dr Hemden was examining her injured knee.

'You may have fractured your patella,' he was saying. 'We won't know until the swelling goes down.'

Mara was struck by his gentle manner. There was no hint of the disapproval he'd expressed earlier, or even the understandable impatience of a man with a huge workload awaiting him.

She approached the bedside quietly, not wanting to disturb the examination. But as she came to stand next to Carlton, Lillian turned her head and looked up at Mara with her undamaged eye. Tears swam there, spilling from the corner and running down the side of her face.

'I'm sorry. I'm so sorry,' she said, her words shaped clumsily by her swollen lips. 'I've spoiled everything.' She closed her eyes and shrank back into her pillow as if she wanted to make herself disappear. The tears still leaked out, running back over her temples and into her hair. On her cheeks, the red marks of the antiseptic had been smeared into streaks. It made her injuries appear even worse.

Looking down at the ravaged face, Mara couldn't avoid the impression that she was now seeing Lillian's inner wounds, drawn to the surface – the same wounds Lillian had relied upon to fuel her performances, but which had also pushed her along the path to alcoholism. It was a pitiful sight. Mara felt a lump of pain forming in her own throat. She reached towards Lillian, running one hand gently down the side of the bruised face and then stroking the girlish plait.

'Hush now, don't worry, don't worry about anything,' she said soothingly. 'It's going to be all right.' She looked at Carlton, willing him to offer Lillian some reassurance as well.

'Of course it is,' he said. 'We'll think of something. I'll get on the phone to LA. Sort out a postponement.'

Postponement.

Mara savoured the word, a guilty joy erupting inside her. For a crazy moment she imagined the film company staying on at the lodge, waiting until Lillian recovered. But that would take many weeks. The more likely plan, she realised, was that they would go home – and then return.

Either way, Peter would remain in her life for a little longer.

'Do you want to send her things over?' the doctor broke into Mara's thoughts. 'So they can go on the plane with her?'

Mara shook her head. 'She's staying here. I've found someone to help with her care.'

'That was quick,' Dr Hemden commented, giving no sign as to whether or not he'd guessed his wife might be involved. 'In that case, I suggest you come back and visit tomorrow. My patient needs to rest now. She needs some time on her own.'

He spoke with certainty, as if he already understood exactly what kind of person Lillian was. His words seemed to have a meaning beyond their context.

She needs to rest, to recover. She needs an escape from her life.

Mara smiled gratefully at him. 'Thank you.'

After they'd exchanged goodbyes with Lillian, Mara led Carlton away. The calm, compassionate presence of the doctor seemed to follow her as she walked back through the ward. She saw her surroundings in a new light. The bare white room was not just a place where Lillian would be treated for her injuries, she realised. It was a sanctuary, where the actress might at last be able to find peace – safe from all the pressures of her world.

The two walked back towards the Land Rover. Kefa and the tracker were waiting there, now deep in conversation with the nurse who had been boiling the surgical instruments. The sun was overhead. It laid burning fingers on Mara's bare shoulders. She was aware of Carlton moving stiffly – like a robot – beside her.

Without warning, he stopped dead.

'Well, that's it,' he said. He turned to Mara, his face an image of despair. 'And we were so close.'

Mara looked at him in confusion. 'What do you mean?'

'We're finished. There's no way to keep going.'

'But – you said you'll arrange a postponement – get on the phone to LA.'

Carlton waved his hand towards the building where Lillian lay. 'I had to say something. The fact is, I've got no insurance to cover this.' He laughed bitterly. 'If it had been the weather, or some other kind of accident – I'd be okay. I could claim the extra costs to re-shoot later. But there was an exclusion clause on Lillian.' He paused for a second. When he continued, he sounded like someone mimicking the wording of a policy. 'The insurer will not accept liability for any event caused by – or in any way arising from – the subject's abuse of alcohol.' Carlton shook his head. 'Of course, it was a risk, taking her on. But she was the right person for Maggie – she's proved that. And I wanted to see her working again. I really believed she'd be okay.'

Carlton spoke in a low voice – almost to himself, as much as to his companion. As she listened to him, it dawned slowly on Mara that he really was defeated. All the time she'd been responding to Lillian's plight she'd been dimly aware of the implications for the film – but somehow she'd expected him to come up with a rescue plan. Instead, he seemed to be saying the production was going to be abandoned.

A numbing silence wrapped itself around them. Mara hunted fruitlessly for something to say. Then a thought came to her. 'But what about those people you talked about – the ones who were going to finish off the film in a zoo?'

'The guarantors,' Carlton said. 'They might try and work out how to shoot the missing scenes later on. But my contract with the studio will be void by then. It's a negative pick-up deal. I give them the film by a certain date – they hand over the money. But if I don't . . . Well, the guarantors will come to some arrangement with the investors. Then they'll sue me – they'll say it's my responsibility because I was the one who employed a lead actress with an exclusion in her insurance. It's a mess, basically. A big mess.' Carlton broke off, staring at the ground. 'One thing's for sure, though. We'll lose our ranch – the place our parents left us. I needed additional investment so I borrowed against it from the bank.' His voice was husky with emotion. 'It's been a Miller property for ten generations. Leonard and I both rent apartments in LA, but Raven Hills is our real home. It's where we belong.'

The pain in his voice reminded Mara of the way John had sounded while describing various desperate plans to rescue his lodge. She could picture only too well the thoughts in Carlton's head: the painful visions of a much-loved home being handed over to strangers. She wished she had some comfort to offer. Instead, she just walked on, prompting Carlton to follow her. She felt that if they at least kept moving they might somehow avoid letting the cloud of despair settle over them. It was unnerving to see Carlton like this – the man had always been so strong, so ready to tackle any kind of problem. It had been these qualities, Mara recalled, that had prompted her to open up to him during that first dinner after the film company had arrived – when she'd told him about how badly things were going at the lodge, and how difficult it was for her being married to a hunter. As she walked beside Carlton, now, she remembered how he'd responded that evening.

'Nearly always, it works out in the end,' he'd said with total confidence. 'You can't see how it will – but then something happens when you least expect it. And suddenly, everything's all right again.'

Mara thought of reminding him of this – of challenging him to act on his own wisdom. But when she glanced at him, she knew it was pointless.

The look on his face was that of a man who no longer believed in fairytales.

FOURTEEN

Leonard was waiting at the top of the path, leaning against one of the tusks, when Mara drove into the car park. He jolted upright, and strode to meet them. As Mara leaned to switch off the engine, he wrenched open her door.

'What's happening?' he demanded.

Mara looked at him in silence for a moment. 'Didn't you get a message from the mission?'

'It just said you were to going there urgently, that's all.' Leonard looked into the rear of the Land Rover, then turned from Kefa to the tracker, his eyes widening in alarm. 'Where's Lillian?'

Mara glanced across to Carlton, expecting him to speak. But he just shrugged, gazing blankly ahead.

'She's been in an accident,' Mara said. 'She's going to be okay – but she's been injured.'

Leonard stared at her. 'Where is she?'

'At the mission hospital.'

Carlton turned in his seat and cleared his throat. 'The good news is, she didn't kill herself, thank God. She easily could have. The bad news is, she won't be finishing the film.'

Leonard's head jerked back in shock. He opened his mouth to speak, but no words came out.

Over his shoulder, Mara caught sight of Peter. She could see from his face he'd overheard everything. He came to stand beside the Land Rover.

'Is she really okay?' he asked Mara, his eyes narrowed with concern.

'She will be,' Mara replied. 'She's in good hands. They have an excellent doctor at the mission.'

'What was she doing out driving on her own?' Peter asked. 'She doesn't know these roads . . .'

'She went into Kikuyu and got drunk,' Carlton said bluntly. 'Then she had an accident.' He turned towards Leonard. 'Consequently, there won't be any insurance.' He breathed out slowly. 'It's all over.'

Leonard strode round the vehicle and leaned into the window to face his brother. 'We've only got a few more scenes to shoot!'

Carlton spread his hands helplessly. 'But they're not scenes you can do without Lillian, are they? You can't cut around them.'

'No, we can't,' Leonard shook his head. 'There must be something we can do!'

Carlton laughed bleakly. 'I guess we could ask the missionaries to falsify their records – say she was sober when she had the accident. But I don't like our chances there!'

Leonard reeled away from the car, clenching his hands. Then he turned his back on them, and crouched down, resting his head in his hands.

Mara turned to Peter. She saw her own emotions reflected in

his eyes; saw his shock and concern, and, running alongside them, his dismay that their precious time together was going to be cut even shorter.

In the tense quiet, small sounds became loud – the distant clanging of pots in the kitchen, the creak of the vinyl upholstery as Carlton stirred heavily in his seat, the buzz of a fly caught behind the sun visor. Finally, Kefa opened the side door and climbed out. The others followed suit. Then they stood together in a group, subdued and silent.

Suddenly, Leonard straightened up and turned around. Mara looked at him in surprise. Where she'd expected to see despondency, there was a strange light of conviction in his eyes.

'I've got an idea,' he announced. He fixed his attention on first Mara and then Peter. 'I need to talk to both of you – in private.'

At a fast pace, he led them to a far corner of the garden, where the trees pressed in around the fence, dark and impenetrable.

'You don't have to agree,' were his opening words, looking at Mara as he spoke. She swallowed; already she felt tension rising inside her. 'I'm asking you to take Lillian's place – to be Maggie again.'

Mara frowned. It didn't seem likely that the solution could be this simple, considering the depth of Carlton's despair. 'Well, if it would help,' she said cautiously. 'Of course I'll do that . . .'

Her voice trailed off as she became aware of Peter, standing beside her – of his eyes widening in surprise.

'The only thing is —' Leonard broke off, as if searching for the right words. After a moment, he seemed to give up and just launch ahead. 'Look, the scenes that are left – they're love scenes.

I always keep them to the end. That way the energy builds during the shoot.'

Mara stared at him as she took in his meaning.

'You can just say no,' Leonard said quickly, glancing from Mara to Peter and back. 'I'd understand. I really would.' There was a short, taut silence. 'But I believe I can find a style of coverage where we won't see Maggie's face. Or if we do, it'll be in deep shadow.' He took a breath, before hurrying on. 'Mara, you've been around us long enough to see how filming works. It'll be broken down into shots. Cut together, it will look like Luke and Maggie are making love. But doing it will be different. Still, I have to say . . .' He paused, a look of uncertainty in his eyes. 'They will kiss. They will touch. All that will happen.'

Mara nodded. She looked at the ground to hide the confusion she felt. Sensing Peter's eyes fixed on her, she tried to imagine what she would see if she met his gaze. Surely, like her, he was torn?

'No one will be in that hut except you two and me,' Leonard continued. 'We already lit the set this morning, so Brendan won't be needed. The shots will all be mute and I'll be behind the camera. So even the crew won't know what's happening in there. Later on, when they see the movie, they'll think we did pick-ups back in LA. The staff here at the lodge will think it's just more of the kind of filming we've already done. No one will ever know it's not Lillian Lane in those scenes. That's the whole point, after all – to find a way to keep her accident a secret and still finish the movie.' Leonard waited for Mara to look up, then he kept talking. A feverish momentum seemed to have gathered inside him, making his movements even more tense than usual. 'Actually, I'm beginning to think it will be even more interesting than if we just filmed it in the usual way. The audience will witness the scene through a grassy screen. The style will mirror the theme of the movie – it's all about hidden, secret things.'

Leonard turned abruptly to Peter. 'So – what do you think?'

Peter was quiet for a long moment. 'It should be easy for me to say yes,' he said finally. 'It's my job. I've done it before. But Mara's not an actress. That makes it different – for both of us.'

'It doesn't have to be,' Leonard argued. 'Sometimes you have inexperienced cast members. Sometimes they're old hands. They're still doing the same job. And Mara's been playing Maggie already. This is just taking it a step further.'

Peter nodded slowly. Mara could see him struggling with the same question that filled her mind. Would they be able to act as though they were in love without it being real?

They will kiss. They will touch. All that will happen . . .

She reminded herself of what Leonard had said, that the performance would all be broken up into bits, one moment cut off from the next.

'Take your time to decide,' Leonard addressed them both. 'There's no pressure. No hurry.' He thrust his hands into his pockets as he spoke, as if to keep their energy contained.

Mara walked a little distance away and stepped in behind a bougainvillea bush, hiding from view. She stared out beyond the lodge grounds to where two small boys were watching over a herd of brown and white goats. She tried to calmly weigh up the factors she should consider. On one side of the scales lay the future of Leonard's masterpiece: the film into which everyone had poured so much effort. The careers of Carlton and Leonard were hanging in the balance. And Lillian's as well. Then there was Rudi's dream of giving up his taxi-driving forever. And the rescue of the Miller family home, Raven Hills.

On the other side, lay all the reasons why Mara should reject Leonard's proposal. She tried to pin down what they were, but her thoughts were vague and confused. In place of words, faces came to her: she saw John, Matilda, Paula and the children. And Peter. She tried to think of how each of them should influence her decision. But the face that kept returning to her – rising up and demanding her attention – was none of these.

It was her own.

It was a bright, strong face – the eyes shining, the lips on the edge of a smile.

She walked slowly back towards Leonard and Peter.

'Well, have you made up your mind, Mara?' Leonard asked as soon as she drew near.

The question seemed to hang in the air, awaiting her reply. But Mara avoided Leonard's urgent gaze, turning instead to Peter. Her eyes met his. Suddenly she was more certain of what she was going to say than she had ever been about anything. When she spoke, her voice was steady and clear. 'I want to do it.'

I want to be with Luke.

Peter looked at her, his eyes like wells – deep and still. He took a slow breath. 'So do I.'

Leonard closed his eyes in relief. Then he smiled, looking suddenly younger. 'Let's get straight onto it, then. I'm ready to go.'

The dress was long and red and made of fine silky cloth. It rustled softly as Mara dropped it over her head. There was no hint of Lillian's perfume on the fabric – the garment had only just been taken out of its wrappings; sheets of crushed tissue paper lay on the bare-earth floor, along with a handwritten label bearing the name 'Maggie'. Mara struggled to ease the dress over her body; even though she'd showered less than an hour ago, she was already damp with sweat and the cloth clung to her skin. But eventually, she settled the dress in place. It fitted perfectly, as if it had been made specially for her.

She stood alone in the middle of the grass hut, barefoot on a woven sisal mat. There was not much light – Leonard had closed the door as he'd left, and there was only one small window – but she could see a few pieces of filming equipment already in place: there was a lamp fixed to a pole in the roof, and the camera tripod lay folded on the floor next to a large, silvery-surfaced board Mara now knew was used to bounce light into a shot. The hut walls would normally have been speckled with pinpricks of daylight, but Brendan had wrapped the whole structure with black plastic from the outside, so that it would always appear to be night.

Mara listened for movement outside, but all was still. She had a strange sense of being caught in a nether realm, a place where time had stopped. Leonard had not said whether she should come out when she was ready, or just wait for him to return. Hovering uncertainly, Mara peered down at the dress. The deep red silk hung in sensuous folds, hugging the lines of her hips and thighs; the neckline plunged low; and slender straps left her shoulders bare. The dress was more revealing than any Mara had seen modelled by lodge clients – more eye-catching, even, than Matilda's silver sheath. It seemed to Mara that a woman dressed in this way could not have been more out of place than in this simple hut. But Leonard had argued that it would make good cinema: bringing together opposites was a way of creating something new. And it made sense in the script. Maggie and Luke decide to dress up for their last evening together, before they return to Zanzibar. They want to remember this night forever. So Maggie, in the red gown, and Luke, in a dinner suit, wander barefoot through the landscape (over ground that has been checked carefully by the hut boys for thorns and insects), glasses of champagne in their hands. They watch the sun sink towards dusk.

Then they enter the grass hut, seeking privacy . . .

Mara turned slowly around, shifting her gaze to the other end of the hut. An African bed had been set up there: a simple wooden frame padded with cowhides overlaid with the pelt of a leopard and a couple of *kitenges*. A single hibiscus flower lay near the centre of the bed, its vibrant red mirroring the colour of the dress. From where she stood, Mara could see the strong curve of the petals with their softly crinkled edges, and the faint speckle of yellow pollen. The flower looked vulnerable lying alone amid the expanse of black and gold leopard skin. Yet at the same time, there was a sense that it belonged there – exactly where it was. It was Rudi's deft touch, Mara knew. This place was his creation.

Mara looked at it all with a sense of disbelief. It seemed impossible that she was really standing here, dressed like a film star, waiting for Peter to come to her.

To lead her across to that bed, and lie down with her.

She clenched her hands, feeling her fingernails digging into her palms. Then she closed her eyes.

It won't be us. It will be Maggie and Luke, she reminded herself. *It won't be real. That's why we can do it.*

Mara jumped as the door scraped open, then caught her breath in surprise. Instead of Leonard's lean figure in the red overalls, she saw a man in a dark suit. It took her a few seconds to realise it was Peter. She'd only ever seen him in light tropical clothes, or khaki safari gear. In his black jacket, and a shirt so white it almost glowed in the shadowy interior of the hut, he looked even more striking than usual.

Suddenly, Mara realised that while she was staring at Peter, his eyes were fixed on her.

'You . . . don't look like you,' he said.

'Neither do you,' Mara replied.

They stood still. An awkward tension rose between them. Mara plucked nervously at the seams of her skirt. Avoiding Peter's face, her eyes settled instead on a bottle of champagne he was holding. In his other hand, he carried two glasses, their stems hooked over his fingers. Following her gaze, Peter lifted the bottle up, showing her that it was only half full.

'We drank the rest outside,' he said.

Mara looked at him in confusion. For a second she pictured him sitting with Leonard, drinking champagne while she was getting dressed.

'We were watching the sun going down,' he added. 'You and me – over by the waterhole.'

'Ah,' Mara nodded. She remembered that the day's scenes were to be filmed out of sequence. 'Did we enjoy it?'

'We did,' replied Peter. 'But the mosquitoes bothered us.'

They both laughed. Mara felt herself beginning to relax. Peter had reminded her that they were now in a world like Alice's wonderland – a place where it was possible to drink the second half of a bottle of champagne before the first.

A place where nothing was real.

He put down the bottle and the glasses and looked around him at the hut. 'It smells like hay in here,' he said. 'It reminds me of a summer job I had once, lifting bales.'

'That's tough work,' Mara responded. She was instantly grateful to him for finding a way to hold back the silence. 'It was one time of the year when I was happy to stay home and help Mum.'

Peter asked Mara more about her life on the farm. They kept on talking, even after Leonard came in and began setting up for filming. They watched as he struggled to mount his camera on the tripod, fumbling with the catches. He refused Peter's offer of assistance, but then kept looking around him as though he had forgotten that there was no crew to summon. When he finally had the camera securely in place, he turned to the task of testing the lighting. First he switched on the lamp in the ceiling, sending a bluish glow over the bed. Then he turned on a second lamp that was set up just outside the window. It threw a wide strong beam of silvery light across the space.

'Looks like moonlight to me,' he said. 'Now, remember how you were, down by the lake? Let's work that way again. The scenes we're going to shoot are memories – flashbacks. That means I don't have to cover every little step. So, you can forget about me. You've read the script, Peter. Just play the scene. I'll grab my shots.'

Mara looked at Peter. His expression told her this was not what he'd been expecting. The approach Leonard described might be easier in one way, but it was much harder in another. It was more risky – more real.

He met her gaze. Mara knew this was the moment when they could take a step back towards a safer path. They could tell Leonard they would prefer him to direct them, move by move, to make them his puppets.

The silence lengthened. Looking at Peter, Mara remembered all that had passed between them – the conversations, the shared experiences; all the steps that had led them to this place. She sensed the same images being played out by him.

It was impossible to tell who reached a decision first – and whether it was signalled by a nod, or a curve of the lips, or the movement of a hand – but, suddenly, they were walking side by side towards the bed. Mara focused on the feel of the sisal under her soles, and then the softness of the beaten earth. She tried to slow her breathing, and calm the pounding of her heart.

'Maggie, you'll have your back to the camera,' came Leonard's voice. 'Remember, both of you, avoid talking if you can. Then we won't have to re-voice Maggie.' He bent to press his eye to the viewfinder. The only sign that he was tense was his faint tuneless whistle. After a few moments, he stopped it; his lips pursed in concentration. In the quiet, parrots could be heard screeching as they flew overhead.

'Okay, Luke,' he said finally, his voice low. 'I'm ready when you are.'

Mara felt like a swimmer poised on the brink of a dive; every nerve in her body strained in expectation. She could feel Peter approaching her, the space between them narrowing, but it seemed to take forever, as if she were caught in a dream. Then, just as she was sure she would collapse and fall, she felt his arms around her, drawing her towards him.

As their bodies came together, she shut her eyes and leaned her head against his chest, breathing his cinnamon smell and the warmth of his body. She felt his lips brushing her cheek, tasting her skin. Then his hands rose to cradle her head, fingers wrapping themselves in her hair. Slowly, his lips travelled across to meet hers, pressing lightly against them, gentle and soft.

After a long moment, he pulled away. Opening her eyes, Mara found his gaze fused to hers. His eyes were wide and dark, shining in the silver-blue shaft of light.

He took off his jacket and turned to drop it onto the bed – but then he paused, looking at the red flower lying there. Carefully he picked it up, resting it in the palm of his hand. He lifted it towards Mara, as if to share its beauty with her, before placing it near one corner of the cowhide. He unbuttoned his shirt, and loosened the cuffs of his sleeves. Stepping close to her, he took her in his arms and kissed her again. Then, cupping his hands over her bare shoulders, he laid her carefully back on the bed. Lowering himself over her, he buried his face in her hair.

Closing her eyes again, Mara abandoned herself to his touch, his taste, his smell. She was aware only of impressions – of lying back on the rumpled *kitenges*, Peter's face above hers; the lock of hair on his forehead falling forward, brushing her brow. Of the red silk, twisting tight around her legs and the tickle of the cowhides.

There was the heat of the lamps and the closed-in air of the hut. Cool blue light playing over skin that was slick with sweat. Her hair lying in damp strands, draping the leopard skin.

His lips moving down her neck, and on over her breasts, wrapped in silk.

Then the slow, careful lifting of the skirt. His hand gliding up from her ankle, smoothing the skin of her calf, moving on towards her knee – and no further.

Dimly she was aware of the boundaries of what was allowed. She felt Peter leading her towards them, reaching further and further, then choosing the moment of retreat. Her skin tingled from the trail of his touch. It was a strong, sweet pain, like the rush of warm blood into limbs that had been numb with cold. As the thaw spread through her body, fresh energy coursed in her veins. She ran her fingers over the strong curves of his shoulders. Then she smoothed her hands over his chest, feeling the soft layer of hair, and the firmness beneath.

Reaching up to stroke his face, Mara felt a wave of joy break through her. She looked searchingly into Peter's eyes. They were frank and open, meeting hers. There was no shadow of uncertainty there – no caution, no holding back.

He grasped her shoulders, pulling her against him. She wrapped her arms around him. And they clung together, as if nothing in the world would ever force them apart.

FIFTEEN

A fire burned in a portable grate that had been set up in the middle of the lawn. Orange flames licked the darkness, sending up bright sparks that danced and whirled in the heat eddies. Tables had been set in a circle around the blaze. Each one held a pool of light, shed by a Tilley lamp placed at its centre. The glass casings were already hot, and the white tablecloths were faintly spattered with the bodies of winged insects that had flown too close. Near the lanterns, green tubes of mosquito repellent had been laid out, along with vases of flowers – blooms of red and gold, smouldering in the muted light.

Mara stood in the shadows at the far end of the verandah, watching the hut boys arranging chairs in clusters. She was wearing the full-length version of her hostess dress. It was loose on her body, and the fabric felt stiff and coarse after the silky softness of Maggie's evening dress.

She had the red dress with her now, folded up in her arms, ready to be returned to Rudi. The faint smell of marsh-mint rose up to her from streaks of mud that stained the hem. She breathed it in, wanting to be carried back to the dreamlike interlude in which she'd walked beside Luke at the waterhole, as the sun sank towards the horizon, spreading fiery colour across the western sky.

They had strolled along the shore while Leonard called his directions. Mara had moved in a daze, focused only on Luke's presence beside her. Her whole being was poised, waiting, for the touch of his hand, his shoulder – even the cloth of his shirt . . .

Mara held the dress closer to her face. Beyond the smell of the mud, she could pick out the fruity scent of champagne. She replayed in her mind the shot in which Luke had opened the bottle of champagne, not watching his hands as he worked, but fixing his gaze on Maggie's face. She saw, again, how he'd prised the cork from the bottle, the loud pop rousing the birds from the rushes. The cork travelling in a long high arc against the sky before falling with a faint splash into the gold-painted water. White foam erupting, running down over his hand and splashing onto the dress. Their laughter ringing out through the air, bright and careless.

The sound of drumming broke into Mara's thoughts. Near the fire, she saw one of the hut boys bent over a goatskin drum, pounding his palms against the stretched hide. As she watched the fluid movements, she was aware of figures appearing from the darkness, and taking their places at the tables: Brendan, the two Nicks and Rudi. The men wore their best evening suits and their faces were smooth and freshly shaved. Faceted wine glasses sparkled in their hands, the globes filled with jewel tones of gold, yellow and dark red. Daudi and the ranger joined them, along with a smiling Carlton; they all held tumblers of the pale local beer topped with white froth.

Mara did not need to scan her surroundings in search of

Peter – she could feel his absence as clearly as she could hear the throb of the drum. She pictured Peter in his rondavel, abandoning Luke's shirt and dinner jacket and changing back into his own clothes. She wondered if he'd been tempted – as she had been – to remain in costume. Part of her had wanted so badly to postpone the final separation from Maggie; but another part sensed the hostess dress would offer her a shield of safety. It would remind her of who she was, here in the real world.

But it wasn't working. In spite of the familiarity of her clothes, Mara didn't feel like herself. A strange vigour still flowed through her. She felt brave and reckless. But at the same time, raw and vulnerable – as though she'd been reborn into a body that was new and perfect, but which had yet to be tested and found strong.

Mara turned to see Leonard approaching, a glass of champagne in each hand. He still wore his red overalls, with the script tucked behind the bib, though he'd exchanged his muddy desert boots for a pair of slippers. Mara guessed he'd gone straight from the location to the bar: his face was red and his stance unsteady. But like his brother, he was beaming with pleasure.

'I can't believe it's all over. Finished!' Placing the glasses on a nearby table, Leonard dragged the script from his overalls. Holding it up for her to see, he flipped through the pages. Every scene had been slashed with a big red tick. 'It's always a great moment, when the shooting script looks like that!' he said with a grin. 'I can't wait to see today's rushes. You're a natural, you know, in front of the camera. I've said that all along. But today there was something else . . .' His voice petered out as he met Mara's gaze. Then he nodded slowly, as if acknowledging something that, deep down, he had already understood: that what he'd filmed in the hut was neither professional nor amateur acting. It was not a performance of any kind. It was real.

Mara just looked at him in silence. She felt no need to respond; it would have been as superfluous as agreeing that day was day, and night was night.

Still watching Mara, Leonard reached for one of the glasses and took a long gulp of champagne. Then, as he lowered his glass, a look of uncertainty came over his face, a tentativeness that was at odds with his usual aura of complete belief in himself. It made him look softer, more ordinary. It was possible to imagine him doing his own shopping or holding hands with a small child.

After a long quiet moment, a smile returned to Leonard's face. 'Those scenes we shot today were more than good, you know – they're groundbreaking cinema. Because I couldn't show who you were, everything about the coverage was unusual. Critics are going to rave about them. Students are going to write essays about them.' His eyes gleamed with excitement as he held up his glass. 'Here's to you and Peter,' he said. 'Here's to us all.'

Mara raised her own glass in response, just as Peter stepped onto the lawn. Her fingers tightened around the stem of the glass. Seeing him there – no longer Luke, but a real person – she felt a sudden rush of doubt. A memory flashed into her head: watching Lillian kissing Peter down by the waterhole, the day of Bina's visit. The passion had looked so real. Maybe what had happened inside the hut had been more of the same. Perhaps it had meant more to Mara, than it had to Peter.

Peter was surveying the scene, clearly looking for someone.

When he found Mara, a smile lit up his whole face. Watching him, Mara felt pleasure flood through her, replacing doubt. She took a slow sip of her champagne. Then, licking the sweetness from her lips, she returned his smile.

As Peter walked towards her, Mara was dimly aware of Leonard excusing himself and wandering away. Her eyes were fixed on Peter. He wore his linen suit, with the tie already loosened at his neck. His hair was brushed back from his face. She sensed a faint nervousness in him; it made him seem young – as if he were, again, the surfer on Bondi beach, barely grown up. As he came close, his eyes travelled over Mara's body – pausing on the red dress tucked under her arm – and then coming to rest on her face. Before they had time to greet one another, the kitchen boy approached them, bearing a tray that held two steaming enamel bowls.

'We are serving dinner,' he said in his singsong voice.

'Thank you.' Mara was puzzled as to why food was being carried to the tables in these plain, simple vessels, the kind the village women used, and not in Alice's porcelain. But concerns about the running of the lodge felt distant to her, and unimportant.

'Good!' Peter said. 'I'm starving.'

As he spoke, Mara watched his lips, tracing with her eyes the perfect bow of his mouth.

'I suppose we should find somewhere to sit,' she responded.

The phrases that passed between them seemed like encoded messages, standing in for all the things yet to be said.

Mara led the way towards the table where Leonard and Carlton were sitting. The brothers were gazing uncertainly at the large bowls of food in front of them.

'There's no cutlery. And no plates,' Leonard said as Mara sat down.

She glanced over the three bowls. One was full of *ugali* – a stiff porridge made of corn meal. Another contained a meat stew; and the third held a dark green sauce, suggesting a potage of wild spinach.

'It's Udogo food,' Mara said, 'from the local tribe.' For a moment she felt surprised by Menelik's choice for the film crew's last dinner, but then she saw how perfect it was. Now the film was successfully finished, after so much hard work and difficulty, everyone was in a light-hearted mood. And the hour was late, which contributed to a casual atmosphere. It all fitted well with eating food by hand from communal pots. She saw, also, that the circle of tables was wider than would have been needed for the usual number of guests. Over near the fire, she glimpsed the Somali construction workers sitting down with Brendan and Bwana Stimu. Tomba and Daudi were deep in conversation with Jamie, while the ranger looked on. And there were still places left for the boys and Kefa. Serving all the food at once, like this, meant even Menelik would be able to join in. Everyone at the lodge would share this last main meal together.

'You eat with your fingers,' Mara explained. 'Like this.' Her voice carried more loudly than she'd planned. People at the other tables stood up to watch her demonstration.

Using her right hand she picked up a small mound of the warm white porridge. After forming it into a ball, she pushed her thumb into the centre to make a little bowl. She dipped it into the spinach *mboga*, then lifted it to her lips. Too late, she remembered a flick of the wrist was needed as the hand left the pot in order to break off the soft stalks. She tried to catch the dangling spinach in her mouth, but instead felt it trailing over her chin. After a moment of embarrassment, she licked it away, and then just shrugged and laughed. Her gesture seemed to strike a chord with the gathering. Within seconds, hands were reaching boldly towards the bowls of *ugali* and an easy chatter filled the air.

As Mara leaned back in her chair, she met Peter's gaze. She wondered if he could see how changed she was. Not long ago, she'd have been nervous and awkward about being the centre of attention, and mortified by making a mistake. Now, she felt relaxed and unconcerned.

Hunger stirred inside her, and she reached again for the pot. Peter followed her example, bending his head close to hers. Together, they dug their fingers into the *ugali*, their hands side by side and almost touching. To Mara, every sensation felt new and unexpected – the *ugali* so soft and warm, the gravy so smooth, the stew so spicy and rich.

After a while, she noticed that the drumming had stopped. In its place, gramophone music – the lilting beat of *A Swingin' Safari* – drifted out to the guests from the sitting room.

Leonard turned towards Mara. 'This is excellent,' he said, licking his lips. 'You've really spoiled us here. We're not going to want to go home!'

Mara's hand faltered, midway to her mouth. She nodded, but could not speak. All she could think of was the way he'd used the past tense – *spoiled*, not *spoiling* – as though the visit of the film company, and Peter's presence here, had already slipped into history.

A dull pain spread inside her, banishing her appetite. She fiddled with the lump of *ugali*, rolling it between her fingers. Then she tried to distract herself by watching Carlton eat. He frowned with concentration as he scooped up a load of meat and gravy, cramming it into his mouth, and then chewing with bulging cheeks. He seemed to be making up for all the stressful days when he had not been able to enjoy his meals. After disposing of several more mouthfuls, he turned to Mara, a dripping ball of *ugali* arrested in mid-air.

'I've got a surprise for you,' he said. 'Now we've got the film in the can, I reckon I can afford to spend a bit of money.'

Mara looked at him in confusion. A few days earlier, he'd paid her the last instalment of the money she was due for accommodation, along with a royalty for the village and also a large bonus he had called her acting fee. She'd had the impression then that he was using up the very last of his resources.

A broad smile came onto Carlton's face. 'When I show the rushes around LA, everyone's going to be calling us. They'll be opening their wallets, just begging for a piece of the action. That means I can postpone paying a few other bills, and help you out instead.' He waved towards the construction workers. 'I'm going to leave these guys here to work for you for a month. They can finish the pool, and build a proper viewing deck out there where those chairs are. That way you'll be ready for the rush.'

Mara frowned, still puzzled by what he was saying.

'Raynor Lodge is going to become a world-famous destination,' Carlton stated. 'A bit like the Fairmont Hotel in San Francisco.' He raised his eyebrows enquiringly, but Mara shook her head.

'I've never heard of it.'

'Hitchcock shot bits of *Vertigo* there,' Carlton explained. 'It's been packed out ever since. The owners must've made a fortune.'

'He's right.' Leonard took over from his brother. 'People love to visit the places where films were made.' He pointed towards the verandah. 'When people see Lillian Lane sitting there, sharing a sundowner with Peter Heath, they'll be flocking to do the same.'

'And they won't be hunters, coming here to shoot,' Carlton broke in. 'They'll be sightseers – families, honeymooners.'

He smiled proudly at Mara. She understood he was offering a solution to the problems she'd shared with him over dinner on that first evening. For a moment, she imagined how simple her future could be: all the visitors would depart; John would return from the Selous; the non-hunting safaris would begin. They'd live happily ever after. But even as she tried to form the vision in her mind, she felt remote from it, as if she now existed in a different realm.

'And of course,' Leonard continued, 'we'll be telling everyone we meet about this place – the food, the service, the setting. Especially the food!' He turned to Peter. 'You will, too, won't you? People always take notice of actors.' A rueful note entered his voice. 'They know who they are.'

'Sure, I'll spread the word, when I get back,' Peter said.

There was a hollow tone in his voice. Mara clasped her hands in her lap. If only they could be left alone together, lost in thoughts of what had happened that day, instead of being dragged towards the future.

'I'll be sending you some production stills to hang on your photo wall,' Carlton added. 'We'll take some more pictures tonight. We need shots of staff and crew together – and lots with Peter, of course.

'We could leave behind a few props,' suggested Leonard. 'A copy of the script.' He pointed towards Maggie's evening dress, a red mound at the far end of the table. 'Some pieces of wardrobe.'

'And there's one more thing,' Carlton announced, pausing to make sure he had Mara's attention. 'You can keep the generator and the two big lights.' He spread both hands in a flourish, like a conjurer showing off his skills. 'Raynor Lodge will now have a flood-lit waterhole.'

Mara nodded slowly as she took in his words. It had been John's dream to find a way to light the waterhole, so that guests could watch the game coming to drink after dark even when there was no moon. But the generator was brand new. And the large lights looked very expensive. 'You've paid me too much already,' she protested.

'It's nothing,' Carlton insisted, 'compared with what you've done.' He looked from Mara to Peter. 'What you've both done.'

What you've both done.

A sudden quiet at the table left the words hanging in the air like an electric charge. Mara searched Carlton's face, trying to tell if he understood what had really taken place between her and Peter. If he did, why was he speaking about her future here as if it lay ahead of her, unchanged? Perhaps he was trying to tell her something by focusing on the bright prospects of the lodge . . .

Mara turned her gaze to Peter. She saw tension in the set of his mouth, and a lost look in his eyes, as if, without direction, he was unsure what he should do, or who he should be. Watching his face, Mara felt the new strength that flowed within her rising up and reaching towards him. Peter had always been such a sure and steady presence, but now, Mara sensed, he needed her to be clear and strong.

'I was glad to do it,' she told Carlton, still looking at Peter. 'It was something I'll never forget.'

Peter smiled, his features softening. 'It was the same for me.'

After dinner, the photography session began. Leonard asked each member of the crew to pose in turn, holding the pieces of equipment relevant to their profession: Brendan with a lamp; Jamie with his headphones and recorder; Bwana Boom with his pole; and Nick, holding the big black camera like a baby in his arms.

Time after time, Peter was summoned to take his place in the picture. Showing no hint of impatience, he rested his hands on people's shoulders as asked, and smiled when he was told to. Watching him, Mara felt a fresh pang of pain. It occurred to her that he probably believed he was doing something for her: for her future at the lodge. She looked at him in despair, as he smiled into the camera. Was there no way to escape thoughts like these? She longed to be alone with Peter – not talking or thinking or making plans, just losing themselves in the softness of the lamplight, and the beauty of the night sky above.

'Your turn, Mara,' Leonard called. 'Come up here with Peter. This time you're not Maggie, standing with Luke – you're the Memsahib of Raynor Lodge enjoying the company of movie star Peter Heath.'

He made them stand so close together that their hips and

shoulders were touching. Mara felt her whole body reaching towards Peter's, her flesh and bones and blood still holding the memory of the freedom they had experienced inside the hut.

'Put your arm over her shoulders,' Leonard called to Peter. 'Move your faces close, almost cheek to cheek. I'm doing a tight shot. Now, smile.'

A second later, it was over. Peter's arm withdrew from her, and their faces moved apart. Then Kefa was brought into the scene and told to stand beside Mara.

'This will be a good one,' Leonard commented. 'We've got the two of you in your lodge uniforms, standing right next to Peter.' The shutter clicked faintly and he rolled on the film. Then he pointed at Mara. 'Now, you step out. Let's get the cook.'

In the moment of turning away, Mara breathed in Peter's smell, drawing it deep into her lungs as if she could hold it captive there. Then she began walking back towards her chair. With each step, she could feel the distance between her body and his growing greater; an image came to her of her soul being dragged out from inside her, and left behind. Somehow, she managed to smile her hostess smile as she passed between her guests. Then suddenly, she could bear it no longer. Weaving a path around the tables, she stumbled away, out of the oasis of light and into the darkness.

The twisted old branch of the fig tree seemed to offer itself as a sturdy barrier that would keep her safe from harm. Mara rested her arms on it and stared into the shadowy distance. The moon was only half-grown, but the sky was clear, allowing a faint light to fall over the land. Her gaze drifted beyond the grey waste of the grassland – broken by the dark circle of the waterhole – towards the rocky outcrop. She traced its outline, thinking, as she always did, how impossible it was to view the shape as a crouching lion once its other name was known. The idea seemed to hold some special meaning for her, tonight. It meant, after all, that reality was not fixed; it could change, according to how one approached it. Perhaps, then – Mara told herself – it wasn't always possible to tell what was real and what was not. Or what was right and what was wrong. And where lay the line between truth and a lie.

Perhaps it was simply a matter of choice, how you looked at things.

Perhaps whatever you wanted, could be yours . . .

Mara closed her eyes, breathing in the fragrance of frangipani and the green smell of the woodland trees that pressed in around her, dense and dark. She imagined silent footsteps made by creeping velvet feet. Watching eyes, yellow and unblinking. She knew it was dangerous to be out here without a gun – not even a cattle stick – and torch. But she didn't care. She felt reckless, as though the new strength inside her made her invincible.

She heard him coming – his footsteps, the snapping twigs, the swish of leaves being brushed aside. She glimpsed the light of a torch beam briefly, before it was snuffed out. Then, he was beside her, a dark shape in the shadows, lit here and there by the glancing touch of the moon.

'I guessed you'd be here,' Peter said.

'I had to get away from everyone,' Mara said, adding quickly, 'Not you.'

He smiled, but only briefly.

'I don't want to leave tomorrow.' He spoke as if they'd already been deep in conversation about his departure, and all that was needed was this final remark.

Mara nodded, silent. Out here on this rocky ledge, wrapped in shadows, they seemed cut off from the whole world. It was possible to imagine they could stay here, in a timeless place, hiding from everything that awaited them. The thought danced before her, holding itself up like a vision.

An image came to her then, a memory of a simple wooden hut with a tin roof, set beside a lake. She saw the smoke rising from a cooking fire. A pair of matching *kitenges* fluttering from a clothesline outside. And a guitar. There had been a guitar, leaning up against one of the doorposts . . .

As she prepared to speak, her heart began to beat faster. 'Once John and I were on safari, a long way from here. We came across a German couple in the middle of nowhere. They were sitting together, drinking tea outside a hut. They weren't missionaries, or zoologists, they were just living there, doing nothing. In the next town, the man who sold us petrol told us they'd gone there just to be alone together. They'd left their old lives behind.'

They ran away together. That was how the man had put it. But Mara didn't want to use these words – they held a hint of panic, and cowardice. Of things that mattered being left behind.

'Their clothes were all worn out,' she pressed on with her story. 'And they only had two cups. We had to get ours from the Land Rover to join them for tea.'

'How did they live?' Peter asked.

'They ate food from their garden. They had all kinds of things planted. Paw paw. Beans. Sweet potatoes. Peanuts.' She smiled. 'I like growing peanuts. I love the way when you dig them up you find all those nutshells clinging to the roots. It feels like a miracle.'

'I'd like to try growing pineapples,' Peter said. 'I've heard that if you cut off the leafy part at the top you can just push it into the earth a little way, and it will live.'

'It's true,' Mara said. 'It's the same with paw paw. You just cut off a branch and plant it in the ground. Everything wants to grow here, in the rainy season, that is.'

'I wish we could do that,' Peter said in a low voice. 'I wish we could just disappear together.'

Mara could hear the agony in his voice, as he was torn between this world and the one he'd left behind. She thought of the photograph of him with his family. The happy, innocent faces of the children. Peter's arm resting on his wife's shoulder. She took a deep breath, her hands tightening on the branch.

'You know we can't.' Her voice was barely more than a whisper. But once the words had left her mouth, she could feel the truth that they held. The solution to a complex puzzle seemed to have been evolving deep inside her, and now it had emerged, clear and definite.

Peter nodded, the pain shifting in his eyes.

Mara took another breath. Now it was John's face she pictured. Not the distant, angry, defeated man of recent months, but the one who had greeted her with such joy when she'd arrived here. The one who had gently bathed her face when she had malaria; who had patiently taught her so many things about life in Africa. The one who had stood with her outside the cave, asking her to promise she would never leave him. She felt as though the land that had witnessed her reply was watching her now. 'Even if you were free, I couldn't be with you.'

'I know,' Peter said.

The note of finality in his voice cut Mara's heart. She felt an impulse to take back all she had said. To insist there was another way. She bit her lip, letting the words of denial pass her by unspoken. For a long moment, she did not trust herself to speak. When she did, her voice sounded light, as if she'd left some large, heavy part of herself behind.

'If only we'd met in some other time – some other place. When we were younger . . .'

'Bondi beach.' Peter's tone seemed pitched to match her own. 'I can see you now, your nose all pink from sunburn, a towel over your shoulders, wearing your new bikini.'

'I didn't have a bikini,' Mara said. 'I wore one of those swimsuits with a little skirt. Anyway, I never went to Bondi, I lived in Tasmania, remember? But even if I had, you probably wouldn't have noticed me.'

'You're right,' Peter agreed. 'I always liked blondes.' He smiled to show he was joking, his teeth showing white in the dimness.

Mara laughed, reaching to push him playfully away. As her hand met his shoulder, he turned towards her. Then he froze, staring into her eyes. Mara looked back at him, her heart pounding in her chest. She withdrew her hand, holding it at her side. She could feel the magnetic pull of his body. But she refused to be drawn by it. Instead, she clung to the branch – both hands wrapped around it, as if it were her only hope of rescue.

In the tense quiet that followed, the sounds of the night – the rustlings of insects, the call of night birds, the distant scream of monkeys in the depths of the forest – seemed to press in close around them.

'I won't write to you.' Peter's words broke into the stillness. 'I'd have to write the kind of letter anyone could read, even if I knew they never would. A friendly letter. I don't want that. I want to remember us as we were today.' He looked in the direction of the grass hut. The small dark shape was barely traceable amongst the matching trees and rocks.

'So do I,' Mara said. She imagined the memory of their love like a seed, smooth and perfect, hidden deep inside a piece of fruit. Safe and secret.

'We mustn't hope for anything more,' she said. Her voice surprised her with its certainty. She felt some deep wisdom was guiding her, giving her words she only half wanted to say, but which she knew to be true. 'We could ruin our lives, always wondering, wishing, hoping, waiting. We could come to hate each other for that.' She turned to face Peter, feeling a sudden urgency, a sense that it was deeply important they understood one another properly; that all was made clear. 'We have to say, now, that we'll never see one another again. It's the only way to keep what we've had.'

'We'll never see one another again,' Peter said. His voice cracked. 'But right now – here – I love you. I can't help it. I do.'

Mara saw the shine of tears in his eyes. 'I love you, too. Deep inside, I always will.'

'I didn't mean for it to happen,' Peter said. 'I should've known from the start it would be different, working with you, because

290

you're not an actress. There wasn't going to be that barrier.' He shook his head. 'But it wasn't just that. It's who you are. I've never met anyone like you before, Mara. I love everything about you.'

A long quiet followed his words. Mara felt a deep sadness wash over her. When she finally spoke, her voice was thin and frail. 'I don't know how I'll survive without you.'

Peter looked into her eyes. 'You will. You're stronger than you think. I've seen it in you all along. I can see it now. You are a strong person.'

Mara drank in his words. She wanted to store them up: a source of power she could call upon when needed.

Suddenly, a beam of light appeared over the waterhole. The swathe of black water was transformed into a shining plain, its surface rippling faintly with the night breeze. Lit from the side, the marsh-reeds threw long dark shadows over the mud banks. Everything seemed painted with silver, like a scene from a dream.

From the direction of the lodge came a distant smattering of applause. A moment later, a second beam came on. Two zebras, drinking in the shallows, were caught in the light, their black and white hides showing starkly against the backdrop of silver. They looked around in alarm, before returning to what they'd been doing. On the far shore, a hippo waddled across the mud. Then a gazelle, delicate and timorous, crept through the light towards the glistening mound of a salt rock, its head bobbing rhythmically as it began to lick.

'They don't seem afraid,' Peter whispered.

'They think it's moonlight,' Mara said.

For a long time the two stood there, watching the animals as they strolled in and out of the floodlight like actors playing their parts on a stage. There seemed no shape to the time that was passing; it could have been minutes, it could have been hours. Then, while Mara followed the path of a waterbuck as it walked towards the edge of the light, she noticed something happening in the shadows beyond. Huge chunks of grey, like pieces of the land itself, were on the move. As they came closer to the light, they became more solid, their shapes clearer. Mara's body tensed with surprise as she picked out swinging trunks, thick round legs, little tails, gleaming tusks. She had never seen so many elephants this close to the lodge. Logic told her that the dry season was nearly at an end, and sources of water were now very scarce. But as she watched the mothers and babies walking deep into the waterhole to drink and play together, and the old bulls standing at the edges, waving their heavy heads as though in amazement at the sight, Mara found it possible to believe that the herd had been sent here, especially. That their presence was a sign of hope.

She turned to Peter, wanting to share the emotions that welled up inside her. As his eyes met hers, warmth flowed between them, deep and strong. In that moment, Mara felt certain all would be well. The seed of love would endure for them – a source of strength that would nourish them both, through all the years to come.

SIXTEEN

Mara stood in the main room, looking around her. Alice's collection of antique crockery was back where it belonged, displayed on the shelves of the dining room dresser. Rudi's first-edition Hemingway novels and the biographies of famous game hunters had been removed, and John's leather-bound classics returned to the bookcase. The zebra-skinned stool was gone, along with all the other items that did not belong here. Mara would be able to report to Carlton that everything was back in its original place. Yet, as she scanned the space, she felt puzzled. The atmosphere of the room seemed different, as if some subtle transformation had occurred. Perhaps it was simply the effect of knowing that so many things had been moved around, even if only temporarily. The grip of the past had been loosened; the lodge was no longer locked in time. Things could be changed again.

Mara ran her gaze over the familiar spines of John's books, coming to rest on a well-worn edition of *Grimm's Fairy Tales*. She stared in silence at the printed gold title of the book, words forming in her head: *Once upon a time, in Safariland . . .*

She closed her eyes on a wave of regret. There could be no fairytale ending for her and Peter – by mid-afternoon, they would have said their final goodbye. Last night, they had promised one another not to keep looking back, and to focus instead on finding happiness in their own worlds. But now, the optimism Mara had felt when the elephants appeared at the waterhole, had ebbed away. The task of facing the future rose up before her like a dark and daunting mountain. The thought of even beginning the climb made her feel tired and empty.

Turning her back on the bookcase, she moved to look out of the window. At the far edge of the lawn she could see the top of the boom pole with its fluff-covered microphone. As she leaned closer to the glass, the four figures clustered beneath it came into view: Leonard, Tomba, Jamie – and Peter. They were recording some extra lines Leonard had written overnight, to help cover for some of the scenes that should have included Lillian.

Mara watched Peter bend his head briefly over a sheet of paper, then lift his face towards the place where the microphone hovered. His lips moved. He gestured with his hands, as though the camera were there as well, recording his actions. Then, as he finished the line, he looked to Leonard for his response. As Leonard signalled his approval, holding up both thumbs, Peter glanced back over his shoulder towards the lodge.

Looking for me.

Mara held on to the thought, hugging it close to her, as if it were something warm and alive. She was about to move to a window from which he'd be able to see her, when she heard footsteps out in the hallway: light, brisk steps, tapping across the polished boards. A moment later, Helen came in. She was dressed neatly, as always, her hair pulled tidily back from her face. But Mara noticed something different about her – Helen was wearing lipstick, a deep orange-red tone that matched her hair.

Helen smiled as she met Mara's gaze. 'The kitchen boy showed me in. I hope you don't mind.' She faltered, looking suddenly unsure of herself.

'Of course not,' Mara said, smiling back. 'It's lovely to see you.' Then her face grew serious. 'How's Lillian?' Carlton had visited the hospital yesterday, but Mara was glad of the chance to get a report first hand.

'She's doing really well,' Helen replied. 'But she's keen to have her things. I was going to send Joseph, but I'd feel responsible if anything got left behind or lost.'

'I think Kefa's already started packing the suitcases,' Mara said. 'I'll show you her room.'

She led the way outside, towards Lillian's rondavel. As they reached the hut, she could hear Kefa moving around inside. Helen hurried straight in to join him, but Mara hovered on the doorstep. Her eyes were drawn along the path towards Peter's hut. She wondered if he'd packed yet. She pictured him folding away the clothes that she'd come to know so well. Zipping the cinnamon aftershave into his toilet bag. Slipping the family photograph between the layers of garments. Then pushing everything down into his duffel bag. Pulling the cord tight at the top.

Mara turned back towards Lillian's rondavel, just as Kefa appeared holding two of Lillian's red suitcases. Shortly afterwards, Helen emerged from the doorway, squinting in the strong sunlight. She was carrying several of Lillian's sketchbooks and the framed photograph from the dressing table.

'Lillian mentioned a photo of someone called Theo. She wanted me to take special care of it. But I could only see this.' Helen held out the picture of the shaggy Alsatian dog.

'That's Theo,' Mara said. 'She thinks of him as her family.'

Helen's green-flecked eyes narrowed with what looked like a blend of pity and disbelief. 'Poor girl,' she murmured. 'Well, anyway, she'll be glad to have her drawing things. Believe it or not, she's already bored, being stuck in bed. She started doing portraits of the girls on the backs of old nutrition charts. She can draw quite well – except she's got no idea how the human body is put together. I had to take in Tony's copy of *Gray's Anatomy* for her to look at.'

Mara caught her breath. It was one thing to think that Lillian would benefit from some honest criticism, but quite another to imagine how she'd react to it.

'She was fascinated,' Helen continued. 'Tony'll be lucky to get it back!'

Mara raised her eyebrows in surprise. 'So, everything's going all right?'

'Oh yes,' Helen said. 'She's sleeping, eating. The girls adore her. She's going to start helping with their lessons when she's a bit better.'

'You're managing okay with the food?'

'Yes, it's no trouble at all. I've been making those one-pot dinners – that way it's easy to carry her meal across to the ward in one bowl.'

Mara almost smiled. 'And there's been no mention of separate dishes?'

'Well, actually, the first time the girls took her meal over, Lillian did say something about that. But Hilary just explained how every-one had to eat what they were given, and be grateful. Nothing more was said.' Helen leaned towards Mara, as though she had a secret to share. 'Tony thinks Lillian needs to stay for at least another week, and maybe longer, to make a full recovery. I hope she does. We love having her.'

Listening to Helen speak, Mara realised that her vision of the mission ward as a sanctuary had proved true. She imagined Lillian surrounded by Helen's daughters, having her hair brushed by one of them, her eyes closed as she listened to the childish voices talk-ing, singing, laughing . . .

'Thank you for taking care of her,' Mara said.

'It makes a nice change having another European woman around. You'll have to visit us, as soon as you've recovered from all these guests.' Helen gave Mara a sympathetic smile. 'I bet you can't wait for them to be gone. From what Lillian's told me, it must have been very hectic around here. And then, of course, you'll be looking forward to John getting back.'

Mara swallowed a lump in her throat, managing only to nod in response. She wished, suddenly, that she, like Lillian, could take refuge in Helen's safe, calm world. At that moment, Kefa appeared again in the doorway. He was holding out the pink sombrero and Lillian's *L'Air du Temps*.

'These are the last items.'

Helen reached for the hat, but left the bottle of perfume in his hands. 'I'm not taking that. Lillian wants you to have the perfume, Mara.'

As Mara took the bottle, her eyes were caught by the frosted glass stopper, formed in the shape of twin doves. She remembered the first time she'd seen it, as Lillian was unpacking her possessions. How romantic it had seemed to her, the way the two beaks were touching, suggesting a kiss. The symbol of love had saddened her then, reminding her of her own unhappiness. She could never have imagined what the next weeks would bring.

Now, as she looked at the glass sculpture again, Mara noticed something that had not struck her before. The birds' wings were spread. The doves were not resting on a branch, but meeting in mid-flight. Seconds later, they would part, and fly on. But the precious moment of their kiss had been captured forever, moulded in solid glass. The thought was strangely comforting. Mara lifted the bottle to her face. Even without removing the lid, she could smell the perfume, rich and sweet.

'It's a beautiful bottle,' Helen said.

'Yes, it is,' Mara said.

Kefa brought the last suitcase from inside. Tucking the smallest of them under his arm, he picked up the other two.

'Shall I take them to your car?' he asked Helen.

'Thank you,' Helen said, inclining her head towards him. She turned to Mara. 'You're lucky to have such a good house boy.'

'House boy,' Mara repeated. As always, the name sounded strange for a man of forty, the father of five children. But now, when she thought about how willingly and expertly Kefa had stepped into her place, taking over the running of the lodge, it seemed wrong as well. 'Actually, he's not the house boy,' she found herself saying. 'He is our lodge manager.'

'I am sorry,' Helen said to Kefa. 'I must have misheard the

kitchen boy.' She looked from Mara's dress to the African man's shirt. 'I should have guessed from your uniform.'

'Please, do not apologise,' Kefa said politely. Then he bent his head for a moment. When he lifted his gaze, Mara saw a faint sheen of tears in his dark brown eyes.

The hut boys were loading luggage into the zebra-striped Land Rovers. The vehicle Lillian had crashed was a sorry sight: the damaged front bumper bar had been removed, the mudguards were missing as well, and one headlamp was broken. As Dudu had described it, the Land Rover 'could still walk, but had only one eye'.

Mara watched numbly as each piece of luggage disappeared from view. Peter was not travelling in either Land Rover – he'd opted to fly out later in the day, along with Carlton and Leonard. But Mara was acutely aware that once the crew was gone, the final parting with Peter would not be far away. The official goodbyes had already taken place. The staff of the lodge had gathered with everyone from the film company on the lawn outside the dining room. Expressions of friendship, humour and sadness had been freely exchanged. Mara had been struck by how different the scene was from the one that had taken place out here in the car park the day the visitors arrived.

Mara became aware that the village carver was hovering beside her, his presence betrayed by the raw green smell of sap. He began a long, formal greeting, enquiring about the state of her home, her work, her food, her health.

'*Nzuri tu*,' she kept saying. 'It is well.'

It is well. It is well.

The words began to sound like a charm. She felt a mad, wild hope that – if uttered enough times – they might contain the power to change the inevitable. To make the impossible come true.

'I have not been sleeping, only working,' the carver said. 'I have made some special carvings.' He smiled, showing teeth edged with black, as if he'd been chewing charcoal. 'Everyone likes them. I have only a few left.'

He reached into his basket and pulled out a sample to show Mara. It was one of the plaques bearing words and decorations, in the style she'd seen before. The letters spelled out Raynor Lodge. Beneath them were two heads shown in profile. The carver had applied the same skill in crafting them that he used to capture the likeness of wild animals: the images were clearly recognisable.

They were portraits of Lillian Lane and Peter Heath.

Mara traced the carved contours of Peter's face with her fingertips. She was reminded of busts engraved on gravestones: symbols of people who were forever lost. She handed the plaque back.

'It's very good,' she said, her voice faint. Then she stared ahead, trying to erase the image from her mind.

The passengers had begun assembling. Over near the archway, Rudi, Brendan, the two Nicks, the ranger and Jamie stood together laughing and talking, smoking cigarettes. Suddenly, a ragged cheer rose up. As Mara looked around, seeking its cause, Tomba came sprinting into view, breathless with exertion and holding a cloth bundle to his chest. He wore new trousers, and his cowboy shirt had been freshly washed and ironed. Grinning broadly, he tossed the bundle into the back of the nearest Land Rover. Mara remembered hearing that Daudi had offered to introduce Jamie's protégé to some wildlife filmmakers in Dar es Salaam. When Tomba's eyes met Mara's he grinned again, his excitement about his trip almost palpable. She responded with an uncertain smile. It occurred to her that she should go and find out the details of his plans. But just as she took a step towards him, she saw Daudi enter the parking area, aiming in her direction. He was accompanied by one of the hut boys, who was carrying a cardboard suitcase on his head. Its side was plastered with a large paper label bearing the words *Government of Tanzania, Ministry for Information.*

Daudi came to a halt in front of Mara. He was dressed in his brown suit, his shoes shining like twin mirrors at the bottoms of his trouser-legs.

'Everything has turned out for the best,' he said. 'This film will be good for Tanzania. People will remember us. Kabeya will be pleased. The president himself will be pleased. You have played your part well.'

'Thank you.' Mara bowed her head. 'I've appreciated all the help you have given. I know Carlton and Leonard are very grateful, too.'

It was true. During the shoot, Daudi had always been ready to offer his assistance, whether it involved liaising with the village people, or helping Kefa bring the Somalis back into line. The only time he'd interfered with the filming was when Leonard had wanted to include some young cattle herders in a shot. Daudi had insisted they be given new loin cloths to wear first, arguing that Tanzanians should not be shown to the world looking ragged and dirty.

'Your husband will be very pleased.' Daudi gestured back over his shoulder at the lodge. 'You will make a good business here, now. But what you need is a Tanzanian partner – an African. That is the path of the future.'

Mara nodded. 'Thank you for your advice. I wish you a good safari.'

Daudi shook her hand, smiling warmly. Then he turned towards the Land Rover.

'Daudi!' Mara called out. 'Wait.'

He looked back at her, raising his eyebrows.

'Take care of Tomba, won't you,' Mara said. 'If he can't find work, send him back here. I'll repay your costs.'

Daudi smiled, but shook his head. 'He is not a child. He is a man.'

Reaching the vehicle, he shooed away the hut boys, who were still collecting tips from the guests. 'You have been paid, that is enough. Do not beg. Where is your pride?'

He glanced back at Mara with a rueful look. She smiled, feeling a rush of affection for this man who was always working towards his vision for a new sense of nationhood, and who seemed undaunted by the task that lay ahead of him.

When Daudi was settled into his seat, the drivers started their engines and drove off, one behind the other. The hut boys ran after them, the pale soles of their feet flashing briefly into view, then vanishing as they pounded the sun-baked earth. Mara waved until the Land Rovers disappeared out of sight, leaving only a thick cloud of dust.

Menelik's coffee was strong and sweet. Leonard, Carlton, Peter and Mara sat in the dining room sipping the steaming black brew from tiny earthenware bowls.

Peter had on the blue shirt he'd worn the day he arrived. Mara rested her gaze on the fine linen cloth, already creased in the heat. She recalled the moment of their first encounter, when she'd mistaken him for a member of the crew and told him to choose another room. It seemed to have happened so long ago, yet it was only a little over two weeks. Sixteen days. Such a short time, yet it had changed everything.

Peter lifted his face, his eyes seeking hers. He didn't speak; the time for that had gone, and everything they had to say to one another had already been said. But a current flowed between them, warm and strong.

The scent of frankincense wafted on the air from a burner Menelik had set up near the door. Along with the quiet in the room, it helped create a sense that a ritual was taking place in here, something deep and old and layered with meaning. The only reminder of normality was the distant sound of the hut boys chattering as they cleaned the rondavels. Mara pictured them brushing the floor of Peter's room, stripping his bed of linen – removing the last traces of his presence.

Carlton stirred, looking at his watch. 'Do you think he'll come?'

'Yes,' Mara said. 'There was a message sent from the mission. It's all confirmed. The plane should be here any time now.'

In the stillness, a moth battered the window with its wings. Minutes passed, timeless.

Then, at last, the faint drone of the aircraft engine broke the quiet – barely noticeable at first, but quickly growing louder, like a swarm of angry bees approaching.

Everyone stood up. The travellers reached for their camera bags, water bottles and jackets. Their luggage was already down at the landing strip, being guarded by some young men from the village, who would also have the task of clearing the strip of wildlife when the plane approached. Mara crossed to the bar and picked up a shotgun and a belt of ammunition she'd laid out ready to take down to the plain.

'So, you're the ranger, now,' Peter said.

Mara smiled. 'Don't worry. I'll keep you safe.' She listened to herself speak, surprised at how normal she sounded.

'Let's go, then,' Carlton said. His voice was loud and over-bright, matching the tones of his tropical shirt.

There was no more talk, after that. Small sounds choked the air. Footsteps seemed slow and muffled. Time stretched out, shapeless, as though they were all lost in a dream.

Then, suddenly, they were outside, walking through the grounds. Carlton led the quiet procession, followed by Leonard and then Peter. Mara came next, the shotgun weighing down on her shoulder. She watched Peter's feet moving in front of her and her stride fell in with his, matching the rhythm of his tread. She was aware of Menelik and Kefa following behind her, and the hut boys and kitchen boys as well.

They passed under the archway, the old tusks curving above their heads. Then they set off along the tree-lined track. Soon they neared the place where a path led to the lookout. Mara saw Peter's step falter, as if, just for a moment, he was considering changing direction. But he kept on.

Emerging from the trees, they stepped out onto the plain. As one, they all stopped, looking up. The plane was in view: a dark bird in the blue sky, growing larger as it approached.

Already, the tribesmen were running along the landing strip, waving their cattle-herding sticks. Geese flew up ahead of them, and grazing animals – small gazelles, and a pair of dik-diks – bounded away, kicking up their hind legs in strange, extravagant gestures of alarm.

The plane circled once above the lodge, flying lower and lower. It was not an aircraft Mara had seen before: like the Manyala Land Rovers, it was painted with zebra stripes. As she followed the others towards the strip, she watched the pilot manoeuvring the plane into a perfect approach. He brought the craft expertly to the ground, both wheels touching down evenly, the wings barely wavering.

The plane came to a standstill, the propellers still roaring, pushing back a blast of air. As Mara stepped forward, ready to greet the pilot, she was met by a volley of dry grass fragments and dead leaves. She narrowed her eyes against the stinging assault, and half-turned her face away. While she was still waiting for the propellers to begin to slow, the pilot's door opened and a man climbed out. He waved a folded map towards her.

'Is this Raynor Lodge?' he yelled through the noise of the engine. When Mara nodded, he looked relieved. 'I'm new around here.' He spoke with a strong South African accent. Holding up one wrist, he poked his finger at the face of a large gold watch. 'We'll have to get going straightaway.'

Mara shook her head in dismay as she took in the meaning of his words – that the departure was going to be hurried, the noise of the engine stealing the chance of last words of farewell.

'I'm on a tight schedule,' the pilot shouted. 'Sorry.'

Mara stared mutely at him for a moment, then signalled to the hut boys to bring over the luggage.

The pilot turned towards Leonard, Carlton and Peter, beckoning them impatiently. 'Come on! Let's get going!'

Peter hung back as Carlton and Leonard hurried across to the plane.

'If you're ever in LA,' Carlton shouted as he reached Mara. 'Look us up.'

'Good luck with everything!' Leonard added.

They both shook her hand, the gesture feeling strange and formal out here on the plains, with the wind blowing dust into their faces and whipping at their clothes. After exchanging waves and smiles with Kefa, Menelik and the boys, they headed towards the passenger door, bent over, cowering instinctively from the roar of the propeller.

Mara turned as Peter reached her side. She stared at him, strands of hair blowing across her face, the ends battering her cheeks. The wind gathered his hair, pulling it back, leaving his face looking bare and vulnerable.

Mara stared into his eyes, a wave of pain rising inside her. In a moment, she felt sure it would burst out, wrenching her apart. She hugged her arms around her body, trying to hold herself together.

Through a film of tears, she saw his hand reaching out across the small space between them. She felt her own hand rising to meet it. Then there was the warmth of his skin meeting hers. Fingers folding over fingers. Flesh pressing against flesh.

For a long moment, their hands clung together, grasping tight, as though it might be possible to fuse them into a single entity.

Then Peter let her go, abandoning her hand to the empty air. Tearing his eyes from hers, he half-ran towards the open doorway, his camera jogging at his thigh, his shirt snapping against his body.

As he put his foot on the fold-down step, he paused for just a second, looking back over his shoulder. Then he was gone, swallowed up inside the craft; his face nothing more than a blurred shape behind the dust-scoured glass of the window.

The pilot closed the passenger door – a hollow bang that cut through the whine of the engine. Then he saluted Mara, and returned to his place in the cabin.

The plane eased forward tentatively, at first, then it bumped away along the runway, gathering speed. The Africans waved and shouted, but Mara stood rigid and silent. Inside her a cry of raw pain rose up, following the path of the plane as it lifted smoothly into the air. Mara watched it climb, higher and higher, until it was, again, a dark bird winging across the sky.

She followed the arc of its journey, across the plains, towards the escarpment. She was dimly aware of the sounds of others leaving, the hut boys chattering as they set off, their voices overlaid with the deeper tones of a man. But she stayed there, frozen, as if by standing still she might be able to prevent time from moving on.

At last, the plane faded to a speck, then disappeared over the far horizon.

'They are gone.'

The voice came to her, soft and deep, accompanied by footsteps, and a rustle of cloth. She breathed the faint smoky perfume of frankincense.

Menelik moved round to stand in front of her, a thin, straight figure, set starkly against the open landscape. A breeze stirred his white tunic and sun glinted from the Coptic cross that hung from a cord around his neck.

The old man looked straight at Mara, his gaze steady and intense. As her eyes met his, Mara felt the power of his presence reaching out to her, breaking in through the haze of her pain. She imagined, in that moment, that he knew everything about her. Like a prophet, he had the power to look beyond what others could see. He understood all that she was feeling. A wave of relief swept through her. Tears welled up in her eyes, then overflowed, running freely down her cheeks.

Menelik made no move towards her. Nor did he seem to feel any need to ask questions or offer words of sympathy. He just stood, watching her weep. A deep stillness flowed out from him, crossing the space between them. Gradually, Mara felt it entering her, bringing a healing calm.

As her tears finally slowed, the old man nodded in the direction of the lodge. 'Now, it is time to go,' he said. There was a gentle look in his eyes, but his tone was firm. He set off towards the track, glancing back, after a few steps, to check Mara was following.

Hitching the strap of her shotgun onto her shoulder, she walked after him, matching his pace, drawn on by his steady steps over the sunburnt ground.

They walked in silence, the quiet broken only by their footfall, and the cries of waterbirds. Soon, they reached the place where the track led in amongst the trees. Menelik turned, again, to look at Mara. There was a faint smile on his face. When he spoke, his voice was strong and clear.

'*Kesho ni siku nyingine,*' he said.

Tomorrow it will be a new day.

SEVENTEEN

Mara stood beside the swimming pool hole watching two of Carlton's construction workers wielding shovels full of red earth. The men were labouring hard, stripped to their waists, sun gleaming off their sweat-slicked shoulders. The excavation was almost complete: the earthen sides of the hole were steep and smooth, the corners square. Soon, the concrete would be poured. Mara tried to imagine a blue-painted pool, brimming with water. But it felt unreal to her, as though it were part of a dream from which she would soon awaken. Turning her back on the workers, Mara cast her eyes over the lodge grounds, taking in all the signs that a new era really had begun. In the ten days since everyone had left, sets of matching tables and benches had been crafted from local timber, and an extension to the shower hut had been built. Over in the compound Mara could see the roofline of the enlarged hen coop. And there was the sound of hammering coming from the other side of the main building, where the observation deck was being assembled. Meanwhile, the hut boys, assisted by some new employees, were hard at work in the rondavels, preparing for the first influx of guests, poached from a tour group by Carlton as he'd passed through Dar es Salaam. They were due to arrive soon.

And so was John.

Earlier today, Kefa had received a message on the newly repaired radio. The Bwana was at Kisaki, Kefa had reported to Mara. He was heading home, direct from the Selous. He wanted to leave his Land Rover in Kikuyu for some repairs. His wife was to drive in and meet him at the Hotel. At eleven o-clock, tomorrow.

Mara felt a twist of panic tightening inside her as she pictured her husband's return. She tried to focus on how excited and amazed he would be by the developments at the lodge. And how relieved, also, when he learned the future of the place had been secured. But even as she tried to evoke these optimistic scenarios, she found herself swamped by a torment of questions.

How could she bear to face John, pretending nothing had changed? And even if she could, surely John would be able to tell – to feel – what had taken place? Sooner or later, she would have to explain what had happened. But what would she say? That she'd fallen in love with another man? That she'd kissed him, and held his body in her arms? The truth was so much more compli- cated than it sounded. She and Peter had made love only in front of Leonard's camera. And the journey they'd taken was not something they had planned. At each step, they'd responded to what was asked of them – to help Leonard and Carlton rescue the film, to protect Lillian, to save Raynor Lodge. They'd done nothing wrong.

And yet . . . Something deep and powerful had taken place between them. Mara could still feel its aura, surrounding her like the heat of the sun. She stepped back and leaned against a jacaranda tree, resting her head on the smooth trunk. As she gazed through the feathery fronds of the leaves, an image of Peter came to her, sharp and strong. She saw the moulded planes of his face. The lock of hair falling over his brow. His blue-green eyes.

She saw his mouth forming the words that seemed printed on her soul.

You're so beautiful. I love you. I can't help it. I do.

Mara folded her arms across her body as the pain of Peter's departure came back to her; the dust and noise of the plane, stealing their last words, the final touch cut short.

She closed her eyes. Peter would be home by now, back with his children. And Paula. A vision of the couple's reunion began to unroll in Mara's mind, vivid and painful. She forced herself to cut it off. Peter's life had nothing to do with her. She would never see him again. Their story was finished. Her future lay here at the lodge, with John.

Mara shook her head helplessly, exhausted by the thoughts and emotions that flooded her body, forming eddies of confusion, and great waves of despair. A deep fatigue seemed lodged in her bones. She felt like retreating to her bed, even though she'd not even made it through half of the day.

Slowly she became aware of footsteps approaching. She straightened up, just as Kefa came to stand in front of her. He smiled, then gestured in the direction of the dining room.

'Menelik has served coffee for you. I have put the reservations book on the table.'

'Thank you,' Mara responded. She remembered, now, agreeing to look at the bookings so she could help Kefa calculate the supplies that would be needed.

'I will check on this work,' Kefa said. He was eyeing the men, who had now laid down their shovels and were taking turns to drink from a water gourd. 'Then I shall join you.'

'Yes. Good,' Mara said. She knew her voice sounded flat, bleak.

Kefa turned back to her, his gaze sweeping her face. 'Don't worry. Everything will ready when the Bwana returns.'

'I know. I'm not worried,' Mara said.

A silence lengthened between them. Mara saw uncertainty in Kefa's eyes. She knew he was anxious about John's return, as well. Since Kefa had been promoted to lodge manager, he'd been enjoying his new authority and the extra responsibility that went with it. But soon, Mara would no longer be the Bwana Memsahib. And what would happen then?

'The coffee is waiting,' Kefa said, a mask of courtesy falling over his face. 'It will become cold.'

The reservations book was a simple cloth-bound diary with a page for each day. John bought one at the beginning of each year, from Bina's emporium. As Mara drew it towards her, she felt the roughness of the cloth where white ants had been at work. The sensation seemed exaggerated, as though she'd lost her reference point to reality. Everything seemed either distant, like the idea of finishing the pool, or too close and overpowering, like the smell of Menelik's coffee, steaming in a cup at her elbow. He had served it in the Ethiopian style, with a sprig of rue immersed in the brew. Usually, Mara liked the unusual twinning of flavours, the herb and the coffee, but today the pungent aroma was enough to turn her stomach.

Pushing the cup away, she opened the book. Flicking past the sparsely filled pages that represented the first half of the year, she reached Carlton's booking. There, a red line running down the middle of each page indicated that the whole lodge had been reserved, day after day after day. Mara knew the information she was looking for lay in dates that were yet to come. But still, she found herself pausing on each of the red-marked pages, as if the day it symbolised could somehow be retrieved.

Reaching the end of the film company's booking – the day when Peter had climbed into the plane and flown away – she made herself move steadily on, the passing dates plotting the journey away from his presence, and towards John's return. The long days and wakeful nights filled with mixed joy and pain.

Suddenly, Mara paused, her hand poised over a page. Lifting her gaze, she met the glassy stare of Raynor's prized buffalo head. But she barely registered its presence. A thought rose up, pressing itself into her consciousness, insistent, like a bird tapping at a window. It had come to her before, but she had managed to push it aside, blaming stress, or the long hours she'd been working. But now she could hide from it no longer. There was, she knew, another meaning to be drawn from all the pages she had turned. Somewhere in that time, her period should have come. She'd never before been more than three or four days late. Yet she knew, without having to the check the dates, she must be nearly two weeks overdue. Right now, sitting here, she could feel that her body had changed. There was a heaviness inside her, a strange fullness.

She bent her head, pressing her face into her cupped hands. She thought back to John's last night, before he had left for Dar es

Salaam. The brief, cold meeting of their bodies. She remembered how they had turned away from one another as soon as the act was done, rolling over, pretending sleep was calling. Yet at that very moment, a new life was being created. A baby that was hers and John's.

Mara tried to conjure an image of herself as a mother, a shawl-wrapped baby in her arms. And John at her side; a proud, happy father. She tried to picture a young boy climbing the trees in the lodge grounds. Or a daughter, the apple of her father's eye . . .

Our dreams are coming true.

She formed the words in her head.

The lodge has been saved, she reminded herself. A baby is coming. It is a time to celebrate.

But the words held no substance, and as she grasped at their meaning, they spun away beyond her reach, like thistledown in the air.

The hotel dining room smelled of stale beer and cigarette smoke and fried food. Mara chose a table near an open window, turning her face towards the fresh air as she settled herself into a chair. Almost immediately, a young waiter appeared at her elbow. He gave her a broad smile.

'Good morning, Memsahib. Can I offer you breakfast?' he asked. He spoke English carefully, shaping each word in turn.

'No, thank you,' Mara said. 'Just a lime soda, please.'

'Can I offer you lunch?' asked the waiter. 'It would be my pleasure.'

Mara raised her eyebrows, surprised at his solicitousness; the staff here were usually less than eager to take orders, even at meal times.

'No, thank you,' she repeated. 'But my husband will be joining me and he may wish to eat.' She glanced towards the doorway. 'I'm not sure how long he will be.'

The waiter bowed his head courteously. 'Please relax while you wait, Memsahib. I shall find you the coldest soda in the fridge.'

Still puzzled, Mara watched him hurry away to the bar. Then she turned back to the window. It opened onto a paved courtyard with a small dry garden bed running along one side. A chicken scratched there, amongst low-growing succulent plants, their leaves green and plump as if they had access to some secret source of sustenance. At the far end there was a grille fence through which a small section of the street was visible. Mara peered past the metal bars, study-ing the scene – anything to avoid letting her thoughts return to the question of what she should say to John. She'd spent half the night trying to decide where to begin; in the dawn, she had returned to the dilemma, but still reached no conclusion. She looked at an old leper, who was squatting in the shade with a begging tin. A couple of young men were sitting astride stationary bicycles, talking to a woman selling bananas. She was dressed in a colourful caftan with a matching turban. She was not from this area, Mara told herself, her build was heavy and her skin too light . . .

Suddenly, Mara's gaze became fixed. There, on the opposite side of the road, was a European man in khaki clothing. He had his back to her and wore a hat that concealed his hair. Still, Mara recognised him instantly. She half-rose to her feet. Now she could see John's Land Rover, parked nearby. A boy, presumably commissioned to watch over it, sat on the dust-caked front bonnet. As Mara shifted her eyes back to John, he lifted his arm to look at his watch. Glancing towards the clock behind the bar, she saw it was only a minute or two before eleven. She nodded to herself. Trust John to arrive right on time after a journey he would have begun at first light, so many miles away.

Several minutes passed before John appeared in the dining room. He'd come via the washroom: in contrast to his creased, stained clothes, his face was freshly washed and his hair neatly combed. Mara stood to greet him, trying to offer a welcoming smile, but John's face looked strained. Mara felt her tension deepening. Perhaps he had arrived in Kikuyu earlier on and carried out some errands. Someone could easily have told him about the film company coming to the lodge. And how his wife had played the part of an actress. On the other hand, after five weeks in the bush on foot, and then a long drive, he might just be exhausted.

John leaned towards Mara, kissing her quickly on the cheek, his dry lips barely brushing her skin. As he pulled away she caught the fresh smell of soap overlaying old sweat and kerosene.

'Sorry, I'm filthy.' He sat down. 'I put the clients on the train at Morogoro and came straight here, up through the Masai Steppe.'

'That's a long trip,' Mara commented. She wondered if her voice sounded as hollow to John as it did to her.

John put his Land Rover keys down on the table. He seemed to study them lying there, for a moment, then looked up, directly at Mara. 'There was no point in going to Dar to see the agent. I've decided to close the lodge.'

Mara stared at him, her lips parted. In the quiet, the creak of a ceiling fan could be heard.

'It's never going to work, I see that now,' John continued. 'The game-watching safaris were just a dream.' His tone was firm, leaving no room for uncertainty. 'And I've decided I'm not going to take clients hunting any more.' He looked down at his hands, resting on the tabletop. 'I've had a lot of time to think, Mara. The people I was with on safari weren't hunters. In five weeks, I didn't fire a shot.'

'What were they doing then?' Mara asked. She was aware she was speaking just to avoid a silence.

'Zoologists,' John said. 'They were doing a transect survey, counting all the animals in a particular area. A couple of them were elephant experts. I helped them track a herd for two weeks straight. One night, they asked me how many elephants I'd shot in my life. Do you know what I answered?'

Mara shook her head.

'I checked my notebook. Two hundred and sixty-seven.' John raised his eyes, looking into Mara's face. 'I made a decision that night. I won't be shooting another elephant. I know I've said that before. But this time I won't be going back on it.'

Mara nodded mutely. She knew she was hearing words that should make her happy. Words she'd longed to hear. But their meaning felt disconnected with her life, her marriage . . .

'I've got a plan worked out,' John went on. 'There was a game department ranger out there with us. He says they're looking for people to work in tsetse control.' An ironic smile curled his lips. 'Finding ways to kill flies. I'll be travelling around. You'll live in Arusha.'

'Arusha,' Mara repeated, trying to hide her confusion.

'You'll like it,' John stated. 'Shops. Lots of Europeans. A very good club.'

Mara picked up a paper coaster and began tearing it apart. Now was the perfect time to tell John she was pregnant. A baby would be part of this new life he was laying out for them. But the simple words she needed to say refused to form. Then the waiter arrived with her drink. As he placed it carefully on the table, shifting a new paper coaster to place beneath it, John ordered a soda for himself.

'Yes, Bwana,' the boy replied. He hovered, then, at Mara's elbow, as if awaiting further instructions.

'Thank you. That's all,' she said.

He leaned towards her a little. 'Memsahib, I am a good waiter. I can wash dishes. I can do laundry.' He straightened up and smiled. 'I would like to work for you.'

'But you have a good job already,' Mara said lightly.

'I want to work at Raynor Lodge,' the boy insisted. 'My cousin has just been given a job there.'

From the corner of her eye Mara could see John frowning as he tried to make sense of this exchange. It was not surprising. When he'd set out on safari, the skeleton staff at the lodge were not even receiving regular wages.

Mara looked past the waiter towards the bar, hoping to discourage him from continuing. She saw the new hotelier, Mr Abassi, coming in from the kitchen. He was dressed smartly in a pressed shirt that was startlingly white against his black skin, and he moved with the air of someone who was perpetually busy. Mara knew he was aware of recent developments at the lodge and was not sure whether he now saw the place as a business competitor, or as an ally in the development of a local tourist industry. Either way, when he met her gaze, Abassi waved and came straight over to their table. The waiter hurried away.

Abassi greeted John first, enquiring about his safari. Mara listened anxiously, concerned he might refer to events that had happened in John's absence. She needed a chance to explain it all in her own way. But she needn't have worried; the greetings moved smoothly from the safari to the health of Abassi's wife and children.

Finally, there was a break in the exchange. Abassi turned his attention to Mara.

'I have most of Kefa's order ready. But we don't have enough whiskey or gin. We expect a delivery this week.'

Mara just nodded. She didn't dare look at John. In the history of the lodge, Africans had never been allowed to take charge of supplies. And now the man John knew as the house boy was ordering alcohol.

'I don't understand,' John said quietly.

Mara swallowed hard, but gave no response.

'What's going on?'

Abassi's face was alive with interest as he took in the rising tension. The waiter, appearing with John's soda, stayed to watch the scene as well.

'We need to talk,' Mara said. 'But not here.'

They emptied their glasses quickly, avoiding one another's gaze, then rose to their feet and left.

They drove the two Land Rovers to Wallimohammed's yard.

There, John took his rucksack from his vehicle and stowed it in Mara's, along with his gun. He did this in silence, as Mara looked on; clearly, this place was no more suitable than the hotel for a private conversation. Now and then, their eyes met, but only for an instant. Mara was glad when one of the mechanics appeared, wiping his hands on a greasy cloth. John led him across to his Land Rover, speaking quickly in Swahili as he went. After heaving up the bonnet, the two bent over the engine.

To escape the heat, Mara crossed to the patchy shade of a straggly thorn tree. She felt tired, again, and daunted by what lay ahead. To distract herself, she thought of her last visit to this place, remembering her mixed feelings of horror and awe as she'd looked at the ruined shed and the burial mounds the elephants had made. She wondered whether John's elephant experts had ever heard of an occurrence like this. Perhaps they had extraordinary stories of their own to share?

Mara hunted for another topic to fill her mind. She recalled her recent trip to the mission, to say goodbye to Lillian. Helen and the girls had been with her when Mara arrived; conversation was limited to Lillian's desire to get home to her dog, her gratitude to Mara and the Hemden family, and her sadness about having to part from them all. Mara had lingered, half hoping for, and half dreading, a chance to be alone with Lillian, wondering if they would then talk about Peter. But the opportunity for a private talk had never arisen.

The bang of the bonnet being slammed shut drew Mara's attention back to John. He was already striding towards her Land Rover, beckoning to his wife as he went. While she was still approaching, he swung open the driver's door, and climbed inside. Mara's step faltered. She reminded herself that John had always driven when they were together. He was, after all, a more experienced driver. And the Land Rover was actually his. But still, as she altered her course, aiming for the passenger seat, she felt as if all her newly found strength and courage were in danger of being stripped away.

Mara watched the last buildings of Kikuyu slide past the window. Soon the Land Rover was passing through an open woodland of thorn trees and bushes, interrupted only by the occasional mud hut and its patch of garden.

John glanced sideways at Mara. It was clear he was waiting for her explanation, now they were in the privacy of their vehicle.

Mara licked her lips tensely. This was still not the setting she wanted for what she had to say. 'Let's not talk, yet,' she said. 'We could stop at the picnic place.'

John frowned, then shrugged. 'All right. If that's what you want.'

Mara picked up his impatience, but pretended not to. She forced a bright tone into her voice. 'We haven't been there for ages.'

It was true. Yet there had been a time – back in the days when she and John still dreamed together about their future – when they had always stopped there for a break on their way home from Kikuyu, enjoying an interlude of peace before returning to the everlasting list of chores that awaited them at the lodge. They used to carry their picnic to a special spot that was a short walk up from the road. And there, from the vantage point of a grassy glade set amid tall pillars of sandstone, they would gaze across the plains at Raynor Lodge. The house and the outbuildings, the paths and gardens were laid out in miniature, like a model village. It was like looking at their lives from an outsider's perspective: all imperfections were wiped out by the softening effects of distance.

Mara took a deep calming breath as the Land Rover ground its way over the rough road. Perhaps, she thought, the place would work its magic on them today. Somehow she would find the right words, and say the right things. The way ahead would become clear.

The midday heat pressed down on Mara's bare head as she followed John up the narrow track, winding through a thicket of low-growing thorn trees. He walked with his usual deliberate step, expertly dodging the prickly branches that reached into his path. He held the gun in his hand. As he moved, the sun gleamed on the oiled barrel. It kept catching Mara's eye. She knew he'd had to bring the gun with him, even though they were only going a short distance from the Land Rover: no responsible person would leave a firearm – let alone a 375 magnum, with its ammunition stowed ready in its magazine – inside an unattended vehicle. Nevertheless, the presence of the gun seemed charged with meaning, coming so soon after John's talk of not hunting any more.

The sound of weaverbirds, twittering as they crafted their nests, accompanied the steady beat of John and Mara's footsteps. They did not speak as they walked, instead continuing the silence they'd adopted during the drive from Kikuyu.

Emerging from the scrubland, they followed a faint animal trail that led them to a steep-sided gully. The track wound on, round the corner, until it ended in a small cul-de-sac. On windy days, Mara and John used to take shelter in there. But today the air was still. They stopped in the place where they preferred to sit – on a natural sandstone bench set in the mouth of the gully, overlooking the valley.

They took their places side by side, a small gap between them. Then they both stared in silence down towards their home. From this position, it looked unchanged. A thicket of fever trees hid the viewing platform and the grass hut blended into the landscape. There were no obvious signs that the place John had decided to close down was now a thriving centre of activity.

Mara opened her mouth as if she were ready to speak, but no words formed on her tongue. She thought about the baby, imagining its tiny form held deep inside her. She told herself that becoming parents would bring her and John close again. But even as she tried to believe that, her thoughts turned to Peter. He was lost to her, she knew, yet his presence seemed part of her every thought, her every breath. She couldn't see how it was possible for her to go on living with John, let alone fall in love with him again. And she couldn't imagine how her marriage would survive her telling him about Peter. She'd considered saying nothing – letting her secret stand alongside John's. But she'd already experienced the effects of remaining silent. She knew how all the unsaid words piled up, creating a wall that could not be breached. She'd thought of revealing that she knew about his affair with Matilda. But she sensed that even this would not be enough to counter John's jealousy, and his belief that he'd been rejected. Finally, she'd examined the idea of postponing any confrontation for a time – perhaps until after the baby was born. Or even longer. But Carlton had promised to hold a screening of the film in the hall in Kikuyu, and – although Mara believed Leonard when he said no one would ever recognise her in Maggie's scenes – she couldn't imagine sitting beside John, watching . . . The fact was she had to tell him now – even though she knew, with a heavy certainty, he would never be able to understand or accept what had happened.

Mara stared silently into the distance, a sense of panic rising inside her. There was no choice, no more time. Her eyes followed the movements of an eagle as it glided in a wide slow circle on outstretched tawny wings. She imagined it swooping down and picking her up, lifting her away out of her life . . .

Suddenly, she felt John's hand on her arm. She understood the gesture instantly – it meant his hunter's ears, his honed instincts, had picked up on something unusual. She saw that John's attention was fixed on the entrance to the gully.

There, the tips of two yellow-white tusks came into view around the rocks, followed by a grey trunk, delicately curved. Then, by degrees, the rest of the animal became visible – the broad head with its tiny eyes, the huge yet gracefully planted feet, the massive chest, the ears that mirrored the shape of a map of Africa.

'She's not bothered by us,' John murmured, though he remained unmoving. Mara, too, stayed perfectly still.

The elephant grazed casually as she walked into the gully. Now and then she swept the ground with her trunk. Mara guessed she was picking up the scent the two humans had left behind: she was treading the same path they had taken.

The giant form was less than twenty feet away. Mara could hear the rasping sound of rough skin rubbing against rough skin as the animal strolled along. She towered over the bushes, a creature of power and majesty, her face, with its leathery deep-lined skin, suggesting the presence of an ancient wisdom.

Mara glanced sideways at John. She saw an expression of awe on his face, too. A look of shared wonder passed between them. It was almost as if there were some link between the appearance, here, of this beautiful animal, and John's pledge never to kill an elephant again. It sent a surge of warmth through Mara's body.

Then the elephant stopped. The huge ragged ears rose out from each side of the head: a clear gesture of warning or annoyance. John tensed instantly. The animal had seen them. With an almost imperceptible jerk of his head, he signalled to Mara to follow him as in one fluid movement he picked up his gun and rose to his feet. He began to move slowly along the track, deeper into the gully. Mara mirrored his actions. At the end of the cul-de-sac, she knew, there was a track that led up onto the rocks – too narrow and steep for an elephant.

John maintained the steadiness of his movements, but increased his pace. Then, without warning, he came to a standstill. Over his shoulder, Mara saw a baby elephant appear – ambling into view, heading from the direction of the cul-de-sac, down towards its mother.

John spun round, grabbing Mara's arm and pulling her off to the side of the track. But thorn bushes pushed in around them, leaving little space to stand.

There was a short, tense stillness. The mother elephant's gaze was trained ahead, past the two humans, to where her baby stood.

Mara found herself thinking in John's voice. *We're in between the mother and her calf. We're hemmed in by rocks . . .*

The mother's head reared up, ears now flapping wildly. Angry trumpeting shattered the quiet.

John grasped Mara's arm again, pulling her back towards the stone bench – moving closer to the elephant, but clearing a path between her and her baby.

Almost immediately, the calf trotted to join its mother, taking shelter behind her. Mara breathed out slowly – but as she turned to share her relief with John, there was another loud roar. The elephant lunged towards them.

'Run!' John pointed up the gully. Then he ran back towards the elephant, shouting and waving his gun.

Mara stumbled backwards, watching in stunned disbelief as the elephant kept coming towards John. 'John! Come back!' she yelled.

He changed his direction, still gesturing wildly. He was luring the elephant away, Mara realised. Away from her.

John stopped, suddenly. He looked down at his gun, his face twisted with torment. Mara could feel his indecision – an emotion she knew to be utterly alien to his hunter's training. A few seconds passed, then he shifted his gun, angling it at his waist. He lifted the bolt up, and clicked it back to engage the round of ammunition. Then he forced it home into the breach. Raising the telescopic sights to his eye, he swung the gun towards the elephant. But before squeezing the trigger, he jerked up the barrel, well above her head.

A shot rang out, echoing across the valley.

The head reared up again, the trunk flailing the air as a roar of fury came from the animal's mouth. Lowering her tusks, she began to charge.

Mara watched John frantically reloading his gun. But she knew it was too late, now – the elephant was too close to be stopped. She just watched in horror as the elephant bore down upon him.

Suddenly, the powerful trunk swept down, wrapping itself around John's arm, and then flinging him into the air. The gun flew off to the side, like a stick tossed into the wind. John yelled – a short, strangled cry. Then he was hurled to the ground, his body thudding onto the earth.

Mara gasped, rigid with terror. Part of her wanted to run to John. But another part of her knew she would only be putting herself in danger. And the baby as well. Their baby.

The elephant raised one foot, seeming to pause for a moment, as if there was still a chance she would relent. But then she brought her foot down, stamping onto the limp figure before her. Mara turned away, facing the sheer walls of the gully. Her breath came in jerking sobs now; her limbs felt weak. Small fragments of sandstone came away as she scrabbled uselessly at the rock.

She heard – and felt – the footfalls of the elephant as it approached her from behind. Desperately, she searched the rocks for some way of escape, but she could see there was none. A strange calmness came over her. She knew she was going to die.

She turned and faced the elephant, her back pressed hard against the rock, her heart thumping in her chest. Small details caught her attention: the colour of the sky, the bumpy surface of the stone behind her spine, the rippling of the animal's loose skin as it moved. She could feel her body's urgent clamouring for sensation. A last hunger before the darkness . . .

It came to Mara only gradually that the elephant had slowed her pace. But her ears were flapping, their ragged edges raking the air as she moved. Mara stared, immobile, as the points of the elephant's tusks came steadily closer. Then she clasped her hands over her belly, some part of her still hoping she could shield this place where a new life had only just begun.

A few feet away from Mara, the elephant stopped. She raised her trunk and waved it towards Mara's body. The pale tip of its nostrils explored the air between them – reaching close, but never touching. It moved from Mara's face, down past her breasts, then hovered over her hands, which were still covering her belly.

Mara looked up, meeting the animal's gaze. The eyes were shrouded in folds of skin, the lashes long and straight. They were moist, gleaming, reflecting the light.

Then they were gone.

The grey head, the trunk, were swinging away. The massive shoulders turning.

The elephant was retreating.

Mara rested her head back against the rock, scarcely able to breathe, as she watched the baby fall into step beside the mother, moving off towards the entrance to the gully.

With slow steps, Mara crossed to where John lay. Her eyes moved quickly over his motionless form, flinching from the mangled, bloody remains of his body, and fixing instead on his face. It was undamaged, with no sign of pain or fear. His lips were lightly closed, his eyes shut. The only sign that John was not just sleeping was the thin trickle of bright blood coming from the corner of his mouth.

Mara knelt and reached a trembling hand towards John's cheek, which was warm and soft to her touch. He looked so young. He might have been a boy, lying there, the one chosen to play the victim in a child's game. Soon he would smile, and sit up, and run off to the next adventure.

A low moan came from Mara's throat. She shook her head, wanting to deny what she could see. She tried closing her eyes, but in her mind she saw the elephant's attack playing out in detail, again and again, each time moving inexorably towards the same nightmare ending.

Tears filled her eyes and ran down her cheeks. She gazed through them, grateful for the blur that helped hide the red oozing from John's chest.

Thoughts began forming in her head, simple and clear, like snatches from a news report.

He could have killed the elephant, instead of trying to scare her off. He drew her away from me. He wanted to save me.

She knew these thoughts would haunt her for many years – perhaps forever. As would the memories of what she had once shared with John, and now lost. Then, there was the painful knowledge of all the things that would never be able to be mended between them. All the things that would never be said.

That one special thing.

Leaning forward on her knees, Mara moved her head close to

John. Some part of him, she felt, might still be conscious: his soul, hovering close, might still be able to hear.

'John. I'm pregnant. With your child.'

She stared at his eyes, closed now, forever. She remembered how – on days when they were clear and bright – their colour matched the blue of the summer sky. But how, too often lately, they were dull and clouded with pain.

It was all over now.

She studied John's face, taking in all the small details she knew so well. His lips, slightly dry after weeks in the outdoors; his childhood scars from unstitched cuts that had spread as they'd healed; his thick fair hair. She sealed these images inside her. Even in the midst of her grief and shock, she was conscious that one day a child would be standing at her knee, listening to the story of their father's death. She owed it to John, and to that child, to capture this moment forever.

This is your father. You are here, at his death. It's all the time you will ever have with him.

A soft swooping sound drew her attention. She looked up to see a vulture settling on a dead tree trunk nearby, carefully folding its ragged wings. She stared at the giant bird – the final proof that death had come. Sudden fury broke inside her. She picked up a rock and hurled it at the creature. The stone bounced against the sun-bleached wood, and the vulture rose into the air, hovering briefly, before landing again in the same place.

'Go away!' Mara screamed. Her words echoed across the valley, as the gunshot had done, and returned to haunt her.

Go away! Go away!

But the bird stayed where it was, the hungry eyes watching, the curved beak held at the ready. Before long, another arrived. And then a third.

Mara knew she would eventually have to walk back to the Land Rover, leaving John here alone. He was too heavy for her to lift. But she would cover his face with stones, she decided, to keep the birds from his eyes. And she would return here straightaway with people from the village – John's gunbearer, and others who would be prepared to handle his body. She would not take him to the Regional Commissioner's office in Kikuyu, as she knew she should. She would take him back to the lodge, to the place that he loved. To his home.

But for now, she refused to set that sequence of events in motion. By staying where she was, swatting away the gathering clouds of flies and preventing the vultures from moving in, it almost seemed as though she could stop time moving forward. In the space she'd created, between what had happened and what would come next, she would gather her resources.

You're stronger than you think. You are a strong person.

Peter's words came back to her, and she grasped them one by one, holding them to her chest like a shield.

EIGHTEEN

Africans began arriving before dawn, emerging wraith-like from the darkness as they entered the circle of light surrounding the lodge. Mara sat at the head of the coffin, which had been placed on a trestle table on the verandah. She felt raw and fragile as she prepared to greet the mourners. She was glad Kefa and Menelik were there, standing on either side of her chair like guardians. They'd been with her through each step she'd had to take this last twenty-four hours – ordering the casket from the Sikh carpenter in Kikuyu, then arranging for Dr Hemden to come across from the mission and write out a death certificate. They'd even taken on the task of preparing John's body for burial. Mara had planned to do it herself. She'd gathered some towels and a bowl of water and carried them over to the bed, steeling herself to lift the blanket and peel away the remains of the shirt, revealing the terrible injuries that lay beneath. For what seemed like an age, she'd stood there, frozen. Then she'd felt Menelik's hand on her arm, steady and cool. Gently, he'd removed the towel from her shaking fingers.

'*Si kazi yako,*' he'd said firmly, as if she were his child. This is not your work.

Mara looked down into the coffin. John's face was in shadow, but his body – wrapped in a white Ethiopian shawl bordered with black embroidery – almost glowed in the half-light. She could feel the deep stillness of death spreading out from the shrouded form.

As each visitor approached, Mara nodded her responses to the murmured condolences. She recognised many of the mourners from the local village. Some had abandoned their everyday shirts and shorts for traditional loincloths or *kitenges*, and several wore mud paint on their faces and bodies. Others had found suits and shirts to wear. They all mingled together, mismatched, like students from different schools. There was one group of men she'd never seen before; their clothes were dusty from the road and they carried travellers' sticks over their shoulders.

'They have walked all through the night,' Kefa commented.

Mara smiled in appreciation. She felt glad so many people had come to pay their respects to John. She understood that for some it was simply an act of courtesy, or even just curiosity. But many, she knew, were well acquainted with John. Some had first met him as a young man, and had watched him grow up, eventually becoming the Bwana of Raynor Lodge. They'd taken orders from him – often curtly issued – and had held out their hands for his money. But they'd also walked over large tracts of bushland at his side, swapping food and stories around campfires, and facing danger together out on the trails. In the complicated ways of this country, Mara realised, they were probably some of John's closest friends.

When each newcomer reached the coffin, they stood still for a time, looking in at John's face and the white cocoon of his body. Now and then, one would stoop to add something – a small leather pouch, a tiny flask of oil – to the collection of objects resting at John's feet. The gunbearer had put the first items in there: an enamel cup, and a spoon and fork from John's camping kit.

'*Vifaa vya safari*,' he'd said to Mara. These are the necessities of the safari.

Menelik had added frankincense, scattering the small chunks of fragrant resin amongst the folds of the shawl. It had been Kefa who'd asked Mara what she would like to contribute. She had chosen John's treasured copy of *King Solomon's Mines*. Now, as she gazed down at the slender, well-worn book, tucked in at the end of the coffin, she remembered opening the cover and looking at John's name written in a childish hand on the title page. A lump of pain came to her throat as she thought of John's loneliness in his English boarding school; his desolate sense of abandonment by his parents. Looking up from the coffin, she peered in the direction of the trophy wall in the dining room, with all its mementos of Bill Raynor. She felt a deep gratitude to the old hunter for the love he'd offered his young apprentice, when John had finally found a way to escape back home to Africa.

Mara gazed down at the book as people shuffled steadily past her. It came to her, suddenly, that she wanted to add something else to the coffin – something linked to her life with John. Excusing herself, she went inside, crossing the sitting room and entering the dining room. There, on the mantelpiece, was the rough lump of stone she and John had found together on a safari way up onto the escarpment during the first year of their marriage. Its milky green colour had caught Mara's eye, and she'd pointed it out to John. When he'd picked it up and turned it over in his hands, they'd found it was dotted with pockets of deep clear red.

'That's ruby,' John said. 'I've heard you can find it up here.' Angling the stone into the sunlight they studied the largest piece of gemstone. It was fractured all through with small lines. 'It's not worth anything.'

'Yes it is,' Mara had insisted. 'It's beautiful.'

John had smiled at her then. 'So we've got to carry it all the way home?' While he was still talking, he'd bent to stow it away in his rucksack. At the lodge, they'd put it on the mantelpiece – their only addition to the Raynors' possessions. Guests sometimes asked about it.

'It's Mara's treasure,' John would say. 'It's worth a fortune.'

Cradling the stone in her hands, Mara walked back through the dining room. In the sitting room she paused, suddenly faced by a large framed photograph that Kefa had recently hung on the wall.

It showed Lillian Lane and Peter Heath standing together beneath a pair of crossed tusks – the entrance to Raynor Lodge.

Mara looked into Peter's face. Her hands tightened on the rough surface of the stone. A longing for the comfort of his presence swept through her with such urgency it took her breath away. But the longing did not feel wrong in any way. Two parts of herself seemed to be running parallel – not touching. In reaching out, in her heart, for Peter, there was no trespass into the grief she felt for John.

Mara stood still, for a moment, overwhelmed by her emotions. Then she made herself push them aside. Peter and John were both gone, she reminded herself. There was just her. She would have to manage alone.

Drawing in a deep breath, she lifted back her shoulders and walked away, returning to her place by the coffin.

Leaning over the casket, her hair falling to cover her face, she placed the stone gently inside – not at John's feet, with the other things, but up by his swathed chest, to the right, close to his heart.

Early sun gleamed off the shiny wooden panels of the coffin as it rested beside the burial hole on a pallet covered with banana leaves. Not far away were the two stone cairns that marked the Raynors' graves: Alice's, with its simple ebony plaque, and Bill's, with its panel of engraved brass. Mara stood beside the coffin, looking out over the plain and the waterhole, wanting to draw into herself the peace and calm of the scene.

From behind her, she could hear the sounds of the crowd: hushed voices, coughs, the whimpering of a baby. The Africans who had assembled at the lodge, and then followed behind the Land Rover as Mara drove the coffin the short distance down to the plains, had since been joined by other mourners. Though she had her back to them, now, Mara could still picture the rows of sombre faces. Bina was there, looking subdued in a simple pastel sari, along with her diminutive husband and several of her relatives. A group had come from the mission, including the whole Hemden family; the girls were pressed in close around Helen, quiet and anxious. There were lots of people from Kikuyu, including a contingent of government officials, Abassi and some of his employees from the hotel, and Wallimohammed as well. Then there was a trio of ageing European men, who had about them the unmistakable air of the professional hunter. It occurred to Mara that they might ask to prepare a plaque for John bearing the motto of their association. *Nec timor nec temeritas.* What would they think, she wondered, if they knew it was neither fear nor rashness that had cost John his life, but a desire to be true to his word.

Mara felt a hand on her shoulder.

'It is time to begin.'

As Mara turned to face the crowd, the pastor from Kikuyu stepped forward. He began reading a psalm, reciting each verse first in English, then Swahili. He followed it with a simple prayer. As he finished, closing his book and tucking it under his arm, people turned towards the coffin, expecting the burial to begin. There was a muttering of surprise as Mara nodded towards the gunbearer instead. The old man stepped forward, a tall, gaunt figure, dressed in neat khakis. Now in his guise as the safari chronicler, he raised one hand, pointing towards the horizon, as though to address John in the realm to which he had already gone. Then, in a voice that was hauntingly high, yet clear and true, he began to sing the story of John's life.

Only when the last words of the chronicler had faded into the still morning air, did the bearers lift the coffin from its bed of banana leaves and move it across to the hole. As the coffin was lowered into the ground on thick sisal ropes, the African women began to wail and sob. Emotion spread through the crowd, the cries becoming louder and more desolate. The grief was not just for John, Mara understood. It was a lament for all the sorrows of life – for the losses that had been endured, and for the emptiness left by things that had never been, and never could be. She let the shared pain wash through her, mingling with her own, and bringing a strange peace to her soul.

The dining-room tables were dotted with abandoned cups and saucers and glasses. Amongst them, like large vessels moored in a cluttered sea, were seven ornate silver plates bearing fragments of the Indian sweetmeats and savouries Bina had provided. Wasps settled there, feeding on the sugar.

The last of the guests had only just left, and the hut boys were beginning the task of tidying up. Mara came to join them. But when she began stacking cups they looked at her with anxious eyes.

'You are tired, Memsahib,' the older one said. 'You should rest yourself.'

Mara smiled, touched by their concern. She sensed also that they were being protective of their roles. They did not want Kefa to come and find them being assisted in their duties by the Memsahib. She wandered through to the sitting room and sat down on one of the cane chairs. Resting her head back against the cushion she closed her eyes. Though she felt numb with exhaustion, she could not imagine sleeping. The adrenaline that had pumped through her body, sustaining her through the burial and then the reception, was still racing in her veins. Snatches of conversations she'd taken part in, circled through her head.

'So you will go home to Australia now,' Bina had said, as if the return of a widowed bride to her family were a foregone conclusion. 'I will miss you very much.'

'Come and stay with us at the mission,' Helen had suggested, as if the lodge were no longer Mara's home now John was gone.

'This is not the time for making decisions of any kind,' Dr Hemden had warned.

Mara had been aware that everyone was watching her responses.

She was conscious that they all thought they understood her situation, when the most important thing of all – the reality upon which everything else turned – was a secret known only by her.

Now, sitting in her chair, Mara pictured her womb nestled inside her body. She knew there were women who remained unaware of pregnancy even after many months had passed, but she had no doubt, herself, about her changed state. She could feel it in her heart and her flesh and her blood. She pictured the baby growing, transforming her into someone else. A mother . . .

The smell of fresh coffee made Mara open her eyes. Menelik was pulling a side table towards her, ready to put down the cup. Mara stared at it for a moment.

'I'm sorry, I cannot drink coffee,' she said.

'Of course,' Menelik responded, already preparing to retreat. 'It will keep you awake. Sleep would be better.'

Mara shook her head. 'It's not that. I don't like the taste or the smell any more.'

A look of dismay came over the cook's face.

'It is because I am pregnant.' She looked up, meeting the old man's gaze. 'With John's baby.'

Menelik kept his eyes fixed on hers as he nodded slowly. Then a broad smile broke over his face. 'Truly, it is good news! When a man dies without children, his life is over. But if his seed is planted he remains. And a wife is not left by herself.'

Mara smiled back as she absorbed his words.

A wife is not left by herself.

A warm silence settled between the two. The clatter of crockery being stacked came from the dining room. Then Kefa's voice could be

340

heard, gently chiding one of the boys for something. A few moments later Kefa entered the sitting room. At the sight of Menelik and Mara, watching one another in silence, he stepped backwards.

'Excuse me.'

'No, come in.' Mara waved toward the other chairs. 'Sit down, please. Both of you.'

She saw the two men exchange tense glances as they moved awkwardly to take their seats.

'I want to tell you that I will not be leaving Raynor Lodge,' Mara said. 'Everything will continue as normal.'

Kefa closed his eyes in a brief gesture of relief.

'But only if you will continue in your positions,' Mara said. 'I will need your help.' She focused, now, on Kefa. 'I am pregnant. I am having John's baby.'

Kefa's eyes widened, as if he were struggling to take in her meaning. 'But you will want to be in your mother's house for the birth of your first child.'

Mara shook her head. 'I want my baby to be born here, in Tanzania, in John's home.'

Menelik tilted his head thoughtfully to one side. 'Then,' he said, after a few moments, 'I will use the words of Bwana Carlton. You must go to Plan B.'

'Plan B?' Mara repeated.

'It is simple. You must summon your mother to come here.'

A laugh escaped Mara's lips. 'That's impossible.'

Menelik looked puzzled. 'You have told me you have many relatives – lots of brothers. Even a man can work in the house if necessary.'

Mara nodded. It was true. Without a woman in charge of the Hamilton household, properly cooked meals would give way to barbecues and serves of eggs and bacon, but no one would starve. And though the house would descend into a slum, with dirty clothes piling up in the laundry, there would be no lasting damage. The expense would not be a real problem, either; the farm had been doing well for years.

'It's a long way to come,' Mara said.

Kefa spread his hands. 'Foreigners come here to play and have fun. Surely a woman who is to become a grandmother would make such a journey?'

Mara gazed at the floor. A vision came to her, slowly growing into focus. She saw Lorna wandering the grounds of the lodge picking flowers, and sitting at the kitchen table swapping tips with Menelik, even taking a walk to visit Lion Rock. Having the kind of adventure she'd dreamed of only for her daughter. Mara looked up, her eyes brimming with tears of longing. 'I will ask her. Maybe she will come.'

'She will come,' Menelik stated. The way he spoke the words made the arrival of Mara's mother sound as certain as the coming of morning after the night.

Mara smiled. She looked from Menelik to Kefa and back. She thought of how lucky she was to have them both to take care of her, along with all the other people who were now a part of her life at the lodge. She thought of Bina, who would be so pleased to hear Mara's news. Of Helen, who would offer so much useful advice; and the girls, who would love the baby.

She had lost John. And Peter could never belong to her. But she had not been left alone.

EPILOGUE

Orange flowers stood up like spears, emerging from the tops of the spiky-leaved aloe vera plants that grew on the rocky hillside. Mara looked down at them from above. She was sitting on a wooden chair perched between two she-oaks. The huge granite boulders of Whaler's Lookout rose up behind her. She could feel their presence there, solid and old, offering shelter from the southerly gales.

Leaning forward in her chair, Mara shifted her gaze to the little wooden cottage built at the base of the hill. She admired its simple, elegant shape, and the symmetry of the six-pane windows set either side of the front door. She took in the sturdy breadth of the stone chimney. Then her eyes settled on the patches of rust that were visible on the seaward side of the tin roof. And the guttering that was hanging down outside the kitchen. She smiled ruefully to herself. When she'd moved into the cottage eight months ago, she'd not realised quite how much work would be needed to repair it. Her brothers had wanted to come and inspect the property before she'd signed the contract, but she'd declined their offer. She had already decided this was the place she was going to buy, regardless of their advice.

Her mind had been made up the moment she'd peered past the faded *For Sale* sign tacked to the verandah and seen the garden stretching up the hillside. It was an exotic jungle of sisal, prickly pear, bougainvillea and aloe vera, planted generations ago, and thriving in the rocky soil. As she'd walked up the hillside, on that first morning, Mara had felt immediately at home there. It reminded her of Africa.

Changing her position again, Mara looked past her land towards the village and the foreshore. The scene was deeply familiar to her. From here, she could see the grassy area that had once been the Girl Guides' campsite – the setting for so many carefree childhood memories. It was a coastal reserve now, and the old pine trees had been replaced with native shrubs, but the rocks and the dunes were exactly as she remembered them. The village of Bicheno had changed a bit since those days – there were more shops and other businesses, and a new sub-division had been opened up. But the place had remained unspoiled. Mara looked at the scattering of roofs clustered around the coastline. Then she gazed along the white crescent beach. Cray boats with bright-painted hulls were moored out in the bay. And there, in the distance, was Diamond Island, edged with orange-lichened rocks, set against the turquoise blue of the sea. Mara smiled. The whole landscape was so beautiful. And now that she owned this little piece of the hillside, she truly felt a part of it all.

As she watched the sun sink low in the western sky, she shivered, wrapping her arms around her body. She wore only a light shirt and jeans. The day had been warm and sunny, but now the chill of a winter's night was blowing in from the sea.

344

She was about to head back down the hill, when she heard the sound of a car engine. Checking the road that ran along the front of her block, she saw a car approaching – a shiny, new-looking vehicle. Even before she identified the hire-company numberplates, she guessed it belonged to a mainland tourist. They liked to drive around slowly like this, inspecting the real estate. As the car pulled up outside her cottage, Mara shrunk down in her chair, hiding herself behind a ti-tree bush. She pictured the tourists commenting on the run-down exterior of the building, and the overgrown garden. They might guess the place was unwanted, that it could be theirs for the asking. But they were too late. Mara felt a surge of pleasure at the thought. This place belonged to her. And nothing would tempt her to part with it.

The chain of the old bicycle rattled as Mara rode down the street. When she breathed in the cold air, the scent of fresh herbs blew back to her from the basket mounted on the handlebars. She'd just picked a large bag of mixed herbs and winter greens to take with her to the restaurant where she worked. They were part of the first crop she'd raised on her land. As soon as she'd moved into the cottage, she'd begun work on a garden plot – marking out a strip of the fertile land at the base of the hill, and fencing it securely against possums and bandicoots. She'd planted a few flowers – some lavender, marigolds and a red hibiscus bush – but most of the beds had been sown with the herbs and vegetables that she planned to sell in the village. Now, as she rode, she glanced down at the basket. The spinach and rocket were plentiful at this time of the year, but the herbs – mint, parsley, sage and thyme – were a bit sparse. She hoped Chantal, the restaurant's owner and chef, would not be disappointed. But if she were, Mara knew she would say so. In the six months since Mara had begun sharing the work of waitressing with Chantal's teenaged daughter, the two women had developed an open, easy friendship. Mara had taken the job temporarily at first, as a way of becoming a part of her new community. Now she enjoyed working with Chantal so much she didn't plan to give it up.

Rounding the long corner that swept into the village, Mara cycled past the run-down holiday resort that occupied one end of the bay. The accommodation wings were dark and empty – no one wanted to stay in hotels any more; tourists preferred furnished apartments, bed and breakfast suites and backpacker hostels. But the public bar was still the hub of local social life. Yellow light spilled from its windows. Mara pictured the place crowded with ruddy-faced fishermen home from the sea, the air humming with voices and cosy with the heat of two blazing log fires.

As she passed the open expanse of the disused bowling green, the musky fragrance of burning eucalypt drifted across to her. Mara was reminded, suddenly, of Raynor Lodge – where smoke from cooking fires greeted the dawn, and returned to haunt the dusk. A powerful nostalgia swept over her. She yearned to be back in the home she had left behind twelve long years ago. Or even just to be in the presence of someone who understood her bond with the place. Her son, Jesse, shared lots of her memories, but he'd married recently, and moved to take up a new job in Melbourne. He and Sarah had invited Mara to come and live near them, and had even picked out a little terraced house in Carlton for her. Mara had been tempted – she and Jesse had been so close ever since he'd been born that she could barely imagine existing without being in constant contact with him. But she knew the moment had come to step back, and let him go.

There had been a time when Mara could have reminisced with her own mother about life at Raynor Lodge. They could have talked, as they had done so many times, of the trip Lorna had made to be present at Jesse's birth. And of how they'd found it awkward at first, being together on their own, with so many years of complex family history lying between them. They always used to share a smile over the fact that, as it turned out, there had been little time to worry about their feelings: while Lorna was still unpacking her suitcase, Mara had gone into labour, two weeks early.

Mara's thoughts turned back to that memorable day. As soon as the contractions had begun, they'd set off for the Mission hospital, with Kefa at the wheel of the lodge's new Land Rover and Lorna and Mara sitting beside him. Her labour had progressed quickly – halfway through the journey it became clear that the birth was imminent. Kefa parked at the side of the road. He helped Mara climb out of the vehicle and move round to the back. There, he raised the side seats out of the way and spread a *kitenge* over the floor.

'You know what to do,' he stated to Lorna. Then he retreated to a respectful distance.

Lorna's eyes were wide with alarm, but she kept her voice calm. 'I know what to do,' she repeated, as if to convince herself. 'I've given birth seven times. I know what to do . . .'

Mara, lost in a fog of pain, was only dimly aware of Lorna timing the contractions and offering advice about breathing. But between the waves of agony, she felt her mother's hand stroking her hair and heard the steady, reassuring tone in her voice. The cycle of agony felt relentless and futile. Then, without warning, Mara felt the urge to push. And only a few minutes later, it seemed, Lorna was guiding the little body out into the world, and lifting it up onto Mara's bare belly.

'It's a boy,' Lorna announced. 'A beautiful little boy.'

For a long time, Mara could not take her eyes off her baby – she just stared in wonder at the tiny hands, the pink feet, the fair hair lying wet against the smooth head. But then, as his first cries filled the air, she looked up, meeting Lorna's gaze. In that moment, she could feel a deep bond, a strength, flowing between her and her mother. And she could feel it reaching out to embrace the baby as well – this new person who was a part of them both, and yet separate and unique.

'He's so perfect,' Mara murmured, touching his furled fingers.

'You were a perfect baby, too,' Lorna said.

Kefa's voice came to them, then. 'All is well?'

Mara smiled, resting her cheek against the tiny downy head. She looked up at Lorna through eyes misty with tears. 'Tell him, yes. It is well. It is very well.'

Then she turned to look out through the open back door of the Land Rover – fixing her gaze on the sky. Deep joy, entwined with pain, welled up inside her.

Here's your son, John. Your little boy.

Throughout the rest of her visit to Raynor Lodge, Lorna had been carefree and alive. There had been no sign of tiredness or headaches; she seemed to have been transformed by the experience of the birth, and her escape from the confines of her world. She'd spent her days showing Mara how to look after Jesse, or helping Menelik in the kitchen. She'd joined Dudu picking vegetables in the *shamba*, and arranged cut flowers for the lodge. While her daughter rested and cared for the baby, she'd taken on the role of hostess, chatting to the clients when they returned with the African guides from their game-viewing safaris.

The precious visit had come to an end all too soon. As they'd made their farewells, Mara had agreed to write weekly letters to her mother – a promise she was to keep over many years, sending lengthy documents plotting every detail of Jesse's life as he grew up surrounded by love and companionship both at the lodge and in the village. Each milestone the boy reached – each accident or illness, and each small triumph – was recorded on thin blue sheets of airmail paper that were then sent on their way across the world.

Though there had been talk of Lorna making another trip to Tanzania, it had never come to pass. Instead, many years later, Mara and Jesse had been reunited with her in Tasmania. Then, at last, they'd been able to share memories face to face – and make new ones. But those days were over, now. Lorna had died a year ago, only a few weeks after Mara's father, as if, in the end, she'd had no choice but to keep following whatever path her husband chose to take. Mara was glad Jesse had been able to spend so much time with her parents during the later years of their life. The boy had even managed to find a place in his grandfather's heart. It was one of the good things to have come out of the agonising decision to leave Tanzania, and Raynor Lodge.

Mara remembered clearly the day she'd made that choice. Jesse had been about to leave for his first term at the Rift Valley Academy in Kenya. Mara had already paid his first term's fee. She'd managed to provide for Jesse's primary schooling by correspondence lessons – as the Hemdens had done – but he was almost thirteen, now, and the time had come for him to go to boarding school. Mara had made a trip to Bina's emporium to buy the tin trunk that would hold her son's possessions. As she'd painted Jesse's name on the lid, trying to quell the shake in her hand, she'd told herself it was not as if she were sending him away to England. Kenya was still Africa. The Academy provided an excellent education. But all the arguments had come from her head; her heart felt hollow and silent. The task of packing Jesse's clothes had proved almost more than she could bear; several times she'd found herself just standing by an open drawer, breathing the familiar boyhood smells of leather, pencils and Airfix glue drying on model airplanes.

Finally the day arrived when Mara and Jesse were to set off for Arusha airport. The tin trunk was loaded in the back of the Land Rover, and all the staff had gathered in the car park to say goodbye. At the last moment, the boy had clung to the elephant tusks at the lodge entrance, refusing to let go. After reasoning with him, then pleading, Mara had been forced to act, peeling away his child's arms, still thin and willowy, and pushing him towards the vehicle. His face – usually so open and alive – was rigid and closed. With his fair hair and blue eyes, he looked just as Mara imagined John might have done, at this age. She sought Menelik's gaze and then Kefa's. They betrayed no emotion – they'd been careful not to influence her decision on this matter. Mara turned back to Jesse, watching in silence as the small figure took slow steps away from her. His big, new shoes, scuffing the dusty earth, looked strange and foreign on his bush-hardened feet.

Suddenly Mara could bear it no longer. She strode to the back of the Land Rover, opened the door, and reached for the tin trunk. She pulled it out and dumped it on the ground. And Jesse turned to her with a look on his face that was still etched on her heart.

'I never want to leave you,' he said. 'Never ever.'

Mara pulled him close to her with a deep sense of relief. 'I never want you to leave.'

But it had meant moving back to Tasmania. Mara understood how vital it was to her son's future that he should have proper schooling and be exposed to a wider world, so he would be free to make a life of his own choosing. She had sold the lodge to Abassi, the hotelier from Kikuyu, on the condition that Kefa be made a partner in the business, and that Menelik – who was on the brink of retirement – be allowed to live on in his room in the compound. It had been heartbreaking, packing up and saying goodbye. But it meant Mara and Jesse did not have to be parted.

Of course, eventually they'd had to go their separate ways. Jesse was grown up, now – making his own way in the world. And he was doing a fine job of it, Mara thought. He was a young man that any mother – or father – would be proud of.

But she missed her son so much that even her bones seemed to ache with loneliness.

Mara struggled to push aside her bleak feelings. Moments ago, she reminded herself, she'd been enjoying her new home, her garden, the village. The future had looked bright. And it was. She knew she would learn, eventually, how to live by herself without feeling lonely. She would work out how to cook for one. And how to find pleasure in eating meals with only the radio for company. She would have to. She had no choice.

Standing on the pedals, she rode up the hill, covering the last of the distance to the restaurant. Soon, she could see the solid façade of the Georgian-era homestead ahead of her. The blackboard advertising French food was already outside in the street.

Pushing the bike in behind the geranium bushes, Mara paused to straighten her black skirt and tuck in her white blouse. She checked that her hair had not come loose from its French knot. Then she unclipped the basket and headed for the restaurant entrance.

The door squeaked loudly as Mara pushed it open. She'd tried to encourage Chantal to have the hinges oiled, but the chef had argued that she liked to be alerted whenever someone arrived. Now, Chantal paused in the midst of chopping, looking across the wide counter that separated the kitchen from the dining area.

'Good evening!' she called.

Mara could tell she was in a relaxed mood. Chantal's favourite Nina Simone CD was playing in the dining room. A glass of red wine stood in reach of the chopping board. And the room was warm, indicating that the temperamental woodstove had been successfully lit.

As Mara placed her basket of herbs and salad greens on the counter, Chantal nodded her thanks. Then she picked up her knife and began chopping again. Her deft, fast movements reminded Mara of Menelik at work in the lodge kitchen with his treasured Damascus blade. She turned away, busying herself with laying the tables. She recognised the mood that had settled over her. It was as if the past had floated in on the fragrance of the wood smoke. Now it was calling to her, appearing in everything she saw.

'Have some wine!' Chantal suggested.

As Mara leaned over the counter to take the glass she offered, Chantal gave her a searching look.

'Have you eaten?' she asked.

'I had a sandwich,' Mara replied.

'That is not enough.' Chantal shook her head disapprovingly, but there was a soft tone in her voice. She often seemed able to pick up on Mara's mood. Mara guessed it was because the Frenchwoman, like her, lived with the memory of another life in another country. Chantal had left Paris fifteen years ago, after divorcing her husband. She missed her home, yet she didn't want to return there – any more than Mara wanted to return to Tanzania. They'd talked together about how these chapters of their lives were over. But they also shared an understanding that sometimes the presence of everything one had left behind felt stronger, clearer, than all that belonged to the here and now.

The first guests arrived, and Mara led them to the table closest to the stove. They were a group of three – two women and a man. They were all a bit overweight and wore comfortable, practical clothes. The man had grey hair and one of the women had a slight stoop to her shoulders; she moved carefully, seeming afraid something might trip her up. As they settled themselves at the table, arranging their handbags on the spare chair and their glasses cases on the table, Mara recognised the traits of people moving from being middle-aged to being old.

It was only later, when she glanced at their faces while reciting information about the menu, that Mara realised the three were probably in their late fifties. Less than ten years older than she was. Midway through naming the fish of the day, she faltered, shocked at the thought. They seemed so much older than she felt herself to be. She understood, suddenly, why it was that – after she'd sold up the family home she'd shared with Jesse in Hobart, people had kept advising her to buy a low-maintenance dwelling, on one level, with easy access. She smiled at the thought of what she'd chosen instead. A wooden shack, with a sloping front deck, peeling paintwork, and guttering that was so rusty it scattered fragments of metal into the wind. It was a place for a person with their eye on the future. Mara found the thought encouraging. As she turned away from the table, she straightened her shoulders and lifted her head. She imagined Menelik, again – no longer chopping food in his kitchen, but standing with her on the plains, the breeze ruffling his robe.

Tomorrow it will be a new day.

Mara returned to the counter with the orders. Lucie, Chantal's daughter, was just emerging from the private section of the house. She was wearing a short skirt, stockings and knee-length boots. She'd applied her make-up heavily, but skilfully, and had straightened her hair so that it hung in a sleek line to her shoulders.

'You look fantastic,' Mara said.

'Thanks,' Lucie grinned. 'I'm going for a counter meal with Andrew.'

'I hope you're not hungry,' Mara said with a smile.

'I know. The food's awful. But I have to make the most of my night off from here.' She turned her head, offering Mara a view of her earrings. 'Do they look right?'

'Yes, I think they're perfect,' Mara said. She felt a moment of pride at having Lucie ask her advice about clothes, in spite of her being even older than the girl's mother. She knew Lucie pictured her as someone who had links with a world that was glamorous and exotic – all because she'd told Lucie, one evening, how she'd once met some famous people while running a tourist lodge in Tanzania. Lucie had not heard of Lillian Lane or Peter Heath or the Miller brothers – the reputation of the award-winning film they'd made together had not survived into the next generation. But still, she had been very impressed.

Lucie slung her bag over her shoulder, ready to go. Then she hovered by Mara, a faint frown on her face. 'I meant to tell you – there was an American couple in here last night. The man ordered the *Crepe Poulet du Mara*. He asked me how the dish got its name.'

Mara nodded. Chantal had created the dish for Mara's birthday, then added it to the menu. Guests had enquired before, about the origin of the name.

'When I said it was named after our other waitress, he seemed really . . . I don't know. He just seemed really interested,' Lucie continued. 'He said he thought he might know you, because Mara is an unusual name. He asked what you look like.'

Mara raised her eyebrows in surprise. 'What did you tell him?'

Lucie shrugged. 'I said you had long hair that was a tiny bit grey.

Dark eyes. Tall. It's okay. I didn't tell him anything else. I began to wonder who he was. He seemed nice, though.'

Mara shook her head, trying to think who it could be. Someone from Hobart, presumably. Or perhaps an old school friend, from up North. Tasmania was a small place . . .

But Lucie had said he was American. A knot of tension formed inside her. She placed the bread basket she was carrying on a nearby table.

'What did he look like?' she asked Lucie. She knew her voice sounded thin and tight.

Lucie eyed her cautiously. 'Like you – not old, not young. I didn't notice really. I kept looking at the woman that was with him. She was so beautiful. She had long, curly red hair, and these amazing blue eyes.'

'Oh well,' Mara shrugged, trying to look relaxed. 'It's not important.'

Lucie looked relieved by Mara's response. She turned to check her make-up in a small mirror that hung on the wall above the till.

Mara looked down at her hands, clasped together so hard that her knuckles were white. Thoughts raced in her head. An American. Her age. Asking about her. And a beautiful woman with red hair and blue eyes. It seemed impossible – yet who else could it be?

Peter.

His face swam into her mind. She saw him in his old blue shirt, his face lit from the side. An easy smile on his lips. Twenty-five years had passed, and yet the vision came to her so clearly that it might have been only yesterday they'd said their last goodbye.

She took in a deep breath, reaching for calm.

Peter.

And Paula.

How could they be here?

It was not so surprising, Mara told herself. Peter was Australian. He'd probably brought his wife back here for a holiday. She pictured him returning to Sydney, showing Paula the house at Bondi beach where he'd grown up, and all the places he used to surf. They might easily have decided to take a trip down to Tasmania as well. Lots of holiday-makers did that. And Peter had said, all those years ago, that he'd never been across Bass Strait.

Then another thought occurred to Mara: maybe he was working here; playing a part in a film. She had not followed his career. During her years at the lodge after John's death, visitors had occasionally tried to open up conversation with her about the actor. Occasionally, someone passed on a piece of information about a new film he was in. But Mara had always changed the subject as quickly as possible. When she'd moved back to Tasmania, she'd refused to let herself check magazines or film guides, or read the entertainment pages of the weekend newspapers. In all the time she'd lived here, she had barely even glimpsed a picture of Peter. She'd never been to see one of his films. She couldn't bear to. And it would have felt wrong – as if she were trying to take possession of him in some way.

Lucie turned from the mirror, the anxious frown back on her face. 'There's just one thing. I think I did say you'd be in tonight. I hope that's okay?'

Mara struggled to smile, hiding a jolt of shock. 'Of course it is,' she managed to say. 'I don't have any enemies!'

Lucie glanced guiltily towards the kitchen. 'Don't tell *Maman*, will you? She'd expect me to be more professional.'

'Don't worry about it,' Mara said. She picked up the bread basket again, bending her face over it to hide the turmoil inside her.

'See you, then.' Lucie waved over the counter to her mother as she left.

As the door creaked shut, Mara spun round, heading for the little service table that stood in the corner. Along with spare water carafes and glasses, it held the till, the order books and the old-fashioned device they used for swiping credit cards. There was also a metal spike onto which order dockets were impaled once the customer had paid. She looked at these first, quickly picking out the third docket down: the one with the *Crepe Poulet du Mara*, and a bottle of vintage Tasmanian red. Tearing the docket from the spike, she glanced over the list of dishes – seeing what he'd eaten, what she'd eaten – before noting the total that had been paid. Then Mara opened the till and rifled through the credit-card receipts until she found the one with a matching figure. The cardholder's name was printed in the top left-hand corner. She gripped the paper tightly, staring at the letters, plain and bold. *Peter M Heath*. Swallowing hard, she studied the signature. It was a scrawl, only vaguely legible. But it was possible to see a P at the beginning of the first name. And the H was even clearer.

As Mara returned the paper to the till, the front door squeaked open. She was still, for a moment, her body stiff with tension, then she turned slowly around.

A young Japanese couple stood there, smiling into the restaurant. Mara gathered herself, picking up some menus and waving the two towards a table. From experience, she could tell by the expressions on their faces that they spoke little English. She was relieved when she saw the woman take out a Japanese–English dictionary; she gave them a simplified description of the day's special dishes and left them to examine the menu. Then she returned to the little table, and stood there gazing blankly down at its polished surface, scored with pale scratches. All that she could think of was that Peter had been here. Only last night, he'd been standing right where Mara was now. And she had known nothing about it. It seemed wrong, somehow. She felt she should have been able to sense his presence, as he'd entered her world . . .

Questions circled in her head. Would he come back to the restaurant, looking for her? Or had he already driven on? She wished she'd pressed Lucie for more detail. Exactly how interested had he sounded? What had been the tone in his voice? And the look in his eye? She tried to tell herself his questions might have been prompted by little more than idle curiosity. The possibility of her being here in Bicheno could have been just a point of mild interest on his journey.

Twenty-five years was a very long time.

The entrees were ready for the first table. Mara collected them from the counter and delivered them to the table. She moved briskly, leaving no moment of stillness during which the guests might try to begin a conversation with her. Then she took the orders from the Japanese couple. Even in her distracted state, she was impressed to see they had managed to understand the entire menu; there would be no need, tonight, to resort to impersonations of a duck, a chicken or a cow.

As soon as she'd taken the orders to Chantal, Mara crossed to the far side of the dining room, opening a door that led into the garden. She stepped out into the cool air, then half-ran along a narrow path towards the toilet block, set at a little distance from the restaurant. Normally, Mara enjoyed picking her way along past the bay tree and the rows of lavender, taking a moment to glance up at the night sky, but tonight she kept her eyes fixed ahead. She bent over the basin in the Ladies and splashed water over her face – welcoming its touch against her burning cheeks. Lifting her head, she looked at herself in the small mould-splotched mirror. Even in the dim light of the single bulb mounted on the ceiling, she could see the marks of age upon her face. Her skin looked weathered. There were crinkles at the outer edge of her eyes. Faint lines gathered at her lips. But her cheeks were still smooth and full. And most of the darkness was left in her hair. She half-closed her eyes, blurring the image. She looked, then, as she had back then. Young, beautiful . . .

Bending over the basin again, she drank from the tap, then wiped her mouth with the back of her hand. Smoothing her hair away from her face, she stepped out onto the path again, hurrying back to her post.

The side door opened silently, letting her slip back into the room without drawing attention to herself. She went over to the counter and was relieved to see there were no steaming dishes waiting there. She noticed that the Japanese woman was struggling to dissect her piece of duckling. Mara headed for the kitchen to fetch her some chopsticks. But mid-way towards the swinging door, she stopped dead. There was a figure over by the entrance to the restaurant. She froze, her heart beginning to pound in her chest. There was something about the way the person stood that she felt sure she recognised.

It was him. She knew it was.

As she turned towards him, she felt as though she were caught in a slow-motion film – time seemed stretched, her movements laboured. Then her eyes found his, just as he stepped forward into a pool of brighter light.

She felt herself drawn towards him, as if by gravity. She crossed the space between them, stopping just an arm's length away. She searched his face. Like her, he had aged a little – there was a touch of grey at his temples, and laugh-lines were imprinted on his skin – but beyond the surface changes, he was the same. He still wore the casual style of clothing she remembered. His hair still fell forward over his brow . . .

A dense silence seemed to close in around them. The clattering of pans in the kitchen became distant. The voice of Nina Simone, backed by an accordion, floated around them, but it sounded like it came from another, parallel sphere of existence. There was nothing real, nothing true – except for the dawning realisation that the two of them were standing there, face to face.

'Come outside.' Peter's voice was low but clear. When Mara did not move, he reached for her arm. 'Please – just for a moment.'

The door squeaked open, shattering the impression of quiet. In its wake, other sounds crowded back in; the hum of conversation, the noise from the kitchen, and music filling the air. Then she was outside, following Peter across a small patio, towards the lillipilli tree.

'I've surprised you. I'm sorry,' he said.

Mara's lips parted. His voice sounded just as she'd remembered it.

'But I . . . had to see you,' he added.

Mara stared at him for a long moment, still trying to take in the reality of his presence. Then she shook her head in confusion. 'How did you know I was in Bicheno?'

'I didn't know until I came in here last night,' Peter said. 'I'm just driving around Tasmania, with Melanie – my daughter.'

'Melanie,' Mara repeated. She almost laughed at herself, realising that her image of Paula had not changed, over time. She'd imagined Peter's wife would still capture the attention of someone like Lucie, when, of course, she'd have aged, too. And Peter's daughter must be about thirty years old. 'She was just a little girl – back then.'

'Yes.' Peter smiled into her eyes.

Suddenly, Mara felt all the years evaporate into nothing. The two of them were back at the lodge, choosing animal carvings for his children.

Then the moment passed. Mara drew a breath. 'What brought you to Tasmania?'

The question sounded bland – cool, even.

As if in response, Peter's tone was light, almost careless. 'We were in Sydney and we had some spare time. I'd never been down here, and it seemed like a good opportunity.' He broke off, looking down at the ground. 'To tell the truth, I wanted to see the state where you grew up. I remembered what you said about going camping at that place on the coast with the French name. Bicheno.

I wanted to see that island with the penguins on it. So we came to take a look.' When he lifted his gaze, there was an expression of apology in his eyes. 'I thought you and John were probably still in Africa.'

Mara stared at him, unable to find any words. What she had to tell him felt so big – and so unlike anything he was expecting to hear.

'Can I visit you?' Peter asked abruptly. There was an urgent edge to his voice. His eyes travelled over her face; he seemed to be taking note of every small detail of her appearance. Under his scrutiny, Mara's hand rose automatically to push back her hair – an old habit, from the days when she'd worn it loose. 'I know we said we'd never see one another again,' Peter added. 'But now I've found you, I can't just say hi and keep going. I don't want to upset your life, your family – I just want to see you, talk to you.'

Mara nodded slowly, a thread of excitement brewing inside her. 'I live up round the corner. There's a little cottage on the side of the hill, under the big rock.'

He gave her a faint smile. 'I know where it is.'

Mara remembered the hire car, stopping in the road, and then driving on. 'You came past this afternoon.'

'Yes,' Peter said. 'The man at the hardware store let me know where to find you. I explained we were old friends.'

Mara looked away. Old friends. She felt a flicker of dismay. Is that what they were? Just old friends, getting the chance to meet up again, after a long time apart . . .

'I thought I should come and find you here first, and ask if I could visit you,' Peter continued. 'You and John. I wanted to check if it would be okay.'

Mara looked at him in silence again. In her head, she repeated his words. You and John. They had not been a part of her world for such a very long time. Biting her lip, she struggled to find the right way to frame what she had to say. Then the words just came out, blunt and brief. 'John's dead.'

Peter's eyes widened with shock. His lips moved as he searched for a response. 'I'm really sorry. When did it happen?'

Mara shook her head. This was not the place and not the time, to tell him what had happened – and how, and when.

Peter didn't push her to answer, he just looked at her, his own eyes mirroring her pain, as though he understood exactly what she was feeling. Then he reached out and touched her shoulder, his hand heavy and warm.

At that moment, the door squeaked open behind them. Peter's hand fell as Mara turned to see the grey-haired man standing in the entrance. He was holding a wine bottle.

'Any chance of getting this opened?' His eyes flicked curiously over the couple. When his gaze settled on Peter, a puzzled look came over his face, as if he thought he knew him, but was not sure where from.

'I'm sorry, I'll be right there,' Mara said. Peering into the restaurant, she could see Chantal placing plates of food on the counter. Turning back to Peter, she gestured helplessly towards the tables of diners. 'I have to go.'

As she spoke, a group of half a dozen people came into view on the footpath outside the front of the restaurant.

'Can I see you tomorrow?' Peter asked.

Mara gathered herself, forcing a smile. 'Come for morning tea, both of you. I'd love to meet Melanie. And hear all about your life – and your family.' The words sounded strained and falsely bright. Lifting her hand in a small wave, she walked away towards the door.

'Mara —'

Peter's voice came after her. She paused, looking back over her shoulder. But the new arrivals had already crowded onto the patio, blocking him from view. By the time she had ushered them past her, he was gone. In the abandoned space, there was just the tall dark shape of the lillipilli tree.

Chantal sat back in her chair, cradling a glass of cognac in her hands. She still wore her apron, splashed with sauces of varying hues. In the stillness of her posture, there was an afterglow of energy – the legacy of the intense activity of the last few hours.

Mara lifted her glass to her mouth. Her hand, she realised, was trembling faintly. She tightened her grip on the stem. She'd not mentioned Peter's visit to Chantal – part of her longed to talk about it with her friend, but her feelings were too tangled and confused to put into words. She pretended to glance idly around the room, her eyes passing over the empty tables, stripped of their cloths, her face a mask, hiding the thoughts and questions tumbling in her head.

Tomorrow Peter was coming to see her – Peter and his grown-up daughter. Melanie. It made sense now, that the two were travelling together; she remembered Peter telling her Paula never liked leaving home. Mara sipped the cognac slowly, letting it sting her lips. The sensation distracted her briefly, but then her thoughts returned to imagining Peter's visit. She would find out so many things about him. Whether he still made wooden furniture. Whether he'd ever managed to persuade Paula to hike with him in the bush.

Whether he had been happy, all these years.

Chantal stirred in her chair, then stood up. 'I'll get some coffee.'

As she headed for the kitchen, Mara stared mutely into the golden liquid in her glass. She could feel herself being drawn helplessly back to the past.

A memory came to her, vivid and strong.

She was sitting in a darkened cinema, a haven of peace and privacy amid the chaos of downtown Dar es Salaam. Rows of empty seats stretched away from her on both sides. The only other people at the matinee screening were a group of Indians. The smell of fried *samosas* and cigarettes drifted on the air.

Mara gripped the armrests with both hands as the opening titles came onto the screen. The film began with the crumbling stone buildings and narrow alleyways of Zanzibar. Lillian and Peter appeared, wearing smart clothes Mara had never seen. They seemed remote and unreal, captured on film; they might have been strangers to her, like any other Hollywood stars. Mara let the first half of the film wash over her in a blur of movement and colour. She was watching and waiting for what was to come.

Then at last, they were there – Maggie and Luke – in the familiar landscape of Raynor Lodge. Walking together, side by side, across the sunburnt hillside. Skimming stones into the flamingo lake. And finally, coming together in the grass hut. Standing close, the moonlight bathing their skin and shining in their eyes. Their arms on each other's shoulders. Their lips touching – tenderly at first, and then with deepening passion.

Mara's eyes filled with tears, the images wavering before her. In the dim light of the cinema, she let herself weep openly, the tears coursing down her cheeks. She relived what they had shared – the laughter, the warmth, the wonder. And the agony of having to accept that she and Peter could not be together. The engulfing pain of that final moment of parting, the plane lifting into the sky . . .

When the film was over, she remained in her seat, struggling to regain her composure. She fixed her gaze on the names that rolled over the screen. *Peter Heath* came first – the printed words looking too plain and ordinary to belong to him. Next came *Lillian Lane*, followed by *Leonard Miller* and *Carlton Miller* side by side in the same frame. There was a long list of the main unit crew, and then, finally, the names of the people who had taken part in the filming at Raynor Lodge. She saw *Daudi Njoma* and *Kefa Nichema*. And *Tomba 'Bwana Boom' Milenge*. *Menelik Abdissa* was acknowledged as *Second Unit Caterer*. Then came her own name. *Mara Sutherland. Stand-in for Miss Lane*. There were some more acknowledgements, then the last line of the credits filled the screen: *Filmed entirely on location in Tanzania, East Africa*.

The music died away, and the screen turned black. As Mara stared into the darkness, she felt as though her life had been suspended. It seemed impossible that she would go back out into the sunshine and continue with her errands. She clutched the back of the seat in front of her and bent over, resting her head on her arms, smearing the tears on her cheeks.

She sat there, motionless, letting images from the film flow back over her. It had been over a year since the film company – and Peter – had come to the lodge. In that time, there had been John's death, and all that had meant. There had been Jesse's birth. The reunion with Lorna. And the ongoing success of the lodge. So much had happened, yet the memories that crowded in on her now were as potent as if the time she'd shared with Peter had been yesterday. She was grateful she'd managed to find an opportunity to see the film for the first time on her own. Very soon, there was to be a screening at the hall in Kikuyu. Mara would be watching the film again, with all the lodge staff gathered around. As Leonard had promised, all of the shots in which Mara appeared – including the ones in the hut – had been seamlessly absorbed into Lillian's performance. No one would ever guess, from watching the film, the truth of what had taken place. Just as long as Mara could retain her composure.

Lifting her head, Mara gazed at the red curtains that now covered the screen. She wished she could just stay here in the quiet darkness, hiding from the reality of her world.

She asked herself for the thousandth time – did she wish she had never met Peter? Never fallen in love with him? Were the precious memories worth the pain of giving him up, or the deep ache of longing she still felt for him? Or the complexity they had brought to her feelings about John? Were they worth the anguish she now faced?

And she knew that they were. She felt their strength, lying deep inside her. Whatever the future might bring, she knew that the love she had found with Peter was a seed that would sustain her.

A seed. Lying dormant . . .

Mara put down her glass, sloshing cognac onto her fingers. Then she stared down at the white tablecloth, her whole body becoming rigid. It was clear to her, suddenly, what Peter had done by coming here and finding her. He'd torn away the careful wrapping that had covered up the past. Now light was shining in, unhindered. Calling the seed back to life.

As Chantal appeared with the coffee pot, Mara stood up, jolting back her chair.

Chantal looked at her in surprise. 'What's wrong?'

'I have to go,' Mara said.

Chantal frowned, concerned. 'Are you all right?'

Mara nodded. 'I'm fine.'

Chantal raised her eyebrows. 'You will tell me later – what is going on?'

'I will,' Mara said.

She was already heading for the door.

In the deserted streets she rode her bike in the middle of the tarmac, steering erratically to avoid potholes. Before long, she reached the colonial cottage where bed and breakfast accommodation was offered. She peered up the driveway to the small parking space, but it was empty. Next, she made her way to the row of brand-new holiday apartments, but there was no sign of the hire car there, either. Nor was it in any of the carports at the motel. Sweating in the cold air, Mara turned in the direction of the resort. As she rode into the car park, she saw the bar was still open – figures moved silently behind the windows, like shadow puppets in a play. Most of the cars parked outside were fishermen's utes and old-model station wagons tarnished with rust. There was a campervan with Queensland numberplates and an ex-army jeep. And that was all.

There was nowhere else for Mara to look, so she turned towards her home. She would simply have to find a way to get through the night, and wait for Peter's visit tomorrow. She tried telling herself it was just as well. What would he – and Melanie – have thought of her turning up, like this, late at night? How would she have explained why she had come? But as she pedalled along, more slowly now, she fought off a growing panic. What if Peter changed his mind and didn't come?

What if she never saw him again?

Wheeling round the last corner, Mara's hands tightened on the handlebars. Ahead, she saw the dark shape of a car parked outside her cottage. She faltered just briefly – then sped towards it. She turned sharply into her driveway, and kept on, riding right up the path to the front door. When she reached the steps, she jumped off the bike, dropping it onto the ground.

Opening the door, she leaned into the living room. Moonlight shone through the side windows and she could see at a glance that no one was in there. She hurried out to the back garden next, sweeping her gaze over the hillside. The jungle of plants looked as though it had been formed from silver; the curved leaves of the aloe vera, their edges lined with spikes and their tips curled into spirals, were like the work of an expert craftsman. There was no wind, and everything was still. The only sounds were the call of a frogmouth owl and the distant hush of the ocean.

Mara searched the deserted hillside once more before returning to the cottage. Walking through the enclosed porch, which protected the entrance from the weather, she stepped out onto the front deck.

Peter was standing there with his back to her, looking towards the sea. At the sound of her footsteps, he turned.

His eyes lit up. 'Mara.'

Mara froze. She opened her mouth to speak, but then just stared at him. Now that she'd found him, she couldn't decide what she should say. All she could think of was that he still belonged to someone else.

'We said we wouldn't see one another again,' she said finally. 'And we stuck to that, all these years.' She shook her head in confusion. 'But now you're here —'

Peter lifted his hands as if to hold back her words. 'Paula died two years ago. She had cancer.' There was a brief silence, dense and deep. Then he continued, his voice soft, yet clear. 'She was determined to beat it – and we all thought she would. But in the end, it was too much for her.' His voice faltered, pain flickering in his eyes. 'I'm alone now.'

Mara's heart clenched with sympathy for him. She understood that whatever difficulties there might have been in his marriage, Paula was the mother of his children. And the two had shared a long journey together. Peter's grief and loneliness were tangible in the air. Mara swallowed a lump in her throat. 'I'm alone, too,' she whispered.

She stared into Peter's eyes, torn by conflicting emotions. There was the shock of hearing about Paula's death. And the sorrow she felt for Peter. But then, too, there was the knowledge, settling slowly in her head, that there was no longer anyone to keep them apart.

She felt a bright flash of hope. A rush of joy.

Then doubts crowded in. How would it be possible for them to reach back past all that had happened and find one another again? And even if they could, would their love be rekindled? Neither of them were the same people they'd once been.

She could see the turmoil mirrored in Peter's eyes. But it was backed with something warm and strong. He'd had time, she reminded herself, to come to terms with this new reality.

Mara looked away, out towards the boats at anchor in the bay, observing the steadiness with which they rode the constant waves. She tried to imagine herself absorbing their calm.

There was a sudden scrabbling sound on the roof. She turned back to see Peter staring up at the guttering. 'What's that?' he asked.

The furry silhouette of a brush-tail possum appeared, climbing along the edge of the roof. At the sound of Peter's voice, it stopped, fixing him with the gaze of a single yellow eye.

Even in the midst of her fraught emotions, Mara had to smile at the sight. 'That's Matata, my resident possum,' she said. 'His name means trouble.'

Peter stepped closer to the animal. 'I haven't seen a possum since I was a kid.'

Mara picked up the excitement in his voice. There was a look of keen interest on his face, as well, that made him look younger – and deeply familiar. She felt her tension and uncertainty beginning to fade.

'He's eaten all the buds off my cherry tree,' she told Peter. 'My neighbours tell me I should trap him and take him away, but I can't bring myself to do it. It doesn't seem fair. He's been here a lot longer than me. And anyway, he's only got one eye.'

'How long have you been here?' Peter asked.

'Eight months.'

'It's a great place.' He spread his hands in a gesture covering the cottage and the garden.

'Yes, it is – I love it,' Mara said. She looked up over the façade of the building. 'It needs a lot of fixing though.'

Peter motioned towards a section of the timber railing close to where he had been standing. Mara saw that a piece of the weathered surface had been cut away, revealing a golden yellow interior. She noticed, then, that Peter held a small penknife in his hand.

'That's Baltic pine,' he said, returning to stand next to it. He chipped off another section. 'Inside, the timber's as sound as the day the place was built. You've got a bit of work to do, but then you'll have a really good little cabin.'

Mara met his gaze. 'I have to find a carpenter.'

Peter let the silence lengthen between them. Then he spoke. 'Well, I'm looking for work. I'm not a professional though.'

Mara brushed back a loose strand of hair, lifting her face towards him. 'You don't have to be,' she said. 'You just begin by pretending. And soon it becomes real.'

She smiled as she spoke. She could feel, inside her, the presence of the young woman in the long red dress. Her hair, untouched by grey, hanging in a thick dark mantle around her shoulders. Her heart brimming with love. Her whole body alive with desire.

Suddenly Mara knew – deeply and surely – that what had become real, back then, was still real now. As she looked into

Peter's face, she felt tears of gratitude welling up in her eyes. Fate had surprised them with a miracle. Whether they had days, or weeks, or months or years to spend together, they would welcome each moment as a gift.

Their story, begun so long ago, so far away, had been cut short. But now – in another place and another time – a new chapter was about to begin.